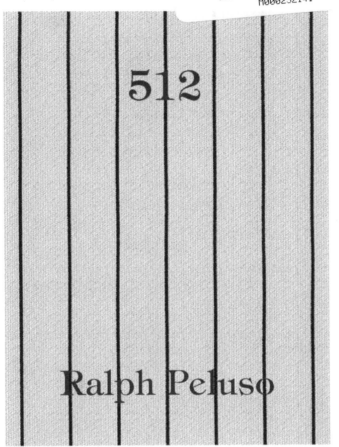

512

Ralph Peluso

Cover Art:
Michelle Crocker
www.mlcdesigns4you.com
Publisher's Note:

This is a work of fiction. All names, characters, places, and events are the work of the author's imagination.

Any resemblance to real persons, places, or events is coincidental.

Solstice Publishing - www.solsticepublishing.com

512

By
Ralph Peluso

First and especially to my lovely and dear wife for the ages, Renee, without her encouragement and selflessness of her time I would not have been able to keep going and 'finish' the story.

To all my children Alicia, Angela and Joe, without whose patience and prodding I would have not gotten to the end.

In memory of my friend, Scott Craig, who had the foresight to refer to me as 'his author friend.'

Of course to my fellow baseball enthusiast and the voice of sanity that rang in my ear, Stuart 'Maddog' McCusker, for pushing me to undertake this project.

Forward

Larry – The Neighborhood Legend
"Heroes get remembered, but legends are never
forgotten." – Babe Ruth

New York City in the 1950's and 60's was a
fertile ground for transforming boys into men.
Every day was filled with challenges. Overcoming
the schoolyard bully was considered a rite of
passage. If you were different, one would face the
wrath of a persistent tormentor. Racism,
stereotyping and criticism of anyone not a member
of the "in crowd" was accepted as normal behavior.
If you were not a member of a social club or gang
you were considered a social outcast. Any outcast
quickly made the target of verbal taunting or
physical abuse, ultimately being drawn into a fight
that where the conclusion was determined even
before it began.

Boys whose athletic skills blossomed ahead
of everyone else were made to be heroes. Those not
so lucky in the genes department fell into to a leper
like caste. Cool uniforms and letter jackets worn
like the plumage of a peacock served their purpose
as the prettiest girls in the school and neighborhood
gathered and fawned over their matinee idols.

Then there was Larry, truly a one of a kind
young man. Of German descent, by the time he was
fifteen Larry stood six feet one inch tall. His wavy
blonde hair always neatly brushed into a duck tail,
except for the one or two curls which gently graced
his forehead. A lean one hundred and eighty pounds
he was a bull, perhaps the strongest boy in the local
high school. Larry never lifted a weight.

With that frame, Larry could run like a dear, no one could catch him from behind when playing touch football. On a dare, the captain of the high school track team challenged Larry to a hundred yard dash.

The track coach upon witnessing the humiliation of his star sprinter offered Larry a spot on the varsity team.

Larry not only could not be covered when playing football, he possessed the strongest most accurate throwing arm. Tight spiral after tight spiral were accurately delivered to his teammate. Regardless of their skill, he always put the ball into a perfect spots; always catchable even by those who did not have great "hands."

His baseball skills were remarkably more profound than each of the two classic street sports. In a sandlot 'pickup' game Larry took a rag tag group of boys across town to take on a different neighborhood team, comprised primarily of high school varsity players. Facing the possibility of an embarrassing loss, many of Larry's friends opted out of playing to go swimming. Larry nearly single handedly took apart the high school baseball players. Only one batter reached base, when the catcher mishandled the third strike allowing the runner to get to first.

Not only did Larry shut down some of the best hitters in Bronx high school baseball, he also embarrassed a two year All – City hurler, by crushing two balls over the centerfield fence. In his final at bat of the game, Larry swung around to bat left handed. Surprising everyone he dragged a bunt up the first base line. The defense was playing him so deep; he did not stop running until he was standing on third. The ball travelled about forty feet and Larry's cunning turned it into a 'triple.' Not done yet, he stole home on the second pitch. Larry had provided confidence for those who played with him and while giving equally important tutelage throughout the game.

His worth as a human did not stop with sports. One time he witnessed a local teen hoodlum with a bad reputation swipe $10.00 from an elderly women. She was buying groceries at Mr. Leonetti's. Trusting the environment she had put her money on the counter. Then she bent over to tend to her thirteen month old granddaughter. Distracted she never saw Bad Bobby steal the money. Larry chased him down for three blocks, finally grabbing Bobby by the shoulder as he climbed up the stoop by his home. Bobby, at first denied the charge that he stole the old woman's money. Then he let go with a roundhouse right aimed at Larry's jaw. Larry easily dodged the blow delivering an uppercut to Bobby midsection which doubled him over. Larry pushed Bobby to the ground holding him there by pressing on the back of his neck. "Tell you what you piece of crap, I will give you ten dollars and you walk it over to Mrs. Bonifacio and you tell her you found it. But if I ever see or hear of you stealing in this neighborhood again I will tell her oldest son Nicky what you did and let him and his mean German shepherd deal with you." Bobby never stole in our neighborhood again, but was shot dead trying to rob a liquor store in Queens six months later.

Larry never played an organized sport. Yet, upon his graduation from high school he received scholarship offers from four colleges for baseball and another for football. One high profile D -1 coach spent almost three hours working his parents so they could convince Larry to continue to his education.

Larry, ever the well-mannered, told everyone there he was going to work for the New York City Sanitation department.

Less than a year later, rather than patrolling an outfield, he was on point in Vietnam. The ambush was sudden. The Viet Cong attacking force of perhaps three dozen caught the Americans in a cross fire. The Cong bullets felled sixteen of Larry's fellow soldiers within seconds. Larry unharmed, retreated back to the unit. Their fate rested on his shoulders. As the Viet Cong snare grew tighter, Larry fended off the attack, hurling grenades at the enemy. His tosses were precise and at an appropriate timing to keep the Cong off balance. Between enemy rushes he dragged man after man to a protected location. Finally, after what seemed like many hours reinforcements arrived. The unit was rescued. Larry had saved everyone's life.

Every other youth neighborhood hero fizzled into their non-descript lives. Larry, on the other hand was now a legend. We all know heroes die and legends live forever.

I often wondered what Larry's life might have been if he had elected a different path. He may have become a professional athlete; he may have gone on to set records, maybe not. But I do know one thing; sixteen other lives would have been cut short in that humid Vietnam jungle.

Larry passed away in 2013, one year after retiring from forty years of service in the New York City Department of Sanitation.

Chapter 1
Ohio 1960

For most of the primarily Italian community of the North Hill section of Akron, Wednesday, August 10, 1960 was starting as a typical miserable, gritty summer morning in the tire capital of the country. The Firestone and Goodyear plants operated nonstop to meet the demand for tires of the post-World War II automobile boom. As the rubber facilities hummed, men worked and endless streams of billowing ebony spewed from the mouths of the half-dozen concrete smoke stacks. This created a yellow haze that lingered in the sky of the city, coating both clothes and lungs with fine black particles. Weather was also not cooperating, as the Great Lakes region was caught in the death-like grip of a two-month-long heat wave. An El Nino condition had developed in the Pacific causing bands of hot dry air to whip across southern California. Stifling pressure-cooker conditions crawled across the states in an easterly direction. The daytime will once again approach one hundred degrees for the 10th consecutive day. The Cleveland metro area has seen less than one inch of rain since Memorial Day. Residents prayed for those brief but refreshing afternoon thundershowers, which did not come.

Pepe awoke at 7:30AM to the usual kitchen sounds and smells of the family breakfast preparation. He leaned his crew-cut head back, sticking his nose in the air. With a deep long inhale, "Hmm. Nana is cooking her homemade sausage and scrambled eggs," Pepe concluded. Accompanying this breakfast feast would be her unusually robust coffee, as dark as the muddy waters of the Cuyahoga River, a meal for a king to start the day.

Pepe scans the tiny bedroom. His brothers Dominick and Bene are still nestled under the sheets. Pepe snaps to attention and jumps from his bed. I will beat them to the kitchen and just have more food for me!

This day is very extraordinary for Pepe. For as long as he can remember, he had been waiting for this day to come. As the youngest of six brothers and sisters, it is finally his turn. Today is a special, almost magical day, one which will be remembered throughout Pepe's lifetime. Today is the day his dad would take him to see his first major league baseball game, the Cleveland Indians versus the Boston Red Sox. The Indians, American League Champions in 1954, were just eight games out of first, chasing those dreaded Yankees, who appear to be stumbling. The lowly lousy Red Sox, as usual, are mired in the basement, 15 ½ games behind. "Why did dad choose this game?" he thought, "it's not like I'm going to see the Yankees." Although Pepe hates the Yankees, he would have rather seen Berra, Mantle, Maris, and Ford, some of the stars he had come to know through the broadcasts heard on his transistor radio. What a treat that would be. Quickly Pepe's excitement took hold again as he reversed his thoughts. "Who cares? I'm going to the stadium to see a real major league game!"

Each of his two older brothers had experienced this rite of passage. Tonio, Pepe's dad, had taken each of Pepe's brothers to their first big league game. This event generally coincided with their selection onto a Tallmadge Little League major's team. Pepe, now 10, had been drafted onto the team sponsored by Luigi's Pizzeria. Pepe has a passion for the game of baseball. He has read whatever he could get his hands on about the sport since the second grade. Mr. Gianfranco, coach of Luigi's, said of Pepe, "He has the keenest mind and interest about baseball of any boy I've seen in 10 years of coaching." Pepe was never sure exactly what the grizzled Mr. Gianfranco meant, but at age ten he achieved the goal of making the majors younger than either of his brothers!

After breakfast, Pepe needed to confront two immediate dilemmas. Should he bring his baseball mitt to the game, and what tee shirt to wear?

His two closest friends, Phil and Bobby, told him if a spectator caught a foul ball without using a glove, the player who hit it out would sign it. Looking with dismay at his hand-me-down mitt, a Rawlings left-handed fielder's edition with the name Johnnie Podres. Pepe thought, "John Podres, MVP of the 1955 World Series, a 7th game shut-out. The Dodgers had finally beaten those Yankees." Pepe spun the glove around and deftly put it on his left hand, three fingers into the thumb slot and thumb into the pinky finger slot. In his family, most times you just had to make do. Unlike his southpaw brothers, Pepe is right-handed. Although he uses the glove on the wrong hand, Pepe is an exceptional fielder, nearly flawless when he gets to the ball. He decides it's best to leave the glove at home.

All of Pepe's belongings are neatly stored in the heavily marred and scratched twenty-year-old mahogany three-drawer dresser that sits in the corner of the room he shares with his brothers. What he could not fit in this old beat-up dresser is stored, usually, on the floor of a communal closet, where ownership is ignored. If it fits you, it is yours, at least for the day. He decided on the faded white, now nearly yellow, shirt with a large number 9 hand scrawled across the front.

This is a predominately blue collar Italian neighborhood. Home for this family of eight was a dingy light green four-bedroom, one-bathroom apartment on the lower floor of a duplex located on Shelby Avenue. Tonio drives a taxi six days a week, earning just enough money to almost make ends meet. This included sending his children to St. Vincent-St. Mary, the local Catholic school, which each would attend through high school. Tonio decided years earlier that his children would be given opportunities he did not have. One of those is a better education, which would provide them a shot at a better life. Today is his day off; nothing in the world could make him happier than an outing with one of his children, especially Pepe, who is the most energetic, athletic and out-going of his children.

Taking Pepe to Cleveland's Municipal Stadium, although an ill-afforded luxury, is as much of a delight for him as it is for Pepe. Tonio has witnessed Pepe's love for the game. The boy would ramble on about baseball for hours. He could quote statistics, game history, rules and of course he could remember the great rhubarbs. Any opportunity to play found Pepe on the sandlots. Today would be special, for Pepe would see the best left-handed hitter of all time take the field, Ted Williams. At age 41, Williams is hitting close to .300 with 19 home runs. This is a phenomenal feat for any ball player over the age of 40. Yes, today would be special. If the Splendid Splinter could manage to hit one out of the field, he would become the second all-time leading home run hitter with 512, behind only the great Jimmy Foxx.

The 39-mile trip to the Municipal Stadium will take a little less than two hours in the family's pale blue 1952 Nash Rambler wagon, equipped with whitewall tires, chrome wheel covers and an AM pushbutton radio. In 1959, Tonio had purchased the car, used, for $400. His mechanical abilities enable him keep it in smooth running condition, despite its age and odometer reading of over 60,000 miles. Recently Tonio rebuilt the straight 6-cylinder engine, so he was confident the trip would go without issue. If he pushed, the car could still reach speeds of up to 50 miles an hour in a mere 21 seconds.

Batting practice is scheduled to begin at 11:30AM, so he and Pepe would need to set out on their journey by 9:15AM at the latest. Tonio did not want Pepe to miss any of the pre-game activities. The players would come over the railing and talk with the fans. Who knows, maybe Pepe might even manage to get an autograph. Tonio thought, *I better tell Pepe not to forget pen and paper.*

Tonio never enjoyed the drive to Cleveland, but he would make the best of the situation. Route 8 could be slow, especially if he had the bad luck to get behind one of the few horse-drawn wagons left in the area, or an overloaded truck carrying produce from a local farm. Tonio would allow plenty of time to get to the stadium, find a place to park, find their seats and settle on food and refreshments. Today's outing will cost almost $7.00. It will be worth it, though.

Cleveland Municipal Stadium, the mistake by the lake, as many referred to it, Tonio reflected. He still cannot get used to that name. He preferred the original name, Lakefront Stadium. Tonio being very old-fashioned, or traditional rather, also preferred League Park, the cozy little ballpark, once home to the Indians, located three miles east of downtown Cleveland. Tonio recalled the good times going to games there with his dad. He remembered vividly the way the three-story red-brick facade jumped out at him, his eyes widening with excitement. Then, of course, there was the bustle of the endless line of trolleys from which the fans emerged before a game, the horns of the autos all adding to the commotion. But most of all, he remembered the inside of the park, the way the lower-level seats jutted towards the field to bring the fans close to the sights and sounds of the players and the game. From where he and his dad had sat, he could hear the umpire start the game with "Play ball." There was a sound associated with every pitch, either a thump as the ball landed in the catcher's mitt or a crack when the batter made contact. Occasionally on a check swing, he could hear the batter groan. An even bigger thrill was the argument which followed a disputed call. He told his dad that it reminded him of the post-Sunday dinner debates conducted by his Italian family. During some of the games, a thin rope provided the only demarcation from the players along the right and left field foul-lines when crowds had bled out from the grandstand. League Park was much easier to get to. He enjoyed the ride along Euclid Avenue, looking at the mansions of families like the Rockefellers and imagining life as part of the very rich. Lakefront Stadium was just too expansive; League Park gave fans a much, much better chance to view a game. Tonio thought there was just too much room between home plate and the stands, and foul territory was just too big. Shortly after Lakefront Stadium had originally opened, the team owners decided to shorten the fences in center field and the power alleys by over 50 feet because too few homeruns were hit. Fans liked and wanted to see more homeruns. Cleveland needed a homerun hitting star.

The uneventful trek north took nearly the full 2 hours allotted by Tonio before he and Pepe parked at the lot closest to Gate D. They arrived just as fans were allowed to enter the stadium. Pepe's eyes widened as he gazed at this magnificent structure for the very first time. Pepe walked into the ballpark, slowly absorbing as many of the sights, sounds and smells as he could. The ticket takers, the food and beverage vendors and the souvenir vendors each provided their own brand of entertainment for Pepe. "Scorecard, get your scorecard, only 5 cents," barked a gentleman whose wrinkled skin reflected years of exposure to the elements. Standing on a wooden box, Pepe thought of the circus. "Can't tell a player without a scorecard," the man continued with a loud and deep raspy voice, the result of one too many cigars.

"Dad, do you think we'll get to see the Indians hit batting practice?"

"Sure Pep, we've got plenty of time."

"Dad, do I need a scorecard?"

"Nah, save your money for something you could keep. Besides, you forgot to bring a pencil."

"Dad, he is selling pencils, too. The scorecard is something I will keep forever!"

"Pepino, its just paper. It will fade. Your memory of today is what will last forever."

"I can use it for autographs!"

"OK," Tonio finally conceded.

"Dad, let's hurry and get to our seats. I don't want to miss anything."

Section 5, Row AC, Seats 11 and 12 was printed on the green ticket stub. Enter Gate D. Gate D was at the furthest end of the main part of the stadium, just before the bleacher entrance. Pepe admired the structure, 45 feet of concrete creating the base of the wall. Above the base rose the coal-black steel upper tier, forming an imposing upper ring. Tonio and Pepe walked hand-in-hand into the stadium darkness on a concrete path. A scant 100 steps later up a slight incline, they emerged back into the sunlight. Pepe stopped. He stared at the giant center field scoreboard in all its majesty. To either side was an advertising billboard. 'Home of the Indians' was in script across the top of the scoreboard, as bright a crimson red Pepe had ever seen. Pepe absorbed the infield, "How did they get the dirt so brown and neat?" The green grass was so bright; Pepe imagined it must have been painted. The foul lines and batter's box, the chalk, all inspired the thought, *If only I could get my shirt as white as those lines.* Pepe's only visual reference was from experience on the dying-grass, pebble-filled baselines of the Akron Little League infield.

Abruptly an imposing man with a fuzzy glove on his left hand, wearing glasses with a bent frame, a silly-looking blue cap and a blue jacket with a badge pinned to the lapel stops the pair. "Tickets, please." Tonio hands the man the tickets. He examines them closely, and then beckons Pepe and Tonio to follow him.

"He's taking us to our seats, son." Tonio responded before Pepe could get the question from his mouth. The man with the fuzzy glove was about 20 feet in front of them as Pepe bounded after him, still skeptical as to his motives. Further and further towards the playing field he strode with Pepe hot on his heels. Tonio just chuckled, as he took two quarters from his pocket. Three rows from the field the man stopped. Row AC, seats 11 and 12, just outside the right field foul pole, just a few feet from the players on the field.

"Wow," was all Pepe could muster.

The man with the fuzzy glove bent over to wipe down their seats. *So that's what the glove is for*, Pepe thought to himself as Tonio handed the attendant the 4 bits.

Pepe began to open his mouth to ask his next question or make his next observation when there was an ear-piercing crack similar to that of lightning during a storm. Then quickly another crack like none he had ever heard. As his mouth went agape, Tonio spoke "Well, son, you just heard Ted Williams hit the ball."

The spellbound Pepe in an excitement-induced trance nearly sat down in the lap of the elderly stranger sitting in seat 13.

"Sorry, sir," Pepe quickly said, somewhat embarrassed.

"That's all right, kid," said the man, with an emphasis on kid. "It's a great day for a baseball game. Baseball was, is and always will be to me the best game in the world," the man said without moving his glance from the playing field. The sound of his voice would remain etched within Pepe's memories for a very long time.

Chapter 2

In the eastern sky, the blazing yellow morning sun was now peering out above the upper rim of the left field stands, bathing the fans seated in the right-field sections in soothing warmth that would build to an unbearable heat as the day moved into the deep afternoon. Pepe pulled the brim of his dark blue baseball cap down onto his forehead, shielding his eyes from the sun's penetrating rays.

"No, Dad, the best lefty pitcher today is Whitey Ford," Pepe commented to his dad, further fueling the debate which started the night before. "I wish we could see him pitch today. Spahn is done and Koufax hasn't done anything yet"

"Oh, Pepe, you're just saying that because you like the Indians and the American League. Spahn will have more twenty-game win seasons from now until he retires than Ford will in his career. Koufax throws harder than anyone in the game, and he's got a paralyzing curve ball that isn't hittable by lefties. And boy, can Spahn hit! Imagine 21 career homers, imagine what he could do if he played every day."

"That Spahn fellow, is he batting above .200 for his career?" more of a rhetorical statement than a question from the old man in the seat next to Pepe. "Boy, baseball changes over the years. Expectations just seem to get milder," continued the old timer.

That thought, somewhat philosophical, a bit prophetic, hit a chord of interest with Pepe. He gazed a little longer at the old man. In spite of the forecast, the old man was wearing a lightweight camel-colored jacket zipped to his chin. On his head he wore a brown tweed newsy cap with a short stiff bill. This reminded Pepe of the comic strip character, Andy Capp. This old guy seems to know his stuff; he had a sense of the past.

"The Spahn kid can pitch, but he ain't much of a hitter," the old man went on.

Just as he finished the sentence, the voice of an invisible announcer boomed from the public address system, "Pitching today for the Cleveland Indians, number 18, Barry Latman. Catching, number 11, Johnnie Romano." After both teams 'starting line-ups were introduced, the voice commanded, "All rise for our national anthem."

As the echoes of the final words of the Star Spangled Banner fade, and the approximately 7,500 fans settled back into their seats, Tonio leans over to Pepe, "Ted Williams is up third. He is the best left-handed hitter of all time. Today you might see a bit of history."

"Gee, dad, he is something, but best of all time?" Pepe shot back.

"Pep, you know his stats better than anyone. Williams can hit for power, for average, and drive in runs. He's the last player have a four hundred batting average"

"Dad, you're exaggerating as usual!"

"Now batting, number 9, Ted Williams, number 9,", so engaged in the debate was Pepe and Tonio that they had argued right through the first two Red Sox hitters.

Latman was into his windup by the time the pair looked up from their debate. The first pitch, a fastball, was just off the inside corner. "Ball One," roared the umpire.

"Best eye at the plate, ever. See that, Pep, that pitch didn't miss by much," said Tonio almost gleefully, as to reinforce his premise.

Before Pepe could respond, Latman was delivering the next offering to Williams. Ball two, on a pitch barely even with the letters of his uniform.

Tonio could not help himself, "Best eye, he's never fooled on a pitch, makes the pitcher work to get him out."

The third offering to Williams was a waist-high pitch on the inner half of the plate, and with a mighty cut, the ball was ripped toward the right field foul pole. Pepe watched as the laser headed directly toward him. The ball was on him so quickly he had neither time to duck nor get his gloveless hand up. The ball appeared to have a destiny with his angelic 10-year-old face. Pepe just froze. Tonio was not paying attention, so he could not react fast enough; already fearing the worst, all he could manage was a helpless elongated cry of "Noooooooooooooo!"

Just as the ball was about to inflict its damage on the immobile Pepe, the old man in seat 13 reached across his broad frame to snare the line drive with his massive tobacco-stained right hand, no more than three inches from the unintended victim.

The few fans seated nearby gave a polite applause but quickly resumed their attentions to the game. "That was close, there, kid. Save the debate for school and watch the damn game. I don't have the energy to save your scrawny butt again," said the old man. "Besides, Williams is good, but not the best hitter ever, right-handed or left-handed. Let me tell you about the greatest hitter the game has ever seen, will ever see. You probably remember him as the best pitcher and his 512 wins.' With a slight pause, in a reflective tone he continued, 'the year was 1914, April 22, I believe …

Chapter 3
Maryland 1902

Summer conditions in Baltimore were settling in early in 1902, with constant stifling humidity from which relief rarely could be found. The summer holidays were still a week away. One oasis for the locals to come and gain refuge from the suffocating elements and insufferable stench of the pigs in the stockyards was George and Catherine's, known as Katie to most patrons, pub. This was a family-owned and operated saloon and restaurant situated on West Camden Street, in the shadows of the meat packing plants, local factories, and warehouses and manufacturing plants. "Pigtown"and the nearby communities was one of the more miserable sections of south Baltimore. The local businesses provided a great deal of the regular blue-collar and working-class customers to the Ruth's establishment.

A slight woman of barely 4' 10", Katie had started feeling the ill effects of her current pregnancy much sooner than in any of the previous ones. Her thoughts focused on the coming long, hot, miserable summer with no relief. The baby was to come in early October. Would she be able to bear working over the next few months? Although only in her mid-twenties, her frail appearance was that of women much older. The combination of constant pregnancies, routine 100-hour weeks on her feet at the saloon and regular bouts with illness were quickly taking a severe toll that would claim her life within the next decade.

Abruptly, there were the all-too-familiar three firm raps on the front door of the saloon. The Ruth's had heard this sound a few times before, made with the end of a patrolman's billy club. Since the large saloon hall room was empty and still, the aggressive knocks created an echo that reverberated across the entire saloon hall. This sent shivers up George and Katie's spines. *Not again, please not more trouble from George Jr.* Katie knew instinctively that her internal plea was to be futile.

Since they were not yet open for business, the couple was in the kitchen, preparing for the expected weekday lunch crowd. By the time the pair had exited the kitchen, Police officer Sean Kearny had shoved open the tavern's front door, dragging the 7-year-old George Jr. by the collar of his dirt-stained blue shirt across the beat-up old oak floor. George Jr.'s shoes scraped along the floor surface, leaving intermittent black scuffs from the little leather left on his shoes, as the muscular 6' 5" Officer Kearny pulled the lad with him. The officer's chiseled face and grizzled look was accentuated by the 3" jagged scar on the outside and just above the corner of his left eye. Although George Jr., was quite big for his tender age, he was no match for the sinewy policeman, who continued to drag him towards his parents with purpose and malice. Each of George Jr.'s knees had meet the ground with some force, as evidenced by a tear at the knee of each pant leg and highlighted with a dash of crimson peeking out beyond the fabric. Regardless, George Jr. fought for his freedom like an eel just pulled out of the murky Baltimore Harbor waters by one of the local fisherman.

"Good day, officer," offered Katie Ruth, her expression outwardly pleasant. "What seems to be the problem?" She was trying her best to hide her fear of the inevitable truth, that George Jr. had once again let his mischievousness and cavalier behavior get the better of him. Katie had grown intolerant of George Jr.'s ritual over the last year. She had long since abandoned any of her maternal instincts when dealing with him. She was now quick with the belt or whip. Shortly before the most recent Christmas, she beat him until she physically collapsed from exhaustion, with George Jr. defiantly smirking at Katie as he absorbed the pain.

The crime that day was George Jr. depositing a wad of chewing gum into the ringlets of the girl who was unlucky enough to sit in front of him on the one few days he attended school.

"Ma'am, for starters, this ruffian is a truant. I know school is winding down, but it's the third time I've picked him up in the past week," Kearny responded in a tone less amicable than that of Mrs. Ruth. Before Kearny could get the next sentence out, Katie saw the cause of the policeman's ire this time. Contrasting his dark blue uniform jacket with its 5 copper buttons were three bright red circular blotches, each about 3 inches in diameter, peppered with pale yellow seeds plastered squarely on his chest.

With his parents working very long hours, George Jr. recently began hanging out with a small band of teenage roughnecks in Baltimore's

Ridgley's Delight section. This was a notoriously tough neighborhood situated between the central harbor district and the Baltimore and Ohio Railroad yards. This young pack of rowdies was quickly gaining dubious fame; their goal was to achieve similar notoriety to that of the Five Points Gang from the Bowery section of New York City.

The Ridgley's Delight gang began with normal childhood pranks, snatching a piece of fruit from a peddler's wagon or getting a night watchman to chase them through the idle railroad cars. There were harmless brawls ending without significant injury. The Ridgley gang's activities evolved into more serious thefts as they began stealing cash from local merchants and small items from local passers-by which could be pawned easily and without notice. The crew had become too well-known in their own back yard by the patrol officers and merchants, so they set their sights on other sections of Baltimore such as Jonestown and Mount Vernon. The one misstep they had was on Lombard Street. Liam, the leader of Ridgley's Delight gang, had snatched a silver cross from the neck of an elderly woman as she slowly crossed the intersection at S. Exter St. Before the gang could run towards the inner harbor, they were cut off quickly, almost out of nowhere, by a gang of much greater numbers and several years older. For this brawl with the Italians, Ridgley's was no match. Most of the gang was left cut and bruised, with their egos more damaged than their bodies. This was a clear and serious message by the Italians: *Stay out of Little Italy*.

Little George endeared himself to Liam during one refreshing spring day of 1902. Little Ruth had become fascinated to the point of obsession with breaking anything by tossing rocks. His targets were things such as windows or glass bottles. He would set up a series of bottles for targets. For hours at a time he would hurl stones of different size and shapes until each of the bottles was reduced to nothing but tiny glass shards. When the gang confiscated the bottle for the valuable bounty, Ruth would just take aim on one of the many factory windows available in the area. As his aim improved, he graduated from breaking random windows to pinpointing an exact window on which to launch his assault.

On this particular day, Liam had wrested two peaches from the local produce market on S. Freemont Avenue, near W. Lombard St. He knew the owner and his wife were in their late 60's and presented no threat to catch him, even if he were seen. Unfortunately he was not lucky. A patrol officer making his routine rounds witnessed the act just as he exited Vincenzo's Barber Shop after a refreshing shave.

The officer yelled for Liam to stop. Glancing back, Liam recognized the predicament and took off in earnest. Liam had been arrested twice since the summer of 1901. Now 14, he could be headed for a stretch in Charles H. Hickey House or worse, Greenmount Avenue and the Baltimore Correction Center. The officer let loose with three long bursts of his whistle. Liam wasted no time and headed south on Freemont. With the whistle pressed between his lips, and billy club in his right hand the officer began his chase of the juvenile. Liam knew if he could get to the railroad yards, he could ditch the cop easily, since there would be too many places to hide between the idle box cars and expansive warehouses, especially the partially-complete B&O Warehouse with its unusual shape. Winding his way through the streets, Liam glanced over his shoulder several times only to find the officer gaining ground. Liam darted east on S. Paca Street, now just two short blocks of his safe haven. The long-legged officer was now eating up ground quicker than at the outset, with cheetah-type strides which appeared to be ever-widening. Liam's forehead was covered in little beads that were beginning to run down his cheeks and his breathing became labored. As Liam approached Russell Avenue, his lead was a mere 30 feet.

Relaxing against the gas lamp pole on the north corner of the intersection was George Jr. George could see Liam straining to maintain his speed as he approached the yards with the "Copper" on his tail. George, fingering the sizable coal chunk in his left pocket that he had snagged from a coal bin earlier in the day, sized up the situation pretty quickly. Although the coal would be useful in his daily ritual of target practice, there was now a more immediate need. George had become quite proficient in hitting stationary targets, but this one was moving. He would have only a single chance at the target; if he missed, there would be no reset. Worse, Liam would most likely be caught and sent

away. George would never again see him. George
adored Liam as the leader of the gang, and he was
the only person George had a connection with.

George raised his left hand to the level of his
head and slightly behind his left ear. He set his
sharp eyes on the target. In a stance which came
naturally, Ruth set his feet just outside of the width
of his shoulders. He perfectly balanced his weight
on each foot. Using his right shoulder as a guide, he
took careful aim on the fast-moving policeman. He
lifted his right foot ever so slightly, moving his foot
toward the target. He began to move his arm
forward. With an ever-so-slight weight shift and
rotation of his right hip, the torque created caused
his left arm to whip in an almost effortless motion.
He let loose the 5-ounce stone, the palm of hand
following through to the target. Ruth put as much
muscle as he could into the toss, grunting timidly.
The throw, with the uncanny accuracy this 7-year-
old had developed, found its mark, hitting the
officer just under the brim of the cap. The unwary
pursuer almost immediately was knocked off his
feet, hitting the ground in a heap. He sat stunned,
blood streaming down his face from the gash near
his left eye. The officer would remain seated for at
least 10 minutes, absorbing the searing pain from
the deep cut on his face and the bruise to his right
knee from the fall. This was just enough of a respite
for his prey and the young Ruth to escape. When
help showed, up five stitches would be required to
close the wound at Hebrew Hospital and Asylum.
"Very lucky" was his physician's opinion. Less than
half an inch lower and the officer would have lost

his eye. The officer was thankful for his luck, since he did not want to be removed his patrol duties and relegated to a boring desk job. Taking him off the streets would have been a blow to his self-esteem. He enjoyed the thrill of finding and putting young hoodlums away for a while. Now he had a score to settle.

Liam was forever thankful to young Ruth, since he, too, would remain free to roam the streets for a short while longer. Unfortunately for Liam, in the spring of 1903 he would once again test fate. After an attempt to steal a veal chop from a butcher shop in Little Italy, Liam was the recipient of two .38 caliber slugs, compliments of a loyal Italian protecting his turf. He had nailed the would-be thief before Liam could make it two blocks.

When the Ridgeley Gang band of misfits was not pilfering or fighting, youthful boredom took over. "An idle brain is the devil's workshop," George Jr. recalled hearing repeatedly from his parents on the occasions they were around. But George Jr. did not object as the gang turned his extraordinary gift into a mischievous game of chicken.

Today's new adventure was to toss rotten tomatoes at anyone who happened into their range of fire when they were loaded with these annoying armaments. Ruth often would squeeze the tomato in his hand too tightly initially, creating an oozing mess. When he could still manage a toss with a mangled tomato, the throw was far short of the target. Or if he got the proper distance, the flattened tomatoes moved uncontrollably, usually drifting harmlessly past the intended target. Finally George Jr. figured out he needed to hold the soft projectile gently, with less pressure in the palm, more in the tips of his fingers. George finally learned to effectively control the speed, flight and angle of the throw. At 7 years old, he was the most accurate thrower in the gang.

On Wednesday, June 11, 1902, the gang, as was typical for a lazy day of summer, was struggling with its boredom. One of the gang managed to rescue a crate of overripe tomatoes no longer suitable for sale and now destined for the garbage scow. An unsuspecting target moved down Russell Street — Officer Kearny, who was daydreaming as he padded along his beat. The streets were empty and things very quiet as many of the spiritless children were swimming down at the Patapsco River, avoiding the heat. Kearny's complacency made him a perfect mark for Georgie to put his skills to the test, a pinpoint throw for the ages, center mass on a cop. Unfortunately for Ruth, he would stretch his luck a bit too far this time.

Georgie's immense need to feel wanted betrayed any prepubescent logic. To get everyone's attention, he always wanted to be seen as capable of doing something no one else could ever dare to do. He assured Liam he could deliver a direct hit onto Officer Kearny's badge. Liam told Ruth to go for it. Ruth fired the first two tosses quickly, each of which hit the officer. Ruth most likely would have had sufficient enough time to escape without capture, had he taken off then. However, Ruth took a gamble which would alter the direction of his life.

He decided to take a third shot. Ruth uncorked a third throw, right on target. Ruth seriously miscalculated Kearny's distance and speed and he was left too close to the fleet prey. Kearny was as mad as a hornet and was making a beeline towards Ruth as he reloaded after the first two gifts delivered to the officer. Just as the tomato once again splayed on impact with the officer's chest, Kearny, using a quick whipping motion, was able to have his club find the outside of Ruth's skinny right thigh. As Ruth's senses recognized the resounding thud, an instantaneous sharp pain followed. The following muscle convulsions caused an immediate 'charlie horse' that slowed Ruth to a crawl as the shearing pain penetrated his young body. With Ruth already clutching his right leg, Kearny delivered a second blow, this time to the left leg, buckling the knee. Sitting on the cobblestone surface, George Jr., in mind-numbing agony, desperately tried to rub the pain from each leg. Refusing to cry aloud, his muffled sounds of fear and hurt would go unheard by Kearny. George Jr. would not allow Kearny to believe he had gotten the upper hand. Snared, George Jr.'s thoughts became focused on the punishment that would be visited on him as he was brought home to face the wrath of Katie.

"Sorry, officer," a now timid-sounding Mrs. Ruth uttered in a tone barely above a whisper.

"Georgie, what have you to say for yourself, dear?"

"Take these stinking pig hands off me. I need to take a look and see how much I missed his badge by." George Jr., the ever-recalcitrant smart mouth, quipped in discourteous manner as he continued massaging his sore legs. Before his remarks had completely dissipated, George tasted the back of Katie's hand as she delivered a swat across his thick lips.

"This place ain't suitable to raise this child. Ya know, Ma'am, he was right here when you had all that trouble a bit back, with the shooting and all. And those young thugs he's been running with. Your place here is always filled with drifters, drunks and roustabouts. No place for a child, even one like this one," Kearny stated in a reprimanding manner.

"Officer, we're at our wit's end. George has become so incorrigible. He is a malicious little animal, not to be tamed. And those God-awful words from his mouth…" a despondent Katie hesitated in mid-response as her eyes welled up. Although she expressed constant anger towards George Jr., here she was face-to-face with the reality of failing as a mother. Only two of her eight children would survive past childhood. She bore a self-imposed responsibility that contributed to her deep sense of failure, but resentment of her failure was turning to hatred of her son.

"What do you expect," retorted Kearny, "given the scum which hangs in these parts of town?"

Silent to this point, the stewing George Sr. had slipped off his food-stained apron, suddenly pounced on Junior and in a single motion, plucked him from the grasp of Kearny and marched him down the rear stairs into the cellar. As George Sr. entered the stairwell, he removed a well-worn barber strop from its storage hook.

The cellar, which was below street level, was the primary storage space for the Ruths' business. Stacks of crates, barrels and odds and ends not only cluttered the basement but also served to muffle any sounds. Very little could be heard in the saloon from the inky depths below. George Jr. knew his screams, even if heard, would fall on the deaf ears of his mother and the revengeful police officer. George Jr. had been beaten before. The elder Ruth, large by standards of the times, could pack a wallop. Although George Jr. would once again try to mute his cries, it would be a battle lost.

The third strike delivered across Ruth's bottom turned a whimper into a wail. Maybe his father and the evil Officer Kearny prevailed in today's stanza because they each could deliver an unchallenged physical beating, but no one would get the better of him. Ruth believed he was mentally and emotionally tougher than either of them. Ruth knew somewhere he would find a place where he was wanted and accepted.

By Friday, June 13, 1902, George Senior knew exactly what he was going to do. The incorrigible Junior was a heavy burden for the family. He and Katie were working non-stop. Katie was in the midst of another very difficult pregnancy. He did not know how much longer she could put in the long, grueling hours in the saloon or deal with the rowdy crowds. The other young ones, also fighting grave sickness, needed constant care.

Junior was out of control, a delinquent at 7 without any direction. He would need more guidance and help than he and Katie could offer if Junior were going make something decent of his life or even simply survive the cruel streets.

At approximately 9:00 AM, the two of them boarded the Caton Avenue streetcar. Their destination today was St. Mary's Industrial School for Boys. Approximately six miles from the Ruth home, at the intersection with Wilkens Avenue, rose the six grey-stone building prison-like compound of St. Mary's, occupying nearly 100 acres. This would be just the right answer, thought the senior Ruth, just the right answer.

Here Georgie would get an education, learn respect and manners. Mr. Ruth realized he just could not manage Junior any longer. Routinely beating the young boy was not a solution. George Senior had considered sending Georgie to St. Mary's following the incident at Christmas. After protracted beating by Katie, the insufferable Georgie returned to school, not as a remorseful soul, but with a heightened sense of meanness. He continued with his campaign of malignant pranks against timid girls, regardless of any further consequence. In his most recent vile antic, Ruth spat out moist heaps of goo into several nearly-full glasses of milk at lunch. This was the byproduct of an enormous chunk of tobacco he had begun chewing in class earlier in the day. With morbid amusement, Ruth watched with simple glee the reactions as the sickened girls began to vomit after a few gulps of the bitter-tasting tainted drink. Ruth, in the solitude of his mind, had won out over Katie.

At that time, George had talked to Brother Matthias Boutlier about Junior and the discipline problems. The Catholic Xaverian Brothers were renowned for their ability to instill discipline and order into the lives of young boys. They were very strict and highly intolerant. When boys graduated from St. Mary's, it was usually as responsible adults with skills sufficient to make a living.

Brother Matthias was born Martin Leo Boutlier, in Lingan, Cape Breton, Nova Scotia. This was a small mining community located on the eastern end of Cape Breton Island. A bat and ball game, was a favorite pastime of the Cape Bretoners as early as about 1838. Matthias and his older brother spent countless hours in pickup games where he learned the ins, outs and nuances of baseball. Along with his reputation of being a master educator and motivator of young men, Matthias prided himself on his prowess at teaching baseball and building competitive teams. Over the past decade, his youth teams had won 4 state championships and 3 times runners-up. During his stint at St. Mary's, Matthias had developed a relationship with Jack Dunn, a scout for the Baltimore Orioles of the International League. More than anything, Matthias dreamt of one day seeing an alumnus of St. Mary's make it to the major leagues. In an occasional private moment, Brother Matthias let his imagination run wild. Maybe there was even that special player to become a star. Maybe.

Shortly before noon, Mr. Ruth and Brother Matthias had finished working out the details for Georgie's stay at St. Mary's. Mr. Ruth did not want this matter in the hands of the courts. As with most immigrant families, he was distrustful of governmental authorities and wanted this matter to be handled by him and his family. Additionally, most juveniles were sent away until they attained the age of twenty-one. Mr. Ruth hoped the time needed to reform Georgie would be less.

Brother Matthias had little hesitation about taking in the young Ruth. He knew exactly how to handle children just like little Georgie.

"Idleness breeds the devil's trouble," Matthias commented. "This little one will get an education, learn a trade and needed discipline. He will become a useful citizen."

Ruth was not quite ready to go. Clutching his father's pant leg, he begged for them to return home. The 6'6" Matthias secured Ruth in a reverse bear hug as Ruth's father laconically walked away, unemotional, without any hint or indication to this wretched goodbye. It was simply an abject display of ill affection as he strolled down the long hallway to begin his journey back to the grime of South Baltimore.

Ruth tried one last attempt to gain the attention of his dad, in the shrillest screech manageable by a 7 year old, "Please, dad! No, don't go. Take me home!"

As the heavy oak front door to St. Mary's closed with a bang, the suddenly abandoned, no longer free to roam the streets Ruth wept. He understood he was home, at least for now.

Chapter 4

The early of life of St. Mary's Industrial school was as uncertain as that of Ruth. In 1866, Archbishop Spalding was dealing with two problems of the day, the loss of thousands of Irish Catholics to the Roman Catholic Church and the burgeoning problem of abandoned, neglected and destitute Catholic children within the largest US cities. These children of very poor immigrant families faced even more imminent issues. With their lack of education or vocational training, even mere survival was doubtful. St. Mary's opened its doors on October 3, 1866, welcoming its first orphaned boy. The school's population grew quickly. Within a few short months, the temporary housing structure was pushed to the limits of its capacity.

Archbishop Spalding was familiar with the positive impact the Xaverian Brothers were having in the other Catholic Industrial schools they ran, such as Lincolndale in New York. The core mission of the Xaverian Brothers was (and remains to this day) working with disadvantaged youth, usually in the inner cities, to give them a sense of purpose in life, provide guidance and direction. The Brothers believed these industrial schools to be an asylum for these orphaned boys from the evils which abounded in the streets. The ages of the students was widely varied. The youngest students were as young as 5, others were in their late teens. No one remained at

St. Mary's past the age of 21, but not a single boy ever tried to escape St. Mary's.

St. Mary's struggled financially, as considerable capital investment was required to complete buildings, add machinery and equipment for proper vocational training. Only through the extreme generosity of private donors was St. Mary's able to keep its doors open. In 1872, it was decided that St. Mary's should be transitioned to a semi-public institution. Unfortunately, in that same year, the most public proponent of the Catholic Industrial effort across the country, and especially in Maryland, Archbishop Spalding, passed away suddenly.

The school's future became even less certain when in 1876, there was a public outcry over the appropriation of public funds to a religious-based organization. Opponents to the efforts of the Catholics filed a lawsuit preventing any additional public funds from going to St. Mary's. Many of the state politicians and general public shared the opinion that the problems stemming from the influx of large number of under-educated, lazy European Catholics, caused by ill-designed immigration laws, was a Church issue.

The courts found a common ground in ruling on a settlement. Per capita investment for St. Mary's was not prohibited, since a significant number of the students were public wards directed to the school. However, the court upheld the argument against appropriations from the general fund. St. Mary's, from the edge of bankruptcy and closure, now was set on course to build up its facilities and forever change the lives of young boys.

After the 1876 decision and completion of the complex, St. Mary's did not deny any boy from the streets entry. They took in those left abandoned by parents who could not afford them, 'street orphans,' delinquents, hoodlums and any other young boy in need of a place to find their way. Many of the students at St. Mary's were court-ordered wards. Other short-term 'inmates,' as the students thought of themselves, came to St. Mary's simply at the request of their parents.

Matthias wasted no time indoctrinating Ruth into his new environment. Ruth was presented with a list of trades and jobs he could perform. Matthias set the ground rules Ruth was expected to follow, the same as the other several hundred boys at St. Mary's. If you did the work of your chosen trade and your school assignments, there would be privileges plus a small allowance.

Matthias was of the Brothers of the Order of St. Francis Xavier. Of the 800 or so students who graced the grounds of St. Mary's, some were like Ruth. Their parents either directly or through the courts had given up on them. Others were true orphans. Of course, there were many who were truly young criminals and vandals. To the brothers, each of these boys was without families, whatever the reason. A boy was a boy and his life could be altered to the good through discipline, vocational training and education.

True to his belief about idleness, the students of St. Mary's had a full, if not exhausting, daily routine. Matthias would vary from this schedule only on Christmas and Easter, the two most devout Catholic holidays, or on days when there was an important baseball match.

The daily routine was as follows.

06:00 AM   Morning bell — students have 30 minutes to wash and dress

06:30 AM   All school Mass

07:15 AM   Breakfast in the dining hall

08:00 AM   Students report to assigned academic classrooms

10:00 AM   Outdoor recess

10:30 AM   School resumes

11:30 AM   Report to dining hall for lunch

11:45 AM   Lunch served

12:15 PM   Recess

01:30 PM   Younger students report for academics; older boys for vocational training

03:15 PM   Religious instruction

04:30 PM   Recess

06:15 PM   Report to dining hall for dinner

07:15 PM   Mandatory reading

08:15 PM   Lights out

This was the daily drudgery for the "inmates" of St. Mary's. The schedule was well planned and designed to allow little time for indolence. If you were late for any activity, you earned an extra duty, usually kitchen cleaning following a meal. Religious education was mandatory for Catholics, but non-Catholic students were encouraged to participate. There was organization, even in recess. The younger boys were relegated to a smaller field, the "Little Yard," and the boys of fifteen and older to "the Big Yard."

Initially, Ruth was not interested in playing by anyone's rules except his own, of course, and made no effort to conform. He was used to being free, with little guidance. On the streets of Baltimore, he went to school when he so chose, awoke each day when he wanted, ate when he just felt like it. If and when his parents decided to mete out consequences, he would simply tough them out.

During his first week at St. Mary's, Ruth continued with his irascible behavior. Ruth had been without any sense of guidance or structure and was not responsive to the rigors of the schedule. Ruth concluded he needed neither school nor a trade. His response when asked about trade was 'food snitcher' — a south Baltimore street term for one practicing the art of stealing fruits and vegetables from the pushcart merchants. This was a skill Ruth had become quite proficient at during his tenure on the streets.

Ruth was fully expecting some sort of whipping after his trade declaration, since the Brother who had made the request was visibly frustrated with Ruth. This little seven-year-old urchin purposely overslept for the all-school Mass service. He refused to pay attention in class on those times when he was physically brought to the class. Ruth got no beating but instead was allowed no sweets after supper. Ruth also lost his free time in lieu of a belt to the rear end. What he did get was a good view of the baseball fields as he peered through the filmy second-floor windows of the library, where he was confined for the next several afternoons.

Ruth was mystified as he watched the boys derive pure enjoyment from baseball, the game which would define his life. He did not understand the game at this point, but he knew he wanted to be part of the activity where there was such camaraderie. Although the sounds from below were muffled, he could see the pats on the back, handshakes and nods of the head when something appeared to have happened. Although surrounded by nearly a thousand people at St. Mary's, he still felt alone. Ruth hungered for the closeness he imagined existed in families and for acceptance by others. He would shortly find that neither of these was to be attained easily.

On the ninth day of his afternoon incarcerations in the library, Matthias visited Ruth for what would be the first of many heart-to-heart chats with "Geawgie," which was how Matthias would refer to him over the next dozen years. Matthias was hoping to reach this lost boy's soul. Ruth was hoping he would be thrown out of St. Mary's and returned home to the delusive comforts of his Ridgley's Delight street family

"Geawgie, what I am to do with you?" Matthias began. "You are a wild young thing. Idleness breeds the devil's trouble. You're going be a very busy young curmudgeon for a while."

Ruth tried without success to breach Matthias's sermon, "I want to go ..."

Matthias, unaffected by the feeble attempt of an interruption and determined to make his points to Ruth, just continued with his message.

"I have assigned one of the older boys to roust you each morning. You will get out of bed. If he needs to, he will toss a bucket of ice water on you. He'll sit next to you in class. He will work with you on your vocational training tasks and any of the extra duties you earned when everyone else is on free time. He will stand with you when we are at service or are saying prayers. Each and every minute of your day, every day, you will feel his guiding hand nearby."

Finally, in a whisper softly exhaled, with eyes cast downward, the final word of his sentence emerged from his lips. "home," managed Ruth.

"Geawgie, we're going to give you a good home, a real, comfortable home, and you will do the things you need to do our way! Understood, Geawgie, understood?" Matthias finished.

Ruth had no quip, response or reaction to what he had just heard. He felt somewhat trapped at the prospect of constant monitoring. Somehow, he would break free and come up to sever these invisible reins.

The Xaverian Brothers, especially Matthias, were noted for ruling the industrial schools with a strict and at most times rigid hand. Xaverian rules were simple, straightforward and administered fairly. Although they set a tough tone, they did not believe in corporal punishment. Only for exceptional offenses and as a means of last resort was punishment ever physical. The usual penalties for bad behavior by any of the boys were the withholding of valuable privileges. One of the most effective punishments (as Ruth would find out later) was being forbidden from taking part in the baseball games and other outdoor activities.

Matthias saw something special in the wild young Ruth. He was determined to change the path of his life. He thought, "If I could keep him occupied, Geawgie will have a good chance in life. He does not lack in determination."

Determined, Matthias knew putting Ruth on a rigorously-controlled and closely-supervised schedule was the right thing. School, vocational training, prayer, chores, and play were all now part of Ruth's minute-by-minute daily routine. The student Matthias had in mind for this job would be ideal. His life had changed for the positive during his tenure at St. Mary's.

Zachary O'Doyle was a strapping 19-year-old who had been at St. Mary's since the age of twelve. He was a thin, undersized lad when he arrived at St. Mary's. Zach now stood 6' 3" tall with broad, very strong shoulders. Brother Matthias had taken a young Zach under his wing after the Jesuit Brothers had rescued him from the New York City streets. Father Maurice Hickey had sent a letter to Matthias, asking him to accept Zach due to overcrowded conditions at the St Vincent's Home for Boys on Staten Island. Matthias agreed and Zach was shipped to Baltimore.

"Big Zach," as the other boys referred to him, was looked up to and well-liked by many of the inmates. Zach was the starting first baseman on the St. Mary's baseball team. He was also an enormously powerful hitter. Twice his batted balls reached the base of the library building wall on a single bounce. No player had ever batted a ball which hit the library building without a bounce.

Born in 1883, Zach was raised in the Mott Haven section of New York. Irish families had begun to immigrate into this area of the South Bronx in the early 1890's. Until that time, Mott Haven was dominated by upper middle-class German families who lived in the newly-constructed exquisite Brownstones. The Irish made their home in the spacious, but drab, multifamily tenements John Mott built to house the working class. Although the Irish served an economic purpose by providing many of the laborers at local factories such as John Mott's Iron Works and for construction of the subway line which would connect Manhattan and the Bronx, they were frowned upon and viewed as social outcasts. Similar to his soon-to-be protégé, Zach was an early delinquent, spending his nearly all of his time finding solitude with others on the street. He ventured to lower Manhattan in early 1896, as a fledgling but 'unofficial' member of the Whyos, the infamous Irish street gang led by Danny Driscoll and the legendary Mike McGloin.

Ruth's crimes with Ridgley's Delight were literally child's play compared to Zach's Whyos indoctrination. No one could join the gang unless he committed at least one murder. "A guy ain't tough unless he's knocked a man out," McGloin would say to anyone wanting to join the Whyos. Knocking a man out was Whyos slang for murder.

At age 13, Zach had prepared himself; he was about to murder a complete stranger to finish his indoctrination into the Whyos. Petty crimes would be a thing of the past. He could make some real money. He could do broken noses for $10.00 and black eyes for $4.00. There was plenty of work to go around. McGloin had targeted a migrant Italian man who had left his family in the old country when coming to America. He wanted to save money and then send for his wife and three young children. Each evening he followed the same path home after a long grueling day on the docks of lower Manhattan. His only mistake was walking the streets alone, trusting he was safe. Every Thursday, which was payday, the man would stop at one of the many local pubs. After more than several beers he would continue his journey home, unsteadily walking along the East River, tired and intoxicated. Some Thursdays he would find a soft place along the river's edge to curl up and sleep. He did not work Fridays. Zach was to bash his skull with a 2x4, clean out his pockets and dump the limp body into the murky East River waters. Then Zach would be a full gang member. McGloin would pick up a few bucks.

Father Salvo of the local Catholic Parish, who also had his ear to the ground on the goings-on with the gangs, caught wind of the plot. Fr. Salvo interceded, convincing Zach this was not a proper path for him to pursue with his life.

The years with Matthias served to transform this reckless, hell-bound soul into a mature, responsible man. Now Zach served as an ideal role model for other boys at St. Mary's. Matthias assigned Zach to shepherd the petulant Ruth through his daily routine. Ruth immediately thought of Liam in his initial meeting with Zach. This took Ruth back to the streets and the brotherly friendship he and Liam had shared.

With each passing day, Ruth became increasingly comfortable talking to Zach. Ruth started asking Zach about the game called 'baseball' that he saw the boys playing in the Big Yard. Zach did his best to tell Ruth all about the game. He explained the names of the positions, the basic rules and how a team would win. Ruth became intrigued with three positions, pitcher, catcher and first base, because that is where most of the action in the field took place. Ruth asked Zach many questions. Who were the best players at St. Mary's? How do you become a good pitcher? Who were the best pitchers? Why was it so hard to get hitters out all of the time? If batters were good if they got three hits every ten times up, why could not really good pitchers get them out all of the times? Ruth bombarded Zach everyday with questions about the game, typical of an adolescent. Ruth also wanted to know who the best and most famous professional baseball players of the day were. Zach told Ruth if he really wanted to learn about baseball, the best person to learn from was Brother Matthias, because he knew it all! Ruth confessed to Zach that he thought once you're famous, everyone likes you.

Ruth wanted to be liked. Ruth wanted to play baseball.

Soon Zach and Ruth were inseparable. They had developed a strong relationship driven by a mutual admiration. As with Liam, Ruth looked to Zach with the same fondness a younger sibling would show towards a caring big brother. Zach shared his experiences at St. Mary's and helped Ruth begin to find his way.

Within months, Ruth had become accustomed to the daily rigors. He even began to look forward to the classes. He enjoyed learning arithmetic. But he especially looked forward to baseball in the 'Yard,' even if he played in the small yard for now. Those times when he did retreat to old behavior, not playing baseball in the yard tore at him from the inside out.

One day Zach mentioned to the naive Ruth that in the not-too-distant future, he would be leaving St. Mary's. Within a year, perhaps when he turned 21. Zach would be fully ready, a grown man then. Ruth never thought he would be apart from Zach. Ruth filled with a sense of anticipated loss and grief. Zach did his best to comfort Ruth, assuring him all would be fine. After all, the Brothers had saved him from the damnation of hell and taught him to be an electrician. They could teach anyone anything.

Zach added that he was now able to go out into the world, make his mark and maybe even start a family, when he found the right gal. Zach let Ruth know that he would always be there for him. When

Ruth graduated from St. Mary's, he could come live with Zach, if he wanted of course.

Ruth felt somewhat better; after all they were family, courtesy of St. Mary's. Zach would always be there for him.

Shortly afterward, Brother Barnabas approached Ruth about a vocation. Patiently he went through the list of possible trade apprenticeships with Ruth, encouraging him to select one. Barnabas told Ruth most boys liked to learn trades which required some physical effort, carpentry, masonry or electrician. Ruth decided to stay away from the physically taxing trades. Rather Ruth tried his hand at being a florist. Although he showed an exceptional amount of dexterity and adaptability, some of the boys began to tease him about working with flowers. Although angered, under the firm suggestion of Zach, Ruth quickly switched to a launderer.

The laundry room at St. Mary's was a dimly lit area of about 400 square feet. The laundry room was always hot and sauna-like. A half-dozen 25-gallon wash tubs for soaking dirty clothes set in a tidy row, lined the center area. Scattered around, most leaning against walls, were dozens of scrubbing boards. There were also 4 hand-cranked mangles, used to squeeze water from the clothing, On the wall lined with shelves were various metal pans, buckets and soap supplies. The show pieces of the laundry room were the two recently donated 'state-of-the-art' wooden laundry machines, each with an agitator paddle. Washing clothes now was much easier with this rubber belt-driven device that was operated with foot pedals. This eliminated pounding and scrubbing clothes against the washboard to get them clean. There was a rumor that a motor to turn the crank would be invented soon. The boys in the laundry room did not believe this.

This was much tougher and more exhausting work than Ruth had anticipated. The turning of the mangle cranks, wringing out the wet clothes, and scrubbing and pounding dirty clothes against the washboard all served to strengthen his club-like square hands, arms and shoulders.

On the biting cold Sunday morning of February 7, 1904, the Brothers and the boys of St. Mary's could see, shooting skyward, orange and red flames and an endless stream dark smoke haze billowing into dreary clouds of the deep harsh winter. Matthias knew something was wrong, very wrong. He had watched as this sooty shroud had spread from a tiny section to the east, the central Baltimore business district, toward the harbor. After an explosion, tremors were felt at far away as St. Mary's the smog engulfed nearly all of the downtown Baltimore, including most of the docks and threatening some of the residential areas. The black haze was now so high and wide that most of downtown was no longer visible. Throughout the day, Matthias could hear the distant clang of the fire engine bells and the unsettling sounds of chaos.

Matthias was not one to sit idly and watch this pending catastrophe unfold. With some trepidation, Matthias gathered the eldest boys, about 50, those ready for emancipation. He sensed the firefighters would need all the capable hands available in an effort to prevent the entire city from burning to the ground. Once the spread of the fire was halted, he also knew there were would be a tremendous amount of cleanup. Brother Matthias called the boys together. He explained to them the situation in downtown Baltimore and the help that was needed to help save the city. Matthias could not give details. The fire was big, but he did not know what they would find, except that they would lend assistance. The boys knew there was risk, but no one complained.

What started as an inconsequential smolder in the basement of the John Hurst & Company building had erupted into a blaze which destroyed nearly one-third of downtown Baltimore before it was finally extinguished. Nearly 1500 buildings were devastated, turned into heaps of ash. The chief reason for this disaster was the lack of standardization of equipment and training. In the Baltimore area, over 600 types of fire hose couplings were in use. The lack of organization and coordination procedures when involving multiple fire companies caused mass chaos. The streets became congested, blocking access for the much needed help.

Shortly after 11:00 AM, a gasoline truck near the Hurst Building exploded from the intense heat emitted by the raging inferno. The roof of the fire-weakened structure was blown completely off. A trolley was knocked clear of its tracks, severing a guide cable which landed on the fire chief and disabled him for life. Most of the downtown structures were wooden, built very high on the narrow Baltimore Streets. This created chimney-like flue conditions with near-perfect drafts, enabling the blaze to spread with unprecedented speed.

When Matthias and his band of inmates arrived on the edge of downtown, their procession halted as they became witness to the mesmerizing sight. Staring down Baltimore Street, a spaghetti-like tangle of fallen wires, fire hoses and cables was strewn around the streets. The sky was black as the night. Each breath they took left a coarse residue in their throats. On the building walls which remained standing, there was a thick, pure white coating of water frozen to the façade and to the telephone wires, creating an eerie winter scene with long cascading rows of icicles between gaping holes. It would have been an idyllic picture at any other time.

The boys joined with a National Guard unit working on Hanover Street. Put to work immediately, they helped by keeping streets clear of debris and onlookers so that the rushing fire trucks could reach their destination.

Thirty-six hours after the start of the blaze, the firemen finally gained control. It took 37 fire companies from several municipalities, the gritty determination of thousands of fireman and volunteers, and a well-established fire line which the men refused to let be broken. Over 86 blocks of downtown Baltimore were completely destroyed. The docks were all gone. The cost of this catastrophe was approximately 150 million dollars and seven lives. Baltimore's Mayor Robert

McLane, who served as a cheerleader in the streets to the firemen working to control the situation, was an emotional wreck as he viewed the acres and acres of smoldering remains of this once-prospering city. McLane was harshly criticized for an ill-fated decision which backfired. Agreeing with the police chief, he issued the order to dynamite several buildings in an effort to stem the fire's hungry march across Baltimore. Two of the buildings did not crumble to the ground immediately, the Hurst Building and a bank on Hanover Street. Hours after the explosions, there was a series of late-falling debris. The sudden storm of wood and iron claimed the lives of six unsuspecting workers clearing the area. They were dead before their bodies hit the street. McLain would not live to see the pledge which he made to the citizens of Baltimore, that 'this would be an opportunity for the city to become a landmark, not of decline, but of prosperity," fulfilled, as he would be dead of a self-inflicted gunshot wound to the head within a few short months. The speculation as to his motive was that he could not live with the results of his decision.

Late in the day Wednesday, Matthias and his physically-bankrupt troop of Xaverian Brothers and brave young men returned to St. Mary's.

Fortunately, Brother Matthias was able to commandeer a few horse-drawn wagons for the trip. Realizing it was going to be a long, cold trek back to the compound, Matthias was very concerned for the health of the students. Some of the severely weakened boys were having trouble walking. Other boys had frostbitten fingers and toes. Fortunately, most of the injuries suffered by the boys were relatively minor, nothing a few days' rest would not cure. A six-mile walk in the dead of winter is a harsh journey, unimaginable when exhausted, dirty and hypothermic. He just wanted everyone now to get home safely, back to the warmth and comforts of St. Mary's.

Ruth was in the laundry room, anticipating the arrival of everyone back from the 'Great Fire.' He knew the laundry load would be big; the soot-stained clothing would be a challenge to get clean, even with the new-fangled laundry machine. To get all the jackets, gloves, shirts, socks and pants completely clean, most items would need just plain old scrubbing on the wash boards.

Ruth was anxious to see Zach, and have him share his tales of fighting the Great Fire of Baltimore. From across the room came the call, "George." It was the all-too-familiar voice of Brother Barnabas, "Come with me. Matthias needs to see you in his office right away."

As Ruth and Barnabas entered, Matthias was standing with his back to the door. "Leave us, Brother. Thank you. We'll be to service shortly."

"Geawgie, there was a terrible accident. It's about Zach." Matthias began

"Where is he, brother?" Ruth asked as his eyes scanned the office. "I have lots to ask him."

"Zach is gone. The Lord has taken him to his new home, where he will remain in peace." Matthias was trembling as the words came forth.

Ruth clutched Matthias at the waist, burying his head against Matthias's welcoming chest in devastating sadness and fear. Ruth was once again alone.

Two days later, with a cold winter rain pelting the assembly of boys, Zach was laid in his final resting place on the grounds of St. Mary's.

Chapter 5
Ohio 1867

Situated in Tuscarawas County just about 50 miles south of Canton, the closest 'big city', is the rustic farming town of Gilmore, Ohio. In the late winter of 1867, McKinzie Young Jr. and Nancy Miller were patiently expecting the arrival of their first child. Two years earlier, McKinzie's father parceled 54 aces of his large 2,000 acre farm as a present to the newlyweds. Little did either of the church-going, well-respected couple, or for that matter any of the other 100 residents of this sleepy community, realize the significant impact this birth would have on American sports history. On March 29th, Nancy Miller Young gave birth to her first son. He would be given the name Denton True. This was more than the birth of a child; this was the birth of the greatest chase in all of sports, and one of the fiercest rivalries.

The Youngs were a third-generation American family with initial roots in Baltimore, Maryland. As expansion into the western frontier began, the Youngs took flight, settling in one of the newly-established states, Ohio, which had become the seventeenth state of the United States on February 19, 1803.

The expansive plains and valleys of Ohio were filled with acre upon acre of untouched fertile fields, driving most of the state's immigrants into agriculture. The Young family, as a result of their service during the Revolutionary War, was able to secure approximately 640 acres of prime farmland.

Over the next several decades, Ohio would become the economic hub and driver for progress within the United States, transforming from untamed frontier into a well-functioning state with over two million residents. Although agriculture drove the initial boom, small townships emerged and grew, providing plenty of work for the masses teeming into the state. There were public works projects, such as building the vital canal systems. As the towns grew up, there were buildings to be constructed, including schools, stables, churches, courthouses and factories. Plenty of strong bodies were needed for the back-breaking construction of the emerging railroads as well.

In 1806, the U.S. Congress authorized the first National Road program, designed to open travel to the western frontier. Private companies were contracted to build a paved road across the Appalachians to points west. The initial phase concluded in 1817 with the road reaching Wheeling, Virginia (It wouldn't become a part of West Virginia until 1863). In 1825, expansion of the road was approved, cutting a swath through Ohio and ultimately stretching to St. Louis, Missouri. Congress believed this would make migration and communication from the industrialized eastern cities to the far western frontier much easier. Ohio farmers benefited, as delivery of their produce and goods to the east coast markets of Philadelphia and New York was now faster.

In early 1867, about the time Nancy Miller was delivering Denton Young into the world, a prominent 29-year-old lawyer, Aaron Champion and a shrewd promoter and wannabe baseball player named Harry Wright rented an eight-acre fenced lot in Lincoln Park behind Union Terminal, about a twenty-minute trolley ride from downtown Cincinnati.

Champion, also the president of the local amateur Cricket Club and enormous civic booster for Cincinnati, wanted to drive economic expansion of the city. He wanted to change the image of the Queen City from the hog capital of the country. Champion believed that he could capitalize on the rising interest in the fledging game of baseball, which surpassed cricket in popularity, to help drive the change he wanted for Cincinnati. Many amateur clubs could, as witnessed by the ability of a New York City team, the Mutuals, now charge for admission. Two years and $10,000 later, most of the monies having been raised via a ten-cent admission, the era of professional baseball was ready to emerge in Cincinnati, Ohio, changing the face of baseball forever from a pastoral sport into a ruthless business. This isolated grass patch had been transformed into a picturesque ballpark, complete with grandstands, a wooden clubhouse, and a freshly-graded, newly-sodded field.

One of the smartest moves Champion had made was bringing in Harry Wright. He was as smart and as dedicated a baseball person as there was at the time in the entire country. The Cincinnati Enquirer stated in a column, "Wright eats baseball, drinks baseball and sleeps baseball. Most likely he probably prays baseball." He was given carte blanche to recruit talent. That he did, bringing much of the well-known area talent to the Red Stockings baseball club.

The flamboyant Wright had his team dress in white knee-length flannel knickerbockers and flaming red wool stockings, offsetting white flannel shirts. The shortened pants were not well received by either the players or the fans, but they have remained essentially unchanged in baseball for nearly 150 years. Wright's goal was to attract attention, get folks to the ballpark and draw people to Cincinnati.

June 1, 1869 saw the first game played by a team where all players on the team admitted openly to being professionals, receiving payment for playing. It took place at Union Cricket Club Grounds as the Cincinnati Red Stockings defeated the Mansfield Independents, an amateur club. Nearly 3,000 fans packed the rickety grandstands or stood along the fence line to watch the well-publicized event. The game itself did not live up to the hype, as the Red Stockings devastated their opponents, winning by a score of forty-eight to fourteen.

Harry believed strongly that the strong amateur clubs of Philadelphia and New York were paying their players, but the payments were being made under the table. The salary for the entire Cincinnati team during the 1869 season was less than ten thousand dollars: Player salaries ranged from $800 to a high of $1,400. This relatively modest sum was four to seven times what the average American farm family, like the Young's, would make in a year. Red Stockings players were bound by contract to the club for only one season at a time. The reason for the limited contract was that Harry Wright prided himself as an extraordinary judge of talent, and he wanted the flexibility to change players as he saw fit, especially if he could woo top talent from another baseball club. The Red Stockings earned the nickname, 'picked nine,' indicating that the team of nine was hand-picked by Harry Wright.

Harry Wright was all business. He did not want to just have a baseball team; his goal was for them to be recognized as the best baseball team in the country. Although he signed the top talent available, he expected them to work. He relentlessly practiced, using creative drills. The team would conduct itself in a business-like manner. They were expected to eat a healthy diet. The players were required to live a clean lifestyle, staying away from tobacco, booze and other vices. He ran the team as he saw fit.

Over the next few years, the performance of the Red Stockings under the leadership of Wright was nothing short of dominating. The team completed its first year of play, winning 57 games without suffering a single setback. George Wright, the reigning superstar of the day, (and incidentally Harry's brother), finished the year hitting over .500

with 59 home runs. That mark would only be surpassed twice in the next 100 years of baseball.

With the winning streak at 92, on June 14, 1870, at the Capitoline Grounds in Brooklyn, New York, in front of an estimated 20,000 frenzied patrons, perhaps the largest crowd to witness a baseball game to that date, the Red Stockings succumbed in the bottom of the 11th at the hands of the Brooklyn Atlantics, 8-7, in what was called the greatest baseball game ever played. A year earlier at the same location, in a game that put the Red Stockings on the baseball map, Cincinnati met the New York Mutuals, beating what many considered the best team in the country. After nine innings, the score was tied at 5-5. Cincinnati was able to plate two runs in the top of the eleventh. With the excited and loud crowd in a near stupor, the Atlantics had the winning runs on with two out. Twice, like wildings, some belligerent fans had run onto the diamond, creating stoppages in play. An easy grounder to their normally sure-handed first baseman inexplicitly went through his legs. Fans began to rush onto right field, creating an obstruction for the fielder. Before the ball could be retrieved, the winning runs sprinted in. Then hundreds of jubilant fans stormed the field, creating a rather dangerous situation for the men from Cincinnati, who tried to retreat while maintaining their dignity. They were pelted with trash, uneaten food, and an endless stream of insults. In the end, the Red Stocking team escaped from the city of Brooklyn with injury only to their pride.

During their fabulous run they took on all comers, of course extracting a price — that being a significant portion of the gate receipts. The team logged over 30,000 miles, playing before large throngs in many cities and under some trying circumstances. Ulysses S. Grant even invited this barnstorming troupe to the White House for a private audience.

The greatest impact of the Red Stockings was on other cities that wanted a baseball champion to represent them and would sponsor professional clubs. Cincinnati's success meant the end of the golden era of amateur baseball.

The Red Stockings collapsed a few years later from financial mismanagement, but professional baseball in America never looked back. It was here to stay.

The Wright Brothers moved to Boston to start a baseball franchise in the new professional league. Again their teams would have great success.

By age 11, Denton Young was putting in long, grueling days on the farm. His formal education, which had taken place in a two-room schoolhouse, had ended. As with most boys raised in rural America at the time, this was at the end of the sixth grade. His value to his family now rested in his ability to handle the demanding chores of farm life. Denton had been a reasonably diligent student, well-liked by his classmates and with many friends. Although Denton did not get the best of grades, he was by no measure an under-educated illiterate.

Life in the Young household was the portrait of a typical, God-fearing American farm family. Their priorities were family, God and chores, in no particular order. McKinzie was a well-thought-of member of the community.

Chores began at the first glimpse of morning sun. There were eggs to be fetched, with some brought to the kitchen for breakfast and others readied for market. On most days Denton would chop a full cord of wood, handle a plow in the field, mend a fence, bale hay or pick apples from their small orchard.

Farm work was back-breaking, dreary work, but Denton still had time for the typical fun of a growing lad. He and the others boys in town found time to fish, hunt or swim in a nearby pond and, of course, play baseball.

McKinzie had become infatuated with the game. He had joined the local team which played teams from surrounding communities on Sunday afternoons, from whenever the weather cooperated to whenever it stopped cooperating, generally April to October. McKinzie would be found patrolling right field. The usual setting for the game was a fallow pasture on one of the resident's farms. His infatuation grew to full-blown baseball enthusiasm. He was determined to teach his boys the game and spent hours with them. He would practice throwing, catching and hitting after chores until it was so dark no one could see.

Denton wanted to pitch, so he would spend extra time learning how to throw a ball. After supper he spent countless hours throwing homemade baseballs, rocks or whatever he could get his hands on, against the barn wall. It did not matter if it was dark; all he needed to do was throw a rock against the side of the barn. If the weather did not cooperate, he would move his throwing practice inside the barn.

Nancy Miller chipped in as well. On many evenings, she could be found making a homemade baseball by using rounded stones for a core, straw and burlap. She somehow found the time to sew several dozen of the makeshift baseballs for Denton.

Young's fascination with the game grew as did he. At age 16 he was nearly 6' 2", very tall for the day. He stood nearly a half-foot taller than his father. From hundreds of hours of farm chores, he tipped the scale at 170 pounds of lean muscle. He was now playing second base and pitching for the Gilmore team.

Denton continued to hone his skills. The side of the barn had taken such an enormous pounding from the barrage of stones and balls that McKinzie nailed a floorboard to the side of the barn to prevent further damage.

Denton's velocity and accuracy improved dramatically as he grew. He would show off his skills to his friends and siblings. His favorite targets were crows. Denton could nail them in mid-flight, knocking them clean out of the sky with a single toss.

While warming up for a game between the towns of Gilmore and Athens, he backed a claim about his incredible velocity by throwing a baseball through the wall of an abandoned barn located near the field. The manager caught wind of what had taken place. In what was no coincidence, the team won every game for the remainder of the summer as soon as Denton became their newest pitcher.

McKinzie ran a very productive farm. In addition to corn, wheat and peas, the Youngs bred a small drift of hogs. Twice every summer, McKinzie would make the nearly 200-mile trip to Cincinnati in order to sell two or three dozen of the hogs that had gotten plump enough to command a good price. McKinzie prided himself in his ability to get his prize hogs close to 275 pounds, well above the average weight of other farmers Along with the hogs; he would also sell other of his produce at the Findlay Market, usually garnering a more than fair price.

The Findlay Market was designed under the direction of City Civil Engineer Alfred West Gilbert. He used an unconventional cast- and wrought-iron frame. This type of construction had been little used in the United States; but the construction was so sturdy that it remains Ohio's oldest surviving municipal market house.

As Denton gained interest in baseball, his tolerance for the long trips to the livestock auction and farmers' exchange market also increased. The Cincinnati Enquirer began publishing less-than-regular baseball reports. Denton enjoyed reading, but mostly he enjoyed reading about the local baseball heroes that played for the Red Stockings.

The Cincinnatians and other Ohioans were among the more avid, loyal and vocal baseball 'fans' or 'cranks.' The American Association Red

Stockings was the second incarnation of the team. They had joined the National League in 1876, but continued to suffer through economic troubles. Some believed the ballpark was just too far from the downtown population center. Even the inclined train system did not help draw fans to the games.

In 1879, under the leadership of their new owner, Justus Thorner, several changes were made. Beginning with the 1880 season, all home games would be played at the ball park closer to downtown, Banks Street Grounds. Next came two ill-fated decisions. In order to sell more tickets, Sunday games were added to the schedule, and with the team's popularity among the growing German immigrant population, beer would be sold at the park. He thought this would keep a steady attendance and the crowd energetic.

Both of these actions violated National League rules. At a special league meeting in October of 1880, the other seven clubs passed a rule prohibiting the sale of alcohol at league parks, even at non-league games, and barred use of the park on Sundays. Failure to comply would mean termination of the franchise. These new rules were directed squarely toward Cincinnati. Unlike the other league cities whose population was rooted in old English puritanical leanings, Cincinnati consisted of a heavy beer-drinking German population. It was customary for Cincinnati's German immigrants to serve beer at all gatherings, and the revenue generated by beer sales and the Sunday games was vital to the Red Stockings. Thorner and manager John Clapp held their ground, thinking the league would cave because of the popularity of the Reds. The league stood firm, and Cincinnati was unceremoniously dumped, replaced by the Detroit Wolverines for the 1881 season.

For locals, reading about their baseball team was more important than ever. In 1882, after a year's absence, the Red Stockings re-emerged, joining the fledgling professional baseball league, the American Association. In that inaugural season, they had taken the league by storm, finishing the season on top of the league, 11½ games ahead of the Philadelphia Athletics and securing a date with destiny.

In an agreement reached before the start of the season, the American Association champions would meet the National League champions. This would be the first-ever meeting between the teams that finished first place in their respective leagues. To mollify the resounding complaints from the Providence Grays, who finished second in the National League, the Chicago White Stockings agreed to a best of nine series with the Grays upon completion of the series with Cincinnati. The Chicago team was heavily favored to beat the team from the upstart league. The concluding game of the series played in Banks Street Grounds saw Will White, a holdover from the National League team; throw his third complete game victory as the Red Stockings completed the sweep of the four game series.

Baseball had been missed in Cincinnati.

If the Youngs had good day at the market, Dent would convince his dad to spend a few pennies to buy a copy of the Cincinnati Enquirer. September 18th, 1883 turned out to be an unusually good day. The McKinzie hogs had earned twice what he had expected. This was a result of severe drought conditions in Nebraska and Illinois that caused the average weight of hogs to be down. In the key exchanges like Chicago and Lincoln, average weights plummeted to nearly 220 pounds. McKinzie's best hog topped 285, with no hog weighing in at less than 265.

"Dent, the Lord has blessed us this summer," McKinzie said after completing his business at the bank. "I've kept a tad bit of cash, let's say you and I stay the night and go see the Red Stockings tomorrow."

"What?" Dent replied.

"This'll be our secret. I don't want the younguns in a tizzy."

"Don't worry. Can we ride the train that goes up the steep hill?"

"Yup, we'll get to the top, and then walk a ways."

Father and son climbed aboard the midnight-colored trolley trimmed in bright yellow. 'Price Hill Incline' was painted on the sides in large Spencerian script. The ride on the steam engine up the steep embankment was extremely slow, traveling the 800 feet to a height of slightly over 350 feet in almost 15 minutes. Price Hills was two inclines running parallel; one was used exclusively for passengers. The Cincinnati inclines were a combination of railcars and elevator systems for the ascent and descent of the dramatic hills surrounding

Cincinnati. The building of the inclines made the plateaus and the land beyond accessible to middle-class residents. Ornate European style houses dotted the tops of the inclines so that those who lived in the city basin could gain respite, even if only for an evening, from the city's increasing pollution, noise and stench of the livestock markets.

Although Denton had been to Cincinnati several times, looking down at the city from a bird's-eye level was a heart-pounding experience. He could see all the way to the city limits at the edge of the Ohio River and out into the lush green hills of Kentucky. The most breathtaking sight was the 'Suspension Bridge' built by John Roebling. At the time of its completion, the bridge had the longest main span (1,057 feet) in the world. With the completion of the Brooklyn Bridge in May, 1883, this mark was surpassed. Nonetheless, the bridge was a remarkable display of architectural design and engineering prowess. Dent was in awe as he viewed the support towers stretching 150' upward.

Six younger children, ascending the precipitous hills via concrete steps, clasping the thin tubular iron rail with each stride and brandishing a broad smile, waved at the passing passenger car. Denton returned the wave and thought, *that climb makes the walk into Gilmore seem easy.*

As luck would have it, the Philadelphia Athletics were in town and were on top of the American Association standings. The defending champion Red Stockings were seven games out with the season winding down quickly, but they had won five games consecutively.

McKinzie and Denton arrived at the park shortly before the start of the game. Two of the stars Denton had read about and wanted to see were 'Long John' Reilly, the 6' 4" slugging first baseman, and Will White, a portly right-handed fireballer, who was once again bearing down on 40 wins.

Bank Street Grounds was located at the intersection of Bank Street and McLaren Avenue, near the western warehouse district. This park was stark in contrast to the spectacular bridge. A wooden frame structure was the clubhouse building for the players. A sign with yellow block letters attached to the eaves simply said, Bank Street Grounds. Bleachers were cut into the side of an embankment. In deep centerfield, beyond the fence, was a flagpole proudly displaying the stars and stripes, which hung dormant in the windless afternoon. The infield was not manicured. Dirt base paths, complete with pebbles, were crudely carved out of the grass plot. Around the playing field was a spartan fence, banners citing the merits of the local merchants. Bavarian Brewing had an emblem proudly displaying their product in both right and left field as did Epply Funeral Services and Embalmer. The field appeared more rectangle than diamond-like. Marking home base was a flat flagstone dug in level to the ground. From home base at a point exactly 55 feet in the direction of second base was another smaller flagstone to designate the pitcher's area. From home base, the foul lines angled at 135 degrees to the outfield fence. The distance was not shown on the fence but was about 340 feet. To drive the ball out of the park in dead center, a batter would need to hit the ball 430 feet and clear the 5 foot fence.

Admission was 10 cents for the Wednesday afternoon game. Nearly 2,500 fans attended the Red Stockings games in 1883. Although this was a weekday game, the Athletics were in first and the Red Stockings needed to win every game to have a chance at repeating their World Series win of 1882.

Neither 'Long John' nor Will White disappointed the Red Stocking faithful. Reilly accomplished a rare feat. In the first inning, he drove a ball between the outfielders to the fence on one hop for a triple. In the 4th, with a vicious swing, he caught the ball flush with the fat of the bat, driving a titanic blast which settled softly to the ground nearly 30 feet beyond the center field fence. Reilly followed with a double and a single in his next two at-bats. The latter was a 'seeing eye' blooper just beyond the outstretched reach of second baseman Cub Stricker, who landed prone. Reilly had hit for the first cycle in the league in over a year. White's accomplishment was not so rare. He pitched his 61st complete game in 61 starts, limiting the powerful Athletics to 3 runs. The Red Stockings had won the season series 9-5, but would finish 5 ½ games behind in third place.

Denton was hooked nonetheless.

With their Cincinnati adventure completed, the pair headed back to the farm. Denton was certain he could play professional baseball. That was all Denton could think about on the journey home. He could throw the ball harder than anyone he had seen in the professional game, and except for John Reilly, he was already bigger and certainly stronger. Plus he still had some growing to do. McKinzie assured the still wet-behind-the-ears Denton that he was right. He did not want to dampen Denton's dreams. Deep down he thought, *Denton will follow in the footsteps of his ancestors and through his blood, sweat and tears build an honest farm life for himself and his family.*

They were both right.

Chapter 6
Ohio 1960

Tonio, leaning in towards Pepe, asked "Son, what do you think so far of your first game?"

Pepe was enthralled, taking in the sights, the sounds and the smells of the ballpark experience. His attention was glued to the men walking up and down the aisles seeking buyers for their goods.

"Hot dogs! Get your red hot hot dogs!" yelled a vendor standing on the dismal gray concrete step less than three feet from Pepe, his dad and the old man. Around his straining neck, hung by a thick canvas strap, was a silver box with columns of steam coming from it. Beads of sweat had already begun to populate his lined leathery forehead. The Indians baseball cap he wore did little to prevent their march down his sun-drenched cheeks.

"Dad, Williams is batting again," Pepe said enthusiastically

"Look. The Williams shift," Pepe instructed the strange old man.

"Named for how they would play Cy Williams."

"Cy Williams? Never heard of him."

"Second-best left-handed power hitter I'd ever seen. Let me tell you about him."

The Indians had positioned the three fielders on the right-field side of second base, the shortstop just behind the bag, the second baseman in short right field and the first baseman on the foul line, ten feet behind first.

"Ohhhhhhhhhhhhh!" the sound arose in unison from the nearly 8,000 fans in attendance. Williams had laced the one-strike pitch into the right field corner. Pete Runnels, the runner on first, scooted to third while Williams, with his familiar elegant stride, ambled into second with a double.

A Williams liner found space between the fielders. Harry Kuenn managed to cut the ball off, preventing Pete Runnels from scoring.

"Almost 42 years old and he can still hit," Tonio lauded. "You see that, Pepe?"

"How many dogs you want?" The old man asked him, distracted from the story he was about to tell.

"Nah, grandma packed some lunch for me," Pepe responded

"Nothing's better than hot dogs at the ball park. Vendor put a dozen down right here for starters. Throw out that crap your grandma made and have some real ballpark chow."

Tonio chuckled, "Old man, ain't nothing better than a homemade sausage hero."

"Better make that 15 dogs. My young friend's ill-informed father has never experienced the culinary delights of a Nathan's hot dog."

"15 hot dogs!" Pepe exclaimed.

"Yeah, kid, that'll get us through the first couple innings. Tell the beer guy to come on over. We need to wash these down with some suds."

During the banter, Vic Wertz strokes the ball into the leftfield corner for a double.

"That kid Mays robbed that guy in the '54 series. Hell of a play. Hell of a play."

A dozen dogs plus three hot dogs individually wrapped in aluminum foil were placed neatly on unoccupied seat number 14.

"That'll be $7.50. Beer man is heading down now."

The old man handed the weather-beaten vendor a sawbuck and said "Keep the change. You load them up with relish and mustard?"

"The works, pops, sauerkraut and onions too. Which one of you has the tape worm?"

"Be quiet. Just get your butt back here by the 4th inning."

"Hot dogs! Get your hot dogs!" Pepe could hear the vendor's bellow fade as he walked back up the grandstands.

"Dig in, kid. They're better when they're hot."

Barry Latman, the Tribe's pitcher, settled in, getting the next two Sox batters out in order.

"Williams may be close to 42, but look at the bush leaguer he's hitting against. This guy couldn't get my neighbor out and he's half-blind!"

Pepe was working on his third dog as Johnny Temple strode to the plate. "These are really good. Thanks, sir."

"Slow down there, kiddo, you don't want to end up with a bellyache."

"We can't tell grandma you chose hot dogs over what she made, she'd be really mad. I'd never hear the end of it," Tonio added.

Temple fouled the second pitch back towards the protective screen behind the plate. Russ

Nixon deftly threw off his mask, located the ball and settled in under it for the first out.

"Beer here! Get your ice cold beer here!" the approaching vendor howled.

"Finally!! Bring your butt over here! We got dogs to wash down," roared the old man. "Line up three. Get the kid some pop, will ya? Where was I again? Oh, I remember…"

Chapter 7
Maryland 1904

In the early 1900's the pace of infant mortality hovered at 14%. The Ruth household was anything but immune from its trauma. Katie Ruth's most recent pregnancy had ended with delivery of a stillborn baby, a boy. This latest tragedy for her came on the heels of the death of another of her very young children from the complications of influenza. Shorty after Zach's death, Ruth returned home at the insistence of his distraught mother.

Anxiety and guilt plagued and ravaged her each and every day. Katie gradually built a false mental image of a loving relationship between her and her now nine-year-old son. Unable to bear the anguish, Katie decided to visit St. Mary's and plead her case. She could not maintain eye contact with Matthias; she sat wringing her hands nearly raw in a passionate attempt at convincing Matthias to let Ruth come home. Although her emotion was virtuous, her logic was feeble.

Brother Matthias knew that the best interests of Geawgie lay in remaining with the rigid life of St. Mary's. In one final act of desperation, the exasperated Katie, with tears from her swollen eyes rolling unimpeded to her chin, fell prostrate on hands and knees, begging the Xaverians to release her young son. With considerable reservation and consternation, Matthias uneasily complied.

Ruth's respite from St. Mary's would not last very long. Quickly Ruth fell back into old habits, only worse. His home life was as unloving as ever. Zach had become a guiding force in Ruth's life. Unfortunately with Zach's untimely passing, Ruth's attitude and outlook turned gloomier. Neither the streets nor his neglectful family provided anything to fill to the loveless void in his life.

Ruth found alcohol and tobacco products comforting. Cheroots were his favorite smoke. It did not matter to him whether he was able to filch a fresh cigar or find a partially-smoked, saliva-laden discarded stogie. Ruth welcomed a dose of strong tobacco flavor.

Within two months, Ruth was picked up by the police for petty theft, a botched attempt at picking a pocket in a crowded farmer's market. The decision was easy; Ruth would be shipped back to St. Mary's.

"Well Geawgie, that did not take long, now did it?" Matthias quipped as he welcomed Ruth back. "You'll be in your old room, so just head on back."

There were no tears shed this time as an unremorseful Ruth again entered St. Mary's, unceremoniously delivered by one of Baltimore's finest.

The final words Ruth heard as he slowly padded down the hallway towards one of the interconnected tunnels that would take him to the dormitory and the sanctity of his room was, "Thank you, Officer Kearny."

Ruth traversed the route back to the dorms very quickly. The dimly-lit corridors provided little deterrence. Once again he was alone, and all the sulking 9 year old wanted to do was to figure out how he could get out of the compound and back to the streets.

With a forcible push, Ruth slammed the door open so that it met the wall behind it with a sharp thud, startling the occupant in the bunk closest to the door.

"Whoa, there, big fella, what's the hurry?" a surprised thin boy with deep-set brown eyes and black hair slicked with several ounces of grease shouted in a nasal voice.

Asa Yoelson was the fourth child of Moses and Naomi. The Jewish couple had immigrated from the Russian providence of Lithuania in 1901. Moses was a rabbi and cantor at the Talmud Torah Synagogue in the southwest waterfront neighborhood of Washington, D.C.

Asa had been working in the burlesque and vaudeville shows. He had been performing at one of Baltimore's more unsavory theaters, the 2 O'clock Club. Reports of teenage girls performing full striptease on the E. Baltimore Street club had circulated Baltimore's police headquarters located less than a block away. A raid ensured shortly. The police were cracking down on all underage performers. The 17-year-old Asa was taken into custody and detained.

The next morning the police contacted Rabbi Yoelson, the strict family patriarch. He told them Asa had run away months ago. He was no longer welcome in the family and they should do with him as they saw fit. Although Jewish, the kind-hearted Xaverian's welcomed him in at St. Mary's.

Yoelson, because of his slight build and gentle voice, appeared a good deal younger than 17. Ruth, because of his size and girth, appeared older than 9. Together they looked like a pair of 14-year-olds.

"Hey, fat boy, don't make so much noise, can't you see I'm resting?" Asa remarked.

"Don't call me fat. Who said you could be in my room, anyway?" Ruth responded

"Matthias, that's all you needs to know. I'm only gonna only be here a few weeks longer. I'll be 18 then and out of here, back to show business."

"You're almost 18, you's a runt! Show business, you an actor or something?"

"Not yet an actor. I sing. I entertain. More talent in my one little finger than in your fat body! Already I've added some class to those dismal singers you call a choir in this dump. Asa is the name. You're Ruth, right. I have heard them talk about you there, big fella!"

"That's right. Let's hear you. If you're so good, let's hear you sing something."

Yoelson vaulted from the bed, arms at his side, palm facing up and began in an enchanting voice:

I've been away from you along time
I never thought I'd miss 'ya so
somehow I feel, your love is real
near you I wanna be.

The Birds are singing it is song time
the banjos strumming soft and low
I know that you yearn for me to Swanee

you're calling me
Swanee - how I love ya, how I love ya
my dear old Swanee.
I'd give the world to be among the folks in
D-I-X-I-E-ven though my mammy's waiting
for me,
praying for me down by the Swanee.
The folks up north will see me no more when
I get to that Swanee shore
"So, what do you think now, fat stuff?"
"Quit calling me that. You're pretty good.
Where did you learn to sing like that?"
"Mostly in Temple. I'm Jewish. You got a
problem with that, fat boy?"
"No."
"Better not. My pop, he's a Rabbi, wanted
me to follow his footsteps. He had me training to be
a cantor. That's a temple singer. But I decided to
go show biz. Besides, I'm not the only one calling
you names round here. Other guys they call you
stuff too, and worse things than fat stuff. Mostly
behind your back, I guess."

Asa could see that Ruth was puzzled by that
statement. Ruth could not imagine anyone not liking
him.

Continuing he added," Hey, I got an idea,
why don't you join the choir? I'll teach you to carry
a note or two. Plus it will keep you from getting in
trouble during services."

Ruth joined the choir as Asa suggested.
Turns out he could hit some high notes since he had
yet to undergo puberty. Ruth rather enjoyed
singing. The dozen or so boys in the choir were

mostly social outcasts, so Ruth quickly made some new friends and enjoyed the camaraderie.

Ruth settled in and quickly evolved into a modestly talented mezzo-soprano, just as Asa envisioned. This added needed range to the otherwise lackluster ensemble. Ruth's singing talents caught the eye of Brother Paul. "Georgie, I did not know you could sing so well," he remarked one day.

Ruth, still quite the wise guy, replied. "I can pretty much do whatever I set my mind to, anything."

On May 26, 1904, after Brother Paul put the group through their final pre-Mass preparation for the May Crowning service, a brief birthday celebration was held in the choir room of the Church for Asa. The May Crowning is a traditional Roman Catholic service honoring the Blessed Virgin Mary as the queen of the heavens. Generally celebrated about May 1st, the celebration at St. Mary's had been a delayed this year to coincide with a visit from Cardinal Gibbons.

Brother Paul could not have been more nervous about the upcoming visit. A visit from a Cardinal is about as important as it can get for Catholics. In the weeks leading up to the performance, when not rehearsing the boys, Brother Paul could be found pacing the hallways, even well after lights out. Paul could not find gentle comfort in a sound sleep. He knew the choir had talent, but the group was anchored by the incomparable Asa and irascible Ruth. Both of these rascals were very unpredictable in their behavior. He prayed each night that they were not plotting something even remotely mischievous. That would destroy the one chance he had to shine in front of a high-ranking Church official that had finally come his way.

Time for Mass to begin was nearing. From the choir loft located in the rear of the flight above the narthex, the choir had an unobstructed view of the nave of the Church. All the 'prisoners' had filed in, filling the pews in an orderly, respectful manner. The Cardinal and his small entourage were the last to enter. Regally, Cardinal Gibbons, dressed in his black soutane trimmed in scarlet, with thirty-three matching buttons and similarly colored fascia and skull cap, deliberately walked to his seat of honor in the front pew.

In the distance, the all-too-familiar clang of a bell snapped everyone in the throng to their feet. Father Michael Agostino was the celebrant. From a sacristy entrance behind and to the left of the altar, he was led in by three altar boys, the one at the head of a small triangle carrying a cross, the two others carrying candles. Father Agostino was flanked by two deacons who would assist him in the celebration of the Mass. Quickly the sextet took their positions; the deacons each on one side of the priest, all three facing the altar with their backs to the faithful. Two altar boys knelt on pillows on an altar step, the third on a kneeler to the left of the altar. "In nomine Patris e Filii e Spiritus Sancti…" so the priest began the Mass.

At the completion of the Communion service, the priests and congregation sit in deep reflection for several reverent moments. The Church was completely still, in a tomb-like silence.

In the background from the choir loft, faintly, the organist commenced the familiar introduction of Opus 52, no. 6, by the famed composer Franz Schubert.

Asa and Ruth arose from their seats and began the somber duet of one of the more cherished arias. Slightly more than three minutes later, with the Church remaining eerily still, all continued to sit, paralyzed by the numbing performance. The unlikely pair had delivered a home run. Their rendition of the Ave Maria drew tears to the eyes of some of the brothers and priests in attendance including the Cardinal. The sweetness, clarity and range of their haunting harmonies were thoroughly mesmerizing and shocking to most.

Brother Paul's ear-to-ear grin was a simple reflection of this, his proudest moment. He knew Asa had vocal range, but *that Ruth,* he thought, *he said he could do it, and he did.*

Cardinal Gibbons left St. Mary's rather impressed. As he finished his goodbyes, he said, "Well, Brother Paul, you keep improving like this, and St. Mary's might someday rival that choral ensemble from Salt Lake City."

As expected, in early September, just a few short months after his 18th birthday, Asa bid adieu to the choir and life at St. Mary's. He would return to life on the Burlesque and Vaudeville circuits. Three years later, Asa would team with a New York City booking agent named Joe Palmer and the celebrated career of Al Jolson was born.

In parting, "Ruth," Asa said, "we'll meet again. You strike me as the kinda fella that really can do whatever he pretty much sets his mind to. See ya, fat boy!"

Although another important person in his life was yet again leaving, this time Ruth experienced no sense of abandonment. The best thing Asa left for Ruth was a bit of that New York City toughness, arrogance and confidence and street wisdom. Silence your critics by doing what you say you can. "Ruth," he would say, "you live with nearly a thousand other fellas. Not everyone will be a friend nor like you. Most will be mean. I'm Jewish, I know. Don't worry about those who aren't your friends. When the world sees your talents, everyone will love you, so, Ruth, choose wisely your friends."

The next several years at St. Mary's were formative for Ruth. He went back to work in the laundry, but he would also remain a key part of the choir until he hit puberty and his voice changed. Even without Asa there to tutor him on his vocals, Ruth was quite good, a real contributor to the choir. Ruth attended classes regularly, excelling in mathematics and English.

Matthias had a special place in his heart for this miscreant child. There had been very little love in his life, and on the very few occasions where he had come dangerously close to a meaningful relationship, life struck back swiftly, delivering an unusually unkind blow.

Wherever you found Matthias, you generally found the young boy. Ruth's parents practiced very little faith in the home. His father was a non-practicing Lutheran; Katie, although born and raised a Catholic, had long since left her faith.

Through the guidance and will of Matthias, Ruth found Christianity and was baptized into Catholicism. On August 15th, 1906, Ruth received the sacrament of first Holy Communion. Within a year, as a result of the daily regimen of Mass and religious education, Ruth's view towards his faith speedily matured. He was now prepared for a mature Christian commitment, and on May 9th, 1907, he received Confirmation.

Matthias was very proud that Ruth had welcomed Christianity so deeply into his life. On several occasions, Ruth had inquired about the life of a priest. Ruth was very much enamored by the wonderful work the Catholic priests and brothers were doing with wayward children such as himself. Matthias was uncertain whether this was in fact Ruth's real vocation or simply projecting self-admiration.

Matthias also pondered whether faith alone had been enough to change this child and eliminate the mischievousness or if his destructive character had simply gone dormant.

Ruth became comfortable with his surroundings at St. Mary. The more comfortable he became, the more his gentle aggressiveness and braggadocio was manifested in his every-day behavior. Usually Ruth would be seen in the recreational yard grabbing 3 or 4 boys at one time and wrestling with them. Once he would have all of them pinned in a giant pile he would declare as loudly as possible, "No one could beat me, no one!"

On one chilly Saturday afternoon in March 1908, from about 100 yards away a voice from the big yard bellowed, "I can, nigger lips." It was John Quig, a recent transfer from the Philadelphia House of Refuge, who relished in his meanness. In the two months since he had come to St. Mary's, he had been in nearly fifty fights. His fists were constantly bruised from the pounding he inflicted on the faces of his opponents. Brother Matthias had recognized the mistake of bringing the pugilistic Quig to St. Mary. It simply was not a fit. Quig resented the regimentation. Matthias believed Quig needed a little freedom and tougher guidance from the mean streets. Matthias was trying to arrange for his transfer to Fourth Ward Industrial School of New York City, where they were better suited to deal with a ruffian like Quig. Quig was no lad though, nearly 20 years old. He was too old and too nasty to stay any longer at St. Mary's.

"Well, you loudmouth oaf, so you think you can beat me?" Quig taunted, "I'll swell your lips bigger than they are."

"This guy is bad news, Georgie," said Louie Leisman, one of the boys Ruth had pinned down. "Real bad news, Georgie. Let's go."

Ignoring Leisman's advice Ruth responded, "Nah, I was simply playing." Ruth, for all his size, strength and arrogant behavior, had only been in a few brief scuffles, usually with those who referred to him as 'nigger lips' because of his large head, full round lips and broad nose.

"So you're a fat chicken, with nigger lips," Quig roared, continuing to jauntily walk toward Ruth.

Brother Paul from the library windows could see the boys, who had stopped whatever game was in progress, begin encircling the small yard. He realized something was amiss. In a flash, he was out of the library, sprinting down the steps two at a time, heading towards the yard. It would take him a full 2 or 3 minutes to get there. At the opposite end of the grounds, Brothers Matthias and Bernard were in the administration building discussing the fate of John Quig when they heard the frantic ringing of the recess bell a full 20 minutes too early. This signal meant trouble, nothing good. Both anxiously headed to the small yard in a full sprint, their brown robes flopping as they ran.

Ruth held his ground, "We're just having some fun, that's all, but if you keep calling me..."

Now within a step or two of Ruth, "Back up your words, nigger lips, you said you could beat anyone," Quig lashed out, the breath of his words touching Ruth's cheek.

"Don't call me that!"

"Or what, what will you do?"

Without breaking step in his hurried march towards the target, Quig delivered the full force of a two handed push to the barrel chest of Ruth, who barely moved. Expecting little resistance from the younger Ruth, Quig was surprised, but he never hesitated as in one fluid movement he cocked his fist, and with destructive fury, he launched a roundhouse right that connected with Ruth's rather large and very dense skull. Quig would not realize for several hours that the impact caused the facture of his scaphoid bone, which would never heal properly.

Ruth, not knowing how to correctly punch someone. Instead using his massive hand, grabbed Quig by the scruff of the neck, bringing him in very close. Quig delivered a left-handed uppercut to Ruth's belly, but he was too close for the impact to cause any real damage. Ruth positioned his right foot behind Quig's legs and pushed as hard as he could, forcibly driving Quig to the ground. Quig landed in a heap, his head bouncing twice off the infield dirt. The supine and sufficiently stunned Quig was now an easy target for Ruth's size-eleven shoe. Without regard for any finesse, Ruth placed his foot directly on his opponent's throat. He pressed down with more than ample force to stop the free flow of air to Quig's lungs, and his face rapidly reddened and neck veins bulged.

"Take back what you said," Ruth demanded

Not realizing Quig was unable to speak, Ruth leaned forward and pressed down even harder, the desperate Quig flailing about aimlessly.

"Geawgie, STOP!" He's had enough," a worried Matthias screamed. "He's not a good person, but you don't want to kill him."

Ruth, unaware of the impact of his strength, immediately halted the counterassault on Quig, who was fading into a semi-conscious state.

"Everyone back to what you were doing, the show is over," Matthias directed the other boys.

"That includes you, Geawgie. I'll deal with Mr. Quig."

Addressing what Matthias would call 'the biggest mistake ever to enter St. Mary's,' told Quig, "You're done here, son. You're gone tomorrow. I'd get you out of here tonight if I could."

An unrelenting Quig, not yet willing to give up his assault, hollered, "Someday I will get you, fat boy, just you remember me."

Ruth cast a disinterested glance back at his would-be assailant and just laughed.

Quig spent the night locked in one of the dorms, closely watched by two of the Xaverians. The next day he was summarily dismissed from St. Mary. Matthias was elated to let New York deal with the problem.

From that day on, no one at St. Mary's referred to Ruth as 'nigger lips,' ever. He had taken down the much older Quig, the toughest thug St. Mary's would ever see on the inside of their walls, without much of a fight. No student wanted to risk seeing what Ruth would do to them if he ever really got angry.

Ruth's body continued to fill out; by his 13th birthday, he had sprouted to a remarkable 6' 2" and weighed nearly 200 pounds. After the incident with Quig, Matthias and Ruth began spending even more time together. Matthias spent hours teaching and honing Ruth's baseball skills and his understanding of the game. Matthias showed him how to hit, throw, catch, run the bases and field. Ruth had remarkable hand-eye coordination, unusual strength and athleticism. Hopefully patience, self-discipline and emotional control would mature as his body had. He would need these virtues to have success in baseball. Matthias patiently waited for the day Ruth would take the field to play in a real game representing St. Mary's.

That day came sooner than anyone expected. Brother Herman strolled onto the small yard, "Georgie, you're needed in the big yard for the game." Brother Herman was the head of St. Mary's recreational and sports programs.

"Georgie, you're going to catch today. Smitty has got the flu bug. Get over to the field and get the gear on."

Believing Ruth had not yet developed enough self-discipline and emotional control, Matthias thought it best Ruth that should start to really learn baseball as a catcher.

On the morning of August 18, 1908, John Smith, "Smitty" to the boys of St. Mary, awoke to chills, body aches, and constant vomiting. Herman and Smitty made a trip to the infirmary, hoping for an immediate cure. It was fruitless. The diagnosis was the flu, and Smitty was simply sent back after a dosage of two aspirin. Not a great talent behind the plate, Smitty had replaced Ray Ryan, the team's legendary catcher, who had signed with the Lancaster Lanks of the Ohio - Pennsylvania League two years earlier. Ryan would spend 11 years in the minor leagues, never being good enough to get a taste of the majors.

Brother Matthias knew of a local sandlot baseball team, the Dunkirk Bays, comprised of mostly 18-year-olds, but Matthias also suspected several of the players might have been a tad older. He had become friends with their manager. One day, Matthias politely challenged him to bring his team for a game at St. Mary's. The Bays had not lost a game in two years, so the game had the potential of significant bragging rights for Matthias.

The catcher's gear consisted of a badly-beaten mask, whose well-worn leather straps barely held the protective mask in place, and a chest protector whose padding had thinned. Although shin guards had been introduced into baseball a year earlier, St. Mary's could not afford such an extravagant purchase.

Matthias timidly sat on the wooden chair in the dugout as he watched as the Bays build an early lead into a commanding one in the top half of the third, 6-0.

Jack Sharrott, who managed the minor league Wilkes-Barre Barons until 1906, yelled from across the diamond, "Hey, Matthias, you know your catcher has his glove on the wrong hand!"

Dunkirk was still threatening in the third. The bags remained loaded but two were out. The Bays' powerful left-hand hitting first baseman confidently strode to the plate. He had already homered with two on in the first. The first pitch was a ball just off the inside corner. Transitioning the ball from glove to hand quickly then whipping his left arm across his body Ruth delivered a strike to the first baseman catching a napping Bay off first for the final out of the inning. Butch Schmidt glared at Ruth, disgusted.

Ruth, batting last in the order, gracefully approached the plate in the bottom of the third, after the first two runners of the inning had reached base. Finally St. Mary's had something to cheer about. With a uniform about two sizes too small, his appearance was both mammoth and comical. As the Bay pitcher went into his windup, Ruth, slightly crouched, in one fluid motion, pulled his hands back towards his left hip, moved his right leg backwards, and turned his right shoulder towards third base.. Ruth continuing to coil drew his right shoulder back further the motion unnoticeable. Rising up as a cobra readying to strike its prey. Ruth stared down his adversary in wait. At the most precise moment he propelled the bat forward, striking the ball with such deadly force that it quickly carried over the center fielder's head to the deepest part of the grounds. In the 15 seconds it took the centerfielder to retrieve the baseball and return it to the infield, all three players scored easily.

Ruth threw out runners attempting to steal in the fourth and fifth innings and picked off a runner at third in the sixth. Ruth homered again in the fifth inning with a runner on to cut the deficit to 6-5. The Bays pushed one run across in the sixth extending the lead to 7-5.

Here Matthias would take a calculated gamble. Matthias decided to bring the 13 year old Ruth in to pitch. Matthias had worked with Ruth and marveled how Ruth could make the ball move to and through locations with peerless accuracy. Ruth could at will make the ball jump late, move down, or back up towards the batter. Doing it in practice was one thing, for sure, but this was Ruth's first real game experience. Matthias was not sure what to expect. Throwing against the Bay's three, four and five hitters made the task even more daunting. The heart of the order trio, each of whom would go on to play for the Baltimore Orioles of the Eastern League, consisted of Jim Clark, Charles 'Butch' Schmidt, and James Catiz.

First up in the inning was the lefty Schmidt, who had homered earlier in the game. Schmidt himself stood at 6'2" and over 200 lbs. His teammates affectionately called him 'Butcher Boy' or simply 'Butch.' His swing was powerful, with a slight downward angle that many attributed to his nickname. His swing path followed that of a slaughterhouse 'knocker' wielding a 16-pound sledgehammer, waiting while perched atop a cattle pen, ready to strike a fatal blow with one vicious blow to the unsuspecting animal. Others, however, believed the name came from his abject inability to field anything cleanly. *Schmidt could butcher picking up a still ball*, teammates thought. 'Butch' Schmidt would go on to play briefly in the majors, each year leading his team in errors.

"Well, the left-handed catcher is now a pitcher," Butcher Boy taunted.

"Geawgie, I need you to get these guys out without letting in another run," Matthias said to Ruth, as he ended his conference at the pitching box.

"Don't worry there, Brother, I can do it."

"Hey, pitch, is that peach fuzz on your face or dirt?"

Ruth, with a heart-shaped discoloration from perspiration on the front of his St. Mary's shirt, peered at his menacing opponent. He knew any mistake might very well put the game out of reach. Ruth manipulated his grip on the ball, bending the index finger of his left hand so his mid-digit knuckle pressed against the seam of the ball. Three pitches later, Schmidt was walking away from the plate, shaking his head from side to side. The belief that he had swung and missed the offerings had not yet sunken in.

"Way to go, Geawgie, way to go," Matthias encouragingly yelled.

"Matthias, where you been hiding this kid? He made my guy look silly. He looks scared, though." Sharrott fired a verbal joust from his dugout.

Ruth had seen Butch's swing earlier in the game when catching. He knew he could hit the waist-high pitch but thought he might not be able to catch up with anything moving down and away. His grip generated the spin to cause the required movement. His third pitch to Schmidt nearly landed on home plate as the batter's mighty swing passed harmlessly above the ball.

Ruth delivered on his promise. Three quick strikeouts as the three best hitters in the Bays lineup were frustrated in their at-bats by the movement and accuracy of Ruth's offerings. However, the Bays still had a lead. The Bays' pitcher had once again settled down, retiring 7 straight since the Ruth homer in the fifth inning. This would be St. Mary's last chance, with the bottom of their order due up.

Inexplicably, the Bays pitcher walked the first batter, and a rare Bay error on a routine sacrifice bunt attempt put runners at first and second with Ruth coming to bat.

Sharrott bounced up in the dugout and was trying desperately to get the attention of his outfielders to signal them to move back several steps. It would not matter. The pitch was already on its way. Ruth turned on the inside fastball, hitting it with such force that the right fielder barely had time to look up as the ball hit just inches below that same second story library window Ruth had peered down onto the ball field from six years earlier. The building had simply stopped the rocket-like ascent of the ball.

Matthias nearly jumped out of his cassock; he could not believe what he had witnessed. This mere boy of 13 years had pretty much single-handedly defeated the Bays. Ruth hit three home runs, had several throwing assists, and had struck out each of the daunting hitters in the heart of the Bays' batting order. The performance simply was worthy of legend. And of course, there was Geawgie's final majestic swing, the first boy to hit the library building on a fly, not to mention nearly reaching the second floor window. These events caused Matthias to ponder about Ruth's limitations. *My God*, he thought, *how far will he hit the ball when he's a grown man?* Beyond the hitting, Matthias further mulled, the pitching instinct! Never in all his years around baseball had he seen such a young, uncultivated talent show the capability to mow down hitters of such a high caliber. "God has blessed you, kid, with an enormous amount of baseball talent. I hope, little Geawgie, that you realize your blessings. God be with this child. Please, Lord, be with this child!"

Chapter 8

"Georgie, there you are. I have got something to tell you," Brother Paul said to Ruth, finding him sitting outside on the steps in front of the four-story dormitory building early one December evening, " My God, boy, aren't you cold? It's freezing out here. You'll catch your death of cold."

Ruth was sitting idly, wearing only what he wore everyday he worked in the laundry, his paper-thin, well-worn, and standard-issue tee shirt.

"Brother Paul, ya know I'm a very tough guy. I'm too tough to get sick, germs are scared of me," Ruth cackled.

"Anyway, Georgie, you will have a new job starting Monday. You are going to learn tailor-making shirts."

"I like the laundry. I like the hard work."

"Understandable, Georgie, but seeing as you haven't picked up a new trade yet, let's see how you do making shirts. Georgie, this is more responsibility and you can make some money. You will report Monday to the third floor of the vocational building, right after lunch."

"How much can I make?"

"That depends, Georgie, on what kind of tailor you turn out to be, how quickly you learn the trade and the quality of your work. The better the shirt is made, the higher the price."

"I guess it'll be OK. Sounds like I don't have a say in the matter. Where is Boss? He and I haven't practiced in a few days." Ruth stated.

Matthias and Ruth had become even closer since the day he began playing for the St. Mary's baseball team. The inmates, out of respect, referred to the gentle giant of a brother as 'Boss.' Many of the St. Mary's graduates claimed to have never heard Matthias raise his voice in anger, except maybe to Ruth. Somehow the pair found three to four hours a day to spend practicing baseball. During the cold depths of winter, Ruth and Matthias would throw and catch for hours in one of the long building corridors, under its pale yellow hallway light. Ruth loved playing baseball. His admiration of Matthias grew when he discovered Matthias could hit a baseball with devastating power. Matthias was the one person Ruth had difficulty getting to swing and miss at a pitch. Matthias had Ruth pitch to him in the big yard daily, and Matthias consistently hit ball after ball over the deep left field fence. Ruth marveled at his ability, and soon he began to emulate Matthias' every movement. He wanted to throw like him, hit like him, take a batting stance just like him. He even began to walk just like Matthias.

One clear, crisp, late September day, after Matthias was finished hitting some thirty of Ruth's best pitches well over the left field fence, a humbled Ruth asked, "Boss, why can't I get you out?"

"Well, Geawgie, I know what you're gonna throw before you do. You throw just fine and can shut down those high school kids you face. Now you have to learn to pitch. Geawgie, it will be hard work, very hard work."

As Brother Paul began to retrace his steps back inside, he turned to Ruth, "Come on, Georgie, let's get you back into where it's warm."

On the following Monday, Ruth reported to his assignment in the vocational building precisely at 1:30PM. The expanse of the third floor replicated the great shirt factories of Glasgow, Scotland. No walls had been built to create the demarcation of classrooms. Instead there were three rows with three large cutting tables in each on the east half of the floor and, three lines of three steam-driven sewing machines on the other. This setup was accented by the bare floor-to-ceiling support beams set about sixteen feet apart. Other than the windows, the only light was generated by the single lamps which hung down from the ceiling on thin black wire to illuminate the cutting and sewing areas directly beneath. On sunny days there was more than ample light, but on cloudy days and in the late afternoons from November to March, in work that needed a level of preciseness, the boys struggled in the shadowy sulfur haze created by the poor lighting conditions.

At initial glance the tailor shop looked like a storm of chaotic activity, but there was a neatly organized process and job responsibility for everyone. St. Mary's had a cooperative effort with St. James School for Boys and The City Tailor for the manufacture of low end, but highly durable, work shirts. Here at St. Mary's, boys would learn the trade and at about the age of 14, be shipped to St. James. St James School for Boys was not as secure or rigid an environment as St. Mary's. There was a storage area in the near corner with piles of webs of cloth. The school had adopted the same assembly-line process as the boys would experience at City Tailor. The boys would learn all aspects of the shirt-making trade, not just the more masculine work of a machinist. There were the stockers, those who had to make sure the cutters had an adequate supply of fabric. The fabric was laid across the cutting table so that a penciler who would lay a previously cut piece on top and then carefully trace an outline from the pattern. Using a razor-like mechanical knife, the cutter then carefully cut the cloth. The cut pieces of the cloth ready to be sewn into a shirt were then put into bundles marked front, back, collar, cuff, sleeve and pocket and delivered next to the hemmers, then to the stitchers, the buttoners and so on until there was a completed shirt. The most exacting part of the process rested with the cuff and collar stitchers, where corners had to be cut to the most accurate measurement so the corners would lay without crease and the collar flat. Shirt-making was a labor-intensive industry in the early 1900's, and the quality and appearance of the finished garment depended on the skills of the people involved in making it. Ruth's incomparable dexterity quickly enabled him to become the best collar stitcher at the school, and he drew great pride from his work. Often, Ruth would be heard bragging that he made the best shirts ever at St.

Mary's. Brother Paul would not argue with that brash statement.

In May 1909, the Brothers decided to ship Ruth to St. James. This would give Georgie more freedom in that it was a school compound without walls, located on Light Street in the Ward 3 section of Baltimore. He had been confined to the grounds of St. Mary's for the better part of seven years. The time seemed right to test fate and see if Georgie had fully departed from the ways of the past. His wages from City Tailor would be deposited into an account held in trust by the Xaverian's at St. Mary, less expenses incurred at St James. Since the Xaverian's ran both facilities, what could possibly go wrong?

Even after a seven-year absence from his old stomping grounds of Ridgley's Delight, the four-block walk from City Tailor to St James proved to be too much temptation for the teenage Ruth. Initially he welcomed the slice of freedom, returning each evening to St James without incident. After less than three weeks and an impromptu reunion with the remnants of his old gang, George began to find comfort in his past ways. Because of his work, Ruth had some cash in his pocket; he was itching for somewhere to spend it. He found it by carousing with his old friends. It had not taken Ruth long to realize there was no regular bed check. Boys were simply expected to obey the rules. Friday Georgie broke the curfew, not bothering to return to the home until mid-morning Saturday. St James had more activity on weekends, since the boys did not leave the home and were busy with their weekend chores of cleaning, laundry and studies. Brother Barnabas, an early riser, was waiting patiently to greet him at the front door. He had become concerned with Ruth's absence when the boy was a no-show at the breakfast table, considering his enormous appetite. Ruth casually strolled through the entrance, stinking of cigars, bad wine and cheap cologne water.

"Good morning, Mr. Ruth," Barnabas politely said.

"Same to you, Brother," Ruth lackadaisically responded.

"Please to my study, thank you."

"Sorry, I am too tired and want to go to bed."

"Now, Mr. Ruth. No discussions, understood?" Barnabas replied in a soft, but demanding, authoritative manner.

A boy's first offense was met with unusual understanding, compassion and no consequence. Boys transferring from St. Mary's had a history of testing the limits early in their tenure at St James; however, they usually and quickly settled into good behavior when the threat of a return to the stricter environment was mentioned. Fortunately, Saturday was an off day from the shirt factory. Missing curfew was one thing, but missing work would have been met with much more seriousness. Barnabas, a believer in second chances, would provide forgiveness only if convinced that offending boy was truly remorseful.

Ruth was very persuasive in his contrition with Barnabas, vowing to toe the line and not to have any repeat performances.

"Okay, Ruth, I trust you. Brother Matthias checks up on you daily. You would not want to disappoint him."

'No. Brother, I won't," Ruth promised.

Within the next few weeks, Ruth was establishing himself as one of the top shirt-makers at City Tailor and a valuable producer for St. James. Better quality shirts, flat collars, tight stitching and clean straight lines all commanded premium prices from the retailers. The pieces completed by Ruth were in this category, generating more income for both City Tailor and St. James. Because of his skills, City Tailor was making plans to move him from the low-end work shirt line to the finer clothes line, making upscale men's dress shirts. The factory owners believed this kid could very well become one of the best shirt-makers on the east coast. Ruth believed this as well, and without any provocation let it be known to the other boys.

"I am the best shirt-maker in the school," Ruth howled in the dining hall one evening during supper.

From two tables down, a vaguely familiar voice echoed, "Little Ruth, is that you?"

"Joe Woods?" Ruth responded with a sense of disbelief.

Joseph Woods, the son of an immigrant Irish farmer, had met Ruth seven years earlier while an erstwhile member of the Ridgley gang.

"Look at you, Ruth. You're a big guy now."

"What are you doing here?"

"Same as you, Ruth, they're trying to make an honest man out of me."

"Why haven't I seen you until now?"

"Cause us older guys work a lot more hours. I'm over at the factory every day and nearly all day. You probably would not have seen me now, except I got cut and needed a few stitches in the hand. So I'm off for a few days."

"Brother, there are two women at the front door," a sheepish student informed Barnabas. He was sitting at the desk in his study as the morning light peered in on the following Saturday.

"Ah….. What? Okay. It's not even 7:00 AM, what do they want?" stumbling with surprise, "Bring them to my office."

"Brother," continued the boy, visibly concerned, "These ladies are a little different."

"How so?"

"Well, for starters, one is smoking a cigar!"

"Okay, I will be right there."

Emma and Betty Johnston were working-class sisters who began hustling in the clubs of Baltimore when each was barely more than 15 years old. Officially they worked as waitresses, but this pair sold more than food and drinks. Their daily wage from waiting tables and the commission they earned from alcohol sales was approximately $5.00. What was written on the back side of the table menu said it all: "need more than culinary joy, ask waitress for details." Providing other pleasures of life to accepting young men and the occasional young woman tripled their earnings. Emma, the taller and older of the siblings, wore a lacy white dress which draped only over one shoulder, leaving the other bare. The hem line was accented with two inches of white frill, and the dress length covered less than one-third of her thighs. She wore leggings of alternating three-inch black and white stripes, held up by black garters peeking out from edge of the gaudy dress. Betty's crimson blouse was cut sufficiently low and the shirt length was short enough to disclose the chunky flesh areas of her bountiful cleavage and inviting midriff. The skin-tight black skirt, which could have been painted on, did little to hide her husky thighs and even less to conceal her trade. The pair had made the acquaintance of Ruth and Joe Woods that prior evening at one of Baltimore's night spots. After hours of sensual bantering and negotiation, an agreement was reached for the boys to share their concupiscent and delightful female company for a few morning hours. The girls were to be done working at 5:00AM, and after some quick freshening, would meet the guys at St James. Ruth handed over $50 in advance for the Johnstons and a third girl whose participation they were to have arranged as well.

"Can I help you?" a mortified Barnabas asked. He had never seen working girls brazen enough to solicit at the home, and certainly none were ever this physically close to him. Emma ascended the steps as she moved within inches of the timid brother.

"Sure, we were to meet our friends George and Joe. This is the address they gave us," Emma responded, with an enticing grin exposing the deep dimples of her cheeks in the process. "They're expecting us for some company and a nice time, you know, father. They's just boys in need of some comfort," reaching with the fingers of her left hand to touch his brown robe, she brought the smoldering cigar to her poised lips with her right. Emma drew a breath ever so slightly, as the dull red burning cigar end became a bright orange, and just as daintily, she blew a soft gray puff of smoke under the nose of Barnabas, who could not withdraw his stare from the exquisiteness of her face. He found himself being pulled into the sparkle of her deep blue eyes, thick ruby lips and captivating voice as she continued. "But if he ain't here, I'm sure other arrangements can be negotiated."

"Madam!! First, I am not a priest, just a brother, and certainly I am not buying whatever you're selling." With beads of perspiration on his brow, he gulped.

"Priest, brother, isn't that the same thing? You don't have no women at home, do ya? I could just provide you a bit of comfort and companionship if you'd like?"

"It's not the same," he responded, dodging Emma's question and silently praying for the fortitude to preserve his vows. "How do you know George and what do you want with him? He's just a young boy."

"We met him at the joint. Big tipper, full of cash and he's paid in advance. But if he's not here, you'll do."

Casually strolling down from the hill on Light Street at E. Baltimore, the untroubled duo ambled towards the home after a long night of

cavorting. Remembering the club Asa had
mentioned, Ruth set out for the 2 O'Clock Club,
made famous because action did not start until 2:00
AM. Perhaps Ruth was also thinking he may have
found Asa still working there. He and Joe passed
the night, and most of the morning, drinking,
dancing and engaging in lascivious conversation
with the ladies wishing to make an extended first
acquaintance. Ruth and Woods finished their
nocturnal activities at Polish Johnnies, satisfying
their palates with generous serving of succulent
sausage meals. Ruth literally ingested three each of
brats, kielbasa, and red hots with all the trimmings.
They had each forked over more than two day's pay
to the Johnston sisters who agreed to a morning
rendezvous of carnal delight. Woods was
convinced the girls had duped them out of a few
bucks, never to see them or their money again.
Neither of the boys had thought far enough ahead to
figure on how they would get Emma, Betty and a
third girl in and out of St. James and keep them
concealed while they were there. It would turn out
to be less of an embarrassment had the girls simply
been a no-show.

Looking up, Ruth saw the unanticipated
scene at the entrance and immediately registered
the magnitude of the problem. "Oh, crap, Joe, we'll
need to think pretty doggone fast."

Neither Joe nor Ruth would finish that
Saturday at St. James. Woods, already of age at 22,
would be released immediately, left to find his own
way in the world. He retained his employment at
City Tailor but now without any association with

the home. Ruth, on the other hand, was allowed to sleep until later in the afternoon, then he would gather his belongings and be brought back to St. Mary's in disgrace, a failed experiment in freedom. To the Brothers it was painfully obvious that Ruth had not yet exorcised the demons within him and suffered no remorse.

"Cousin Emma!" shouted Ruth as he ran, arms extended in a last desperate effort to save the moment, "You made it. Come on over here and gimme a big hug."

"George, cut the nonsense, you'll get no refund, and we're going home. This is too stinking strange. Come on, Betty, let's go."

Ruth abruptly stopped. His eyes were downcast, squarely focused on Barnabas' feet, shoulders slumped. Once again, when left alone, Ruth was not able to constrain his destructive impulses. More than anything else, however, Ruth was deeply troubled by the further disappointment his behavior would cause to Brother Matthias. He feared that this might be the last straw and Matthias might abandon him as everyone else in his life had. Ruth did not realize that Matthias saw a lot of good in 'Geawgie.' He knew that Ruth could very well become the perpetual overgrown child whose immaturity and impulsiveness would plague him for a great deal of his adult life. He also knew Ruth had a heart of gold, especially when it came to the younger boys. Most weeks he would use all of his earnings to buy candy for the 'kids.' Each Friday, Ruth resembled the Pied Piper, with throngs of small boys flocking to him in the small yard and following him as he pranced about. He would dodge them momentarily, then dispense the sweets to each and every one. Along with his enormous generosity was enormous baseball talent, too. Ruth's career as a pitcher almost did not happen, as Matthias returned him to his former position behind the plate. Geawgie was boasting to Brother Matthias in typical Ruthian fashion that he would hit 100 homers in games played over the summer, adding, of course, if he faced the St. Mary's pitchers he could probably make it to 300. "So, Geawgie, you think you can do better?" Matthias questioned. Ruth chuckled as he spoke. "Brother, it's a merry-go-round out there. Heck, I won't lose a game." He would come darn close to accomplishing both for Matthias, who waited at the entrance to greet the returning son to St. Mary's.

"Geawgie, of course you know the way. I do not know if I can give you any more chances. Prostitutes, drinking, smoking, breaking curfew? I just don't know anymore. Maybe you need to be back on the streets. The priest will be by to hear confessions tomorrow at 8:00 AM. You had better be first in line."

These words penetrated Ruth to his core; his worst fears might soon be realized. Carrying a suitcase in each hand, he painfully took the long, slow walk of shame back to his empty room. There was to be no roommate this time. Ruth would be alone in his own contrition.

With each day that passed with neither of his parents coming to retrieve him, Ruth's sense of relief grew. Matthias neither scolded him nor administered harsh consequences. Frustrated by his failure to make any progress with the young boy who had so much potential, Mattias grew icy-cold in the relationship. This punishment cut deeper to Ruth's core than any corporal punishment could.

Ruth was restricted from participating in any of the baseball games, told only to remain standing on the berm between the yards in isolation. It tortured Ruth to watch the other boys participate in the ball games. Besides the team which played other schools and sandlot teams, St. Mary's had several dozen intramural teams or dormitory teams.

Ruth believed firmly that Matthias would come around and their relationship would reignite. Five days later he was proven correct. Casually approaching Ruth, Matthias nonchalantly flipped him a glove and said, "Join the boys in the big yard for tomorrow's game. You're pitching." Matthias did not break stride as he went past, when he got about fifty feet away he turned and fired a ball at Ruth, grazing his left shoulder, "A couple of months ago you would have had it," he said, continuing with his departure. For the first time since the incident with the Johnston sisters, Ruth was relieved and thankful. Matthias granted him yet another reprieve, and unexpectedly, he was not demoted to a 'dormitory team' from the 'school team.' The next day, Ruth walked the first two batters he faced, hit the third, and although one of the base runners crossed the plate on a ground out, he did not allow a hit in the game.

Fall came earlier than expected that year in east, and because of several days of heavy piercing winds and cold rain, the last seventeen games of St. Mary's season were cancelled, although the team did manage to play nearly eighty games during the summer. Ruth, according to his own count, amazingly hit ninety-six home runs, but more importantly by everyone else's count, he only lost one game he pitched of the 35 games he started, allowing less than 2 runs a game on average. Ruth would never play catcher again.

On Tuesday, July 30, 1912, the temperature in Baltimore reached 91 degrees with humidity hovering near 85% and created a suffocating atmosphere in which even the healthiest of individuals found it difficult to breathe and handle routine work duties. Katie Ruth was finishing the routine chores of her usual long day in the restaurant, cleaning up the numerous messes and spills, rinsing spittoons, washing grimy dishes, stacking chairs on tables and mopping floors to make the place presentable for next day, at which point the cycle would repeat. She had been fighting a persistent cough since April, attributing it to a summer cold which she just could not shake. She had recently lost her appetite, resulting in a dramatic weight loss. Her plain, tawny dress hung loosely from her body, making her appear more malnourished than she was. Suddenly, without warning, her weakened muscles gave out, her knees buckled and she fell to the floor in a heap. Hearing the sickening thud, Ruth Sr. rushed in, scooped her up, and carried the limp body of his wife to the hospital. She was diagnosed with advanced lung disease, dehydration and exhaustion. One day later, she was transferred to the Municipal Tuberculosis Hospital. Even death would not come easy for Katie Ruth, as she struggled to meet the peacefulness of death for nearly two weeks, finally succumbing on August 11, 1912.

"Geawgie, please pack a few things, you're heading back home for a stay," Matthias addressed Ruth in a private conversation in the dining room.

"Why Brother? I do not want to leave."

"It's about your mother, she's not well, and so you need to go home to be with her."

On August 10th, Ruth was released from St. Mary's. He was brought directly to the hospital ward his mother shared with five other terminally ill patients. Ruth could manage only to stare stoically at his comatose mother, whom he found barely recognizable. She weighed less than seventy-five pounds, and her facial features were dramatically depressed, almost corpse-like in advance of her passing. Ruth displayed no emotion, no connection to her. Any of his feelings or thoughts was an enigma, bottled inside of him forever as he looked at her silently. If Katie had been at all responsive and able to open her eyes, she would have looked in disbelief at the enormity of the young man whom she had given life to, now standing over her.

The funeral service, attended by a scant handful of mourners, mostly patrons of the restaurant, was held at St Alphonsus Catholic Church, a parish comprised of primarily German immigrants which was located at the intersection of Saratoga and Park Streets. From there, the tiny procession trekked to the east side of Baltimore, taking Katie to the Most Holy Redeemer Cemetery for her burial. Katie's grave would be as nondescript as her life, marked by only a simple stone. Ruth returned to St. Mary's for his final stretch before his release for good.

Ruth's baseball diamond notoriety began to grow during the next year and a half. St. Mary's own weekly publication, The Saturday Evening Star, reported the highlights of the baseball team's game with particular focus on the now almost-legendary exploits of the young pitching and hitting star, Ruth. He was spectacular in the final weeks of the 1912 scholastic season, limiting local high school teams to less than one run per game. Powerhouse St. Stephens had not lost a game in six weeks, and had swept games against St. Mary's Industrial three straight years, including an early season 16-3 drubbing. The season-ending showdown now loomed on the horizon. With Ruth firmly entrenched on the squad, St. Mary's would have a fighting chance.

Chapter 9
Ohio 1880

Messer Street Grounds, home to the Providence Grays in 1880, was an irregularly-shaped ballpark. Left field was extremely short. Conversely, straightaway right field was over four hundred thirty feet, while center was just about three hundred twenty feet deep. To all observers, that section of the field appeared cavernous. There was a twelve-foot fence all along the outfield. Mike Dorgan of the Grays, leading the game against the Buffalo Bisons in the bottom of the ninth inning, took a deeper defensive position in right field than normal. Dorgan wanted to avoid any balls getting past him for an extra base hit. It was very difficult and a rarity for a player to hit a ball out of the park, as evidenced by there having been only eight home runs hit at Messer Street Grounds all season. The first two batters of the inning were retired rather easily, but Dorgan was fidgety nonetheless. He was a relatively weak outfielder; he had little range and a poor throwing arm to boot. To this point in the game, no Buffalo player had reached base yet. Silently, he prayed the ball would not be hit his way. Although Providence was the host team, the prevailing practice in 1880 was to flip a coin for last at bats. Pud Galvin, pitcher for the Buffalo Bison, was coming to the plate. Galvin had not gotten a ball out of the infield in his two previous at bats, but Dorgan did not adjust his defensive position, remaining in this deeper-than-normal location. Galvin took a long stride with his front foot towards the pitch; with his hands high he took a big cut. The ball made contact near the end of the bat, resulting in a weak humpbacked drive toward the large empty green space in short right field. With the ball hit directly at him, Dorgan froze for a brief moment. After the slow initial reaction, he frantically began racing in from deep right. He darted forward as best he could, losing his cap as he extended for the ball with his bare hand. With his fingers spread, Dorgan managed to grab the sinking soft liner on a single bounce. Using every ounce of his momentum, he fired a strike to the stretching Joe Start at first just as the inexplicably trotting Galvin, who thought he had an easy hit, was getting there. Time hung suspended in the next anxious moment. Then the umpire raised his right fist, thumb up, "you're out!" John Ward had done it; he had retired all twenty-seven batters he faced, and just five days after Lee Richmond of the Worchester Ruby Legs had accomplished the same feat. Casually, Ward removed the handkerchief from the pocket of his gray-and-black-striped baseball shirt and wiped his brow clean. There was no self-gratifying celebration, fist pumping or animation. The sparse crowd offered no standing ovation nor extended cheering to recognize the magnitude of this accomplishment; they simply clapped at the victory for the Grays. Since two pitchers, both of whom would go on to have mediocre careers, had thrown shutouts with no one reaching base within a week, not a soul following the game would have believed how rare a baseball feat this would become. The daily New York Clipper's report of Ward's effort described the pitching and defense in every way perfect, a 'perfect game' by the Grays. The term did not directly address the pitching effort, but rather the team's performance. Those newsmen beginning to follow baseball across the country most likely believed such games, with pitchers retiring every batter in order, would become routine, most likely weekly occurrences. The term 'perfect game,' attributing the success to the effort of the pitchers, would not become common baseball jargon until 1908, when the feat was accomplished by Addie Joss of the Cleveland Naps against the Chicago White Sox. More importantly, it would be nearly a quarter of a century until a pitcher would throw the next 'perfect game.'

In early 1888, Denton Young finally returned to his rural home in Gilmore, Ohio, after spending nearly three years with his father on a relative's dairy farm in Nebraska. McKinzie Young had decided the best thing for his son's future was for him to learn the farming business inside and out, and the best way was to do that was for him to spend time on a much larger working farm. McKinzie had some distant cousins who had built a sizable dairy farm outside of Omaha. This would provide Denton a perfect chance to learn more about building and operating a profitable farm than he could in Ohio. Denton would continue to play baseball in Nebraska, but it was not at the competitive level of the eastern United States. In addition to the money he made working the dairy farm, the teams from Cowles paid him $20 per month to play. A series of the semi-pro teams in

Nebraska collapsed from financial pressure. Denton had little trouble finding new clubs, since in the 27 months in Nebraska he failed to lose a single game. Shortly after his return, Denton would make two life-altering decisions: he would join a semi-pro baseball club playing out of New Athens, Ohio and he would propose marriage.

Despite his absence from Gilmore for a half a decade, he quickly became reacquainted with a curly-locked auburn cutie from the farm adjacent to the Young's, Robba Miller. Denton initially met her when she was eleven. From the time of his first glance into her fiery green eyes years earlier, Denton had been smitten. On the fateful day they met, he had set his mind that he was to marry her and build a long prosperous life together. Robba was now 16 and had blossomed into a radiant young lady while retaining the rural charms inherent in her tomboy ways. Denton would be celebrating his 21st birthday, soon to be responsible for his own decisions. Throughout his years of absence from Gilmore, he wrote her on a less-than-regular basis; she responded with even less regularity.

Denton was persistent and fortunate. The Young and Miller families, because of the sustained absence of McKinzie and Denton, the two oldest males, had developed a routine of sharing the Sunday midday meal following the weekly religious service. This nascent tradition continued after their return. Once Robba's initial coolness and hesitancy towards Denton melted, they began taking extensive walks which grew into spending more and more time together. Robba's heart finally fell to Denton as they began to share a common picture of their future.

Denton, armed with just a modest country boy education, made a habit of reading about baseball and discovered that there were owners willing to pay players an obscene amount to play for them. He calculated that if he could play professionally for about five years while working the farm in the off season, he could save enough to buy a significant tract of land and fulfill the dream of the long blissful life he dreamed of sharing with Robba. Denton was passionate about baseball. Baseball would provide a clear path for him to earn the money he needed to buy a farm to fulfill his much bigger passion, to make Robba happy.

Young led the New Athens team to the tri-county championships in 1888 and 1889, not only with strong pitching performances but also with his sparkling play at second base. Playing most of the season without the use of a glove, he could make the routine play look casual and the hard play appear routine. In a time when most semi-pro baseball scores could have passed for those of football, Young held the opponents to less than a handful of runs in games he pitched. By late January 1890, he received several offers to play minor league baseball. Desperate for talent, the Canton Nadjys sent their business manager to the Youngs' farm to try to lure Denton to play for them. The expansion of the professional leagues diluted organizations of their talent. Canton, a competitive club, was pressed to find quality players to replace those lost and willing to pay handsomely. Mr.

William Heingaotonk, who doubled as the field manager, was a straight-shooter with little time for idle conversation. He got right to the point.

Sitting around the kitchen table Denton and McKinzie listened to Heingaotonk as he started his appeal.

Looking directly at McKinzie, "Mr. Young, Canton has affiliations....," he began.

"Excuse me, Mr. Hh...einga...otonk," stumbling to find the correct pronunciation, Denton interrupted.

"Please, son, call me Bill."

"Well, that's the problem. I am a grown man, twenty-three years old. This is my decision, so kindly address me accordingly, or you can go back north."

"OK, how about if I call you Denton? We have three professional team affiliations and can just about promise that someday you'll pitch with one of those clubs. I am prepared to offer you $40 now and $40 a month for the season," somewhat dismissive of Denton, he continued.

McKinzie stuck his hand out, saying nothing. His index finger pointed toward his son, letting Heingaotonk know who would make the decision.

"Well, Bill, that's a tidy sum, but I already have a higher offer from..."

"$60," Bill rudely interrupted..

"Dad, I am not sure they learn manners up in the north side of the state, but they seem to have money. You have a deal."

From his coat he produced a simple contract, then reaching into his pants pocket, Heingaotonk pulled a wad of bills, counting out twelve five-dollar bills. He handed them to Denton with the admonition, "Now go buy yourself a glove." Denton made his mark on the document. He was to report to Pastime Park in North Canton on March 1. Just as quickly as he had arrived, Heingaotonk was gone, onto to the next prospect.

Denton deposited himself on the kitchen chair, relieved and now with more money than he had ever had in his hand, ready to take the next steps in his life: a marriage proposal and professional baseball.

McKinzie was perplexed by at what had just transpired in the blink of an eye. His son had gone from a farmer's son to an independent man and professional baseball player.

"Well, son, I am off to bed, we got chores in the morning. Please wake Jesse and Alonzo. It's time they started to take on more of the responsibility around here." McKinzie had already started to think about life after Denton left.

"Right, dad, I'll be along in a moment."

The pieces of Denton's life were beginning to fall into place. He bought the glove a few days later, but not before he made his first purchase, a modest sterling band he would place on Robba's finger at their marriage ceremony — assuming, of course, that she agreed to marry him. Denton hoped their wedding would take place shortly before he was to leave for Canton. He sat back in the wooden kitchen chair, closed his eyes and drifted off to sleep, very much the picture of contentment. His dreams took him to the day of his wedding.

In his dream, relatives and friends from Gilmore were invited to the Young's farm for the afternoon celebration to unite the happy couple. Nancy Young had spent the previous day preparing white wedding cakes, cooking food and decorating the farmhouse. Robba spent the day hiding at the far end of her farm, sitting with her back against a 100-year-old oak tree. She had become too much of a lady to climb the tree any longer. The families had arranged for the preacher to perform the ceremony at high noon. Robba decided on a small wedding party, selecting her sister Mary and cousin Irene to serve as bridesmaids or escorts.

"Robba," Mary and Irene called out in unison, "It's time to get you ready."

The procession was simple. Robba would lead the way. In a plain white dress, she approached the preacher with slow, purposeful strides. She was followed by Mary and Irene, then her mother and father. Denton waited for her, standing to the left of the preacher. The celebratory meal afterward was equally simple, an assortment of freshly-cooked meats and home-grown vegetables. After the celebration was done and the guests had left, Robba went back to her farm, packed up her things and moved into the Young's, now a married woman. She and Denton would be at each other's side for the rest of their lives, complementing one another.

Reality woke him up. From the front porch, McKinzie called out, "Denton, come quickly. Mr. Miller is here to speak with you, son."

"I understand here, boy, you planning to ask Robba's hand in marriage. Is that right?"

"Yes, sir, that's correct. I was planning to come see you today."

"Well, this train's left the station. She's all in a tizzy. How do you plan on supporting her and a family?"

"I have a plan, sir. I—" He was cut off in mid-word by an increasingly angry Mr. Miller.

"Son, if you're talking about baseball, it will be a cold day in hell before I allow her to marry someone who will be on the road away from home half the year, making peanuts. Son, you need to make an honest living."

"Mr. Miller, I pledge to you I will not marry Robba until I have at least one thousand dollars in the bank. That will be enough for us to buy a place, have some savings and start our life on the right footing. That's my pledge to you, if you pledge your blessing in return." Denton extended his right hand.

Mr. Miller grabbed Denton's hand and shook it firmly, "Son, you do that, you will have my blessing."

Friday, February 28th, was a sad day in Gilmore. Robba had not spoken to her father since the incident at the Young's farm weeks earlier. Each time she saw Denton, she burst uncontrollably into tears. She feared losing him to the temptations that surrounded baseball players. He'd be spending week upon week on the road, and she'd heard the stories of carousing and drinking. Denton stood over her, his arm wrapped around her tightly as she heaved from the heavy sobbing. He assured her of his enduring love, his pledge of faithfulness and that he would return with enough money for them to start their lives.

On March 1, 1890, he arrived at Pastime Park at 9:00AM. A creature of habit, Denton was up at first light and sauntered to the field about an hour ahead of everyone else. In his bag he had three baseballs. He decided to practice his throwing some while waiting for other players to arrive. Walking off the appropriate distance of about fifty feet, he placed two balls on the ground and took aim at the side of the wooden fence surrounding the grandstand. An hour later, every board in a section of the fence covering about ten feet was splintered, broken, or knocked out.

"Well, I'll be," Heingaotonk commented as he arrived. "Looks like a cyclone has come through here."

"I guess I was throwing a bit too hard for that old fence," Denton responded sheepishly.

"Denton, we just put that fence up last year. It wasn't that old."

Talk of the arrival of this new fireballer to Canton spread rather quickly. The magnitude of the damage grew as well, as the story spread from fan to curious fan in the Canton area and then beyond. By the time the news of the right-hander with the cannon-like arm reached the Cleveland Spiders office, he had knocked the grandstands down with a single pitch. Davis Hawley, a part owner of the Spiders, contacted their top Canton scout, Cash Miller, inquiring about the exceptionally-hard throwing right-handed pitcher now called 'the Cyclone.' Miller assured him that Denton Young threw as advertised. By June 1st, they decided to go see the phenomenon pitch. They arrived at Pastime Park the next day.

"What gives with this kid, the Cyclone? Seventeen hits, ten runs and he looks rundown."

Canton was, unarguably, a terrible club. They only had nine position players and four pitchers. If someone were hurt, generally a pitcher would fill in and play the field. Cyclone could play second, first and catcher. Two days earlier, when chasing a foul popup, Cyclone stepped on a bat, turning his left ankle. As a result of this injury, Cyclone was extremely cautious in his follow-through, unwilling to land with full weight on his foot after the delivery of a pitch. As a result he could not muster the velocity everyone wanted to see.

"The kid's working with a sore ankle, he can barely walk, but he's still out there playing every day. Doesn't miss a game," Miller said in return.

"Well, I'll need to see him again before we make the investment."

"Just bear in mind, this kid has pitched two games where he allowed only one hit."

"What about the 15-2 game he lost?"

"Mr. Hawley, our fielders made twenty-one errors. He didn't have a chance."

After the game, Cash Miller tracked down Young. He wanted to let him know that the owner of the Cleveland Spiders of the National League would be coming to watch him pitch again. After today's performance, there was concern that he, Young, was just another oversized farm boy with a strong arm and not enough smarts to pitch at the next level. Miller added that Young would need to pitch the game of his life to reverse this impression. Young's dream of pitching in the major league was on the precipice, in danger of derailing before it would get started. The prospect of returning to the Gilmore farm, without the money he thought he would make, enough to buy that place of his own, weighed heavily on his mind. He would have proven his father right, even though McKinzie had never discouraged his dream.

"Look, Young, I'm not going to throw you to the wolves. Make sure your ankle is healed before you pitch in front of guys from the big leagues again."

Young made a few relief appearances and a spot start or two while waiting for the ankle to heal fully. In mid-July, he told Cash Miller that he was recovered enough and was ready to go.

On July 24, 1890, McKeesport, who was battling Canton for last place in the Tri-State league, was in town. During the pre-game routines, George Strief, the squat crusty thirty-three year old catcher with no further ambitions about making it in the big league, approached Denton. He knew all the tricks of the trade and prided himself on mentoring the young Cyclone.

He asked Young, "How are you feeling? You set for the big day?"

"I'm feeling pretty good. Maybe I can make something special happen. George, I'm 23 now, maybe it's not meant for me to play at the next league level. I fear I blew my chance weeks ago. I guess I'll just be going back to the farm and forty years of dirt plowing."

Strief responded, sensing Young's unease. "Hey! Snap out of it! We're in last; McKeesport is next to last. But there are several thousand people and scouts here, and they're not here to see two miserable last-place teams play. Young, they've come to see *you*. Show them what you've got. I'll put a couple of extra pads in my glove, so just let her rip."

Strief knew how important Young's performance in the game would be, and what it meant to him. Young talked about Robba so often he felt like he knew her, although they had never met. He genuinely liked the Cyclone and hoped the kid would make it in the big time. Strief would help him any way he could.

Young, finished with his warm-ups, was standing in the pitcher's box, peering at the semi-crouched Strief. *Is he grinning?* Young thought to himself. The batter stepped into the batter's box. Young put his right foot on the pitcher's box line, readying to deliver the game's first pitch. The umpire, looking out from behind Strief, yelled, "Play." Young raised his arms over his head and sent the first pitch toward home. Strief with his glove chest high, his arm fully extended and elbow locked, received the pitch with a thud. As the umpire was about to raise his hand for strike one, Strief fell forcibly into him, both catcher and umpire tumbling to the ground. No one had noticed that Strief had lifted his toes, putting all his weight on his heels, knowing since he was off-balance, this would knock him backwards to the ground and, for a little extra emphasis, he could take the umpire with him. The desired effect was achieved. Most of the crowd and scouts were in awe. The umpire picked himself up, dusted off his dark blue Prince Albert coat and trousers and politely repositioned himself. Fearing he could not react quickly enough to a ball coming at his head, the umpire did not take the position behind the catcher but behind Cyclone in the pitcher's box. "Play," he cried and Young delivered the next pitch.

On August 6th, the Chicago Colts were back in National League Park for a double-header against the Cleveland Spiders. Adrian "Cap" Anson, standing in foul territory outside of third base, was lightly tossing a ball to his third baseman, Tommy Burns. Anson was regarded as a cunning baseball player, in some of the local writers' opinions, a baseball genius. During the years from 1880 to 1886, his Chicago teams had won five pennants. Some of the innovations to his credit were the hit and run, moving players to back up one another on throws, batting signals and the use of a third base coach. Many viewed him as the premier judge of baseball talent at the professional level.

"Hey, Cap," Burns asked, "isn't that the kid from Canton?"

"I think so. Looks like they have the farm boy pitching today. He's somewhat of hard thrower, nothing special. Bad player going from one bad team to another," Anson cockily answered. "We'll beat them as easily today as we did yesterday." Anson was correct at least as it concerned the second game of the day, in which the Colts prevailed 7–1.

Cyclone did deliver something impressive and special, just thirteen days earlier. After all eyes at the ballpark witnessed the 'devastation' of Young's first throw, the urban legend of the man whose pitches could reap the destruction of a cyclone was now implanted in the mind of each McKeesport player. Strief's antics had yielded positive dividends. Most of the McKeesport batters did not want to step into the batter's box. Of course, they could not get close enough to the plate to afford a good swing at his pitches. They were tentative. Young pitched Canton to a 4-1 victory, not letting one batter reach base on a clean hit.

Young was not aware of the pre-game comments of Anson. The Spiders, with Young hurling a gem, secured their 25th win of the year. The powerful Chicago club could muster only three hits to go along with their single run. A fervent Anson sought out the Spiders manager, Bob Leadley, after the completion of the second game.

"Bob, you want to sell the farm boy? I will pay you triple what you paid!"

"Anson, you'll need to talk about purchasing Young with Mr. Hawley. I only handle them on the field."

"I am going to get him, Bobby. Boy, I missed the boat with him. I completely missed the boat."

The Spiders would finish the season winning nineteen more ballgames, playing just well enough to avoid the cellar. Young would win eight of those games, completing his first professional season at 9-7. He, however, gave up more hits in the next seven weeks than he had allowed in nearly a half a decade. At the conclusion of the baseball season, Young returned to the farm in Gilmore and to his love, Robba, just in time for the fall harvest.

Chapter 10
Ohio 1892

As autumn slipped towards winter, the daily breeze was gaining its cold feel. Young had just finished raking the barn as Robba came bouncing through the open barn door. Her hair was pulled back in a long pony tail. Young's face lit up when he saw her. His heart thumped as she approached. He was deeply in love. Unlike the daylight of autumn, this reaction never lessened throughout his life, whenever he saw or spoke of her. Young had never had another girlfriend, nor would he ever share intimate moments with women other than Robba.

"Bobby!" Young shouted as he walked briskly towards her. He threw his arms around her, "I have $460 saved in cash. There's a tract of land I can put a deposit on."

"Slow down a bit. Dent, you've only been in the professional league a few months. Do you think it's wise to spend all that money now?" she answered.

"Most everyone thinks I will have a pretty good career and make some good money."

"Don't be foolish. Grown men playing a boys' game for money? It's just a craze. People can take families and watch games in their town for free."

"Bobby Miller, I know I promised your father we'd wait until I had enough money to buy that farm, but let's elope. I have the preacher ready. We won't tell anyone but …"

"Why, Denton True Young! You are a man with a plan!"

Early that Saturday, Denton 'CY' Young and Robba Miller were married. The simple service was attended by no one. Each had agreed to hold the marriage as their secret until Young had purchased the land for the farm. Maybe they would only need to keep the secret for a year, two at most.

"Denton, what if I become with child?"

"Bobbie, it does not matter. We'll be happy. But . . . we'll cross that bridge when we come to it, and, tell everybody if we have to."

There was another secret Young would keep inside for a year. The owners of the farm, which he had eyed to spend his life on with Robba, declined his offer and down payment. The only reason given was that they had changed their mind. He did not share this with Robba until after he inherited the family farm, several years later.

The Cleveland Spiders were considered the most inept hitting franchise in the fledgling National League when they moved over from the American Association. The addition of George Joseph 'Nig' Cuppy to the pitching staff to complement the league's now most-dominant pitcher, Cy Young, and the capable John Clarkson, who had been released from the Beaneaters earlier in the season, enabled the Spiders to complete their dramatic ascent, winning the second half of the split season and earning the right to a showdown with the powerful Boston Beaneaters. Cuppy and Young would serve as teammates for all but one of Cuppy's years in professional baseball.

The shadow of the League Park grandstands stretched over the infield as the sun began its afternoon descent to the west. It was Monday, October 17; nearly every seat in the ballpark save only the double-deck grandstands was already filled as the anxious Cleveland throng continued to file into the ballpark. Today was opening day of baseball's championships, the series reinstituted after a one-year hiatus. The first pitch was scheduled for 3:00 P.M.

The fencing of the extended single-deck grandstand was draped with red, white and blue bunting, adding to the festive aura of the park. The outfield fences were cluttered with signage of thriving businesses: Sherwin Paints, Quaker Co. and PJ Haberdashers.

A modest breeze out of the north, cooled by the waters of Lake Erie, put a moist chill in the air but kept the six flags atop the grandstand waving steadily.

"Nig, seems like there is more interest in baseball now than there has ever been before. How many people you think will come today?" Young asked Cuppy.

"I don't know. Why the concern?"

"My Bobby seems to thinks professional baseball will not last."

"When all is said and done, ten thousand people will be here, easy. Maybe eleven thousand."

"Nig, I think you'll have a better career than me. Twenty-eight wins in your first year. Without you we would still be middle-of-the-road nobodies."

Although Cuppy did have a better season, Young dominated the league, winning 36 of 48 decisions and allowing less than 2 runs a game. The Beaneaters were a strong run-producing club scoring at a rate of 5.7 runs per game. Led by their incomparable field manager Frank Selee, what they lacked in power, they made up for in speed and an aggressive style of base running. For the season, the Beaneaters swiped 338 bases and had 203 doubles.

"Chief," referring to Young as most of his teammates did, Cuppy responded, "you're too modest and too much of a gentleman. They'll talk of you as the best there ever was when you're done."

"Clarkson has 300 wins already. Come on, I have what, about 70? I'm going back to the farm for good, after maybe one more year. I'll have all the money I need. Besides, there's rumor of the owners reducing the salaries, cutting roster sizes to save money. My Bobby might be right. Professional baseball may be short-lived."

"Chief, you're too humble. By the way, Pud Galvin has almost 400."

"Humble, hah. I'm already 25. Pitchers like us don't last. They generally quit before they're 35. Besides, I'll already have hell to pay. Chances are I'll miss the harvest because of the playoffs. I won't get back home until nearly November. This profession is costing me money."

Young walked out onto the field from the wooden dugout to begin his pregame warm-up routine. His opponent to start the series, pitching for Boston, was Jack Stivetts. Jack was built much like

Young, standing 6' 2" and already had over 100 professional victories. Stivetts had had just as much success in the 1892 season as Young, racking up 35 wins and yielding a paltry total of 140 runs for the year. Unlike Young, Stivetts was feared as much for his hitting as he was for his pitching. Stivetts would retire at the age of 32 after 11 seasons, only nine of which he could effectively pitch. He amassed 203 wins.

Cy Young and Jack Stivetts hooked up in what may be considered the best game ever played in the professional baseball postseason. The pair dueled throughout the afternoon and into the early evening, with neither giving an inch. The weak-hitting Spiders were simply overwhelmed by Stivetts, who yielded only four hits but walked three other batters. Young's challenge was much more daunting, and his effort was consequently more spectacular than that of Stivetts, allowing just six singles and issuing one free pass. Inning after grueling inning, Young kept the powerful Beaneaters lineup off-balance using his explosive and incredible ability to spot the ball. Cleveland mounted a rally in the bottom of the ninth as Jesse Burkett reached third base with two men down. Burkett was stranded there thanks to an outstanding fielding play by first baseman Tommy Tucker who had lunged to his right snatching a hard hit ball out of the air for the out. The twenty-second of the long line of goose eggs was lifted on to the scoreboard as the third out in the eleventh inning was recorded by the Beaneaters at 5:03PM. The afternoon dusk had drifted into near-complete darkness. Graciously, the umpires stopped play. The game was officially recorded as a tie, with neither team having scored a run.

For the Cleveland faithful, this was devastating disappointment, a game they felt certain the Spiders would win. Clarkson was announced as Cleveland's game two pitcher. Boston had pretty much roughed up their former mate since going over to Cleveland in midseason. On the other hand, the Boston starter, Harry Staley, had been practically surgical in his cutting through the Spiders lineup whenever he faced them.

The South End Grounds pavilion, home of the Beaneaters was unprecedented in its architecture as a baseball field. The medieval 'witches cap' turrets on top of the magnificent grandstands made it one of the most distinctive ballparks of its time, conjuring images reminiscent of Camelot. It was one of baseball's first double-decker parks. In the spring of 1894, it would burn to the ground because of youthful vandals who ignited some rubbish, leading to the Great Roxbury Fire. Boston was tough to beat on their home field winning fifty four of the seventy five game played there. Nothing changed during the 1892 post season.

One week after the series began; it came to a non-climactic close. Officially over on October 24, 1892, for many the outcome was never in doubt. Boston finished the dismantling of the Spiders by completing the 5-0 sweep and avoiding a budding controversy.

League officials had decided that game six and seven would be played in New York City. They believed games played there would bring larger attendance and wider exposure, helping the league get on a better financial footing.

Nick Young, league president, promised the players bonuses for those two games of $5,000, more than double what they'd receive from the entire series.

The Beaneaters were furious about this decision, since those series games would take place in their home park. Nick Young and owner Arthur Snoden bluntly "suggested" to team manager Frank Selee that in the interest of the game the team let up a bit. The players unanimously told Selee they had no interest in extending the series more than necessary.

The Spiders, without help from their opponents, simply did not have the firepower to produce the required wins needed to prolong the series.

Young had his worst performance of the playoff. He yielded eight runs, gave up eleven hits, including a pair of doubles, a triple and a home run. Young made an error and walked three batters. Cleveland managed three runs in the top of the third inning but the usually reliable Young could not stop Boston's hit barrage, relinquishing the lead two innings later. The final score was an embarrassing 8 to 3 loss.

The thirteen Beaneater players got to share a $1,000 bonus. The Spiders got to share half that. The league magnates capriciously reduced the post-season payoff. Young and his eleven teammates would each earn an extra $41. Most groused about some but Cuppy was distraught. He told Young he really needed the money that was promised. Young had sufficient cash to fulfill the promise he made to Mr. Miller, so there was no reason to hold on to secrets.

Without prompting, he gave his share to his teammate.

The official wedding ceremony between Robba and Young took place two weeks later, on November 8, under the skies of a perfect autumnal Ohio day. It was just as Young had seen it in his dreams. Robba had shed her boyish image. Now, as the bride-to-be, she was radiant in her white wedding dress. After the ceremony, she joined Young on his family farm, this time to stay.

The winds of change began to impact professional baseball during the winter of 1892. Hard-throwing pitchers like Cy Young were dominating the landscape. The professional leagues were pirating not only each other's players but entire teams. After the 1891 World Series the American Association, in existence for a decade, finally folded, the result of the impact of two previous events. One was the formation of the Players League in 1890, which siphoned off talent and gate receipts. The other was the shift of its cornerstone franchise, the Brooklyn Bridegrooms, to the National League. Players were demanding more money; if they did not get it they would jump clubs and or leagues.

The American Association, thought of as 'The Whiskey and Beer League,' was looked down upon by the rival National League, which would have liked nothing better than to see this low-life nuisance of league disappear. What was the appeal for their fans, cheap tickets and cheaper booze? Besides, the cities of the American Association were considered second-rate river cities. From 1884 to 1890, the champions of the American Association and the National League met to determine the professional champion of baseball. The National League continued to maintain its restriction on the sale of alcohol at games and preferred to keep more of a family picnic environment. Because of their financial stability, they were able to consistently attract the league's better players. Although the National League lost the playoff series in 1889, they delivered a crushing blow to the rival league from which there would be no recovery when they convinced the champion Brooklyn team to switch affiliations. Brooklyn was a city of prominence and should be associated with a more refined league. In the following year, Brooklyn would again emerge as champions, but this time as representatives of the National League.

The baseball championship format of 1892 did little to generate any increase in fan interest, which had waned after the collapse of the American Association. The excitement of seeing a 'World Series' champion crowned was now gone. However, pressure was mounting from another renegade league led by the fiery, charismatic Ban Johnson. In 1893, post-season play was once again absent, but effective with the start of the 1893 season there was one dramatic change.

Nicholas Young, during his tenure as National League president, ruled with a heavy, if uneven, hand. Most of his decisions satisfied the desires of the more powerful team owners. He had little tolerance for rowdyism, violence on the field or player disruptions. He believed the National League was 'Major League Baseball,' because of the cities the teams represented. He was a moving force for the formation of the league, serving as league secretary-treasurer until his election as league president in 1885. He remained in that capacity until 1902. He believed that if the owners made money, the league would grow stronger and attract more teams. Nicholas Young also believed each owner should have an exclusive territorial franchise that included rights to any player within that area.

The league batting average had dropped to an all-time low of .245 and showed no indications of reversing its course. America was changing; the idea of a pastoral game in a peaceful glen was gone. Fans wanted action and plenty of it. Although fights and lack of sportsmanship on the field was behavior he detested, baseball crowds erupted with passion when the occasional rhubarb erupted. Most of all, fans wanted runs. The two best run-scoring franchises consistently drew the biggest crowds and made the most money for the owners.

By a vote of 10-1, the owners agreed to eliminate the 'moving start' pitchers had in delivering a ball to an awaiting batter and to move the point at which the ball must be released back towards second base. Until now, the pitcher could deliver a ball from anywhere within a 12 foot by 3 foot rectangular box. The front line of the box was fifty feet from the batter. The pitcher's box was eliminated, replaced with a foot-long rubber slab 60 feet 6 inches from home plate. The pitchers would also need to maintain contact with the pitching rubber, so they had no more moving starts toward the batter.

The final series game debacle against Boston and the impending decision to move the pitching distance back ten feet weighed heavily on Young's mind. As fall scampered out and the biting winter winds blew across the Ohio plains, this crisis in confidence grew, gnawing at him every day. Training camp, beginning with a grueling train ride to Jacksonville, was set to begin in just about eight weeks. Although Young statistically had one of the best seasons in history, with 36 wins and an earned run average of 1.98, Cleveland management expressed a desire to cut his pay. During the year, he was criticized by his manager and other players for a lack of toughness. Young was strong-willed in his faith and personal belief against fighting or violence of any kind, and for that matter, against acting in other than a gentlemanly manner. Earlier in the season, in a game against the Reds, Charlie Comiskey, who would be a central figure in the 1919 Black Sox scandal, took exception to the aggressive spikes-up slide at first base by Cupid Childs of the Spiders. Childs was following the orders of manager Patsy Tebeau. After taking over the club, he chided his players for not being tough. "I want a team who looks at the opposing team with hatred. If you want to play for the Spiders, you must be a fighter. I want a team of fighters." Comiskey, a feisty player who was not faint of heart, immediately went after Childs, tossing him like a rag doll. The Spiders, most of them wielding a bat, raced to the aid of the undersized Childs. Baseballs were thrown at unsuspecting players. Cincinnati joined the fray with an equal amount of weaponry. After nearly thirty minutes, one of the more vicious fights in baseball's history, peace was brought about by members of the press and management officials from the Spiders.

After reading the next day's newspaper account of the fight, Tebeau called Young into his office. Every newspaper account highlighted that the only non-combatant in the melee was Cy Young. Even one Mennonite player from the Reds had stepped in to defend the honor of his team, but not the gentleman Young. Tebeau unleashed a wrath of derogatory statements and foulest challenges to Young's manhood that would have made a sailor blush.

"You're a gutless nobody, Young; I will not have a gutless pitcher on my team. Cowards like you will never amount to anything in this game." Tebeau cooled off a few days later. Young had threatened to leave the team because of his demotion to the bullpen. A subsequent discussion between the team owners and Tebeau resulted in the return of Young to the starting rotation. Tebeau barely spoke to Young for the remainder of the season, upset that he had to play a pitcher whose intestinal fortitude was questionable. At the conclusion of the series, Tebeau did not refrain from his further criticism of Young, claiming his unwillingness to fight showed his cowardice and led to his team's defeat.

"Bobby, I am thinking about skipping baseball and just working the farm," Young addressed Robba in his usual polite manner as they were preparing for the traditional family Christmas gathering.

"Why, what's wrong, dear? Why the sudden concerns?"

"There are changes. They want the game to be more for the hitters. I am not much of a hitter. There are pitchers who can hit as well as they can throw, " Young added, but despite his vow to never keep secrets from Bobby, he did not disclose that he hurt his arm in the second series game and it was still bothering him, even now. He believed that his sore arm, more than anything else, had contributed to his ineffectiveness in the deciding game of the series. Tebeau thought Young's abysmal performance was for another reason which he shared with him nose-to-nose at the conclusion of the game.

"But I hear tell you're one heck of a pitcher."

"Well, that remains to be seen. They've moved where we can pitch from ten feet farther away from the plate. We also have to be touching this little twelve-inch piece of rubber. We can't take a step any longer."

"Hush, now!"

"Bobby, now that's a pretty big difference in distance. I won't be able to pitch as often, so they'll cut my pay even more. Maybe it's just not worth being away from home so much."

"You know your dad. As much as he complains that you're not here, he is most proud of his son, the professional baseball player. Heck, when you're away that's all he ever talks to our friends about after Sunday services."

"There's talk of adding more teams, traveling further west and more games. I barely help around here already."

"Denton Young, surely you're not ready to give up now?"

"I just don't know, Bobby, I just don't know. Plus, the manager hates me."

"You'll just have to win him over."

Young spent the next several weeks in deep consternation, mulling his personal uncertainties and the structural changes surrounding the upcoming baseball season. Players had very few rights and even less options. Professional baseball owners were on the verge of agreeing to a commonality of ownership, sort of a 'trust' amongst the twelve league teams with a maximum limit on player wages of $2,400 per year. Of course, there was no minimum amount a player could be offered. In one bad season, a player could go from riches to rags without any recourse, except to play for one of the other two-bit leagues.

Finally, at the insistence of Robba and McKinzie, Young decided return to the Spiders for another year. The $2,400 salary for playing was much more than he could make on the farm; they could build a little nest egg. If he did not perform well from the new pitching distance, well, worst case, he would return home but with some money. Because of the bitterly cold Ohio winds and the labor of his farm chores, Young's arm was not improving as he would have hoped. Maybe six weeks in the Florida warmth and sunshine, along with daily exercise and limbering was the recipe he needed to heal.

Young's concern about the pitching distance proved to be much ado about nothing. His 1893 season was a near repeat of 1892, winning 34 games. Some pitchers would lose their effectiveness in the 1893 season because of the distance, but Cy Young would not be one of them. However, he could already feel the effect of the pitching from the further distance on the health and strength of his right arm. Near the end of the 1893 campaign, Young sought out Clarkson to help him change his mechanics. Clarkson added two important elements to Young's repertoire of weapons. Clarkson showed Young a new and untried grip. Young held the ball in the palm of his hand with all five fingers around the ball, thinking how uncomfortable it felt. Clarkson told him to use the identical motion as his fast ball, but with this grip the velocity of the ball would be cut nearly in half. Clarkson called it the slow ball. Under Clarkson's tutelage, Young converted his big sweeping curve ball to one with a very late downward break.

Following spring training, Young once again sought out John Clarkson for help. Clarkson would teach Young how to deliver the ball using a different shorter windup, narrower angles and further changing the movement of his curveball.

Young watched with trepidation as the pitching stars from before the distance change began to fade from sight. Clarkson, his personal mentor, would be done after the 1894 season, as his win total declined from 33 in 1891 to 8 in 1894. Young continued with his winning ways. He was more impacted by the incompetent management of the Spiders than by his own decline.

At the conclusion of the 1898 season in which Young went 25-13, winning 25% of the Spiders games, Young approached Frank and Emmit Stanley Robinson about a raise. He had strung together nearly a decade of solid seasons and wanted an increase in his pay to $10,000, well above the league cap. He had heard that other standout players of his time were paid more than the stated maximum. Young threatened to leave baseball and return to the farm, which was also prospering. Also, Robba had yet to bear them a child. Desperately each had prayed for a large family, which wasn't to be. Young attributed their failure to conceive to his extended time away from her. If the Robinsons did not acquiesce to his wishes, he would just leave baseball. He was nearly 32, his best years might already be behind him. With a shade over 231 wins, he would be thought of amongst the good pitchers. Pud Galvin's win total was not even in the remotest of his thoughts.

"Young, the Spiders cannot afford to pay to $5,000. You will earn the same as last year next year, the league maximum of $2,400. Plus, Patsy Tebeau will no longer be the Spider's manager. I know he didn't care for your style," Frank Robinson offered.

Cy knew the amount he requested was a long shot, but with Tebeau gone, it became more palatable. "You have a deal," he responded as he shook hands with the Robinson Brothers, signing the contract moments later.

Emmit Robinson, quiet and all business, spoke before the ink on the paper was dry. "Young, one more thing before you go. The Robinson Family has purchased the St. Louis franchise. With all the growth to the west, that will become our showcase team. You'll be joining a few of your Spider teammates there. We've traded you. Good luck."

With the sudden force of an unexpected blow to his midsection, Young felt all energy drained from within him.

"Oh, and Cy, don't think about not meeting your obligation to play. We'll take your farm. Think about the bright side. You should beat the rest of the league easily," Frank closed with a smirk.

Young did think about the bright side. He would finally be rid of the cantankerous Patsy Tebeau, and $2,400 was still an awful lot of money. There was nothing he could do; he had signed a contract. When he told Robba what had happened, she was supportive and told him the time away would be about the same. She would come and visit when they played Cincinnati, Louisville and Cleveland.

New Sportsman's Park, called League Park after 1899, was a sanctuary for pitchers. The fences in left field were nearly five hundred feet and center field was further. Right field was closest at three hundred feet. The distance from home plate to the stands was one hundred and twelve feet. This was an ideal pitcher's park.

Young was full of enthusiasm as be boarded a train heading for Little Rock, Arkansas for preseason training. He had found out that Nig Cuppy had also been traded, and Cy was looking forward to the reunion.

Walking through the gates onto the ball field, Young was greeted with a familiar voice and an all-too-familiar tirade of insults.

"Well, boys, there go our first place dreams. Meet the gutless wonder, Cy Young. He's the coward from Ohio."

The hostility Tebeau exhibited towards Young continued well beyond the incident of the 1892 midseason, manifesting itself in 1896 as the forever bullying and unrelenting Tebeau persisted in abusing Young.

The owners of the National League teams agreed that a 'World Championship of Baseball' series would be continued in 1894. Baseball leadership in baseball decided that the participants in the Series were to be the teams finishing in first and second place during the regular season. By 1896, frustrations for the citizens and players of Baltimore were at a boiling point. In 1894, the Orioles, with a remarkable late-season run that included an 18-game win streak to capture first place, were swept by the John McGraw-led Giants from New York. McGraw pulled every dirty trick in the book during the series, but that was only one source of the disgruntlement.

William Chase Temple initially indicated to major league owners that revenues from the Temple Cup Series would be split, with 65% going to the first-place regular-season finishers, rewarding them for the travails and success of the long season. Throughout the year, Temple was heavily lobbied by the owners that gamblers would influence the outcome of the series if there was no incentive for the players to win. Temple reversed course immediately prior to the start of the Temple Cup, crushing news to the Orioles players. A deal was struck at the eleventh hour for a 50-50 split. Reluctantly the Giants' John McGraw agreed but pledging revenge on the field, a four-game sweep. In 1895, the Baltimore Orioles once again finished first, losing in five games this time to the Tebeau-led Cleveland Spiders. Play on the field could at best be described as dirty. Kid Gleason had sent a Spider player to the hospital with lacerations from a slide where he used his spikes with surgical precision on their unprotected legs.

Tebeau was brutal in his use of Young down the final stretch of this season, at one point using him for five consecutive days, winning each of those games. Nonetheless, Young was dominant in his performances and the Spiders had earned their championship. Baltimore was in a near-riot stage after Young pitched the masterful final game, but the police were able to maintain civil order. In

1896, for the third consecutive year, Baltimore captured the regular season crown, but there was a sense of uneasiness festering within the blue-collar town that had lost two straight Temple Cup series. Adding fuel to the fire were allegations by Baltimore's Ned Hanlon that some of the teams down the stretch had thrown games to the Spiders. The war of words between the Cleveland and Baltimore players and their faithful rooters escalated, sucking the already pent-up Oriole faithful into spewing incendiary words at Spider fans and players.

The 1896 series was marred at the outset by rowdy and unruly fan behavior in Baltimore. Playing at Union Park, an undersized field tucked in between local tenement buildings at 25th and Barclay Streets, fans strategically lined the rooftops, preparing their assault on the Spider players every time they came within range. On the field, Ned Hanlon's Orioles matched the nature of their barbaric fans. He vowed to see blood spilled rather than lose another series. At the turn of the century, the culture of the country was generally one of gaiety and a polite social environment. That gentility was not the case on the baseball diamond, though, especially in Baltimore. The team was chastised by the league officials on several occasions during the 1896 season. The Orioles were known for the perpetual taunting of their opponents that accompanied their dirty style of play. Although the Orioles manager was creative as he brought new and innovative tactics to the game, like the introduction of the bunt and the sacrifice, Hanlon also introduced the knock-down pitch and the spike-high slide to prevent double plays. Many believed he did not mind losing a game if he won the body count.

Baltimore fans adopted fully their team's style of play, and their rooting merely complemented it. As a result, they were more than prepared for the series against Cleveland. As the teams readied themselves prior to the start of the first game of the 1896 Temple series in Baltimore, the Spider players received a hostile greeting through a cacophony of sounds from cow bells to horns to drums, followed by an endless storm of cabbage, rotten eggs, tomatoes and an assortment of other fruits and vegetables when they veered too close to the stands or buildings. When the fans' arsenal of food was depleted, they resorted to hurling coins along with their insults. Tebeau expected his team to be of equivalent fabric, fight back with more fervor and win consecutive titles. Whether it was the incomparable and intimidating Baltimore line-up with six .300 hitters or the equally intimidating environment, the Spiders proved no match for the hostility, faltering badly and losing the 1896 series in five. Tebeau again put the responsibility on the shoulders of Young, whom he expected to be the team leader.

Young had made the mistake of sharing his concern for the team's safety. A sea of crazed fans followed the team from Camden Station and assembled in front of the Anchorage Hotel at Fell's Point the night before the series was to open. Quickly an effigy of Spider players was hung and burned near the entrance to the hotel lobby. Several players, led by Cuppy and Tebeau, were heading back to the hotel from a nearby brothel. A scuffle erupted, just yards from the front door, between Spider players and the Orioles fans. Fortunately, several more Spider players were watching through the glass door and were able to step into the fray and wrestle potential teammate victims inside. Young, one of the onlookers, did not step forward to help. This did not go unnoticed by Tebeau, "I will deal with you when we get through this!" he shouted at Young, brandishing his fists. The players involved in the brawl suffered a few scrapes and cuts but no serious injuries. One fan, however, was not as lucky, sustaining a broken nose and fractured skull, courtesy of a brand-new 35-ounce Louisville Slugger. The fans screamed for blood, threatening to storm the hotel. Bottles and rocks smashed the windows of the door and first-floor rooms. A second fire was ignited within feet of the lobby door while a third blocked the rear entry. The near-riot scene resembled a fort under siege by a rival army. Half the growing crowd of about one hundred blocked the alley to prevent any players from escaping. Inside the hotel, players broke tables and chairs to create makeshift weapons in preparation for an attempt to escape or to defend themselves. Young, of course, not believing in violence, recommended a period of prayer. Tebeau was outraged, restrained by Spider players as he turned on Young, screaming, "Go cower on the floor, you yellow bastard!"

"Patsy Tebeau! Please do not tell me you're a manager," Young said sarcastically, expecting more restraint from a person responsible for others.

"No, I am your teammate, first. I'll be watching your back, you coward, even though you obviously don't watch any of ours."

In a gentlemanly voice with words that cut to the core, Young responded, "Good to see you, too, Mr. Tebeau. I hope the evening goes well for you."

Seven Perfecto regular field players had been traded from the Cleveland Spiders along with pitchers Cuppy, Young and Jack Powell. Tebeau proved to be a soothsayer, however, as the St. Louis team finished fifth in 1899, adding to the frustration of the Robinson Brothers, who also saw the Spiders plummet to the bottom of the league standings with a miserly twenty wins and one hundred and thirty four losses. This was the final nail in the coffin of the Cleveland club, which ceased operation at the conclusion of the embarrassing season.

Tebeau, after lobbying the Robinsons to install him as player manager just before the start of the season, took heavy criticism for the team's lackluster results. He, in turn, continued his relentless assault on Young. It did not matter that Young led the team with twenty-six victories and registered an earned run average of 2.58.

St. Louis in 1900 continued to underperform under the dogmatic reign of Tebeau. The constant personal attacks on Young were finally taking their toll. Cy's record for the season would end up at 19 wins and 19 losses. After ninety-two games of futility with the Browns, eight games under .500 and sinking in the standings, Pasty Tebeau was fired and gone from baseball for good. Young would finally have some peace of mind. Tebeau would impart no further on-field revenge.

Chapter 11
1914 Baltimore

"George! Has anyone seen George?", the long-time St. Mary's 'inmate' Stevie "Maddog" McFarland yelled to the crowd of boys huddled in the gymnasium, fighting the chill in the air and debating their next indoor activity. The squat but powerful Maddog had replaced Ruth as the catcher on the St. Mary's baseball team. Brother Matthias had told him to find Ruth with a sense of urgency that frightened him. He had frantically searched several of the compound's buildings and Ruth's usual haunts but had come up empty.

Aided by the northeast winds blowing in from the frigid Atlantic and across Chesapeake Bay, Baltimore remained wrapped in a blanket of low, gray, nearly black clouds which had dropped sleet and ice on the city for the last three days. Outside activities had been cancelled once again at St. Mary's. The boilers were stressed, barely generating sufficient heat to prevent the near-freezing pipes from bursting at the joints and creating a watery mess.

"No, he's not here," a unified response was murmured from the throng. Another boy yelled, "Try his room. The lazy oaf is most likely still sleeping."

Maddog thought to himself, *Of course. Only place I did not think to check.*

Saturday, February 14, 1914, could very well be the day Matthias had longed for. Hastily summoned to the office of Brother Paul, now the superintendent of St. Mary's, Matthias arrived to an audience of Brother Gilbert, Fritz Maisel and Jack Dunn.

Jack Dunn had spent his life beating the odds. He had grown up in the tough section of Bayonne, New Jersey. The sleepy rustic community had been transformed into a dirty, smoke-filled center for oil refineries, led by giants Standard Oil and their largest competitor, Tidewater Oil.

As the pastoral quality of the town changed, so did the attitudes of the local youngsters. Nearly every boyhood activity now was intended to prove one's street toughness. On this particular day, during a game of chicken, the stakes were dangerously elevated as the venue moved to the local railroad yard, adjacent to the 8th Street station. The Victorian-style building was recently completed, with its modern compass-point spire extending skyward, and it became the finishing point. Seven youngsters were lined up, awaiting the signal to go. The challenge was to race, at top speed, across the 15 sets of railroad tracks, disregarding the moving trains which could come from either direction and at different speeds. The trick was to match your running angles to get ahead of the slow-moving locomotives. If you did not risk beating the train, or if you stopped, you faced not only verbal ridicule but also a physical pounding to the shoulders and legs, which of course made the walk home extremely long and painful. Dunn was not the most athletic of nine-year-olds, but he was bright. He faced every challenge with a can-do attitude. This was the third time he was being forced to run the yard; twice before he had failed. As a result of the beating after his second failure, it took nearly two weeks for the purple bruises to disappear from his legs and arms and to be able to walk without a limp.

Rail yard activities were generally consistent. The trains were moved along fairly laboriously, and the maze of intersecting tracks dictated strict enforcement of speed restrictions. On the 'go' signal, Dunn took off with a mental vision of how he would run the course. His plan was flawlessly executed. With one more stretch before the final sprint up the slight embankment, crossing the last set of tracks and the quick hop up a single step to the finish line, feeling confident he was home free, Dunn decided to glance backwards to see how the others were faring. He had begun to step easily in front of the lumbering Constable Hook train that was headed for 22nd St. to cross the next-to-last set of tracks, but the move proved to be careless. His misstep caused him to tumble, rolling across the tracks to narrowly escape the closing Constable Hook train. The engineer sounded the whistle, alerting the reeling Dunn to the approaching threat. Picking himself up, Dunn saw the dilemma; the commuter train headed south towards the beaches was late. If the train pulled out before he could pass in front, all would be for naught and he would face the consequences. Angling hard south, Jack had five cars to outrun before the locomotive. He heard the conductor's cry of "All aboard" and saw the train begin to move.

Dunn's timing was nearly impeccable, just ahead of the end of the station he crossed paths with the engine. That night in the hospital, the attending doctors recommended amputation of his left arm, fearing deadly infection in the crushed, disfigured limb. His family decided to run the risk.

Although Dunn would never be able to lift his arm above his head, he managed to play seven years of professional baseball. In one of those years he pitched, compiling a 23-14 record. Realizing he would never reach stardom, Dunn studied the mechanics of the game, of baseball players and even more importantly, the business. In 1908, with a $10,000 loan secured from the legendary owner of the Philadelphia Athletics, Connie Mack, he bought the Baltimore Orioles, the team he had managed in 1907. Dunn convinced Mack through his semi-arrogant passion and conviction that he could build the Orioles into a minor-league powerhouse which would provide a steady stream of major league talent for the Athletics.

Jack Dunn was not only the owner of the Baltimore Orioles; he also served as the team's chief scout and manager. Right now, Dunn was in search of a left-handed pitcher. Brother Gilbert was the baseball coach at Mount St. Joseph; for the second year in a row, his team was enjoying unmatched success on the strength of their southpaw phenomenon, Ford 'Rube' Meadows. At a recent tournament in South Carolina, Meadows had pitched consecutive shutouts against Boston College, Holy Cross and Georgetown as well as a complete game victory against the powerhouse

Fordham Rams. Dunn cajoled Gilbert into a meeting between them and Meadows. Dunn extolled the rewards of playing in baseball as a profession, assuring Meadows he had the talent to become a star. What Gilbert had not told Dunn was that Meadows came with attitude. His responses were obstinate and condescending towards Dunn, who angrily walked out of their meeting. Internally, Gilbert was happy that Meadows would remain in school, but he also feared losing the kinship with Dunn. Gilbert told him of a lefty pitcher named Ruth at St. Mary's. Although Dunn had only seen him pitch once when he came on in relief, he could tell that Ruth had terrific stuff and pinpoint accuracy. He would be able to sell Dunn on Ruth not only for the merits of his pitching, but also his ability to hit and versatility in the field.

Not wanting to lose a second prospect, Dunn contacted a player he had recruited into the professional baseball ranks from the Baltimore area, Fritz Maisel. Since signing his contract, Maisel had become somewhat of a free spender who liked having flashy possessions. Dunn knew Maisel owned the most luxurious and most expensive model car made in 1913, the Cadillac limousine. The solid black car was large, extraordinary and could accommodate seven passengers. The Model L had cost Maisel a whopping $3,250. It did not matter to Fritz, who anticipated a long and prosperous baseball career. According to the 1913 product brochure, the limousine found its greatest sales 'among those who place luxury, comfort, ease, richness, taste, dignity, elegance and refinement above all price consideration and are satisfied with nothing short of that which represents these qualifications in the highest degree.' The driver's compartment was three-quarters enclosed, with storm curtains provided for added protection in inclement weather. Five passengers could be accommodated in the rear compartment; two of them sat on revolving seats that folded flush with the body sides when not in use. The passenger compartment was trimmed in the best blue broadcloth. Silk curtains and a speaking tube for communication with the driver were included.

Maddog found Ruth sleeping in his overalls with two woolen blankets pulled tightly over his body to his chin.

"Wake up, Georgie; Matthias wants to see you NOW!"

"Why? I ain't done nothing wrong I can think of," Ruth said as he began to sit up and wipe the sleep from his eyes.

"I dunno, Georgie, must be something. He told me to tell you to go straight on to the big guy's office, Brother Paul's."

"Crap. That's not good. Maybe they're kicking me out for good this time? But I can't think of anything I've done."

"Better hurry on over and see. Come over to the gym when you're done. That's if you're still an inmate."

Although Ruth's father was still alive, St. Mary's would have legal guardianship over Ruth until he reached the age of 21.

Dunn, a man of little time for idle talk, got right to the point. "So tell me, Matthias, can this kid pitch?"

'Mr. Dunn, if you have ever seen Geawgie, he can pretty much do anything."

"Look, Brother, I am not interested in the anything. I want a left-handed pitcher, period."

Bouncing with all of the subtlety of an earthquake, Ruth entered.

"Brother Matthias, you wished to see me?" said a puzzled Ruth, surveying the crowd.

"Let me see if I got this straight. Gilbert, you say he can pitch but you've only seen him once, briefly. Matthias, you're giving me no straight answers. Joe Engel says he can pitch, but he may have got that secondhand as well. Look, I need a lefty pitcher, that's all."

Looking to the man-child Ruth, "Kid, can you pitch and would you like to be a professional ballplayer?"

"Yes, sir, I can pitch."

"Fritz, find a ball and a couple of gloves. Take this kid over to the gym and let me know what you think. Also, talk to him about life in the professional league. Come back in a half hour. I have business with these gentlemen."

"If Fritz likes what the kid has, I want him playing ball for me in two weeks."

Brother Paul responded, "Ruth has been with us for about a dozen years. This is his home, we are his family. How can I be sure you'll keep him safe? Plus, legally, we must care for him until he is 21."

"Brother, I will pay Ruth $600 for his first year, plus I will donate $1,000 to St. Mary's. In exchange you will assign legal guardianship to me, he will become my child. The legal papers will be here Monday."

When Ruth and Fritz returned, Dunn signaled Brother Gilbert and Fritz that they were leaving. Dunn did not bother to ask Maisel the obvious question since he knew the answer. Joe Engel, a player with the Washington Senators, had in fact seen Ruth pitch. A graduate of Mount St. Mary College in Emmitsburg, MD, he was invited to pitch the alumni game. The main venue of the day was a varsity game against a Baltimore school for troubled boys, figuring them to be a cupcake opponent. On the mound that day for St. Mary's Industrial stood a lanky fellow with a large head and features. All the lean lefthander managed was to strike out 20 batters and blast three long home runs in a thorough thumping of the Mounties varsity team. Stunned by the dismantling of his alma mater, Engel relayed the events of this game to Dunn when asked about local pitching prospects. Dunn trusted Engel's judgment.

"Ruth, I will be back in two weeks to take you on a train to the Carolinas for spring training. You'll be playing professional baseball. Have you ever been on a train ride?"

Turning for the door and not waiting for an answer as he let go Ruth's hand, Dunn and his troupe were gone as quickly as they had arrived.

Ruth shook his head, "Nope," in a belated response to Dunn's rhetorical question.

Dunn looked across the spacious backseat of the Cadillac at Gilbert as the car made its way through the slick Baltimore streets, "Well, Brother, this kid you touted as the greatest pitching prospect of all time better pan out, or I'll be heralded as a complete bumpkin. Christ, I'm now his legal guardian for two stinking years."

Gilbert reminded Dunn, the kid could hit as well.

Not one to miss a trick, as the legal documents were being prepared, Dunn instructed the attorneys to show Ruth's birthday occurring in 1894 rather than 1895. If his prospect did not work out, he would be off the hook; if Ruth were successful; he would sell his contract and be off the hook. Either way his guardianship would last only one season.

Brother Paul, Brother Matthias and Ruth stood in awkward silence for several seconds that seemed like hours. Finally Paul broke the tension. "George, you are ready for this. You have all the God-given tools. We've seen you grow up. This is your time; you'll make it real big."

Matthias was more comforting to Geawgie, trying to make him understand all the ramifications. Letting him know, too, that if things did not work out, he was welcome back at St. Mary's.

George slowly traipsed back to his room, concerned about his future, about what was to become of him outside of the structured safety of St. Mary's. Reflecting on what had taken place with a feeling of abject abandonment; he was right in his original thoughts of earlier when he was abruptly shaken from the peace and quiet of his St. Valentine's Day nap: *They were finally getting rid of him for good.*

Chapter 12

Fear, uncertainty and doubt raced through his mind, consuming the entirety of Ruth's daily thoughts. He bombarded Matthias with questions during the final days preceding his final departure from St. Mary's. Ruth was concerned about the tiniest and most trivial of details. He asked Matthias over and over again which uniform he should take to wear. How would he know when and what to eat? Which bats would he need and how many? Which mitt to take? Who would wake him each day?

Matthias assured Ruth over and over that playing professional baseball was a business. The team would provide all of what he needed. "Geawgie," he would say, "Playing baseball for a living is different. The game just does not end when you want it to. It is a job for men. When you leave, the one thing you are clearly going to leave behind is your boyhood."

Ruth shared quiet, tearful goodbyes with only the closest of his friends. He reluctantly agreed to a modest farewell dinner that spread across the school's three cavernous dining rooms. Ruth had been at St. Mary's for an unusually long time, by now he was completely entrenched as 'one of the boys.' Although not an orphan, the emotional abandonment provided a bond with all the orphans who did make the journey through St. Mary's towards adulthood. As large and as imposing of a figure Ruth had grown into, he was still a child emotionally stunted and fragile. When the hundreds of boys cheered him, Ruth's sense of impending loss of the kinship and parental guidance overwhelmed him.

Brother Paul encouraged Ruth to address the boys, "Say something, Georgie."

Ruth, visibly shaken, chest heaving from withholding the tidal wave of sobs, began, "Fellas, each time I go to bat, I'll be thinking of each of…" Unable to finish the sentence, shoulders slumped and head lowered, he turned to Brother Paul, who comforted him in a warm fatherly embrace.

Brother Paul said to the students, "Georgie will be back before you know it. He expects you to follow his progress in the newspapers. Let's have a cheer for one of our own!"

Together Brother Paul and Ruth then left the dining room; the inmates exploded into a wild and thunderous ovation for Georgie that could be heard all the way back to Brother Paul's office. Matthias was waiting for them there.

Brother Paul addressed Ruth once again, "Georgie, you have superior skills and have always accomplished what you set out to do. I have all the faith in the world you'll play good. We'll say a prayer for you every day."

"Brother Paul, you mean play well," Ruth responded.

Mathias finished helping Geawgie gather all of his minimal possessions and pack them into two rather small but well-worn and tattered brown suitcases. Sensing Ruth's trepidation, he decided to share some advice in hopes it would finally take root. 'Geawgie, the world can be cold and cruel.

Not everyone you meet will look out for your best interests. We've prepared you as best we could. When you came to us, you were a wet-behind-the-ears baby. You leave today a man, playing baseball in a man's world, not in the sandlots. It is a job, a job for men and a job you're prepared for."

Meanwhile, Brother Paul sat at his desk and pulled Ruth's file, making his final and simple notation in the official personal record of one George Herman Ruth, "Released to play professional baseball for the Baltimore team on March 2, 1914."

Ruth's final exit from St. Mary's was as unceremoniously somber as his arrival in 1902. Ruth and Matthias walked out the gates of St. Mary's and Ruth climbed into his awaiting ride.

At 1515 N. Charles Street stood the enormous beaux-arts Union Station, completed just three years earlier. Architect Kenneth Mackenzie Murchison demonstrated his eye for detail and extravagance as the two-story station was built on raised land, and its grand entrance, the fluid columnar symmetry and arched windows provided decorative accents against the flat roof line. The building was the bright star in the otherwise dreary skyline of Baltimore City. Many thought this structure was constructed as a response to rival New York City's Grand Central Terminal.

Union Station accepts trains from the north—south routes through two tunnels. The Baltimore and Potomac Tunnel, finished in 1873, with its steep grades and sharp turns limiting the speed of the trains, created lengthy delays for travel to the south. At the time, the 1.3 mile stretch was perhaps one of the worst bottlenecks in the entire nation's rail system. The Union Tunnel, the northern entrance, also opened in 1873. It was bored to accommodate three rail tracks, with a long gentle slope and was perhaps one of the more reliable train routes in the country.

Not on this day. Led by the cruel, biting winds of an Alberta Clipper, a harsh late-winter blizzard had swept down from the northern plains into the central United States. Turning east along the Great Lakes, the storm picked up considerable moisture along its path as it barreled into the east coast, slamming Philadelphia, New York City and the New England states. The severity of this dangerous winter mix of ice and snow had halted all train travel from and into the northeast US.

Jack Dunn had met Ruth outside of the iron gates of St. Mary's and drove crosstown to Union Station. As he stepped from the car, Ruth stood in awe of the station. He had never seen such an intricate building. Over the past decade, Ruth, except for his brief period of freedom, had been primarily confined to the St. Mary's compound. Seeing the buildings of downtown Baltimore was a new experience. Jack and Ruth ascended the exterior steps and advanced into the chaos.

The sight of this sea of humanity halted the pair. There were hundreds of travelers everywhere in the spacious lobby. Most travelers were trying to make the best of the situation, sitting on their assortment of luggage or lying down on the cold marble floor, using clothes as makeshift pillows, blankets and bedding. There was nothing to be done except wait out the delay.

"George, the train will be leaving on time, from Track 10," Dunn told Ruth.

"Where are we going again, Mr. Dunn?"

"Oh, I'm not going, George. You and your Oriole teammates are going to Fayetteville, North Carolina. It will be warmer there, much warmer. You've got a little over 8 weeks to get ready. I'll be down in a few days. Let's get to the platform."

At 6:15PM, Jack Dunn and George Herman Ruth boarded the silver passenger car to begin the ten-hour journey south. Ruth was extremely tentative. For the past dozen years, he had rarely left the comforts and security of St. Mary's, the place he called home. Now he was embarking on a journey to a strange and distant place, leaving the city of his birth for the first time in his life. He was leaving with a man he had met a scant two weeks earlier. Ruth was unsure of what would become of him.

'Guys, this here is George Ruth, the pitching star from St. Mary's.' Several of the Orioles players were already on board, grabbing sandwiches and whiskey to ready themselves for the traditional overnight card game. A few nodded at Ruth, but most just went on with their business.

Ben Egan was a bull-like man, 6 feet tall and over 200 pounds. He was a career minor-league catcher with several 'short cups of coffee (baseball slang for short stints in the majors), and he approached Ruth with his hand extended, "Ruth, I'm Ben, Ben Egan. I'm your babysitter for the trip. Don't go giving me any trouble." Egan was as angry and frustrated a person as one could find. Dunn had discovered him playing for the Utica Pent-Ups of the New York State League and had highly recommended him to Connie Mack for stints with the Athletics, twice. The results were a disaster each time. Egan compiled a .165 batting average, and for all of his strength, he managed to miss hitting a single home run. Finally, to save face with Mack, Dunn purchased his contract and elevated him to chief rookie caretaker.

Handing Ruth a couple of sawbucks, Dunn said, "Egan will take care of you, Georgie. He's not much of a player, but he is a damn good babysitter for stars passing through on their way to the bigs. A damn good babysitter."

"That's right, Jack. I'll take care of this valuable big baby for you," said Egan, in a mocking tone. 'Big' Ben Egan clearly resented Dunn's characterization of him.

Dunn turned and climbed back down the steps, leaving the station without hesitation or glancing back towards the train. He had bigger issues commanding his attention, like the health of his franchise.

There were almost twenty people in the close confines of the rail car, including Ruth, other Orioles players, sportswriters and non-player team staff. But life had again dealt Ruth the lonely card. In just a little over two weeks, he was literally abandoned and cast to the lot of strangers, not once, but twice.

For Egan, this was his fourth trip south with the Baltimore club. Although on the outside he was jovial, the clown at the party, internally he was extremely bitter over his own failures and inability to stick with a major league club. Year after year he watched rookies come up and eventually pass him by on their way to the big leagues. As a result, he took a certain pride in his ability to make the rookie's life as miserable as possible during the first few weeks of spring training. In past years, he convinced rookies there was any number of imminent calamities destined to occur on the nearly half-day train ride.

Three years earlier, a pair of wet-behind-the-ears players freshly recruited out of the cornfields of Indiana nearly jumped from the moving train, scared to wit's end. Egan, with collusion from other veteran players, had circulated a rumor that a prisoner sent to death row for a series of grisly multiple murders had escaped from New York's Sing Sing prison. The murderer had been seen heading south and may have boarded a train for Miami. With other veteran Oriole players in on the gag, the plot thickened. Egan and his conspiring pals, throughout the early evening and with increasing intensity, circulated gradually more detailed talk that the murderer assuredly was on this train. He was desperate to reach the Mexican border. A signal was devised to notify all players if and when it was confirmed the fugitive was on board. On the signal, players were to hurry to the cargo car at the rear of the train. There would be safety in numbers, but more importantly they could retrieve bats from their stowed gear to arm themselves.

One of Egan's devilish playmates was assigned the overnight watch from 2:00 AM to 4:00 AM. During dinner and the evening card game, the conductor, who was also in on the antics with the help of a $20 tip, relayed confirmed sightings of 'Butcher Al Bilotti' in one of the forward dining cars, enjoying a leisurely meal. He added that there was little need to worry, since the Butcher had not moved from that location for hours. The Butcher was known not only for his heinous acts of barbarism but also for gorging himself with a pre-blood fest food orgy. At 10:00PM, all of the Orioles were ordered to their berths for lights out. The two rookies, as usual for the trip south, shared a berth. This provided little comfort, as the restless pair could not get a wink of sleep.

At approximately 2:45AM, three of the Oriole veterans charged into berth 13A shouting, "Skipper says play ball!" This was the signal for everyone to assemble in the baggage car. In a flash the vets were gone, running toward the back of the train. The rookie pair, already on edge, jumped from their berths, following as quickly as possible. While running towards the meeting spot, the duo took little notice that the train was eerily silent with a lack of general commotion. What they did hear were several well-planned screams and thuds. With the baggage car now in sight, the fear inside of them was increasing. Instead of seeing teammates milling around with bats and other weapons in hand, the area was empty, a deathtrap. One rookie broke the tension, "Inside the baggage car, that's where everyone is." Full of nervous energy, the first rookie burst through the unlocked door, tripping over an unseen piece of luggage and awkwardly landing on the supine body of Ben Egan. Egan wasn't moving. The rookie's hands were covered in a sticky warm substance. *Egan's blood*, he thought. Was Egan dead? Cowering, he crawled on all fours, seeking a hiding place amongst the piled luggage.

The second rookie, looking toward the rear door, froze in a terror-captured moment. There, against the moonlit window, the rookie could see the ominous threatening profile of the Butcher. As the Butcher turned toward the rookie and approached, he raised his right hand, exposing the 15-inch carbon-steel-bladed, extra-wide edge machete. With the reinforced wooden handle, the machete measured over 27 inches in length. On the farm where the rookie had grown, his family had dozens of these rugged and dependable cutting tools. These were used for the toughest of jobs and provided maximum leverage for chopping, cutting and slicing. Even if the edge were dull, most anyone could slice and filet the toughest of game as easy as a pat of butter. The hair on the neck of the petrified rookie stood out as he abruptly attempted to reverse his course. The door behind him was closed and locked. Had he somehow pulled the door closed after him and mistakenly locked it in the process?

His only avenue of retreat blocked, the rookie noticed the side window and darted towards this dangerous path of escape. A decade of baseball training had honed his already cat-like reflexes as he reached the window just precious seconds ahead of the Butcher. He opened the window quickly.

Perhaps he could survive the leap from the speeding train, but he was sure that to stay meant certain death at the hands of the Butcher. The rookie turned his face to the cold night air rushing in as the train hurtled along at nearly 60 miles an hour. He climbed hurriedly to a position with both feet on the window's ledge; the rookie was perched ready for this dangerous jump. The jump did not happen; he had moved too slowly, and a mammoth hand snatched his collar, jerking him back into the car with great force overwhelming his own strength. The flailing rookie, wildly screaming in panic, was dragged back into the darkness of this death chamber. Fearing the imminent end of his brief life as he was tossed backwards onto several suitcases, he closed his eyes, made the sign of the cross and searched his memory for one final prayer. All that came to mind was Psalm 23. The rookie muttered softly, anticipating his demise, "The LORD is my shepherd; I shall not want. He maketh me to lie down in green pastures; he leadeth me beside the still waters, he restoreth my soul. He leadeth me in the paths of righteousness for his name's sake. Yea, though I walk through the valley of the shadow of death, I will fear no evil, for thou art with me; thy rod and thy staff, they comfort me." "What you saying, rook? Get up. You're not going to die, at least not today." said Egan. Egan and the other Orioles erupted in uncontrollable laughter. This was the best prank ever. The puzzled rookies, realizing that they'd been the butt of a cruel prank, sheepishly walked away.

Sensing a naiveté in the young Ruth, Egan, the
perennial imp always on the lookout to pull a mean
practical joke, was itching to rattle this large,
immature youngster. Egan and the other veterans
decided to repeat the caper of the escaped killer
successfully pulled off three years earlier. Several
things would work against Egan here. Although
Ruth had a boyish persona, he was very aware of
the things which went on around him, he was not
easy to scare and lastly, Dunn had warned Ruth of
Egan's antics with rookies, especially those who
were highly touted.

During the team dinner, rumors of the
Butcher's escape from New York State's maximum
security prison began. The conspirators intensified
the situation with talk that he was somewhere on the
train heading south. Egan licked his chops at the
prospect of seeing the enormous rookie cringe with
fear. As ordered by Egan, the veteran players
shunned Ruth from the card game, directing him to
his berth for an overnight nap. The routine to be
followed was carefully reviewed with Ruth.
"Remember, if you hear 'the skipper says play ball,'
we meet in the luggage car, got it?"

"Yup, I got it," said Ruth, adding, "but if I
sees this butcher fellow I'll handle him."

"No. He's a killer, a cold-blooded killer. Just
get to the luggage car."

A few minutes before 3:00AM Ruth heard
the pounding on his door and the alarm signal,
"Skipper says it's time to play ball!"

As casually as if he were taking a Sunday
stroll, Ruth left his berth and made his way to the

rear of the train. Pulling up on the luggage car door handle, he forcefully kicked the door open. Carefully he stepped inside and reached over the travel trunk blocking his path, grabbing the unsuspecting Egan by the throat and lifting him with one hand half a foot off the ground.

"I've got him, I've got the butcher," Ruth screamed.

In his left hand, he held what would become his trademark, a 42-ounce club of a baseball bat. He yelled, "I'm going to brain this murdering son-of-a-bitch!"

The grip on Egan's neck was so firm and strangulating he had trouble breathing. The pressure on his larynx was so crushing that he could not project a single sound in his defense.

Ruth raised the bat high above his head, preparing to deal a fatal blow, "You're a dead man, Butcher!"

The veterans in the car, now worried for Egan, screamed in unison for Ruth to stop. The cacophony was either not discernible or ignored by a straining Ruth as he raised his prey even higher.

Feebly Egan squeaked out a few words, "Please, Georgie, don't kill me, please," as his arms and legs fell limply to his sides.

Ruth let go of his overpowering hold and watched Egan fall to the floor in a heap. "Well, tough guy, you ain't so tough now, are you? It's easy to pick on one of the hayseeds fresh from their farms, but I ain't no hayseed and you ain't so smart. If you plan a prank, get your facts straight. All trains from the north have been delayed on account of the blizzard. There's no way could someone coming from the north could get to our train, you big idiot!"

Egan responded, "You're one strong bastard, Ruth. Let's start over. I'm Ben Egan."

Ruth's right hand was met by Egan's as Ruth pulled the embarrassed catcher from the floor, "Now, you're supposed to be looking out for me." Egan and Ruth roared in laughter, soon followed by the rest of the team.

"Let's get to bed, we've got a long day ahead of us tomorrow," someone bellowed.

Egan and Ruth, from that moment on, had an iron-clad friendship. The two biggest players on the team in stature, they loved to compete, brawl and mix in plenty of playful mayhem. Egan helped Ruth with his preparation into professional sports. When Dunn showed up in Fayetteville two weeks later, his eyes lit up when he saw Ruth, who had trimmed down.

"Wow, Georgie, you look good. You working hard?"

"Egan's taking good care of me, like you told him. I played all eight games since I've been down here. I pitched two games, and I do not think I gave up any runs. Played two as catcher 'cause Egan needed a break. Played three in the outfield and in one game, I played all nine positions, just as I did at St. Mary's. And Mr. Dunn, I'm not tired at all."

Dunn turned his attention to find Egan; this wasn't any way to protect his prized investment. Egan explained that Ruth was a strong as an ox and played the game with such ease he could most likely pitch and play every day. Egan had never seen the like. He added that in their first game against Savannah, Ruth not only pitched a complete game shutout, but hit two balls into the swamp past the right field fence and had two triples to boot. Egan added," That's quite the player you got there. He's no babe in the woods." Dunn thought maybe this babe is the real thing, a once-in-a-lifetime find.

The Orioles broke camp on April 18, 1914, heading back north to Baltimore for the opening series of International League play against the Buffalo Bison

Ruth was casually warming up; the manager had tapped the youngster to start the second game of the season. The midmorning sub-freezing temperatures had quickly risen to 83 degrees by game time. Many of the players had stripped off their woolen sweaters and jerseys, choosing to loosen up in tee shirts. Not Ruth.

He was engaged in a light conversation with Egan, when he heard the soft voice of a youngster and turning, he saw a girl about nine years old with long blonde curls, big blue eyes and an even bigger smile. "Hey, mister, you sweat a lot"

Ruth wiped his forehead with the sleeve of his sweater.

Eagan, sensing a moment to needle Ruth, chimed in, "This here is George Ruth, our newest player. Yeah, Ruth here is just a wee bit older than you."

Several of the other Orioles nearby chuckled.

"Mister Ruth, good luck today," she chirped.

"Mr. Ruth!" exclaimed Egan loudly. "He's just a babe like you!"

"Shut up, Egan, you're a horse's ass," Ruth answered. "Girlie, come on back. Let me show you how to pitch." Daintily placing a baseball in her right hand, Ruth instructed her to follow what he did. He rocked back twice each time taking his big hands over his head then to his waist as he leaned back then forward. The lass followed his lead. "Do that, then take your right hand towards your target and let go. Go ahead now; let me see you do that." Gracefully the little lady did it and threw the ball directly to Ruth. "You did it!" he shouted as he ran three long steps towards her, wrapping his arms around her in a gentle bear hug. She disappeared briefly. "Keep the ball," he instructed.

"Thank you, Mr. Ruth, and good luck." Turning, she ran back to the clutches of her family, who stood frozen by what they had just seen. *It's a good man who can take the time to make a child light up with joy*, her father thought, *and a very special man.*

A noticeably uncomfortable Ruth took the mound. Although the final outcome records the contest as a six-hit shutout 6-0 victory, Ruth nearly did not make it out of the first inning.

Hitting will always be more of a crowd-pleaser than fielding when watching baseball. A long hit driving in the men on bases is the dream of ballplayers at every level, including professional players. There is no man in baseball who would not rather hit for .300 than field brilliantly, and the spectators share this sentiment. There is one fielding stunt that is the most brilliant and spectacular play in all of baseball. It only happens once a generation, but when it does happen it is written swiftly into baseball history. This is the unassisted triple play.

Cornelius 'Neal' Ball had spent seven inglorious years battling to gain his place in the big leagues. His career batting average was a paltry .262; his fielding was no more noteworthy, committing 216 errors in just over 2,500 chances. In Cleveland during a game against the Red Sox on July 19th, 1909, Cornelius 'Neal' Ball vaulted all at once into the historical limelight by recording two remarkable feats. First, he performed this rarest of all plays. Racing, Ball took a ball on the fly, twenty feet rear and right of second base, thus putting out the batter. He hastily scampered to touch second base, retiring the runner trying to come back from third. Jake Stahl, running with his head down, was unaware the ball had been caught by Ball and he was barreling from first base. Ball launched himself into the path of Stahl, tagging him for the third out. This was the first unassisted triple play recorded in professional baseball history. Later, Ball caught a soft line drive to end the game, giving him a ninth putout for the game, breaking the record for putouts by a shortstop in a game. In a single summer afternoon, Ball had etched his name into professional history.

The first batter connected solidly with the game's first offering from Ruth and ripped the ball towards left field. The quick-reacting Ball ranged deep into the hole between second and third. Racing hard, he backhanded the ball and in a single motion threw a BB to the first baseman, recording the out.

The ever-compassionate Egan yelled to Ruth, "What are you doing? You served that weak-hitting Alice a meatball!"

Strolling to the plate next for the Bisons was none other than Joe McCarthy. He was beginning his eighth season as a minor leaguer but his first with the Bison's, having been sold by the Wilkes-Barre Barons over the winter. The diminutive McCarthy, although listed at 5 feet 8 inches and 190, was actually several inches shorter and probably weighed 150 pounds soaking wet. He had little prospect of ever reaching the major league, instead doomed as a career minor leaguer.

Joseph Vincent McCarthy was born on April 21, 1887, in Philadelphia, Pennsylvania on the same Girard Avenue where Benjamin Shibe had been born 49 years earlier. During his early indoctrination into baseball, his father gave him an A.J. Reach and Co. Cock-of-the-Walk gleaming white horsehide professional baseball, manufactured by J. Shibe and Co. of Philadelphia.

Ben Shibe was a major force in the popularity and development of the baseball. It was his business savvy that helped turn what had been a nascent game at his birth into a multi-million dollar enterprise by the time of his death. A co-owner of the Philadelphia Athletics, Shibe would be at the forefront of some of baseball's most dramatic early evolutionary changes, from baseballs to stadiums. With baseball's popularity on the rise following the end of the Civil War, Shibe joined his brother John and nephew Dan, who had worked for a company that made cricket balls, in founding John D. Shibe & Co. Ben thought that by getting children playing baseball at an early age, the sport would become immensely popular. The new company focused its attention on making an assortment of baseballs for children which could be used for play in the inner city and not wear out as quickly as the balls used by the professional leagues. The company churned out many different brands of balls, such as the Skyrocket, Bounding Rock, Red Dead Balls, Red Stocking and the Cock-of-the Walk. Their company supplied others, such as Alfred J. Reach, from the company of Reach & Johnson. Reach and Shibe were friends, and by 1882 Benjamin Shibe and A.J. Reach formed a new company, which after a series of name changes, became A.J. Reach and Company. A.J. Reach decided to leave the retailing behind and concentrate on strictly manufacturing. By 1883, the Reach factory was making 1.3 million baseballs and 100,000 bats per year.

Ben Shibe was not only a manufacturer; he had a passion for the game and for general baseball operations. Shibe developed a deep love for and understanding of the game in spite of a physical disability. He directed the Shibe Semi-Professional Team, which produced many professional players. During the 1880s, he became the principal stockholder in the Athletic Club of the American Association. All of his savvy business ways did not prevent the club's bankruptcy in 1890. Many believed Shibe was in the business of baseball solely to make a buck. The fact is that he made many baseball-related investments in teams that would never produce a penny of profit. Of course, the publicity generated by those teams certainly didn't hurt his sporting goods business.

Shibe made two significant contributions by altering the cover of the baseball and the core of the ball. Throughout the mid-1800s, there had been a problem with the stitching on the cover of baseballs. Usually the tips of one "S" were fitted on either side of the waist of the other, so the stitches always 'drew.' Since the cover was not smooth, the hide never had full protection. Shibe tried to fix that problem for many years, trying many different methods, always coming up short of the perfect design. Eventually he discovered that the nature of the spherical ball required the stitches to be grouped closer together at the end of the "S"—to be even with those at the waist—in a decreasing space of separation. Using 116 stitches, it worked perfectly. In 1889, Shibe's nephew, Daniel M. Shibe, was awarded U.S. patent #415,884 for the design. In 1909, Shibe made arguably his biggest contribution to the game with his company's invention of the cork-centered baseball. The result was a livelier baseball which was introduced in the 1910 World Series and used in all games beginning in the next season. In 1911, major league baseball experienced its second explosion of offense. Players could now drive the ball further, turning a greater number of singles into doubles, and doubles to triples. Shibe, however, simply thought that the new ball's greatest value was that the ball was more durable.

In 1901, the American League gave its Philadelphia franchise to Connie Mack. In order to compete with the established National League Philadelphia franchise, Mack needed a local backer who would give the newcomers instant credibility and prestige. He also needed capital. Ben Shibe was just the right man. Reach was a minority stockholder in the Phillies, and Mack made it clear he intended to raid the Phillies for players, so Shibe hesitated to invest in the team. At the same time, he also believed a second major league was good for baseball. Reach felt the same way, and at his suggestion, Shibe agreed to buy 50 percent of the club. Mack had allocated 25 percent from his own share to two sportswriters whose voting proxies he held, giving Mack and Shibe equal power. That way, neither man could do anything the other didn't agree to. In practice, they never disagreed, and Shibe left the running of the team and all the baseball decisions to Mack. When Mack wanted to buy out the two sportswriters' shares in 1912, Ben Shibe loaned him the money instead of letting his sons buy them and put 75 percent of the stock in Shibe hands. Trusting in Mack's able leadership, Shibe's franchise captured six American League pennants and three World Championships during his 21 years as team president.

On January 5, 1903, Ben Shibe opened an envelope with a Girard Avenue return address. He still had great affection for the street of his birth. The letter was written by a soon-to-be 16-year-old whose aspiration was to become a professional baseball player. A similar letter was sent to Connie Mack. They decided to watch the local play in a high school game that spring. Shibe did, and after the game, he advised Joe McCarthy to get an education, because he had zero chance of a career in baseball. Not so easily dismissed, McCarthy pleaded his case throughout his high school years and while at Niagara University, repeatedly asking for a chance, a tryout with the Athletics. McCarthy pointed out that what he might lack in ability and size, he made up for in smarts. In one of his letters, he even played 'King for a Day,' advising Connie Mack what changes he would make to the way the team and the league were being run. Each and every letter written over the next five years went unanswered. McCarthy became bitter, and his bitterness increased with each ignored letter. McCarthy saw some brash local players, with marginally more talent and a lot less work ethic than he, held up as stars and moved onto the major leagues. McCarthy's steel will and indomitable spirit drove him harder, vowing to make a name for himself in baseball so he could show every stinking, over-hyped athlete how the game is played.

Now, glaring from home plate out towards the pitcher's mound, McCarthy stepped into the batter's box.

"Come on, Ruth, throw some heat at this little dish rag," encouraged Egan, slamming the physical stature of McCarthy.

"The big fellow looks unsteady," McCarthy shot back, ever so politely.

"He is Dunn's latest baby destined to be a star, the baby Ruth." Unbeknownst to Egan, the statements literally made McCarthy's blood boil.

Stepping toward home plate and rocking backwards in a protracted arm motion from waist to head, Ruth took two big wind-ups and delivered a fast ball directly under McCarthy's chin. The force that McCarthy used in yanking his head away spilled him onto his boney backside.

Egan erupted in laughter. "Good show, Babe, good show. Now get the next one over."

None too amused, the agitated McCarthy moved back in the box, avoiding the three next wild offerings, earning a free pass to first.

"A real star, this kid's a real star." McCarthy chirped.

Flustered, the inattentive Ruth took a wind-up; McCarthy immediately took off from first, stealing second without a throw as Egan scurried to keep the low throw in front of him. "Hey, pitcher, this is a thinking man's game. You don't seem to me like the type that does a whole lot of thinking. Now a hit gets me home."

Ruth, determined to throw a strike, finally delivered a pitch. Murray, batting third, hit a fly to shallow center. McCarthy held at second. The clean-up hitter, Ben Houser, then mistimed a Ruth off-speed pitch and hit a weak pop-up between the mound and first base. Ruth, waving his glove at Gus 'Kaiser' Gleichmann, another large man for the era, moved in for the catch. Gleichmann called "Mine" and they both stopped. McCarthy, now standing on third, was chortling at the sight of the behemoth figures watching in disbelief as the feebly hit ball fell to the ground. Once again, Ruth apparently forgot the situation with a man on first as he went into a full windup. The slow-footed Houser then stole second.

"Hey, catcher, does this budding star know how to play?" McCarthy yelled at Egan with tears of laughter rolling down his cheeks.

Egan walked out to settle Ruth down. "George, I know this is your first game, but come on. Hickory can't hit the ball if it's high and tight." Ruth delivered the hard inside pitch right into George Jackson's midsection. Jackson had spent the previous three seasons with the Boston Rustlers and was not happy being back in the minor leagues. He was even less pleased about being plunked in the stomach by a 19-year-old rookie, so he took exception and started to run towards Ruth. Egan, anticipating this, had already come out of his catcher's stand and grabbed Jackson from behind.

"Listen, Hickory, he's just a nervous kid. No need for problems here."

"Okay, but if it happens again, I'll bloody someone. My cleats are sharp."

McCarthy, not missing a chance to put down another 'rising star,' called out, "Hey, Babe, Egan isn't going to be around to protect you all the time."

The sixth batter to face Ruth in the first inning was another major league retread, a pesky little hitter named Wilbur Charles 'Roxey' Roach. He had learned the art of slapping the ball around from a major league teammate with the New York Highlanders, Hal Chase. With the count 2-2, Ruth dealt another creampuff of a pitch and Roach smoked a two-hopper straight up the middle. *A sure hit that would score at least two runs*, Ruth thought as the ball went quickly past him and he headed to his cutoff position behind third, anticipating a throw there.

"You're out!" Ruth heard from behind as he ran toward the third base foul line. What he did not see was a majestic play by Ball, who had ranged far to his left and then, diving full out, managed to prevent the ball from getting into the outfield and from a prone position, managed an accurate toss, forcing Jackson at second.

McCarthy shook his head, "A bit of the luck there, Egan, and he's a bit lucky. We'll get him next inning."

The line score was no runs, one hit, and no errors. The Orioles were fortunate that no runs were scored in a bizarre start to the young lefthander's career. McCarthy's prediction did not hold up. The Bisons failed to move a runner as far as third the rest of the way, as Ruth recorded a six-hit shutout in front of a raucous crowd of fewer than 200 faithful fans.

A dejected Dunn watched. With such an abysmal crowd, it appeared that there was not much he could do to prevent the imminent and inevitable end of the Orioles. There was some nice raw talent on the team, but Dunn realized that with the sorrowful attendance, he was not going to be able to pay the players enough to keep them from jumping to the rival Baltimore Terrapins of the Federal League. Of course, there were also many other owners willing to overpay for young prospects and washed-up veterans. Nascent players, like the young Ruth, with unlimited potential, needed valuable time to develop. Back in his office, a pensive Dunn sat in the dark, contemplating his moves to save the ball club. Perhaps he even regretted pulling the youngster Ruth from his safety net at St. Mary's. Soon, maybe all too soon, Ruth was again to be displaced, landing in the cold money-lusting hands of some other owner. Dunn sensed that it would not be long before he would dim the lights for the last time in his Orioles office. "From the day he was born, this poor kid never had a chance."

Behind the strength of the pitching staff, the Orioles played competitive baseball and were perched in second place behind Providence as the calendar approached Memorial Day. The Federal League, driven by the ambitious commissioner, James A. Gilmore, was supported by wealthy and powerful financiers including oil baron Harry F. Sinclair, ice magnate Phillip Ball and George S. Ward of the Ward Baking Company. Under this leadership, the league declared itself a major league for the 1914 season. Gilmore, as expected, was routinely raiding the financially struggling minor-league teams. Dunn had increased Ruth's salary to $200 a month after the lefty recorded an eighth consecutive win. Desperate to raise operating capital, Dunn began shopping Ruth. His first stop was his former partner and financial backer, Connie Mack.

"The kid's good, very good. What's his record now?" Mack inquired after Dunn finished his sales pitch about Ruth. Mack continued supplying the answer to his rhetorical question, "13-4, right. That's quite an impressive start to his career. But to be perfectly honest, I want punch in my lineup top to bottom. Ruth's hitting, what, .230? He swings wildly; pitchers with little skills are fooling him."

Dunn impatiently interjected, "At St. Mary's, he was a killer at the plate. He pounded the ball all over the park. He'll come around. But this kid is so strong; he could probably pitch damn near every day. Sort of like Radbourn or Young."

"No, Jack, I've seen this story before. Schoolyard hero, professionally he can't catch up with the pitches that move. You know them all: the spit ball, the shine ball. And especially the ones where the pitcher cuts the baseball with their belt buckle. He has a big hole in a vicious swing, no chance. Every now and then he'll hit one a mile. If I was looking for a pitching prospect, I'd take him off your hands. As it is, unless he learns to hit better, though, no dice."

Sitting quietly in the corner of Mack's Broad Street office, barely noticed by Dunn when he walked in, was Charles Albert 'Chief' Bender. The Chief was one of the standout pitchers of the early 1900's. Despite having to withstand the nearly daily barrage of racial slurs and demeaning comments by the obnoxious fans, throughout his professional career he always carried himself with dignity and grace and he remained a kind man. Bender made three significant contributions to baseball. He created the slider, known as the 'nickel' changeup. The grip resulted in movement on the ball delivered towards the batter which created a shorter, sharper break than the curve with the speed nearly that of a fastball. Those familiar with the Athletics say Bender introduced this pitch on May 12, 1910. On that day, each Cleveland Nap batter he faced failed to produce a hit. Second, he made an art form of stealing the opposing team's signs. Mack would position Bender as the third base coach on the days he did not pitch to capitalize on this skill. Bender had an innate sense of a player's abilities that he used in the evaluation of other ballplayers. Mack routinely asked his opinion of minor league prospects and their player capabilities at different points in their career. Bender was honest and accurate. Mack especially used Bender's talent when Mack was ready to make a contract decision.

"See the Chief over there, Jack; he doesn't think much of your kid, doesn't think he'd fit in, either," politely said the ever-dapper Cornelius "Connie Mack" McGillicuddy, Sr.

Although not a tyrant, he ran his ball club in a very organized and disciplined manner. He would only look for players with quiet and restrained personal lives, having seen many players destroy themselves and their teams through heavy drinking in his playing days. Stories of Ruth's excesses had already begun to surface around the league. He ate in excess, he drank in excess, and he smoked and caroused frequently. Mack himself never drank; before the 1910 World Series he asked all his players to 'take the pledge' not to drink during the Series. When Topy Hartsel told Mack he needed a drink the night before the final game, Mack told him to do what he thought best, but in these circumstances "If it was me, I'd die before I took a drink." Hartsel heeded the advice. By 1911, the temptation of alcohol became too great, and he did not return to the Athletics. When asked about the discarded outfielder, Bender gave thumbs down; Hartsel was done in baseball.

Dunn decided to go north and talk to John McGraw. He hopped on the train at Philadelphia's Broad Street station, the nation's largest passenger terminal at the time and in less than 5 hours; he was in McGraw's Manhattan New York Giants office.

"What's on your blessed mind that you would come all this way to see me? You're pretty much in deep with the other league. I'm guessing you have money problems. I'm also guessing you're here to peddle a player or two. But if you're talking to me, then no one reputable is buying. Okay, I'll listen," the straight-shooting McGraw said.

Starting from the first time he had become aware of Ruth and his abilities, Dunn recanted the tale to a thoroughly-enthralled McGraw. The Giants manager leaned back in his chair, shaking his head from side to side as one often does when trying to register disbelief.

"Jack, that's some heart-warming story. You had never really seen the boy play, but going by what some robe-wearing Catholic wannabe baseball manager brother tells you, you sign the lad. You make him homeless and now you want me to be his caretaker. I'd like to bail you out, but not now. If he seasons a bit more and develops into a little bit of a threat at the plate, come see me then. Really, Jack, another Cy Young? With his strength and a lot of prayers, he may have a better shot at being another Roger Connor."

McGraw bid Dunn goodbye and good luck as they closed the meeting by shaking hands. Nonetheless Dunn was wondering if McGraw and Mack were right, maybe he had read too much into the kid's talent. Dunn grew even more impatient with each passing minute on the slow train ride back to Baltimore. The more he dwelled on his dilemma, the more he became desperate for an even rasher move. The Providence Grays were coming into town for a series. Ruth had contained the powerful Gray line up twice already.

Joe Lannin, orphaned at the age of 14, migrated with the flood of French-Canadians from Quebec seeking work in the booming textile mills of New England. However, arriving in Boston, the ambitious young man chose to work instead as a hotel bellman. Not well educated, Lannin possessed great interpersonal skills, a sharp wit and was a great listener. The rich New England bluebloods spent hours in the hotel lobby and restaurants, talking about their investments in the commodities and the real estate markets. Asking questions and taking advice from those who would share it, Lannin amassed a tiny nest egg which, through savvy commodities investing and the purchase of several undervalued hotel chains, grew faster than imaginable. By 1912, this self-made immigrant owned a string of golf courses, hotels and apartment buildings. In 1913, with several other investors, he now held a controlling interest in the Boston Red

Sox. Baseball in Massachusetts had caught fire and developed a strong rivalry with Mack's Athletics, snatching the pennant in 1912 from the Athletics, who had won it for two straight years. By 1914, Lannin had bought out his partners to become the sole owner.

Preparing for a stretch run, as the final few weeks of the season was referred to in baseball, Lannin traveled to Baltimore to look at some of the highly-profiled Providence Grays players. Dunn sought out Lannin to engage in a conversation about Ruth. Lannin, possessing a soft spot in his heart for the essentially orphaned Ruth, listened with true compassion.

"I agree the boy can pitch. I hear, though that Gilmore has offered him tidy sum to go play in the Federal League for Hanlon's team," Lannin offered. "He needs to understand that if he did sign with any team in the Federal League, Johnson will bar him for life from playing in the American League, even long after those guys fold."

Caught completely off-guard and mildly surprised, the stoic Dunn did not tip his hand about the concern raised by Lannin. "I've already spoken to Ruth. He's not going anywhere. He's looking forward to playing on a real major-league team, not some two-bit fly-by-night struggling organization."

"I'll take you at your word that you have the boy locked up," Lannin remarked as he and Dunn shook in agreement on the deal, which was to send Ruth to the Red Sox for $2,000.

Immediately after the game, as Ruth was leaving the field heading toward the club house,

Dunn approached him, asking if Ruth could come up to his office after showering, letting him know he had some very interesting things to tell Ruth which he believed would make him happy. Nearly an hour later, as Dunn was sitting back in his black leather office chair, relaxed for the first time in several weeks, puffing the Boston cigars Lannin had given him after consummation of the deal, Dunn heard the rude loud raps on the door which could only be made by Ruth.

"Come on in, Ruth," encouraged Dunn. "I was beginning to wonder if you'd forgotten about me."

"No sir, Mr. Dunn, not at all."

In the most impersonal of manners and without any sense of tact, Dunn immediately continued, "Son, you're going to the majors, you are now a member of the Red Sox. They'll increase your pay to $300 per month. Mr. Lannin is a real fine gentleman. What do you think, George? This is your dream, to play ball in the major leagues."

The normally effusive Ruth peered down at Dunn over his broad nose and deep set eyes. With the teeth-baring grin of a Cheshire cat heightening its sense of smell in response to a perplexing situation, or simply to ferret out an unsuspecting rat, Ruth responded.

"That's real nice, Mr. Dunn. But I have this piece of paper signed by Mr. James Gilmore here telling me they're going to pay me $10,000 just for signing to play for the Baltimore Terrapins. Then they'll pay me $1,000 a month to play. See, it says right here, contract with Mr. George Herman Ruth.

He also tells me that some of the top American and National League players are going to play next year."

Dunn interrupted the Babe as he took a short breath, "The owners will never let that happen."

"Mr. Dunn, it's already happening. He told me the players in both the National and American leagues are not happy. They're treated poorly. Not paid what they're worth. They're lied to. In the end, they're cast aside like a pair of old, worn shoes."

"Ruth, some owners are like that, but Mr. Lannin is a good man and he'll take care of you."

"Stop before I get angrier than I am and rip that empty head of yours from your pencil neck. I was told by Brother Matthias that you'd take care of me! The club has money problems and so you sell me. You really think I wouldn't hear tell of you shopping me up and down both leagues?"

"This is your chance, Ruth. I *am* taking care of you. I'm getting you to the majors."

"No, no, no. You need cash and I'm the best asset you have. You care more about your bank account than you do about me."

"Ruth, if you go to the Federal League, the American League will bar you from returning. You know what that means? You'll never play for any American League team, ever again. Never, George, never! Most of the owners are vindictive men. Once they kick someone out of baseball, it's for good."

"Like Mr. Lannin?"

"George I am your legal guardian. I will forbid it."

"Mr. Dunn, you gave up that right when you agreed to sell me. I'll play out the season with Boston. That will be my only commitment. If necessary and they kick me out, so be it. Then I'll move on. One thing I do know is that someday I am going to sit in your seat and nobody will tell me what to do. You know about my dreams? I will tell you, Mr. Dunn. I am going to break all the records. After I'm gone, everyone will remember me."

"Ruth, you're not that good. Not yet, anyway. Oh, you beat up a bunch of ragtag high school kids on a playground. I did shop you around, and the fact is, no one would touch you. They say you cannot hit at the major league level and your pitching is not up to that caliber, either."

"That's crap! I know what I can do. And that is anything I set my mind to!" Ruth added, now yelling at the top of his lungs.

"Maybe you can, but you don't take care of yourself. George, for your own sake, just don't tell Lannin you have a contract. Wait and see how things go for you in Boston. If you tell him about the contract, you'll be gone."

"I'll wait to tell him, but only until Mr. Gilmore sends me the ten g's. That's when I'll announce I'm leaving."

"George, did Gilmore sign the contract?'

"No, but he gave me his word. He said I would have the money next week."

"You trust him, George?"

"More than I trust you right now, that's for sure."

"Well you're off to Boston for now, anyway. Good luck, and if you get your money, I will pray you've made the right decision."

Ruth turned away in disgust, off once again to pack his things, now for a distant, much larger city. No longer did he bring the baggage of abandonment. Ruth was now convinced he would need to make his own way in life, making his own decisions.

He looked forward to playing back in Baltimore with the upstart Terrapins for a new league. It would be the fresh start he needed. Plus, he would be loaded. The $10,000 would arrive soon. Then Ruth would be set for life.

Chapter 13

In the wee hours of the tepid summer morning of July 11th, 1914, Ruth stepped onto a train bound for Boston's Back Bay Station, his life in motion again. Several hours after arriving in Boston at 10 AM, "the Babe" was making his major-league pitching debut against the Cleveland team at Fenway Park.

The Cleveland Naps struggled to stay out of the cellar. The team was in decline; their once proud slugger Nap Lajoie was nearing the end of a long career. Although unhappy and surrounded by ineptness, Shoeless Joe Jackson continued to put up terrific numbers.

Tris Speaker patted Ruth on the rump as the Red Sox took the field to begin the game. "Kid, don't worry about a thing. These napkins will fold pretty easily." Ruth immediately admired his new teammate.

Allowing two singles in the first inning, Ruth found himself in immediate difficulty. Lajoie was stepping in to hit, with Jackson on first and leadoff hitter Graney at third. Lajoie topped the first pitch, sending the ball trickling toward the third base line. Being left-handed, Ruth was already following through in that direction. Quicker than anyone expected, Ruth pounced on the ball and nailed Graney at home plate. The slicker and quicker Shoeless Joe Jackson motored all the way to third. Ruth, walking back to the mound with the ball, was in disbelief when he saw Jackson waving at him from the bag at third. Ruth needed one more out to end the inning. As he took his stretch position on the mound, he stared at Lajoie on first, and peering over his right shoulder, he saw the cocky Jackson edging towards home. Ruth stepped off the mound. With utter disdain for the youngster Jackson did not move back towards the base. Jackson now had Ruth engaged in his personal cat-and-mouse game. Ruth stepped on and off the rubber quickly. The fearless Jackson was now several more feet from third. Ruth drifted toward first, stumbled, landing on his left knee. Jackson turned to run for home with the first run of the game. The dumbfounded Jackson was met by player manager Bill Carrigan as he looked up in anticipation of crossing the plate. With a tag right to his chest, Jackson became the final out in Babe Ruth's first professional inning. Four months out of St. Mary's and he was already showing the guile and poise he needed to outsmart one of the top major leaguers.

Relying mostly on speed and guile, Ruth took a 3-1 lead into the seventh. He was scheduled to bat in the bottom of the inning, but then the Naps rallied with three singles to tie the contest. In his first two at-bats against lefthander Willie Wilson, Babe had struck out and flied to right. When his time came again, Boston manager Bill Carrigan sent up veteran Duffy Lewis to pinch-hit. Lewis promptly scratched out an infield single and came around to score. When the lead held up, Babe Ruth had secured his first major-league game victory.

The Red Sox players were taking their turns in the batting practice cage before the next day's contest against the Naps. Speaker and Carrigan were among the group milling, ready to jump in and take their swings. Strolling ever so casually from the dugout, the Babe approached, carrying what appeared to be a club.

Speaker spoke in his most diplomatic manner asked, "Whatcha got there, Ruth?"

From the crowd of players a voice rang, "Something to kill his dinner, most likely."

The Babe, somewhat annoyed, retorted, "A brand new bat which none of you are man enough to handle." The lumber in his hand measured 36 inches long and weighed 45 ounces. "When I hit one, you'll strain your neck to watch it sail."

"Ruth, pitchers do not need to take batting practice. This here is for the field players," Speaker said.

Ruth was still annoyed. "Who's going to keep me out? Not any of you twerps."

Ruth stepped through the narrow, netted gate into the cage towards the plate, even though Duffy Lewis was still occupying the batter's box. "Get out. I'm taking some whacks," the belligerent rookie demanded. Lewis responded by sticking the knobbed end of his bat squarely into Ruth's chest as the bigger man approached. Wrapping his mammoth left hand around the bat handle, Ruth easily yanked the bat from Lewis and tossed it toward the pitcher's mound. "Didn't I make myself clear? Get out. I'll show you no one's good enough to hit for me. No one!"

The veteran Lewis grabbed Ruth's uniform shirt with both hands as the two started to wrestle, but before either could get seriously injured,

Carrigan and several other players grabbed Ruth in an effort to pull him out of the cage. Ruth, now incensed, fought with the rage of a trapped bull. Seven players held Ruth's arms at his side as they tried to drag him through the tiny portal. Finally Carrigan interceded and instructed Ruth to leave the field and take the day off.

After he settled down, a sullen Ruth sat quietly on a stool in the windowless end of the locker room, completely indifferent to the events on the field. His mind drifted to thoughts of playing in Baltimore. He did not care to be in Boston. He held the upper hand. After all the check from Gilmore would arrive soon and he would be gone. So let them ban him, he'd play for twenty years in the Federal League.

Unfortunately, Ruth only demonstrated infrequent bursts of power in Baltimore, and he had hit barely above .200 in the minors. Pitchers in the majors were not expected to perform well at the plate. In spite of that, the brash youngster would argue for more time in the batting cage each and every day during ensuing weeks. Several times, Carrigan had to break up shoving matches between the Babe and other players. Soon Ruth's status became clear when he discovered one day that his teammates had sawed the handles off his bats. He was there to pitch, not hit.

Led by the merciless Ty Cobb, the Detroit Tigers batted the Babe around fairly easily, knocking him out of the box early in his second start. Carrigan advised the Babe he was perhaps not ready to pitch in the majors and Fenway was not a kind place for lefties. Babe was relegated to the bench, where over the next month, he watched former Orioles teammate Ernie Shore meet instant success on the mound.

Each day that the surly rookie watched the Red Sox play while he sat on the bench; the burning anxiety within him grew. He alienated his teammates each and every day with his routine behavior, which became cruder. Before most games, he went on wild eating and drinking binges. When he did get into the game, his play was devoid of any passion, fundamentally lackadaisical. The Red Sox were a veteran hardnosed team and did not tolerate this behavior. Ruth had quickly become an outcast.

For any newcomer, the Red Sox would not have been an easy ball club to break into at the time. In 1912, playing in the brand-new Fenway Park, the team christened the inaugural season with a World Series championship. For the 1914 season, most of the core of the team had remained in place. Carrigan was clearly the established leader, a no-nonsense manager who served double duty as the daily catcher. Donned with the nickname 'Rough' for his playing style and discipline toward players; he expected nothing but 100% effort from the players.

The outfield trio of Tris Speaker, Harry Hooper and Duffy Lewis was among baseball's best. Speaker was the jewel, as he was widely considered one of the game's greatest hitters and fielders. Larry Gardner was a solid third baseman and above average stick. The indestructible ironman Everett Scott became the regular shortstop in 1914, where he would remain for the next 1,307 consecutive games, becoming the first baseball player to play in more than 1,000 consecutive games and completely shattering George Pinckney's streak of 577 games. Scott was so dedicated to the game that at one point he played with one eye closed from a puss-filled boil. Even a nasty slice across the ankle, which bled through his stocking for the next week and had been delivered by Ty Cobb, could not deter Scott from taking his regular spot in the lineup.

The pitching staff was also very deep, with a combination of veterans and newcomers. Joe Wood and Ray Collins were the mainstays, and youngsters Shore (10-4), Dutch Leonard (19-5), and Rube Foster (14-8) each contributed, forming a powerful pitching group. Ruth was nothing more than an afterthought at best. He had not only become a leper and a malcontent, he was a distraction. Most of all, he was expendable.

In Baltimore, Ned Hanlon continued actively trying to add more marquee talent to his roster. After a long and successful managerial career, he pondered why he had decided to invest, becoming the principal shareholder for this fledgling team in a start-up league. Although the Terrapins were only a few games back, the attendance dragged. Otto Knabe was a solid manager; Vern Duncan and Guy Zinn, transplants from the majors, had been added but had not developed the rapport with the community. Although the team was playing hard, Hanlon was frustrated. Brooklyn, Chicago, St. Louis and

Pittsburgh all competed with major league franchises within their cities but they all had consistently larger gate draws than the Terrapins.

Hanlon hoped the answer was sitting opposite him. This would be his coup de grace, stealing the Athletics' best pitcher right out from under Connie Mack. Chief Bender was in the middle of another outstanding season with the Athletics. He had, however, become increasingly disenchanted with Mack's treatment of older players. In confidence, Mack told Bender at the year's end that Eddie Plank, Home Run Baker and Eddie Collins were to be sold. Bender more than understood how ruthless the business of baseball was, and Mack was as cold and calculating as any other owner. Loyalty was not a word in Mack's vernacular. Bender knew the day would come when he would be gone with no pomp and circumstance. He decided to reach out to Hanlon while he was still thought of as having value to a club.

"Well, Chief, I look forward to having you pitch for the Terrapins next year. We're just a few wins away from being champions," said Hanlon. "If the Ruth kid were to pan out, we just may have something special, something real special."

"I don't know what you're fixing to pay Ruth, but I wouldn't waste my money. The kid does not have the self-control," Bender said.

"The kid is a Baltimore legend. He can hit the ball a long way and has a great arm."

"Your money," Bender replied with a shrug. "He has trouble hitting bad major league pitching, and I hear he had trouble getting any of the Tigers out. Cobb thought he was a joke. Plus he's been nothing but trouble in Boston."

Reaching to the middle of his desk, Hanlon picked up the $10,000 bank draft, tore it up and tossed the pieces into his trash can. "Thanks, Chief, it was Gilmore's idea anyway. He can deal with the kid. I'll give you an extra grand out of what you saved me."

By mid-August everyone within the Red Sox organization had had enough of the Babe, so Lannin sold his contract to the Providence Grays of the International League. This rival of the Baltimore Orioles had been just purchased by Boston owner Joe Lannin.

His teammates did not shed many tears at his departure. Some of them, in fact, cheered openly when they heard the news about the unproven rookie. The final straw occurred during warm-ups before the scheduled game on August 16th. Ruth was standing behind Joe Wood, the scheduled starter who was loosening his arm. Carrigan's return throw to him was low and off-line, the ball skidding towards the observing Ruth. Wood yelled out to the passive Ruth, "A little help there, rook." Ruth indifferently spread his legs, giving a mock salute as the ball passed under him. Wood became incensed and threw his glove at Ruth. The Babe, in turn, unleashed an expletive-laced verbal assault on Wood and his entire ancestry. Carrigan intervened once again, sending Ruth to the clubhouse, this time telling him to pack his things.

Arriving to the solemnity of the clubhouse, the fuming Ruth kicked over a table and punched a hole in Woods' locker door. Part of his internal anger was driven by the news he had received that morning. Hanlon would not honor Gilmore's commitment to him. There would be no ten thousand dollars; no fresh start for him to look forward to just another broken promise for Ruth to endure. He hurriedly dressed, storming from the club house in such a huff that he did not notice the pair of men sitting in the corner, engrossed in conversation. Speaker was bent over, tying the laces of his cleats while espousing his opinion on the changing business climate of baseball, when he was distracted from his thoughts by the unruly commotion. He looked up just in time to see the whirling dervish speed past. In the wicker rocking chair next to him sat a quiet, dapper, middle-aged man dressed in a three-button brown wool suit, a bright white shirt and a tie fastidiously matched to the shade of his suit that, despite his barrel chest, had the look of a successful business man.

"Who's that?" asked the visitor.

"No one of any note, Cy, just another youngster with a chip on his shoulder who's rapidly making a mess of his life."

Chapter 14
1903 Boston

October 1, before the scheduled first pitch, well over 15,000 New Englanders had filed into the expansive Huntington Avenue American League Baseball Grounds ball park. Each of the 11,500 seats would be occupied and 3,500 other patrons would dot every possible vantage point to peer at the game, some with an obstructed view, each rooting passionately for their team. The ballpark, completed in May 1901, was billed as the home of the Boston-American League Ball Club. This was done to woo fans away from Boston's National league team and its aging park.

Although no team nickname was officially on file with the American League, local newspaper writers, with sparing regularity, referred to the team as the Pilgrims. Others just called the team the Americans, as a way of differentiating them from their National League counterparts. The baseball park had been hurriedly constructed on grounds formerly occupied by a circus, built to expansive dimensions and it included some quirks not seen before. One such strange feature was a tool shed in the field of play, although it was well over 500 feet away from home plate, and a treacherous sand pit in deep right center, which at times made outfield play comical. The long abandoned rail tracks which had served as a terminal point to the circus cut through the vacant end of the grounds. Less than two football fields' length beyond stood the outfield wall of the home of Boston's struggling National league team. Fans who sat in the upper tier of that park could see the modern home of the Pilgrims. For the owners, it was a painful, irritating reminder of the nascent league with its better financial backers and its new parks with their larger crowd capacities.

This was an historic day in professional baseball. Once again, teams from opposing leagues would battle on the field to crown a consensus champion under agreement by the professional leagues. This post-season play was officially dubbed the World Series.

After nearly three years of open and hostile warfare, the leaderships of the National and American leagues finally came to their senses. Each league was bloodied and battered, losing key stars and feeling the devastating financial wounds resulting from their enmity. A three-man panel National Baseball Commission was established to arbitrate disputes and lay the groundwork for how the leagues would coexist. Through the work of the National Commission, post-season play was reconstituted to the delirious delight of fans, who had been praying this day would come. The final format of the best-of-nine series was the brainchild of Barney Dreyfuss, owner of the Pittsburgh Pirates, who in late September convinced his counterpart from the Pilgrims to expand the series from the single-game playoff suggested by the National Commission. While the Commission was initially hesitant, Dreyfuss gained their approval when he allowed the series to open in Boston. The

Commission had determined that the National league team would host the meeting between the leagues, since they were the older team.

On Sept. 18, the day after Boston clinched first place and one day before the Pirates did so, Dreyfuss and Killilea signed the agreement for the series. Still, the series was nearly doomed before it started. Players had caught wind of the plan for the extra games, and they vowed to boycott the series and leave for their off-season homes if they were not handsomely compensated. Dreyfuss and Killilea set out to quell the strike threat from his players over the extension of the season. They agreed to amend their contract to provide each player a share of the Series gate. Killilea further satisfied his players by including a more than generous incentive for bringing the championship home to Boston.

Dreyfuss was less magnanimous. Without a rival league to lure his players away, he stood firm in his position. He considered the series as part of their personal services contract to the Pirates. If any of the players elected not to play, there would be recourse; no boycotting player would be offered a contract for 1904. This would essentially put those players completely out of baseball, since the American League teams were barred from offering them work.

At 11:30 a.m. on Sept. 28, every member of the Pirates team, an unhappy group of 15, boarded the train at the Pittsburgh and Lake Erie Station for Boston and a date with history.

In 1900, the American League had opened for business, making the claim that it was the true major league, and its teams began furiously raiding the National League. The attacks of this wave of free agency had been so effective that by 1903, many of the National League teams were left with few talented players. The Pirates escaped more or less unscathed through the tumult, dominating the decimated league by capturing three straight league crowns. The Pirates breezed through 1902, winning the pennant with a 103-36 record. In 1903 the outcome was again the same, although with a bit more of a struggle, finally salting away the title in late September. Honus Wagner and an outfield that included two players hitting over .341 led the way for Pittsburgh. Fans expected that the Pirates would prevail against a team from the younger league.

For game 1, the normal pre-game activities of batting and fielding practice were abandoned because the crowd was unmanageable. Patrons, predominately composed of men attired in three-piece black business suits, hijacked the field. Fans were milling in every area of the field. Others were crossing the field, taking a direct path to the grandstands from the ticket booth just beyond the left field foul pole. Some were simply engrossed in watching and admiring the players in their attempt to get ready for the game. Some others merely congregated and chatted. No one stood out in this blended, ebony-clad sea of humanity. Beyond the left field fence, in the shadows of the arched white sign which marked the entrance to the baseball grounds, John F. Fitzgerald, Mickey "'Nuf Ced" McGreevy and Patsy Tebeau stood, engrossed in a private discussion. This unlikely triumvirate received little notice from the patrons rushing to get into the ball park.

The Pilgrims manager selected Cy Young as the first-game pitcher. Since joining the Pilgrims in 1901, he had logged three very productive years, compiling a 93 and 30 record. During the course of the 1903 regular season, he had completed all but one of the 35 games in which he was the starter. At 36 years old, there was little evidence he was losing any effectiveness. However, this game proved disastrous for Young, who yielded four runs in the first frame alone. In the 7th inning, Young enabled the weakest hitter of Pittsburgh's outfield trio, James Sebring, to sneak into the pages of baseball immortality by driving one of Young's pitches into the right-field stands with the first official World Series home run. Although down 7-0 after the long poke, Young stayed in to finish the game. The Pilgrims were on the short side of a 7-3 first-game result.

Last to leave the park was a dejected Young. He had toughed out nine innings, but this day, his best just hadn't been enough. His Pilgrim teammates encouraged him and supported his efforts, knowing full well that without him, they would not be in the series. Young decided that the walk alone back to the hotel was the best remedy for him. Nearly an hour and a half after the final out, Young embarked alone on the one-mile journey, leaving through the left field exit.

"Well, Young, I see old habits die hard," a familiar voice called out. Glancing up, he saw, leaning against a nearby telephone pole, the last person in the world he expected.

"As gutless as ever," Tebeau, relishing Young's failure, taunted the already downtrodden Young.

"Gave it my best, Mr. Tebeau," Young said, answering respectfully as always, "That's all one can do."

"Doesn't matter to me. I made a lot of money wagering against you, and I'll make a lot more before this series is out. I wish you the best, Cy, all the best to you." Tebeau walked away, vanishing into the shadows as if he were vapor. Young vowed to himself that he would show this nemesis and win a few games. The Pilgrims would emerge to be crowned baseball champions.

Five days later, the Boston squad faced a perhaps insurmountable deficit — down 3 games to 1 with the next three games to take place at Exposition Park in Pittsburgh. Hometown cooking was just what Honus Wagner needed, heating up as he rapped out three hits in the game.

Fred Clarke skipped over both twenty-five-game-winner Sam Leever, who left after an ineffective opening inning in game 2 but was well rested, and sixteen-game-winner Ed Doheny, who had not yet pitched in the series, deciding to use the less-than-formidable Brickyard Kennedy to start game five. After the 7th inning, the Pilgrims' brutal pounding of Kennedy was brought to a halt, with Boston well in front, 11-0.

Clarke would have Leever and Deacon Phillippe rested for games six and seven as the

Pirates readied to close out the series at home. Although finishing the game six contest, Leever once again was batting practice fodder for Boston as the Pirates fell in a second straight humbling home loss. After a day of rain, the series continued in Pittsburg on October 10th. The Pirates' fate remained unchanged as they lost for a third straight time. Now the team was facing a return trip to Boston while hanging on the precipice of elimination.

An early Nor'easter blew through New England, unleashing its bitter rain and delaying the game eight until October 13. Cigar and cigarette smoke bellowed in a steady stream from the Third Base Saloon. This was a local pub owned and operated by McGreevy for over a decade. Uncommonly busy for a Monday, the crowd overflowed out onto Ruggles Street, creating a queue to enter. The pub's proximity to South End Grounds made it a popular hangout for many baseball fans, the Boston Beaneater players, south-side Irish and German working stiffs, politicians and of course, a heavy dose of gamblers. The saloon always did a brisk business and even more so when there was baseball being played in either of Boston's professional parks, but today was an unusual exception.

McGreevy loved baseball, and he set the atmosphere as a baseball haven, accenting the ambience with baseball paraphernalia. The walls were lined with photos, drawings and crumpled or tattered scorecards. In every corner of the pub there were used player bats (some with cracks or broken in two), old worn-out spikes and even player shirts. He loved chatting the game and being around the players. His nickname, "'Nuf Ced" came from the line he used to end any heated debate among patrons about baseball for which there would be no peaceful conclusion. With the successive rain-outs, the anxious fans and participants sought out the close-by refuge in droves, knowing McGreevy would be telling baseball lore and readying the hometown throng for game 8.

Former Massachusetts State Senator, John 'Honey Fitz' Fitzgerald, was in his customary place of honor, leading the Royal Rooters. The all-brass band was dizzying the crowds in its delivery of the Pilgrims fight song. A parody of mocking insults was launched at the Pirates, to the music of the theme from 'Tessie.' An even larger ensemble of nearly 50 had travelled to Pittsburgh. Their purpose was to provide a distraction for the Pirate players, especially their leader, Honus Wagner. Third Base, with alcohol flowing easily and patrons in a frenzying hypnotic serenade so loud, made any conversation impossible. The Rooters were relentless in the playing of the theme. When the vocal chords were tired, they just played the tune, even louder, hour after hour, after hour, after hour...

"Honus, why do you hit so badly?
Take a back seat and sit down
Honus, at bat you look so sadly.
Hey, why don't you get out of town?

Finally, to the delight of some, Honey Fitz proclaimed, "Time for refreshments." He strolled to a table in the back of the saloon where Tebeau awaited with Frank Wallace, an Irish mobster.

Without the ear-piercing sounds of the band, conversations could return to normal. Gamblers and patrons readily exchanged cash, wagering on the outcome of the series and of the next game. Nary was an effort made to even attempt to hide what was going on. The working-class Irish and Germans fans placed small bets, just a few bucks. Close to the start of the game, the high rollers would enter the scene. Most activities halted as heads turned to watch. With a pause in the chaotic atmosphere, savvy bettors listened; they'd try to follow the money. One Pittsburg rooter, returning from a downtown tour and dinner, strolled in, laying 8-10 odds and slapping $10,000 down. "I will be back to collect after game 9." This emotional but ill-advised wager shifted the betting odds creating longer odds if the underdog Boston were to win. It did not take long for Wallace and his ever present sinister grin to plunk $20,000 down on Boston to win.

There had been troubling rumors in baseball during the last three years, centering on gambling in the sport. Teams were said to not play hard when engaged in meaningless games while betting against themselves. Many in the sport turned a blind eye to the practice, seeing this simply as a way for the players to augment their paltry pay. Prior to the start of the 1903 season, several of the Pirate players had received warnings from League President Nicholas Young, who was thought of as a weak patsy for the owners during the years he served. Harry Pulliam, who succeeded Young, left the reins even looser and focusing on settling the war between the leagues and stopping the attrition of players from the National League. Throughout the season, he dedicated little time to deal with this minor annoyance of player gambling. Gambling was ignored more in 1903 than in any other season.

A concerned Wallace, in a sound barely above a whisper, "I hear Dreyfuss has changed his mind about the player bonuses. Should we be concerned?"

Tebeau commented with conviction, "I heard that as well, but the players are still angry."

Fitzgerald, in a tone both forceful and scolding, added, "There better be no surprises, Patsy. I have my political future riding on this as well as the money. One cannot make his constituents angry."

"Tebeau, if you're a church-going man, you ought to pray everything pans out like I want it to. I do not want to come find you," Wallace threatened. Rising, he bade them good day.

Fitzgerald, furthering the conversation, "Use the Royal Rooters if you need to, in any way. Understood?"

"Yes, Mr. Fitzgerald understood."

Several of the Pilgrim players, including Young, were eating at a table on the far side of the large tavern room. Tebeau could not resist the opportunity to confront Young. Young, watching Tebeau stroll towards him, decided to speak first.

"Well, Mr. Tebeau. What do you have to say now, after my two straight victories? I hope you did not lose that much money."

With a sinister chuckle, Tebeau chided,
"Lose, Young, lose on you? Are you that naïve? I
made more money on you with your wins than in
your loss. Do you really think you could beat the
Pirates? You could stop Wagner. Young, you were
drummed out of the League as an overweight
washed-up pitcher three years ago. You're dumb.
Goodbye, Young." Roaring in uncontained laughter,
Tebeau departed, walking out into the rain storm.

Young stunned, reeled as the crowd noise in
the pub became hazy. His head spun in near-vertigo
as he digested the impact and implication of
Tebeau's words. He cleared his mind and thought,
*maybe Wagner was just having a rough spot, and
all players go through them. Wagner's not a God,
he is human.* 'I'm not going to have Tebeau get the
better of me, not again. He wants to get my goat.
There's no way the Pirates would intentionally lose
the series.'

Extra police and security had been hired in
anticipation of the sea of humanity that would
descend upon Huntington Grounds Park on October
13, 1903. The temperature reached a comfortable 65
degrees once the storm finished its pummeling of
Boston. To prevent the unruly crowd from reaching
the infield, a protective rope had been set up on the
perimeter, along with Boston's finest. People were
everywhere, climbing up telephone poles and even
sitting atop the outfield fencing, while others found
a way to sneak in to occupy the seats of other
unsuspecting patrons. An even starker visual was
the vivid contrast of cultures at the park. The blue
collar and very poor were vying for any spot from

which they had a view of the players, while the blue-blooded hobnobbing social elite and wealthy were assured of their box seats. Regardless of social status, the scene was one of merriment, the result of many being intoxicated or on their way. For hours before the game, there were laughter, happy greetings and hope as the Boston hopeful readied for the joyful moment.

The Royal Rooters, blasting 'Tessie' incessantly, managed to get onto the field surrounding the Pirate players, preventing their pre-game warm ups. The target of their disconcerting pre-game antics was starting pitcher Deacon Phillippe and shortstop Honus Wagner. The antics seemed ineffective as Phillippe pitched a decent game, allowing just three runs on eight hits. Wagner and his batting mates did not hold up their end, managing only a feeble four hits against Bill Dinneen, who gained his third win in the series.

The gate from the series was extraordinary, with well over 100,000 spectators purchasing tickets and many more buying food and drinks from the hawking vendors. Each Boston player received a bonus of $1,000. Barney Dreyfuss decided to include his owner's share in the amount he gave to the Pittsburgh players, making their purse higher than that of the winning Boston team. There was speculation that some of the Pittsburg made as much as ten times wagering on the outcome of the series. Team owners brushed it aside as just speculation and rumor and did little to investigate.

Cy Young with his World Series bonus, championship, and personal accomplishments secured, headed back to Ohio for some well-needed rest. He had passed both Pud Galvin and Kid Nichols during the 1903 campaign, now standing alone at 379 wins, the all-time record.

Chapter 15

Robba stepped through the weather- beaten front door; she looked tenderly at her husband and thought *My Denton, the picture of serenity.* Quietly she stood on the expansive front porch which wrapped around three-quarters of the faded white farm house. Robba admired Young as he sat back in the wicker rocking chair, absorbing the last of the warming rays of this late fall day into his leathery face.   The nights had already begun to capture more and more of the daylight hours.

The dozen years of marriage had slipped by quickly, but Robba's devotion and love towards Young had never waned. Young was the pride of his home town and of his family, far exceeding the dreams of many local baseball heroes. 'Cyclone' Young was finally thought of as the best pitcher baseball had ever known. Robba cherished Young's accomplishments just as if they were her own. The farm house and grounds were in need of some maintenance and repair, painting, replacement of wood siding and planks, rails on the fence line, all in addition to the upcoming fall harvest. Family and friends pitched in to help from time to time, but not enough to make up for all the minutes, days, and years baseball had stolen from their time together.

She did not harbor any ill will or suppress angry feelings towards Young, in part because she knew that, after all, his baseball career could not last much longer. Young would be 38 years old before the start of the next season, and he had amassed over 400 wins to his credit. What more could he want to accomplish in baseball? Young had just completed another brilliant season, highlighted by the first perfect game recorded in the American League on May 5 and the first since the pitching distance had been moved back to 60' 6". Whatever Young would decide, she would support him. After all, she would have the rest of her life to share with him. Her only regret so far was that the marriage had failed to produce a child. Robba realized that her youthfulness was slipping away more quickly than Young's ability to deliver a baseball. With each passing season, the harsh chores and routines of the farm were slowing sapping her resolve, until suddenly she realized the best of her child-bearing years were probably gone. The void in her heart, she knew, was no greater than that of Young's, as both longed for children, he perhaps even more than she. If Robba attributed in any way the lack of her ability to conceive in their union to baseball, she never let a word fall from her mouth to Young's ears, knowing with all certainty that would end his relationship with baseball. If they were meant to have children, it would happen when and as the Lord saw fit.

Robba watched Young occupying his usual front porch spot. Relaxed in his rocking chair, leaning back, eyes shut. Young was such a good man, she thought. He looked so at peace. As she stepped toward him, one of the oak boards creaked.

Young jumped from his chair, the rocker slamming into the wall behind him. "My dear, you startled me."

"Sorry, Denton, I did not realize you had fallen asleep."

"Not sure I was really napping, more like just lost in my thoughts."

"A penny, Denton, a penny for your thoughts, you seem so jumpy."

"I've been doing a lot of thinking about baseball. Not sure I want to go on. Each time something goes not as expected, there is always talk about it not being on the level. Somehow my abilities seem to be at the center of the controversy.'

"I don't understand, Denton. What do you mean?"

"Robba, remember last year when we beat the Pirates in the series to become baseball champions?"

"No. Series? What's that?"

"Oh, Robba, you know, the World Series, to see which of the two leagues is better. Remember when you came up to Boston to watch us play Pittsburg, last year."

"Yes, of course. How could I ever forget that. Boston the World Series Champions!"

"Talk after we won from most people was that we could never have beaten the Pirates if everything was on the up-and-up."

"How is that at all possible?"

"It's the gamblers, darling, the gamblers. They line the pockets of some of the players with cash. Then those players do not try their very best. I think they are told to lose."

"You really think that some of the players do this?"

"Look at what happened this year. On the last day of the season, Chesboro throws a wild pitch with the winning run on third, in the bottom of the ninth, no less. We come back to win first place, beating out the Highlanders."

"Who is Chesboro?"

"Jack Chesboro, just the best pitcher in the American League."

"I thought you were the best."

"Thanks, darling, but Jack won 41 games this past season."

"So why would he throw the game away?"

"Money, Robba, it's always the money. With no playoff between the two leagues, this is the only way for players to make extra money."

"There was no series this year?"

"No, because the New York Giants owner is mad about the American League having put a team in New York to compete with the Giants. And their manager hates the American League. So the team declined the invitation. Some folks believed he would change his mind if the New York Highlanders, who were in first during most of the season, were not the American League representatives in the series."

"So they paid the New York players to lose the game, so that maybe the Giants would agree to play in the series?"

"Now you're starting to understand."

Robba chuckled, glancing down passionately at Young. She was never one to hide the depth of her love. Equally, Young was an open book to her. Her eyes could penetrate into his soul and see his deepest thoughts. She did not let on, but she understood more than he realized, "Besides they do not even remember your given name anymore …Cyrus." The common name many players and sportswriters came to call him. The loving couple began to laugh aloud as Robba wrapped her arms around Young's broad shoulders from behind the rocker, the top of his head resting against the softness of her bosom. The couple lingered savoring the moment.

After the 1904 season and the boycott of the informal post-season championship, Young was not only determined to remain in baseball but also to lead the Americans back into the World Series. The absence of the post-season matchup between the American and National league winners prompted the league presidents to act quickly. The result was the establishment of ground rules for post-season play. The fiery John McGraw, known as "Little Napoleon" by the press and fans, Mr. McGraw to his players and "Mugsy" to his enemies, applied the dirtiest of the tactics of the old Orioles as well as the tactics of inside baseball, the hit-and-run, the stolen base and the scientific game to achieve success. The Orioles were the roughest team in a rough age, baseball in the late 1890's.

The new league under Ban Johnson was trying the shed the image of a second-rate league of beer-drinking thug baseball players ready to fight at the drop of a hat. In 1902, Johnson, then president of the American League, had suspended McGraw, the manager of the Baltimore Orioles, for his repeated assaults on the umpires. The latest on-field incident by the Orioles resulted in Johnson issuing an indefinite suspension order to McGraw.

The lowly Orioles, already destined for the cellar by mid-July, were playing a meaningless game against Connie Mack's Athletics. In the third inning, Tully Frederick 'Topsy' Hartsel drove a ball into the left centerfield alley. Between innings, tired of being a doormat to the league and especially fed up with losing to Mack, McGraw told his players to do anything, and that meant *anything*, to prevent any more runs from scoring. In full stride after rounding first, Hartsel headed to second. Politely, Orioles second baseman stuck his foot out successfully sending Hartsel tumbling down onto the infield dirt. Billy Gilbert, who had come onto the baseball scene from nowhere, had a striking resemblance to Patsy Teabeau. Gilbert played one season then disappeared as if an apparition. Looking up, Hartsel saw the ball still bounding away from the outfielders, so he quickly got back to his feet and hustled past second, heading to third. Jack Thoney, playing third, firmly planted his 5' 10", 180-pound frame in front of Hartsel with left foot raised spikes glistening in the sunshine.

"Head home and I will slice you, orders from Mr. McGraw." Thoney bellowed in a hoarse, gravelly voice. Hartsel halted his advancement and stood meekly on the bag. Hartsel knew no one dared not to obey an order from McGraw.

Without warning, Thoney brought his foot down onto Hartsel's right shin, cutting his flesh cleanly and added, "Just so as you know not to go nowhere."

When word of this brutal incident reached Johnson, with everyone clearly pointing to the demanding McGraw as the only instigator, the consequences were quickly meted out, and Lil' Napoleon was sent packing. McGraw's personality was shaped in Truxton, New York, where he was born in 1873. His mother and four of his siblings died in a diphtheria epidemic. John McGraw came to love baseball. It was a way out for the young McGraw. An unsympathetic father was neither any help to him as a maturing young man nor to his baseball career. McGraw's father had been a Union soldier in the Civil War and he hated baseball, favoring the Irish game of "Shinny" instead. Young John was beaten often, one time for breaking a church window and another for breaking a merchant's window, but most of the time from taking on more than just one other young man at a time in a fight.

McGraw was the living embodiment of the rough spirit of the 1890's, carrying the 19th century's hard-bitten and take-no-prisoners ethics into the 20th century. If a little player or umpire blood was spilled in order to win, then so be it. McGraw was foul-mouthed and a mean-spirited SOB to any one or team he considered to be a threat to the success of his teams. He made fun of people and their weaknesses. He made an art of pushing their hot buttons. Barney Dreyfuss was a frequent target of McGraw, due to the Pirate owner's thick German accent. Losing to the Pirates and Dreyfuss in 1903 had left him seething. Seeing the Pirates falling to the American League brought out the worst of his hatred. Whatever the reason for the Giants winning in 1904, the fate of the World Series that year may have been foreordained.

Johnson simply had had enough. McGraw's threats of retaliation were not idle; as he signed on to manage the New York Giants, he immediately brought over with him certain star players: 'Iron Man' McGinnity, Roger Bresnahan, and Dan McGann.

Young returned for another season in 1905 and started the worst stretch in his fabled career. During these next two years, Young won only 31 games whiles losing 40.

During the 1906 season, Young began to tinker with a variety of slower pitches with a great deal more movement. At 39, his fastball was now several feet too short to retire major league batters with any consistency. By season's end, he had amassed 21 losses and for the only time in his career, failed to post a shutout.

On July 5, 1906, an exhausted Young walked into the dingy clubhouse at the Huntington Avenue baseball park. The second game of the July 4th doubleheader concluded the thirty-day road trip that had begun with a visit to Cleveland. The sting of their 6-19 record in this stretch was not lessened by the 9-3 win against the Senators, who were challenging the Americans for rights to reside in the American League basement. At 7:00P.M., the worn-out Americans boarded a train at Union Station for the trek from the nation's capital back to Boston. Most of the players did not find the comfort of their beds until after 2:00AM. Restless during his abridged night's sleep, Cy somehow found a reserve of energy sufficient to drag himself early to the ballpark, arriving shortly before 10:00AM. He hoped to find peace in the quiet of a deserted windowless clubhouse. Old Jojo, who had to be at least 75 years old, was the only other person there.

"Mr. Cy, I did not expect to see anyone here for a while. Game don't start until 2." Jojo said in a surprised voice, as he readied the uniforms for the players. "A letter come for you shortly after the team left. I put it in your locker. Been there for some time, three weeks at least, I imagine."

Cy nodded his head and waved in a gesture of acknowledgement to Jojo as he passed. Picking up his pace, an apprehensive Young quickly reached his destination and pulled open the metal door of his spartan locker. The edge of the white envelope was peeking over the front edge of the eye level shelf. Anxiously he reached for the envelope, and gathering it in his hand, he ripped it open in one motion as he seated himself on a nearby stool. The return address in the upper left-hand corner of the small envelope was simple enough, Peoli, Ohio. Young knew immediately it was from the only woman with whom he had ever had a relationship. Robba did not make it a habit of writing much, usually news about someone passing. Three years earlier, Cy received a letter telling him that Robert Miller, Robba's father, would be moving in with them because he had not adjusted well after his wife had passed away. Just last fall, Robba wrote to tell that her mother's sister passed away from the mysterious stomach ailment which claimed her mother's life as well. Cy sensed another of the older generation passing on, and once again he would not be there to comfort her following the loss of a relative.

"My Darling Denton, the Lord has answered our prayers, finally, and He sees fit to bless us. I am with child. Denton, you are to be a father. The next phase of our life as parents is about to begin. Don't worry, my dearest; the birth of our child will occur months after the end of the season. I am not only well but aglow with pride. Just the thought that I carry our precious gift of life makes my heart ache with even more love for you than ever. Your loving and devoted wife, Robba."

Young sat back, stunned by the news. At 40 he would become a father. *This is it. After this season, I can retire. I can go back to working the farm,* Young thought. He had some money, not wealthy by any stretch but well enough off. *Finally I can put this aching right arm towards something more worthwhile than slinging a baseball.*

A distracted Cy Young pitched out the balance of the 1906 season with the ineffectiveness of a rookie bush leaguer and to what had become an opera of boos. On October 5th, the Americans lost for the 105th time that season. Young cleaned out his locker, packed and locked his two brown steamer trunks and set out for home on the last train headed towards Cincinnati. He would reach Peoli by mid-afternoon the following day.

Robba, seven months pregnant, greeted Cy warmly at the entrance to the farm. Her face was beaded in perspiration and her once light-blue dress was darkened with the efforts of her chores. She threw her arms around Cy, kissing him openly on the lips.

"Robba, are you okay? You're covered in sweat from head to toe. Should you be doing all this work?"

"Oh, Denton, I'm fine. I'm surprised you're home so soon. I would not have expected you for a few more days."

"I could not wait to see my beautiful lady."

"Stop, now, Denton, look how round I am. How can you say I'm beautiful?"

"Robba, you were right. You do glow. You are having our baby. How can you think of yourself as anything but beautiful?"

The fall days passed quickly, and on a deep, dark December evening, Robba gave birth to a baby girl. Irene Palmer, a young Irish midwife from Peoli, told Young that the birth was not at all troubling for Robba or the child. Mother and daughter had come through the ordeal just fine. For a first child, Robba's labor was relatively short, just six hours. Young softly gathered the baby girl in his arms just as the morning sun began to peer through the east-facing window of their bedroom. Gazing into the pinkness of her soft round face, he understood the depth of his responsibility and realized what his parents had experienced, knowing they had protected many fragile treasures. Doc Brandt arrived by mid-morning and declared mother and child healthy, verifying Irene's opinion.

On Sunday a week later, the families and friends gathered in celebration of the child's baptism. The Young's meager farmhouse was teeming with people, most inside but others braving the winter cold, eating and having conversation on the front porch. Although the day was bright and sunny, each time even the gentlest of breezes was felt, it was a vivid reminder that winter was still in full swing.

Yet to announce his retirement, Young was blasted with perpetual questions of his intentions about baseball by nearly everyone who attended. The relentless leader of the onslaught of the badgering was McKinzie Young.

"Denton, you have done all you could in baseball, and besides, it is a young man's profession. Time to give it up, son; you have a wife and new baby to take care of. Your focus should be on them," McKinzie chided his son.

"Dad, don't you think I know that? I just want to make sure the family is provided for."

"Son, your mom and I have made it many years with less than you have already. Your priority is your family!"

"I know, dad, I know. That little girl just tugs at your heartstrings, doesn't she?"

"Yes, she's quite the little angel. Son, you should be proud. I am certain that once you give up baseball and you're here full time, you'll have a few more children. Robba's healthy and strong."

"Dad, let's get back to the festivities, we'll talk of this later, Okay..."

As the winter nights turned ever longer and darker, consternation grew inside the Young farmhouse. Without any warning, the baby suddenly stopped suckling from Robba's breast. The baby girl struggled to put on weight, and the pain from severe colic increased, causing a never-ending cacophony of wailing from the feeble infant. Any relief for the parents came when, from pure exhaustion, the baby fell asleep and the crying ceased, at least momentarily. Cy, in an effort to comfort the struggling child, helplessly cradled her in his arms for hour upon hour, withstanding not only the piercing cries for help but also the sharp ache which had developed in his shoulder. Each was relentless. A Doc Brandt visit to the Youngs' home had become a daily event, but everyone was equally unsuccessful in their attempts to bring the child some relief.

"Maybe we should take her to Columbus, to the new medical hospital at the University there. Doc Brandt just doesn't seem to be helping her,"

"Robba, the Doc said it isn't uncommon. Once the colic is gone, she will get back to normal."

"We can get in the car and be in Columbus before the morning."

"Robba, she'll be fine."

"Denton, I'm scared. When will her bout with this colic end?"

"There is nothing to worry about. My mom says I was the same way. The Doc will be here again at the end of the week and she'll be fine. She's been quiet today and resting better."

At 8:30PM, Young and Robba headed off to their bedroom for what they hoped would finally be a quiet night. It had been nearly a month since the crying had started and only today had there been any sustained respite. The house was peaceful at last, but strangely so. The large snowflakes blanketing the ground added to the scene's tranquility. The beleaguered couple easily drifted away into an unconsciousness of sleep as did the suddenly tranquil and completely exhausted child.

Young stirred a few minutes after 1:00 A.M, raising his head from the pillow. Thinking he may have heard the faint cries of the child, he sat up for a moment, carefully listening. He heard no further sounds. *Please God, one night of rest for all of us, please.* Young placed his head back on the pillow, listening intently for further cries, but to his relief, none came. He closed his eyes and escaped back to the comfort and solitude of his dream world.

In 1907, the Americans made a significant decision, moving preseason training to Little Rock, Arkansas, where it would remain for the next two years. Travel to Little Rock was much more difficult than the previous southern locations.

The Boston Americans began a spring training ritual began in 1901 that would last for decades. In early March, every Boston Americans player would assemble at Boston's historic South Station. United the team would trek to spring training.

On the short walk from the terminal, across the elevated footbridge to the covered platform, the players were greeted with a cruel reminder of winter's fury as remnants of passing Nor'easters would bite against their exposed skin. The under-ventilated roofs trapped both steam and smoke, adding a haze to the already eerie scene. From the platform, the team boarded a train heading for spring training. The first training site was located in Charlottesville, Virginia. The first complete game recorded for the newly organized Boston franchise was a 13-0 victory over the University of Virginia.

During the next five seasons, the team selected the state of Georgia for its preseason training. After completing their first season, the Americans picked Augusta, Georgia, for their 1902 preseason headquarters. The following season, the team shifted their training camp to Macon, Georgia. The 1903 Boston Americans won the World Series, and then, being superstitious, the team elected to remain in Macon for spring training through 1906.

For Young, the camaraderie with the other players softened the loneliness he felt when leaving Robba and the comfort of having family nearby, which made the time on the uncomfortable journey pass a bit more quickly. However, in March of 1907, Young did not travel to Boston to join his teammates at the train station. He remained in Peoli with Robba as long as he could, not leaving until the last possible moment. The soliloquy of Young's twenty-four-hour journey to Little Rock began with Young and Robba silently packing what he needed into their 1906 Harrison Model B touring car. After the brief goodbye, Young motored along the dirt road for nearly 60 miles across the middle of Ohio to the state capitol. From here, Young boarded the train heading south to Cincinnati and on into Memphis. From Memphis, Young would catch yet another train, "The Rock," the Chicago and Rock Island Railroad Company's finest and swiftest passenger train, reaching his final destination and rejoining his teammates.

For the 1907 season, Young's determination was driven by different events. He was ready to drop baseball, work his farm, grow his family with Robba and remain firmly entrenched in Peoli for the rest of his life. On that cold January night, baby girl Young had lost her battle. Less than one month after gathering in happy celebration of the birth, the family gathered once again, this time to lay the tiny infant to rest in the family cemetery on the grounds of McKinzie Young's farm. Complications from the 'easy birth' would cause Robba to become infertile, extinguishing Young's lingering dream of a family. Robba and Young vowed never to speak aloud about the birth and immediate loss of their child nor their desires to have more children. The mere mention of either would create a hard-to-dismiss, painful recollection. They would instead remain dedicated to the happiness each brought to the other and the joy they would have through their nieces and nephews. Although separation now would create more loneliness than at any other time in their lives, Robba urged the Cyclone to return to baseball.

Young now needed to remake himself to have any future success in the game. His overpowering fastball was literally gone. The fear it had instilled was now a fading memory for hitters. His focus for any makeover would be in mastering balls which moved: a slow curve, a drop and a screwball (a pitch that broke back towards right handed batters). Young rebounded with back-to-back 21-win seasons in 1907 and 1908. He tossed his third career no-hitter on June 30th, 1908, finishing second in the league in complete games with an astounding 30, fourth in wins and second in ERA with a spectacular 1.26. Despite of all his efforts, though, the Boston Red Sox, the now-official name for the franchise, could not manage to win more games than they lost, completing the season with 75 wins and 79 losses.

Ed Walsh and Addie Joss were clearly the two best pitchers in the American League, but at 41 years old, Young was not very far behind. Before the final curtain would go down on his career, Young would win nearly 200 games after the age of 35, a remarkable feat in any era. However, he would never again pitch in the World Series.

On February 18, 1909, Cy Young was traded to the Cleveland Naps for Charlie Chech, Jack Ryan (who would have a combined 27 wins between them in their career) and $12,500 in cash,. The Naps narrowly missed earning a World Series berth, finishing half a game behind the Tigers in 1908. They believed that the powerful pitching combination of Joss and Young would be enough to propel them to a pennant. Unfortunately, fate had another plan in mind. Although the re-mastered Young was somewhat effective, Addie Joss began to inexplicably fade. Unknown to anyone at the time, Joss was suffering from the early stages of the effects of tubercular meningitis, the disease which not only abruptly cut his career short but would take his life within the next year.

During the 1910 baseball campaign, the Cleveland newspapers began to report that Young was struggling on the mound. Two factors impacted Young's ability to win more games. First, his problems on the hummock did not stem from his arm strength or ability to deliver effectively a baseball. Young's once lean and muscular athletic body was betrayed by the years. Every off-season since 1904, Young gained weight at an alarming rate, nearly 10 pounds a year. When he reported to spring training in February 1910, Young tipped the scales at 260 pounds. His once-lean frame had been transformed into a beer keg on legs. He still possessed skill and pitching savvy, but running and bending to field ground balls was becoming more difficult every day. Hitters changed their tactics when facing Young. On days when Young could overwhelm batters with his command of the pitches, bunting became the hitting weapon of choice. No longer graceful, Young was unable to chase down even the most routine of balls hit relatively close to him. When he did make a play, there was a fair chance he would stumble. If, with a runner on third, the ball escaped the Naps catcher, the runner could just about walk home. The lumbering Young was now too slow to beat even the least swift of runners to the plate. The Naps lineup had become anemic. On several occasions, they failed to score a single run during a game pitched by "Old Cyrus," now his common nickname.

The American League was peppered with new darlings of the game. Christy Mathewson had just won his 250th game; many of the beat reporters believed he would one day pass the "ancient one' in victories. The New York Times touted the Yankees most promising young prospect, Russell Ford, and he possessed all of the pitches of the day. On July 14, 1910, the future and the past were set to square off in New York's historic Washington Heights at Hilltop Park. Washington Heights is the highest point on the island of Manhattan. Hilltop Park had become the home of the Highlanders in 1903 and had hosted two historical outings. Two years earlier, on June 30, Young threw the last of his three no-hitters. Then just two months later, in a weekend series with the hometown New York club, Walter Johnson hurled 27 impressive shutout innings over four days. At that time, New York City 'blue laws' prevented the playing of games on Sunday.

Today a personal milestone for Young was at stake. If he prevailed against New York, that would give Young his 500th win. *Five hundred wins and I will retire after this season,* Young ruminated.

The Yankees team was comprised of relative baseball youngsters at nearly every position, many of whom were probably still being irritated by their diaper pins when Cy pitched in his first professional game. Ford, the rising star, kept the hapless Naps off-balance the entire day. His only mistake was yielding a solo run in the bottom of the first, primarily the result of his errant throw on a routine grounder. The Yankees rarely caught up with Young's assortment of off-speed offerings and pinpoint accuracy, but when they did, they drove the ball long and hard. However, Young was done in a single half-inning, the fourth, a fielding error and wild pitch putting across the final runs in Cleveland's 4-1 loss. Although Young was not successful, the hometown crowd of nearly 7,000 wildly cheered him at the game's conclusion. The blaze of his flamethrower-like right arm now clearly gone, the crafty old man matched his young adversary for most of the afternoon.

The next day, the New York Times described the Washington Heights scene as a crowd filled mostly with grey-headed folks urging on Cyrus Young to beat these brash baseball newcomers who were out to set the world on fire. These fans had seen it all before, but they were here to cheer on the big man with the magnificent record. The zip to his fastball had been eroded by time, and the magical twists of his curves and drops were not nearly as magical any longer. The crowd knew the odds were long, but each person in the crowd knew Cy could size up his enemy and cut them to ribbons. The New York fans remembered him in his heyday and they acknowledged a true gentleman of the game, as gracious in defeat as he was humble in victory, a valiant warrior with no more battles to fight. The article added, "If the old man is to gain a 500th win, it will need to be against an inferior team to the Yankees."

The New York Times had steadfastly refused to refer to the New York baseball team as the Highlanders, tagging the nickname 'Yankees' on them since their move to the Washington Heights location. The Times claimed this was meant out of respect for playing on a site which was steeped in Revolutionary War significance.

On July 24, 1910, Cy Young did face an inferior team and recorded his 500th major league win in a masterful 11-inning performance against the Washington baseball club. It was his third win of the year. Young toiled, mostly ineffectively, through the next two months but would manage four more victories.

Reporters gathered round him at the end of season. He was besieged with questions about his future, speculations that the Naps were going to send him to the minor leagues, concerns that he could not keep up with the younger, faster players.

"Gentleman, please. I have at least three more good years left. I can get to five hundred and fifty wins, I am pretty sure of that," Cy advised his audience. "I just need to take a little better care of myself this winter and maybe not eat so much of Robba's wonderful home-cooked meals. I'll knock a few pounds down. I *will* keep up with the young ones. Five hundred and fifty wins and I will be done. This is a total so large that it will take someone with mythical talents to surpass it."

The offseason was no kinder to Cy as his weight continued to balloon. By July 29, 1911, Young had appeared in his last game as a Cleveland Nap, struggling the entire season. On August 14th,

Deacon McGuire and Charlie Somers invited Young into the owner's office.

"Cy, I'll come right to the point," Somers began "We're sending you to the minors so you can shed a few pounds and then see if you have anything left. Your arm is just not doing what it is supposed to. You know, getting hitters out."

"Sir, Deacon knows I can still pitch. Don't you, Deacon?"

"Sorry, Cy, you're done. Got to go with fresh talent," Deacon responded.

"I am sorry to have to say," Young continued, "that I will not accept a demotion to the minors."

"I understand how you must feel, but a demotion to the minors is in the best interests of everyone," Somers replied, "There is no more to be said."

Young turned to walk out of the office and in a muffled voice, said, "Mr. Somers, I am not going to the minors."

The next day, Young was released unconditionally by the Naps. Five days later, he was on the mound for the Boston Nationals, informally called the Rustlers, returning to the city that was the site of many of his triumphs. Briefly rejuvenated by the change of scenery, Young won three of his first five games with the Nationals before faltering badly. On September 22, 1911, Young hurled a five-hit shutout against the Pirates notching, his 511th career win.

On Friday, October 6th, in the second game of a double-header, Young hoped he could repeat the magic of his previous game against Pittsburg as the Nationals travelled to Brooklyn to face the Trolley Dodgers. The nickname had been adopted by franchise owners in the 1911 and 1912 seasons to honor the citizens of the New York City Borough who had to duck and weave in order to avoid the many trolleys car lines that crisscrossed the Brooklyn Streets. Residents of the once-proud city of Brooklyn had seen their identity diminished when Brooklyn was annexed by New York City on New Year's Day, 1898. Throughout the succeeding decades, the Brooklyn faithful would remain proud of two things they could call their own, the Brooklyn Bridge and their beloved Brooklyn baseball team. Unrelenting and critical newspaper reports had sarcastically tagged the team with the nickname the Bridegrooms (meaning never a bride) — unfortunately because of the team's penchant for finishing second. In reality, the six players were married in 1885, and in honor of those unions and a new ball park in Washington Park, the team was christened with that name which had stuck until a merger with the Baltimore team in 1899. Ned Hanlon, the then-owner/manager of Baltimore, suggested the name Superbas, after a popular traveling vaudeville troupe named Hanlon's Superbas (though he had no relation to the troupe). The Brooklyn populace was in need of an identity and for no other reason, had a complete and abject disdain for the opponents of the Trolley Dodgers.

A chorus of boos and expletives greeted the 44-year-old 'Old Cyrus' as he lumbered slowly to the mound of the ballpark in the Park Slope section of Brooklyn. The covered grandstands teemed with fans, although Brooklyn was 33 games behind the league leading, and despised, New York Giants who resided across the East River. Beyond the open outfield, thousands more stood to jeer the man with more victories than anyone could imagine. Each inning was a testament to the sheer willpower of the indomitable pitcher. Young, barely able to retrieve errant throws to the mound, somehow managed to make it through four painful frames.

During the forgettable 5th inning and 8 consecutive base hits, three doubles, a triple and four singles, Young was mercifully removed from the game, failing to record an out in the inning and yielding 13 runs for the game. The eighteen thousand fans cheered the effort of the rotund Young in what would turn out to be his final walk from the pitcher's mound in a professional baseball game. Young was humbled by the show of admiration; he had been pitching for twenty-two years, but he finally felt he was revered by the fans for his achievements.

On October 6th, 1911, in Baltimore, Maryland, an obnoxious, overstuffed left-handed pitcher who currently called a 'reform school' home had just retired the side for the ninth consecutive inning against a local rival Catholic High School team, St. Stephen the Martyr, completing an 8-0 perfect game. During the game, the rambunctious teenager also launched three balls into the creek just behind the right field fence. As he trotted around the bases on spindly legs, he tipped his cap to the wildly cheering crowd of all seventy-five students in attendance who happened to have nothing else to do that day, and with a grin from ear to ear he taunted his opponents.

Chapter 16

After the season, Young returned to Peoli, unhappy with how the season had ended. His aching right arm had worsened since the end of the season, even though he rested it daily. Convinced that a trip to John D. 'Bonesetter' Reese would rejuvenate his tired limb, he and Robba headed to Youngstown, Ohio.

John D. Reese was born 6 May, 1855, in Rhymney, Wales. He was taken in by an ironworker named Tom Jones, who taught him the trade of bone setting, a term Welshmen used for the manipulative treatment of muscle and tendon strains, not the setting of breaks. Reese remained under Jones' tutelage until he left for the United States in 1887. In this country, he became a renowned healer and trainer in the early 20th-century, one who was known for his ability to get injured athletes 'back in the game' and get injured actors back on the stage. Although he gained wide visibility as the nation's 'baseball doctor,' Reese reportedly 'drew no line between rich and poor patients.'

Reese enrolled at Case University medical school, but left after only three weeks before completing any formal studies, to pursue alternative medicine and complementary healing practices. During his long career, Reese delivered alternative medical care to a clientele that included industrial workers, celebrity athletes and heads of state. His work brought him considerable recognition within the Welsh-American community during his later years. At the time of his death in 1931, Reese was regarded as a national figure and his passing was marked by the *New York Times*, which printed a detailed obituary.

By the 1920s, Reese was a national phenomenon. In 1923 Time magazine wrote: "His deft fingers developed Reese into an outstanding and nationally famed expert at rehabilitating errant bones." His eclectic group of patients included all-time baseball greats such as Cy Young, Ty Cobb, Rogers Hornsby, Walter Johnson and John McGraw. Reese's viewed his involvement with baseball players as a sideline. He preferred baseball players but worked with other athletes. The primary focus of his practice was treating his one-time colleagues, the mill workers of Youngstown. Reese's unique ability to manipulate muscles and ligaments put working men and ballplayers alike back to work, giving him the reputation of a miracle worker in some circles.

Reese's growing celebrity never distracted him from the essentially humanitarian nature of his vocation. His compassionate and egalitarian approach to medical care was conveyed in a brief article that appeared in a local newspaper about a year before his death. The article stated: 'Athletes, theatrical people, rich men, poor men, bakermen, and no, not thieves, but others in all walks of life have made their way to the home of John D. Reese to have him lay his healing hands on their broken bodies and restore them to health and usefulness.'

But Reese also had a darker side, and he may have facilitated the first known use of performance-enhancing drugs in baseball. In the mid-1890's, Bonesetter began dabbling in Ayurveda medicine. This is a system of traditional medicines and elixirs native to the subcontinent of India practiced in parts of the eastern world. One such compound was the "elixir of Brown-Sequard." This was essentially a sweetened, aromatic solution of alcohol and water containing testosterone drained from the gonads of an animal. Pud Galvin, after losing several games in a row, found youthfulness return to his tired arm after using Brown-Sequard.

Young had twice before visited 'Bonesetter,' and each time the results produced 'comeback performances,' after the 1900 season and again after the 1906 season. Each time, Young was believed washed up with the help of Bonesetter he bounced back strong. Reese's combination of acupuncture, herbalism, chiropractic, nutritional supplements and homeopathy got him back on track. The rehabilitation programs worked like magic.

"Denton, do you think that Doctor Reese can help you again this time?" Robba prodded her husband. "You're closing in on 50, there, Denton. You know, you're not a spring chicken," she chuckled.

"I am not yet 45, darling, and you're not a spring chicken any more, either." The couple roared in unison.

Robba knew how stubborn Young could be and that he truly believed he could pitch a few more years at least, but she, more than anyone, could see how he had changed physically. He was no longer able to control his weight. Routine chores around the farm were increasingly difficult for him. She would coax her strapping young nephews and a few of their friends to help the 'old man' get a few things done around the farm. Once he could bale hay all day, but now, after a few painful minutes, he needed to rest. In her heart, she hoped Young would accept the inevitable. Baseball is a young man's game, and the time had come when he needed to leave it for them. She hoped he would walk away before he was embarrassed by the ruthless owners or worse, severely injured. She was leery and concerned about the crazy concoction Brown-Sequard that Young would be ingesting. Drinking a mixture that included testosterone from a monkey just didn't seem smart.

"Good luck, Denton," said Robba as she stretched to wrap her arms around the neck of her husband in an embrace which lasted longer than any either could remember for any of his previous departures for spring training.

"Robba, everything will be fine," he said. Reaching for her hand, he placed in it a brown pint bottle that had no label. "I know you were worried about it. I just couldn't bring myself to drink this stuff."

"Thank you, Denton, and Godspeed."

Young arrived in Hot Springs, Arkansas, on March 1, 1912, only slightly energized after three weeks under Bonesetter's care. Maybe if he had taken Reese's magical potion, he would have seen significant improvement. Young had met with Johnny Kling, manager of the now-renamed Boston Braves. No promises were made for a spot on the roster. Kling outlined several conditions which, if met, would earn him a roster spot, but the conversation included no guarantees for a regular spot in the starting rotation. First, Young would need to get his weight down. Second, he would need to have effective and decent showings in the pre-season games. And, third, he would need to accept delegation to the bullpen until called on to start. Only after these conditions were met would Young be given a place on the team. Otherwise he would be sent to the minor leagues and have to work his way back up from there. Although Young agreed, he knew he would not accept an assignment to the minors. If they sent him down, he would just walk away from the game.

After several weeks of hard work trying to get himself into playing condition, Kling and Young agreed that he just did not have anything left.

The New York Times headline on March 15, 1912, was succinct, simply to the point.

'Young Quits Baseball- Famous Pitcher too Fat and too Old to be Useful to the Game any Longer'

The gallant effort just did not produce the results he needed. The younger, more athletic players added to Cy's discouragement, but he came to grips with the reality that all of his baseball skills had eroded one day at a time. His playing days were over. However, he had amassed a small fortune and could go back to his agricultural interests and his love in Peoli. Once there, though, it would not take Young very long to realize that he was not much of a farmer. Soon after, he came to understand that he was not an astute businessman, either.

"Ballplayers do not have much business sense," he commented to other members of his church congregation after Sunday services. "I guess we just go on for too many years, being told what to do by the manager and following the rules of baseball to have any business sense when we are done with baseball. Fortunately, I have enough money from baseball for me to live comfortably the rest of my life."

Retirement in Peoli would not be kind to Young and Robba. The old guard of both the Young and Miller families began to pass away, slowly but steadily. Young and Robba began to hunt and breed dogs more than he tended to the needs of the farm. Following Young in another of his father's paths, Young became a Mason and quickly climbed up several degrees. Folks of Peoli began to refer to him as the gentleman farmer. He would always warmly welcome visitors into his home. Mementos of his playing days were prominently displayed in the living room. For anyone who would listen, he provided in careful detail what each meant to him. There was the trophy commemorating his 500th victory and baseballs from his Temple Cup and World Series triumphs. Young had slipped gracefully from baseball legend to model citizen of Tuscarawas County.

Quickly becoming bored with the unfulfilling regimen of retirement, Young began travelling to the major league baseball cities to see some of the games and catch up with his old pals. During his stint with the Spiders, Young had befriended a local Cleveland entrepreneur, Davis Hawley, who was also serving as the Secretary of the Spiders at the time. It was Hawley who had refused Cap Anson's offer of $1000 to buy Young for the Chicago Colts in 1890. From that day on, he and Hawley remained friends. Hawley had built several hotels, including Hawley House, which he sold to his brother so he could start the Cuyahoga Savings and Loan Company. The pair could not have been more of a mismatch. Young was a farm boy who spoke very few words and whose use of descriptive adjectives was limited. He enjoyed life's simple pleasures as God-given. Hawley, in contrast, had mastered the art of effusive gab. When asked what he was wearing to dinner that evening, Young's response was a brown or black suit, shirt and a tie. Hawley, on the other hand, if complimented about his dinner wear, would elegantly present the excruciating detail on each element of his attire. A suit was transformed into melodic chronicle from the lineage of the wool to the training of the tailors. The tales that Young had to offer spoke of him practicing his fast ball by tossing walnuts against the barn door and in spring and summer, waking, leaving the house at 5:00AM to walk 20 miles to play in a baseball game and then returning home in time for supper. What his stories lacked in color and imagination, they made up for in his down-home honesty.

"Cy, the fabric of this suit is 100% pure cashmere, from the fibers of cross-bred Tibetan and Tartary goats imported from China, spun and de-haired in the Blackstone Valley. My tailor, Fedele 'Fedie' Cicco, came to the US in 1910. He trained in the art of custom tailoring in Milan under the finest Italian tailors. He is attentive to every measurement and stitch. Yes, notice the stitching, the tightness in the lining to the fabric. The cut-line of the sleeves is perfectly straight. The lining is made of pure silk. The supplier says this silk fabric is directly descended from silkworms from the Chinese Goddess of Silk, the Lady Hsi-Ling-Shih."

Young knew baseball. He knew how to make a ball move in different directions. He also knew some about farming, hunting and fishing, but he did not know a silkworm from a bloodworm or what the thread count should be in his cotton shirt. Young was a good listener, and he could listen to Hawley talk for hours. When allowed the chance, Hawley would do just that. Any subject of the day, he could command with authority, from United States politics and the economy to sports.

Hawley had been trying to convince the conservative Young to start investing his money; simply keeping it in a bank was not a smart financial strategy. Young resisted both the enticing temptations and risks of investment over several of their occasional lunches.

"Cy, business in this country is going to really explode next year. That democrat Wilson has a real shot at taking the presidential election. He's got very progressive ideas. If he is elected, there will be an end to corruption and monopolies. Government will help ensure that the concept of free enterprise is successful."

In the early years of American history, most political leaders were reluctant to involve the federal government too heavily in the private sector. In general, they accepted the concept of laissez-faire, a doctrine opposing government interference in the economy except to maintain law and order. This attitude started to change during the latter part of the 19th century, when small business, farm and labor movements began asking the government to intercede on their behalf. By the turn of the century, a middle class had developed that was leery of both the business elite and the somewhat radical political movements of farmers and laborers in the Midwest and West. Known as Progressives, these people favored government regulation of business practices to, in their minds, ensure competition and free enterprise. Congress enacted a law regulating railroads in 1887 and one preventing large firms from controlling a single industry in 1890. These laws were not rigorously enforced, however, until between 1900 and 1920, when Republican President Theodore Roosevelt (1901–1909), Democratic President Woodrow Wilson (1913–1921), and others sympathetic to the views of the Progressives came to power. Wilson, in his first term, used tariffs, anti-trust, currency control and taxes to successfully prime the pump of the US economy.

"I expect cities to grow dramatically; people will travel more as getting around the country gets easier. Better railroads, heck, I understand Henry Ford is very close to being able to mass-produce his Model T. Think about it, Cy, there will be a great many new hotels, grand hotels, that will be built across the country. I'm raising money to start an encaustic tile company in Ohio. I think you will triple, maybe quadruple, your money in 5 years. These will be wildly lavish hotels. Each one will have an enormous lobby, suites with multiple bedrooms, bathrooms and Turkish baths all needing uniquely designed tile floors. We will provide the tile. Fedie Cicco, he is originally from Calabria, Italy, have I mentioned that? He thinks that with the tariffs on imports the new administration will levy, everyone will buy American rather than the very expensive Italian marble."

Hawley generated a great deal of passion when he told of his vision to capitalize on the next tsunami of economic growth. His conviction about the business finally broke Cy's resistance and he agreed to invest a little more than half of his life savings into the venture.

Hawley's analysis was right on many fronts. In the next decade many glorious hotels, with magnificent lobbies, foyers and steam rooms were built in the major cities including several in downtown Cleveland. Ford did introduce the assembly line in 1913, and cars rolled out of the factory in record numbers. Automobile and rail travel did continue to improve and the general population took a big interest in travelling within the country.

However, there were several factors Hawley did not anticipate. He invested in a company using older methods of manufacturing the tiles. Competitors produced tiles with more distinctive quality in the colors, more details to the patterns and designs, and more resilient to wear and tear. That was a minor problem. Improvements in manufacturing technology served to reduce kiln drying time from seventy hours to two, and that was an insurmountable competitive advantage. Further, architects, investors and owners of these fabulous hotels did not mind spending the money on imported granite. Each wanted entrance and foyers which made a statement and impression.

A scant two years later, on January 1, 1914, the Great Lakes Tile Company of Barberton, Ohio closed its doors forever. Each individual investor and several Cleveland banks which had loaned money to Great Lakes Tiles would receive no return, their investment gone.

Cy Young's small fortune became smaller. Once again, Cy Young would turn to baseball to make a living.

Chapter 17
Massachusetts 1914

As recalcitrant and incorrigible as Ruth was, he was nonetheless troubled when reprimanded for his actions. Providence, Rhode Island is forty-one miles from Boston, but it was a slow, lonely trip for the 19-year-old Ruth. As much trouble as he was for Boston management and the veteran players, he was turned out from his baseball family. The ramifications of his actions troubled him deeply, but what troubled him more was the failure of his new teammates to accept him.

Exiting the ball park from the doors on Brookline Avenue, a dejected Ruth, the entirety of his earthly belongings in hand, began the nearly mile-long journey from Fenway Park to the Back Bay Station.

Fenway Park, opened three years earlier, was constructed on reclaimed marsh and swamp lands with low acidic content, "fens," on an odd-shaped land parcel which most believed lacked any real value. John I. Taylor, owner of both the Boston franchise and Fenway Realty Company, thought the name chosen for his ballpark would help his other businesses.

Glancing back at the two-story brick structure, while taking a deep heaving breath, Ruth wondered if he would ever set foot back in a major league stadium. The American flag atop the entrance sign 'Fenway Park' stood stiff. A late-day thunderstorm quickly approached the city. In no hurry, Ruth welcomed the relief and distraction provided by the cool, sudden downpour. He would make one more stop before leaving town, most likely for good.

Lander's Coffee Shop was located on Dartmouth Street, across from the train station. Just weeks earlier, he and Ernie Shore had set foot from the train station onto the Boston Streets for the first time. Peering from the glare of the midmorning sun, Ruth caught site of the glass windows with the large stenciled printing 'Diner Good Food.' He told Shore he was hungry and needed to eat. Sitting at a table next to the windows, Ruth ordered ham and eggs with coffee. A speechless 16-year-old slender waitress stood with pencil and pad in hand as he clarified the order, "That is an order for seven ham-and-egg breakfasts, one for my good friend here and the rest for me." She was even more dumbfounded when the gregarious teen finished his meal. She and Ruth made small talk and exchanged some laughs. She had never seen anyone with quite this appetite in the four months she had worked at Lander's.

Ruth would become a frequent visitor to Lander's during his five-week tenure with Boston. He confided in the waitress about his loneliness and not being accepted by the veteran players. They would make fun of him and call him names every chance they had. He knew they resented him because he was more talented in every way than any of the players on the team and if given the chance he would show them. Ruth, as a manager, would not tolerate such nonsense. No, he would be a true leader, no letting humiliation of young players run so rampant. Under his leadership, teammates would pull together and win. He would win more games as a manager than anyone before him had done. Given the chance, he would do more with his arm, bat, glove and mind than had ever been seen.

She, in turn, would tell Ruth that he needed to control his temper and bide his time. Eventually he would shine. Ruth said he knew only one way to do things, to fight for his place. If they were mean to him, he would just give it right back.

The soft-hearted waitress soon became his best and probably only friend in Boston during the summer of 1914. Glancing out through the front windows she saw the recognizable figure approaching the restaurant, seemingly not at all bothered by the heavy rain shower. The clothes were hanging from the familiar silhouette like a clump of limp noodles on a spoon.

Water raced down from the brim of his once-tan hat, now dark brown from the drenching. Ruth pushed open the door to the coffee shop with his foot just as the demure waitress arrived at the entrance. He proceeded to his favorite table that looked out onto Dartmouth Street, with rain dimpling the abundant puddles.

"Helen, the usual, please. I am going away on a trip. Maybe even for good." He handed her a wet, crumpled $20 bill. In exchange, she handed him a warm dry towel. To the cook she called, "Jake, incoming order: six cheese burgers, three fries and two chocolate shakes." She knew what the usual late-day meal was for this young giant, but she also knew when something was wrong. She had become very fond of him in the brief time since they first met.

"Going one way to Providence, dear," Ruth said in response to her question. "Thanks for the towel."

Pulling up a chair, Helen asks, "Tell me what happened, George."

Ruth recanted the events of the day, regretting that he did not heed her advice and hold his temper. She provided comfort to the gentle giant, got him dried off and well fed. She also provided reassurance that he would return to the Boston Red Sox and accomplish amazingly wonderful things on the baseball field.

"Just like the storm of today, this storm of yours will pass. You'll be back here by the spring and you will never look back."

"Helen, whether I come back to the Red Sox or not, I will come back for you." Ruth eased himself from his seat onto one knee and softly caressed her hand. "Helen, will you marry me?"

Although the pair had been dating little more than two months, she hardly knew anything about him, except that he very much wanted what she wanted: a family life. She accepted.

With just the comfort of knowing Helen had consented to become his wife, Ruth left for Providence with more confidence than he had felt just a few hours earlier.

Ruth's August 20 debut for the second-place Grays included the type of drama he would soon be enjoying on a regular basis. Pitching before an overflow crowd of 12,000 — then the largest ever to see a baseball game in Rhode Island — he earned a 5-4 victory and helped his own cause by tripling twice.

This performance was the springboard to a pennant for Providence, with Ruth going 9-2 in less than a month's work. Recalled to the Red Sox for the final week of the season, he drew a start from Carrigan and gained his first of many victories (along with his first major-league hit, a single) against the hapless New York Yankees.

Nobody in Boston really noticed. Up the street from Fenway, the 'Miracle' Braves were completing a last-to-first climb up the standings that would culminate in a World Series sweep of Connie Mack's mighty Philadelphia Athletics.

****

On October 17, 1914, another important event in Ruth's life would go unnoticed. Ellicott City, Maryland is a small village, approximately 10 miles southwest of Baltimore, on the banks of the Patapsco River. It sits in a small valley surrounded by several hills, and in the fall, this setting provides a cornucopia of colors from the trees densely covering the hills. St. Paul's Catholic Church, dedicated on September 13, 1838, was the only Catholic Church between Baltimore and Frederick. The exterior of the church was gray granite from a local quarry. The interior had been upgraded at the conclusion of the Civil War from the original plain, simple interior to frescoed walls, a Scottish marble altar flanked by carved wooden angels, a silver crucifix and elaborate German silver chandeliers, a tabernacle in white marble and a brass door. Other additions included tinting the glass windows and two marble side altars. In 1896, the steeple, topped by a Celtic cross, was added.

At this hidden jewel of a church in the sleepy town there was excitement, at least for the fifty or so people in attendance. The local son, the rebellious teenage George Herman Ruth, was to be married to Helen Woodford.

Helen had spent most of her life in South Boston with her parents, who had emigrated from Newfoundland to the States to find work. Her humble beginnings rivaled Ruth's, except that her family life was stable. At the age of 13, without completing an eighth grade education, she began working to help with family expenses. Because of her lack of any other skills, she began waitressing, bouncing from one sleazy coffee shop to the next. As a young attractive girl without any attachment, she had to become adroit in the ability to fend off unwanted advances. She had left a job at the Waterfront Diner because the dockworkers pursued her relentlessly. The last incident ended in a brawl when a brawny merchant shipman, rebuffed by Helen, became physical, nearly tearing the left sleeve of her dress off. Fortunately, two gentlemanly sailors on leave from a Navy ship docked in the harbor came to her aid. Fisticuffs ensued, which left the merchant shipman down for an extended nap. In utter contrast, although starved for affection and attention, Ruth was always kind and attentive to her and never physically forceful.

Helen considered Ruth quite the catch; he looked at her in much the same way.

Ruth's father declined to attend the ceremony, as did Jack Dunn, both most likely thanking their lucky stars that Ruth was now someone else's problem.

Chapter 18

In 1541, Spanish explorer Hernando de Soto, the discoverer of the Mississippi River, was the first white person to visit the 'Valley of the Vapors,' as the Ouachita Tribe called the area. De Soto and his conquistadors lingered for several months, enjoying the rejuvenating waters of the warm, mineral-laden springs. To de Soto's surprise, the springs were 'neutral ground' where the loosely affiliated tribes of the Caddo Confederacy and other tribes local to the Mississippi Valley, including the Tula, who had had brutal and bloody battles with the Spaniards, would gather in peace to enjoy nature's bounty. So peaceful were the tribes when in Hot Springs that a Caddo spiritual chieftain presented a maiden to de Soto as gift for the pale strangers in this strange new land as the explorers readied for their departure.

For centuries, warring tribes honored the long-standing tradition of peaceful coexistence when in the Valley, even when it meant watching your enemy recuperate. Three hundred fifty-four years later, the harmony was broken.

During 1803, Thomas Jefferson commissioned the first US exploration into this area of the recently-completed Louisiana Purchase upon hearing of a peaceful healing center from his friend William Dunbar from Natchez, Mississippi. Dunbar, a chemist, George Hunter and a dozen soldiers set out in December of 1804. The first white settlers began arriving in 1807, led by Jean Pierre Emanuel Prudhomme, the ailing owner of a

Red River plantation who had heard about the healing hot waters from the Natchitoches Indians. He built the first permanent settlement at the springs and lived there for two years. Isaac Cates and John Percifull, two trappers from Alabama, joined him there. Cates remained a trapper, but Percival envisioned a great future for the springs. In 1809, Percifull, the enterprising young frontiersman, began renting rooms to visitors captivated by the water's curative powers. By 1832, others such as Ludovicus Belding set up boarding houses for visitors coming to enjoy the healing waters. In 1832, President Andrew Jackson made Hot Springs the first Federal Reservation in the area surrounding the city of Hot Springs, in an effort to conserve its natural resources. It was the first piece of America protected for future generations, becoming America's first national park. This action sparked a lawsuit between the original landowners and the US Government that went on for nearly five decades.

The outbreak of the Civil War left Hot Springs with a declining bathing population. After the Confederate forces suffered a devastating defeat in the Battle of Pea Ridge, in March 1862, a march on Little Rock was inevitable. The Union troops stood poised to advance on the Confederate stronghold. Confederate Governor Henry M. Rector decided to move his staff and state records to Hot Springs. Union forces under Major General Frederick Steele watched the Confederates retreat as Major General Sterling Price maneuvered his remaining Confederate troops out of the Arkansas capital, thus returning Little Rock to Federal control in 1863 and giving the Union effective control of the strategically important Arkansas River Valley. Steele decided to follow the weary rebel forces that had suffered heavy casualties to Hot Springs with the intention of finishing his assault, following the orders of President Lincoln to punish the rebels dearly. Poised for an attack, Steele watched as the unsuspecting soldiers of the Confederacy bathed in the warm baths, trying to recover. Rather than mercilessly unleash an attack, Steele rode into the town with a small contingent. The Union force began to enjoy the serenity and take a tiny respite from the taxing havoc of war. Towns surrounding Little Rock and those in the Eastern Theater were ransacked and brought to smoldering ruins by Union cavalry regiments; pastoral Hot Springs was spared.

After several weeks of rest, Steele's cavalry unit returned to Little Rock. By September 2, Union reinforcements and Arkansans opposed to secession had arrived, bringing the strength of Steele's army to around 15,000 men. He, too, turned his efforts to the east.

The thermal waters that give Hot Springs its name are one of nature's most bewildering phenomena. The springs are nestled in the central Ouachita Mountains along the forested southwestern slopes. There, the 47 hot springs gush forth nearly a million gallons of 143 degree water daily. These waters begin as rain water that is absorbed through crevices in the earth's surface. It is then warmed and mineral-enriched as it percolates deep underground, rising as temperature increases and eventually flowing back to the surface, laden with over 20 minerals.

The first bathhouses were basically tents erected on wooden poles and made from canvas. Eventually these were replaced by wooden buildings and log cabins, still shabbily constructed. During periods of heavy wind and rainstorms, they collapsed regularly, eroded from wood rot or burned down because of careless visitors. By the early 1900,'s the bathhouses that now lined 'Bathhouse Row' were exquisitely-built structures replete with marble, brass and stained-glass accents. Most housed state-of-the-art mechanotherapy machines, gymnasiums and beauty shops to help visitors seeking instant cures feel better about themselves.

By 1915, several major league clubs, including Boston, Chicago, Pittsburgh, Washington and Brooklyn made Hot Springs their spring training headquarters. Players, too, came for the peacefulness of the area and to use the springs to refresh their bodies in anticipation of the long, arduous baseball season to come. Although players were rivals on the field, friendships were renewed during preseason. The 'games' between the clubs were exhibitions and kept good- natured. Centuries of a tradition of tranquility and peace would disappear as a result of the arrival of one George Herman Ruth. Innocently enough he stepped down from the train in Hot Springs on March 1, 1915. Locked arm in arm with his unsuspecting newly-betrothed bride, only he knew the plan hidden behind his smile. The Fordyce Hotel and Bath was set for its grand opening. The building was a testimony to the rising popularity of the springs. The beige terracotta exterior and aquatic images had an inviting appeal. Welcoming guests were the elaborately detailed lobby, with its walls lined in veined Italian marble, pink marble staircases rising to the second floor, cherub fountains flanking the spacious room and ambient light streaming in from stained glass windows above every transom. Ruth and Helen became the first officially-registered guests.

The Fordyce featured the most modern of rooms for medicinal relief. There were men's baths and ladies' baths, but most important to Ruth's plan was the private men's vapor bath. This room, in addition to marble walls, tile floors and nickel-plated fixtures, had several shallow vapor tubs, each with a gradually-sloped walk-in ramp. In this private room, fashioned after the Roman tradition, men were required to wear a toga when lounging and be naked when they chose to enter one of the walk-in tubs. There were also small marble benches on which the men could relax. This room was part of a separate wing of the hotel completely private, apart from the ladies and men's general facilities. The door could be secured shut from either the inside of the bath or, most critical to Ruth's plan, the outside.

Ruth was not assured of a spot on the Red Sox major league roster when he arrived in Hot Springs. Ruth was fortunate and undoubtedly very lucky, although he did not realize how much. Baseball was once again in flux. He had joined the Red Sox at a very opportune time, at least financially. The establishment of another baseball league during 1914 and 1915 — the Federal League — had forced American and National League owners to pay higher salaries to keep rising star players from jumping ship. This practice did not necessarily hold true for the established stars of the game, who already commanded a higher salary, more than they knew the Federal League owners would be willing to pay. Siphoning the young talent, though, would erode the foundation for the future. Higher pay found its way down through the ranks, all the way to rookies and young players with talent, where a few dollars went a long way. To pay for increased salary of the youngsters, the owners would slash the compensation for the older and aging veterans. They also threatened lifetime bans if a veteran were to jump leagues. Although several players did make the leap, the ownership strategy eventually did the trick; the Federal League did not survive much past the end of 1915 season, and National and American league owners returned to their skinflint habits. This strategy benefitted Ruth directly because he was one of the most sought-after young talents.

In a move to protect their interests and forestall the inevitable, the owners of the Federal League had filed an antitrust lawsuit against the American and National Leagues in the Federal District Court of Northern Illinois, claiming collusion and monopolistic practices were used to drive the competing league bankrupt. John T. Powers, President of the Federal League, with the unanimous consent of the owners of the six teams, selected the venue presided over by Judge Kenesaw Mountain Landis.

Judge Landis was a powerful but enigmatic figure. He had been a star baseball player on the Logansport Indiana High School team and had a deep passion for the game. At age 17, he suddenly left school to work in the judicial system in South Bend. Upon earning his law degree in 1891 from Union Law School in Evanston, Illinois, he opened a law office in downtown Chicago, in the same ward once represented by the strong Chicago political boss, 'Honest' John Comiskey, father of Charles Comiskey. In 1910, Landis represented Charles Comiskey in a contentious real estate dispute after the White Sox abandoned South Side Park for the newly-built spacious Comiskey Stadium in the middle of the season.

For the hundreds of cases and clients he handled before being appointed to the Federal bench by Teddy Roosevelt in 1905, he showed a penchant for defending the rights of the oppressed. In 1907, he was the presiding judge over the Standard Oil antitrust trial. The giant oil conglomerate controlled all facets of the oil industry in an unchecked manner. Their dominant position in the market led to predatory pricing, hidden rebates, discrimination in distribution means, each action targeted towards the destruction of any competition. Landis, in an arrogant and headstrong decision, ordered the largest fine ever levied against a corporation, $29 million. Judge Landis, although a brilliant adjudicator, made several critical errors during the trial. Two years later, his decision was set aside. Standard Oil was ultimately broken up after a suit was brought by the Justice Department under the Sherman Antitrust Act a few years later.

His father, when living in Georgia, fought for the Union and was a strong abolitionist. Judge Landis himself was not, however, a friend to the black man. For example, as he took on as a personal agenda the banishment of Jack Johnson from boxing for transporting a white woman over state lines for the purpose of prostitution. On October 18, 1912, Johnson was arrested on the grounds that his relationship with Lucille Cameron, although the couple was at the time engaged to be married, violated the Mann Act against 'transporting women across state lines for immoral purposes' due to her being a prostitute. Cameron, soon to become his second wife, refused to cooperate and the case fell apart. Less than a month later, Johnson was arrested again on similar charges. This time the woman, another prostitute named Belle Schreiber with whom he had been involved in 1909 and 1910, testified against him, and he was convicted by a jury in June, 1913. The presiding judge was Kenesaw Landis. The conviction made despite the fact that the incidents used to convict him took place prior to passage of the Mann Act and that the sole witness recanted an early testimony and was offered immunity on trumped-up solicitation charges. Landis issued the sentence of one year and a day in prison and relentlessly ensured he was prohibited from boxing ever again. Landis, the future commissioner of baseball, blocked blacks from being signed into the major leagues.

Had the Federal League owners selected another federal district, the outcome, and indeed the entire landscape of baseball might have been forever different. Landis proved again that he was a puzzle and no friend to the upstart little guys. Time was of the essence for the Federal League. Although the established leagues were independent rivals, their collective practice to drive salaries up was increasing the losses sustained by the Federal League. The league filed an emergency brief requesting an injunction to provide immediate relief. Landis refused to issue the restraining order, but he also let the lawsuit languish in his court for over a year. The failure of Landis to act quickly accelerated the league's bankruptcy after the 1915 season. When commenting on the decision of the Federal League to fold, Landis offered the following, "Well, they failed to make any profits, so what do you expect?" This was an interesting observation, given that the premise of the lawsuit was that the antics of the rival baseball leagues were in fact an effort to accomplish exactly that.

The failure of the Red Sox in 1914 to surpass the Athletics in the race for the pennant, finishing 8 ½ games behind, undoubtedly led to salary disputes in 1915. Lannin was furious and put the blame squarely on the shoulders of the team leaders, who would fight to avoid the severe pay cuts he was attempting to make. The Red Sox had some of the most celebrated players of the time. Tris Speaker was the team's centerpiece, the best all-around player in the game. Lannin offered a contract cutting Speaker's salary from $15,000 to $9,000. Although Speaker had refused to sign this contract, which he considered an insult, before the start of spring training as was customary at the time, he still decided to attend. Speaker made this decision even after Red Sox owner Joseph Lannin announced there was no negotiation and instructed Speaker that he could go play for the Brooklyn Tip Tops for all he cared. Lannin knew the Brooklyn team had offered Speaker only $8,000. The frail-armed Smokey Joe Wood, coming off a mediocre 1914 season, was offered a meager $5,000, slightly more than what Ruth would make. Throughout his career, he blamed Jack Stahl's overuse of him in 1908 for his chronic arm problems. Wood, who with very little market value lacked leverage, when threatened with release, caved in and decided to report to camp. Initially, he had planned on returning just before the start of the season, so he arrived in Arkansas on March 3. Lannin, not missing an opportunity for *harmony* with the players, inflamed the situation further by fining Wood $250 for missing the first two days of spring training.

The Boston players were very optimistic with their stars and young talent under wraps; after all, the fans and players believed the Red Sox were a team with championship potential, capable of finally overtaking the powerful Athletics.

Lannin did purchase a hard-hitting outfield prospect named Malcom 'Mal' Barry from Connie Mack's minor league franchise, the Jersey City Skeeters, as an insurance policy since Duffy Lewis, one of the infamous million-dollar-outfield trio of Speaker, Hooper and Lewis, was hurting.

Reflecting the times, everything would change next year. Shortly before spring training broke and the players were to head north, Speaker was sold abruptly to the Cleveland Indians for $50,000 and two unknown players. Fans in Boston were shocked and dismayed by the alarming news. Speaker brought in the largest amount ever paid for a player, but no one except Lannin cared about the money when the cost was a .345 lifetime hitter and the leader of the 1915 World Series champs. After a successful campaign in 1915, Wood demanded a significant pay raise. Instead, he was summarily released, effectively marking the end of Wood's baseball career. A year later, he joined his friend and roommate Speaker in Cleveland for an abbreviated stay.

The Red Sox was a team loaded with talent. Ruth offered something much different; he possessed the ability to play in multiple positions. He had a real chance, if only he could keep his nose clean. Not savvy enough to be aware of all the goings-on around baseball at the time, the naïve, immature Ruth arrived in spring training with a much different agenda, to seek revenge on those veterans who had showered him with constant humiliating insults that ultimately led to his being sent to Providence. Even if he had been forewarned and told to behave himself, the petulant man-child would not have been able to control himself.

Founded in 1902, the Alligator Farm and Petting Zoo owned by Jack Bridges was quickly becoming a standard attraction for the diehard baseball fans that had travelled from the north to watch and socialize with players from their hometown teams. Most had never seen an alligator up close and personal. The farm featured several alligators over sixteen feet in length. In 1906, one female visitor to the farm, an unthinking tourist, held the leash of her pet terrier a bit too loose while enthralled with the mass of gators in the "pit". The frisky black and white pup, agitated by the goings-on, jumped down and quickly edged its way under the lowest rail, roaming just a few feet towards the brown water, closer to the wooden fence than the single gator basking on the slope of the mud pit apart from the twenty or so other gators. In the blink of an eye and with the fury of hell, the reptile lunged and snatched the helpless pet with such force that the stunned owner's shoulder was nearly yanked from its socket. The hard-hearted and thoughtless Bridges mundanely commented, "That is one lucky alligator, strawberry shortcake in just one bite. That certainly beats a muskrat for dinner." Sally Curtain, the terrier's owner, stared blankly at the shredded end of the leash; now missing a dog, for a few moments, then fell to her knees, sobbing uncontrollably. To warn future visitors of the danger posed by these ancient reptiles, Bridges had a small gravestone placed in the main pit, near the point where the gator finished his meal, which read, "In Memory of the Fox Terrier Swallowed Whole – 1906."

During the decade since the farm was opened, Bridges, in addition to capturing large gators and keeping them as an attraction, also became adept at breeding these deadly animals as well as several related species, including African crocodiles. He believed, correctly, that tourists would pay handsomely for these unique pets. He also knew that most of those he sold would never survive either the trip north or the cold climate long enough to become a mortal threat to the new owners. Most visitors to his farm could not tell the difference between gators, crocs and caimans.

Bridges had a separate section of the farm where he was attempting to raise the Nile crocs to full maturity. "Monster" crocs twenty feet or more in length and weighing upwards of a ton, he thought, would be quite the attraction. Bridges ran out of patience with the slow-growing reptiles. Now he had too many juvenile crocs and he needed to offload a few. He thought perhaps he could find a zoo or another farm to take them off his hands.

Nile crocs have narrower longer heads than alligators, with a v-shaped snout and provide a more menacing appearance since one large tooth along the lower jawline is exposed. Juvenile crocs in a high gait can gallop at speeds approaching seven miles per hour and possess a wicked bite. Once they've latched onto small mammal, the croc will maintain the vise-like grip for hours.

The afternoon was moving towards dusk when Ruth emerged from the Alligator Farm. With a devilish glow on his moon-shaped face, he strolled proudly towards an awaiting car. His eyes darted toward a pair of platinum blond women who sashayed past him, both wearing flimsy cotton dresses. In most circumstances Ruth would have passed some sarcastic remarks, but he let them proceed without a word. In each hand he carried a small cage. Returning to his automobile, his thoughts were on his plan for revenge.

Helen sat patiently in the passenger seat, waiting for Ruth to return from an unexplained errand he just needed to run. She couldn't imagine why he had dragged her out to this awful, dirty, smelly place or what he needed to buy here.

With a bounce in his step and whistling, Helen did not understand what errand would have made Ruth so happy. Ruth placed the two cages in the back seat as Helen, frozen in her seat, spoke, "What on earth, George! What are those creatures?"

"Nothing, Helen, it's simply a well-deserved present for some of the boys."

"Those things look dangerous."

"They're just babies. They can't do much harm," Ruth said before he proceeded to giggle, slyly.

"My God, look at all those teeth! Can they get out of the cage?"

"No, you're safe."

Bridges never thought to even question Ruth what he planned to do with the six juvenile crocs he had just purchased. For him it was an easy six hundred dollars. Nor did he understand some of the questions Ruth asked. Most folks, when they purchased reptiles, have questions. What and when to feed them? What is their temperament? What is proper housing? How big do they get? How long do they live?

Ruth was more interested how badly could someone get hurt if they were bitten? When are the crocs most aggressive and active? Could he return them in a few days?

Bridges said he would always take the critters back, but of course there would be no refund.

On Saturday March 6th, the Red Sox would hold an intra-squad contest. No admission was charged and it was open to the public. This 'game' among the Red Sox players was meant to provide a venue to remove some the winter's rust before the preseason exhibition schedule started the following week. Innings and score were not tracked; the game would start at noon and end at 4:00PM. The players could then go back to their hotels and have time to relax and absorb the waters of the healing baths.

Ruth was neither gracious nor cordial during this meaningless competition. Pitching in the second inning, Ruth attempted to buzz a fastball under the chin of Speaker, instead catching him square on the jaw, splitting the skin for some six inches. Adding more fuel to the fire, Ruth proceeded to plunk Hooper in the back and Mal Barry in the arm.

Lannin was watching from the dugout with manager Bill Carrigan. Each openly expressed his dissatisfaction with Ruth, yanking him from the game. As Ruth sauntered towards the dugout, the million-dollar outfield came at him with the ferocity of a hungry dog towards raw meat. Ruth threw up his hands in a passive, surrendering manner, and apologized.

"Sorry, boys, the pitches just got away from me. I'm sorry. Just a bit wild today, that's all. I haven't worked out the kinks yet."

Speaker still wanted a piece of the youngster, but Smokey Joe held him back.

"He's just a kid, a baby, that's all. Let it go, Tris."

"Yes, please accept my apologies. Tell you what, come over to the Fordyce. I'll buy dinner. We'll drink some gin. We'll take a vapor bath in the private facilities. We'll relax and bury the hatchet. You boys come over to my hotel at 6:00PM. Okay?"

Wood accepted on behalf of the five players. By 8:15 P.M., the quintet was wrapping up cordially, but the tension in the air could be cut with a knife. The guests each ordered the most expensive steak on the menu and had several gin cocktails. They agreed Ruth would pay dearly for his disrespect towards them. After dinner, Helen, graciously and in her most soothing voice, thanked each of the players for being their guests at dinner. She added that it meant an awful lot to her husband. Ruth instructed Speaker and crew how to get to the bath. He added that there were six private tubs, climb in and enjoy. He would bring back some cigars and some Old Tawny port. Helen said her final farewells, bidding everyone a peaceful and safe night, and made off for the suite with Ruth.

The unsuspecting band of five left the dining room, making their way along the path plotted by

Ruth. Carefree, they strolled down the long corridor to the other side of the hotel for the private men's bath. In the anteroom, 5 of the white wraparound togas were neatly laid out. Opening the door, the bath was vacant. Ruth expected that at this time of night, there would be very little risk of anyone else making use of the room.

Ruth had convinced each of the players to use the comforting walk-in vapor bath, as it would sure help ease their aches and pains. Lewis, moving a bit slower than the others due to his leg injury, was the last to enter the tub.

Speaker announced, "This is good, but a quick nip of the port and let's get out of here. I'm not at all comfortable butt-naked with five other guys, especially that big oaf. I'd still prefer to flatten him."

"Tris, we can jump him and beat the crap out him. Barry is his equal in size," Wood added.

"Guys, we'll make nice and leave. When I'm healthy, he'll be gone. With the big guy over there and all our pitching, there ain't any room on the club for him. Lannin will cut his losses and send him packing back to Providence. What the hell is taking him so long, anyway?" Lewis remarked.

"Probably pitching woo with the little woman," Speaker interjected. The room erupted in laughter.

Ruth noticed a robe on the floor next to each tub as he entered the room.

"See how easy it is to fall away into dreamland," Ruth bellowed, ignoring the subdued chuckles.

"We have a long season ahead as teammates. Let's let bygones be bygones," said Wood.

All except Speaker agreed, still seething from the blow to his face.

"Sorry I took so long, guys, had to go to the can," Ruth said, coming into the view of the players in the tubs. Hidden behind a small statue of a water nymph were the twin cages. The steam room was at the optimum temperature for croc activity, and they were hungry. Ruth reached down and unlatched both locks, allowing the doors to swing open on their hinges. He then moved quickly out of the room, locking the only exit from the outside.

"Happy birthday and Merry Christmas, here are your early presents! You can use the poles with the loops to capture my little friends and put them back in their cages. Be careful, they pack a mean punch," were the instructions he gave as he left.

The exit portal sealed with a thud and silence overcame the room as the five tried to process what had just taken place. The effusive steam further filled the air, serving to cloud and restrict everyone's vision. The crocs raced from captivity. The quiet was broken by the sound of the cadence of one hundred twenty claws ticking with each step on the tile as they scurried towards freedom and their prey. Pausing to assess the first target, the croc peered at Mal Barry, "What the hell?" he exclaimed in a fright. The croc got into range of its target too quickly for Barry to move away safely. With the lightning quick snap of its head and jaws barely discernable to the naked eye, the upper half of three of Barry's toes were caught in the grip of the famished reptile. Barry's career abruptly ended as flesh shredded and soft tissue was destroyed.

A startled Barry, screaming, unleashed three punches into the croc's snout. The reptile released the foot. Barry stumbled from the tub, not bothering to use the ramp which was blocked by the croc. He managed to hobble away despite the piercing pain. Blood spurted from the gashes on his foot. Only through the power of his will did he manage to elude a second croc by leaping onto one of the white marble bench seats. Using a toga, he managed to wrap his foot and stem the blood loss. The pain was unbearable and he needed help fast.

Wood and Hooper were lucky; none of the crocs had managed to find them. The pair made their way to the door, only to find it locked. They starting pounding their fists on the wooden frame, cursing every element of Ruth as they now realized what had occurred. He'd set a trap for them!

"Open the door, you bastard! You'll be sorry for this! Barry's bleeding pretty badly! He needs a doctor! Open up!" Wood yelled. His face was red and the veins on his neck were popping out and ready to explode until every ounce of air in his lungs had been exhausted.

Lewis, frightened beyond belief, stood as frozen as if his eyes had met those of Medusa. One of the croc's snaps came too close, nipping his thigh and creating only a 'minor' laceration which would require a few stitiches. Speaker, with cat-like reflexes, avoided each croc. "Stand on the benches. They can't reach you."

Speaker found one of the poles Ruth had mentioned and managed to get the loop around the neck of the aggravated reptile, carefully placing it back in its cage. "That's one down. How many you think there are?"

Wood, Lewis, Hooper and Barry each occupied a bench, a comical sight. Buck naked, hopping and yelping each time one of the crocs lashed out at them. Ruth watched from a small window, howling in uncontrollable laughter from the depths of his belly. He had not thought through how to get the crocs back into the crowded cage, but if things got out of hand, he could simply open the door and lock the predators in the room, making it the hotel management's problem.

Speaker successfully gathered a second croc and locked him in the cage, but from there he was not sure what to do. Upon securing a third croc, all he could do is hold it at a distance.

The thrill of the moment wore off after about 10 minutes; Ruth had had his fun and was ready to end the shenanigans. No sooner had Ruth unlocked and partially opened the door than all five players, in their birthday suits, made for the exit. Expecting they would be furious, Ruth bolted for the safety of his room. He knew there would be hell to pay the next day.

Not worrying about any scandal from running unclothed through the hotel, Barry was taken to the hotel lobby to get some medical attention. The head waiter was able to secure five linen table clothes for the gentleman to limit further exposure.

Lannin and Carrigan called for a closed-door meeting with the participants in the fracas. Neither the French-Canadian Lannin nor the Irish Carrigan was big on forgiveness.

"Ruth, you owe me for what I paid for Mal. He'll never walk right again, thanks to you. As a player, his time is done. Big talent wasted, thanks to your stupidity and insolence. I hope you can fill his potential in the outfield. He hits a ball far as I have ever seen, or at least he did. If I had an option, I'd get rid of you now. Carrigan here agrees. Isn't that so, Bill?" Lannin lectured, uninterrupted.

"Ruth, you're trouble and I have little use for ya." Carrigan added.

"As for the rest of you, I'm telling you. NO trouble. It's over. Shake hands and get your rear ends out of my office."

The Red Sox went on to win the American League pennant by 2½ games over the Detroit Tigers and then completed their championship run by nipping the pesky Phillies in each of the four games they won to capture the World Series.

Carrigan, true to his personality of holding a grudge, used Ruth as the fifth starter and only in ten other games when he did not pitch. Ruth compiled an 18-8 record, starting only 28 games and appearing in four others to mop up losses. His win total was 5th in the league. Walter Johnson led the league in victories with 27, but started two dozen games more than Ruth. Each of pitchers ahead of him pitched in at least 10 additional games. Ruth managed to lead the Red Sox in home runs with four, remarkably since he only had 103 at bats, equaling the combined total of the million dollar outfield with more than 1,800 plate appearances and only 3 behind American League leader Braggo Roth.

Carrigan and Lannin, both blinded by their disdain for the behavior of this emerging star, destined to become a legend, decided to bench him for the entire World Series, save for one meaningless at bat. Carrigan used a rotation of Ernie Shore, Rube Foster and Dutch Leonard. Shore and Foster each had one more win than Ruth, but Leonard did not. The Phillies and the Red Sox had trouble scoring runs in the series, but Carrigan failed to find an opportunity on the field for a player with a .315 batting average and who led the team in home runs.

Ruth confronted Carrigan during the series and was instructed to take a seat and be quiet. "Kid, I don't like you. I don't like left-handed pitchers. If I had my way, you wouldn't be on this team. Sure, you hit 4 homers. Can you imagine what Harry would have hit! As far as pitching, you did good, but I would rather you pitched elsewhere."

"You'll look back on this day with regret after I have broken all of the records, pitching *and* hitting. I'll enjoy watching this series, but this will be the last time I watch," Ruth vowed.

Chapter 19

The winds of change swept across New England. Notable players gone from the Red Sox were Tris Speaker and Smokey Joe Wood. Tris Speaker was banished to Cleveland in exchange for emerging Sam Jones, Fred Thomas and the unheard of sum of $55,000. Speaker was replaced in the outfield by the immortal Tillie Walker, whose lifetime on-base percentage was six points less than that of Speaker's lifetime batting average, not to mention that Speaker is considered by many baseball historians as the finest defensive center fielder ever to play. These events did not matter to the throngs of Red Sox faithful crowding into a chilly Fenway Park on chilly April 12, 1916, for opening day. The grandstands were gaily decorated with American flags and bunting. The enormously patriotic crowd rose spontaneously to give rousing renditions of the Star Spangled Banner. The Royal Rooters were present in overwhelming force. An entire section of the grandstand was given over to the three hundred band members with their instruments and another three hundred singers, creating the environment of a lively cabaret on an alcohol-filled Saturday night. The music and singing kept the crowd in a fever pitch during the entire afternoon. On hand were several high-profiled politicians braving the cold in their fur-lined coats, the Governor of Massachusetts Samuel McCall, Lt. Governor Calvin Coolidge and Boston's Mayor James J. Curley. Each time a Red

Sox player was introduced to bat; there was a stadium-shaking welcome. The loudest of all ovations was given to the introduction of "the player replacing Tris Speaker in the outfield, Tillie Walker."

As the fans cheered for Walker while he moseyed to the plate, the despondent Hooper sitting in the dugout remarked, "In all the years I played with Speaker, it was 'I got it,' 'you get it,' never did we come close to running into each other. How can they cheer for this bumpkin? As much as I want to blame you for Tris' being gone, it ain't your fault. It's the greedy bastard, Lannin. But you better back up your mouth, kid."

Boasting the strongest pitching in the league, the Red Sox were once again poised to challenge for baseball supremacy. In a surprising move, Bill Carrigan handed the ball to Ruth to pitch opening day. Walker did not disappoint the hopeful Red Sox fanatics. In the eighth inning, after furiously racing after and nabbing a fly ball deep in the right field, he unveiled a powerful and accurate throwing arm, unleashing a breathtaking throw that reached the catcher without bouncing to douse the runner attempting to score and preserving the win for Ruth and Boston. The fans left the ball park believing they had just witnessed the first remarkable play of the next 'Tris Speaker.'

Five days later, Ruth once again took the mound. This time his opponent was the man who had now established himself as the best pitcher in baseball, Walter Johnson. Over the previous six seasons, Johnson had led the league in strikeouts five times and in wins for the most recent three years running. He had already captured baseball's pitching Triple Crown of most victories, lowest earned-run average (a measure of runs allowed every nine innings) and highest strikeouts of opposing batters. In the same years, he also led all pitchers in complete games, shutouts, winning percentage and innings pitched, dominating in seven of pitching's top measurements. The pair had squared off once before, with Ruth emerging victorious.

"Ruth, you're facing Johnson today. It is time for you to get your comeuppance. He's something you can never be, GREAT. Oh, yeah, and he's a decent human being," Carrigan warned.

Walter Perry Johnson was the second of six children born to Frank and Minnie (Perry) Johnson on a rural farm, four miles west of Humboldt, Kansas. In August 1907, during his rookie campaign, Johnson was called upon to face the Ty Cobb-led Detroit Tigers. As the tall, lanky right-hander with his extra-long arms hanging seemingly half way down his thighs, Johnson took his position on the mound, one of the Tigers imitated a cow mooing and hollered at Senators manager Pongo Joe Cantillon, 'Get the pitchfork ready, Joe — your hayseed's on his way back to the barn.'

The easy side-arm delivery of Johnson caught the Tiger hitters completely off-guard as the ball buzzed past them with eye-opening velocity. The acerbic-tongued Cobb ripped the first two Tiger batters, questioning their intestinal fortitude as they bailed out away from the pitch. "You chickenshits, hang in there and hit the goddamn ball, he's a nobody rookie!"

Cobb, an intimidating left-handed batter who would amass over 4,000 hits in his career, stepped in to face the gangly youngster. "Okay, try to throw your best by me," he shouted.

Three pitches later, the embarrassed Cobb, mumbling to himself, walked slowly back to the dugout, dragging his bat behind him. Years later, he would admit to fearing he was in danger from the sound of the ball hissing towards and past him, so frightened he simply froze.

"Boys that may be the most powerful arm ever turned loose in a ballpark. The ball came at me with the devastation of a big old train," he said, his steel-grey eyes glancing down away from his teammates as he took his seat. No Tiger player had the courage to criticize Cobb, even after taking an undeserving verbal lashing.

Johnson is considered to the greatest right-handed pitcher in baseball history, the hardest thrower of his time and most likely any era. A phenomenally successful pitcher, he spent most of his career anchoring pathetic Washington Senators' teams. For twenty-one years he suffered with the Senators, winning 417 games with a remarkable lifetime winning percentage of almost 60%. This was unprecedented, since the Senators won only 46% over their games over that span. The anemic batters of the Senators provided Johnson little help. Of the 279 games he lost, 65 of those he suffered when the Senators were shut out, twenty-seven by the score of 1-0.

In the rain-shorted affair, the Red Sox had pounded out 11 hits and 5 runs against Johnson while Ruth minimized the damage of the eight hits he yielded for his second victory of the young season, a 5-1 win. After the completion of the sixth inning, the skies had opened up and rain teemed down so quickly that puddles formed in the infield within minutes. The umpires, after waiting nearly two hours, ended the dreary day early for players and fans, calling the game.

Ruth and Johnson met four more times in 1916, but the fireworks did not begin until the game on September 12th. In their next three head-to-head contests, Ruth and the Red Sox were victorious by scores of 1-0, 1-0 and 2-1, neither pitcher conceding a home run. The second of the 1-0 games lasted 13 innings, with both hurlers dominating the opposing hitters. Whenever the pair faced off in 1916, Ruth brought more than his best; he had a passion to beat the man considered the best. Ruth desperately sought to climb to that throne and absorb the adulation.

The final frame of their timeless confrontations during the 1916 season occurred on September 12, only three days after the fourth meeting. This was the final home game for the lowly Senators, and owner Clark Griffith wanted to treat his fans to the pitching of Johnson one more time. The brilliant pair once again locked up in a duel. The 21-year-old Ruth, now quickly establishing himself as the best left-hander in the game, and Johnson, the fireballing right-hander closing in on 230 careers wins, held the opponents in check for most of the afternoon.

With no score into the ninth inning, Ruth, with Hooper on first, unleashed a mammoth high fly ball that went soaring upward to the blue sky and away towards the flagpole located in dead center field over 420 feet way. When a ball hit the base of the wall, the contours of the outfield fence, a right angle protrusion and the shadows cast from a nearby woodshed worked to deceive the outfielders, rendering their ability to judge which direction the ball would carom useless. The ensuing race to prevent an inside-the-park home run was on. All of the spectators were on their feet watching as Elmer Smith raced after the mighty poke. The beautiful motion of baseball is evident in these situations. From the dugout, players on the hitting team move to the top step, cheering the base runners' advancement moving safely ninety feet at a time, while the defensive side players took up the same position to watch in helpless anxiety. The defensive players on the field move to different places on the field, knowing that with any slipup, they may need to make a play. Johnson had moved from the mound to back up the catcher. The right fielder moved towards the foul area behind first base. The first baseman was moving towards second base, in case a second relay was needed. Shortstop George McBride jogged into position in short left field, hoping for a chance to relay. McBride possessed a rifle for a right arm, but he had the accuracy of a Colonial musket.

Hooper scurried around the bases, reaching home easily. The fairly fleet-of-foot Ruth decided to savor this romp around the bases, believing the ball would not be easily retrieved.

Rounding second, Ruth decides to tease Johnson. "Hey, Walter, how did you like that one? Not sure if I hit the entire ball, though. Throw me another of those fabled fastballs next time, and I'll put it out there in the street," bellowed Ruth.

Not watching the action closely, Ruth had not noticed the ball bounce directly back into the waiting glove of Smith, who quickly fired a perfect strike to McBride. From 160 feet away, McBride carefully sighted his target, Eddie Foster, who was straddling the third base bag, ready to nail the loafing Ruth.

"Run, Ruth, run!" Hooper yelled when he realized the situation unfolding on the field.

It is a tradition in the nation's capital for the President to attend and throw out the game's first pitch of the year. The Presidential box resides on the third-base side of the stands behind the home team dugout. Woodrow Wilson, an avid baseball fan, decided to attend not only opening day, the standing tradition, but also the final home game. His popularity was high at the time and the November elections were only a few weeks away. The visibility was good. With all the commotion around the Presidential box as well as his security, the chief executive is never involved with balls in play.

After hearing Hooper's exaltations, Ruth, now about two-thirds of the way down the base path, went into full stride, hoping to salvage a triple. McBride unleashed a throw that hurtled with the velocity of a rifle shot. The sounds of the stadium crowd paused in an eerie hush, with everyone watching McBride's toss and anticipating the capture of the runner at third.

McBride's ball appeared to accelerate as it flew past the hard-striding Ruth, whose chance of a triple seemed to be fast disappearing. Unexpectedly, however, the projectile continued to rise. And rise. It sailed above the outstretched glove of Merito Acosta, the left fielder who was backing up third and right into a surprised President Wilson's hands.

"Well, Johnson, I'm good, very good, but sometimes I'm just plain lucky. Looks like I got you again," Ruth proclaimed as the umpire awarded him home on the overthrow.

Ruth took the mound, needing just three outs to keep his winning streak against Johnson intact. With one out, Ruth started to labor. The next batter earned a trip to first base on after four pitches wide of the strike zone. Upset, Ruth plunked the next hitter square in the back. Senators now occupied first and second. The next offering induced a routine one hop ground ball to shortstop for what was a certain game ending double play. On the transfer of the ball from glove to throwing hand it was dropped. The bases were loaded the bases for the light-hitting catcher John Henry. Although hitting a paltry .250 it was significantly better than his career average that hovered slightly above .200. The first offering from Ruth was a curve just above the dirt and closing in on the front foot of Henry.

With a swing better suited for the golf course than the baseball diamond, Henry somehow managed to pick the ball clean off of his shoe top, getting the barrel of the bat on the ball. He unloaded, drilling the off-white sphere past a diving Larry Gardner. The ball continued down the left field line, and when it was retrieved back into the infield, Henry stood on second, having knocked home two runs and tying the score. Carrigan, believing Ruth was physically spent, brought in his sufficiently rested long-time teammate, Ernie Shore. Ruth was sent to play right field.

Shore was born March 24, 1891 in East Bend, N.C. He and Ruth became teammates from the time Ruth began playing with the Orioles in 1914. Shore had come to baseball through the New York Giants organization. His major league career began a trend toward his apparent affinity for bizarre pitching performances, Shore gave up ten runs during a ninth-inning relief appearance for the Giants in June 1912, yet somehow he managed to earn the save. That game still holds the NL record for most runs scored in the ninth by two teams (seventeen).

From the Giants, he moved to the Baltimore Orioles, uniting with Ruth. The duo was sold, in arguably one of the most one-sided transactions in history, to the Red Sox in the summer of 1914 for $25,000. A week later, July 14, Shore made his American League debut and fared much better, pitching a two-hitter and beating the Indians 2-1.

Despite starting the season late, Shore undoubtedly would have been a Rookie of the Year candidate had the award existed in 1914, going 10-5 with a 2.00 ERA and less than a combined walk and hits per inning pitched. It was merely a warm-up, however, for his 1915 campaign.

Shore went 19-8 in his first full season, posting a magnificent 1.64 ERA, third best in the league. He stamped an exclamation point on the pennant-winning season by hurling a 12-inning, 1-0 shutout against Detroit in September.

Shore returned to earth a bit in 1916, as his ERA jumped a run to just better than the league average. He still managed to win 16 games. Again, the Sox went to the World Series — this time against the Brooklyn Robins. Shore cruised through the Robin lineup in Game 1 before running into trouble in the ninth, needing Carl Mays to close the game out. In the clinching Game 5, however, he was masterful, hurling a complete game three-hitter, giving up a lone unearned run to give the Sox their fourth World Series win in 14 years and second in a row.

Although Shore had earned two World Series rings and had three consecutive seasons as one of the AL's best starters, Shore would forever be best remembered for the circumstances of his relief appearance on June 23, 1917. On this day, Ruth was on the mound for the Red Sox. He walked the Senators' leadoff hitter, Ray Morgan, on six pitches, arguing on all but one of the calls. Unable to control his rage, Ruth complained even more vigorously between the batters. Home plate umpire Brick Owens, finally hearing enough about his ancestor's intelligence, ejected him. Incensed,

Ruth threw down his glove in protest and charged the paralyzed umpire. Ruth delivered a roundhouse right that caught Owens squarely on the chin, knocking him to the ground. Six Red Sox players subdued Ruth and escorted him from the field. Shore was called from the bullpen. Also ejected in the rhubarb was Ruth's battery mate. Morgan, sensing there might be hesitation, decided to attempt a steal off the new battery, to no avail. With the base runner retired, Shore went to work, not allowing a single man to reach first as the Red Sox won, 4-0. The Red Sox players celebrated this unique perfect game.

Ruth did not like being pulled from the mound, especially with Johnson in line to earn a win at his expense. He'd proven all season he could battle Johnson for as many innings as it took. The Red Sox were hanging on to a slim lead in the standings as the 1916 season wound down.

The slender Shore recorded the final out of the ninth, forcing the game into extra innings. Johnson completed the tenth, although he was roughed up for another run. Shore did not experience the same good fortunes as he would when he relieved Ruth in the infamous 1917 contest. In the bottom of the tenth inning, before he could retire a single batter, Washington pushed across two runs. The final run scored all the way from first base, as a hesitant right fielder misplayed what most on hand at the ballpark agreed should have been a routine out. Charging furiously after a late start on the softly dying line drive, Ruth managed to kick the baseball nearly all the way back to second base.

The teams shared a long, narrow, dank corridor to get to their respective locker rooms. Although Griffith Stadium was barely five years old, the concrete and steel structure did not take well to the intensely humid weather which stifled Washington D.C. from May through October, and the green paint on the walls was already peeling. Ruth saw Johnson ahead of him and jogged to catch up. With the meat hook he called a hand; Ruth smacked him on the back and said, "You got us today, good job." Ruth recognized the enormous talent that the "Big Train" possessed, knowing that if he were to be considered the best pitcher, that Johnson set the high water mark he would need to surpass. "Train, you still have not beaten me, though."

"You're pretty good. That was a nifty little dancing act out there. After the way you booted that ball around, I think you should just stick to pitching. You probably cost Shore the game, I do not think I could have gone another inning."

"I lost it in the sun."

Bursting into uncontrollable laughter, Johnson clutched his sides and then the youngster around the scruff of the neck, "Ruth, the sun went below the roof line in the eighth inning. Just admit you're not much of a fielder."

"I tell you what I'll admit to, they'll remember me as the best hurler there's ever been, not you!"

"Ruth, you just don't pitch enough. How many games have you pitched in this year? 30? The only reason you pitched again today was simply as a stunt by the owners because you and I have had great battles. You need to push your manager so you pitch in 50-60 games. He avoids pitching you in Boston because you're a southpaw. I'm not the guy you're chasing, anyway. Cy Young, he's your target. 511 wins, that's a whole lot. I'll be lucky to catch Mathewson. Pitch more games and you just may be lucky enough to become the most memorable lefty ever, but a lot of things need to go your way. As far as you catching Young, never happen."

The Red Sox, who were locked in a three-team race with the Tigers and White Sox, fell into third place in the standings and a half-game behind after the loss to the Senators. There were nineteen games left to play, with critical series against Chicago and first place Detroit.

On the half-day train ride to get from D.C. to St Louis, invigorated by Johnson's challenge, Ruth approached manager Bill Carrigan, telling him he felt strong enough to pitch nearly every day. If he were given the chance to pitch in as many games as Walter Johnson, he would win just as many, if not more games.

"Bill, I know you do not like pitching me in Fenway Park, but I can win there. Hell, I can lead the league in wins if I had the opportunity. If I was my manager, I'd pitch me every other day. Nobody, I mean nobody, makes good contact with anything I throw. The ball park doesn't matter," Ruth pleaded.

"Tell you what. You'll get your chance. Pennock hasn't done much and the little guy is tired. You'll have your chance. I'll get you four, maybe five starts. But if you blow this, Ruth, I swear…"

Not giving Carrigan a chance to finish his sentence, Ruth swept him up in a bear hug, nearly snapping his spine. The little guy was the diminutive Rube Foster, who claimed he was 5' 7" but was probably two inches shorter. He began to labor in the dog days of summer.

Carrigan, somewhat true to his word, started Ruth four times between September 17th and September 29th. Three of his outings produced shutouts, including the pennant-clinching game on September 29th against New York in Boston for his 23rd victory of the season, just two wins behind Johnson. It was also his ninth shutout, and his earned run average fell to a remarkable 1.75. Although he pitched in forty-four games and over 323 innings, Ruth did not yield a single home run. At the tender age of twenty–one, Ruth had swiftly ascended the baseball ladder and was firmly established as the best left-handed pitcher in the game.

However, Carrigan, without any explanation, elected to skip Ruth, his most effective hurler, in the final three-game series against the last place Athletics, preventing Ruth from having any opportunity to pull even with Johnson for league lead in victories.

Gamblers had occupied the first base field pavilion seating section in Fenway Park since the park opened in 1913; as the 1916 season drew to a close, the infestation was so rampant that the section was avoided by general customers. Between one hundred fifty and two hundred gamblers now occupied the same seats for every home game. They congregated with a willingness to bet on anything from balls and strikes to the outcome of the game. Speculation persisted that the Irish and Jewish gamblers had connections and clever communication signals worked out with the certain players to aid their betting cause. Leader of the pavilion pack, the powerful but very local bookmaker and gambler Joseph 'Sport' Sullivan, was always planted in his usual conspicuous position, two rows back of the home team dugout.

Chapter 20

Arnold Rothstein was born in New York City, the son of a respectable Jewish businessman. His father, Abraham Rothstein, was a wealthy businessman and was dubbed by New York governor Al Smith as 'Abe the Just.' He was a pious man with a reputation for philanthropy and honesty. The elder Rothstein contributed to and served as chairman of New York's Beth Israel Hospital. Abraham's older son became a rabbi. Abe saw his youngest son as a very quick thinker and extremely brilliant with figures, but also a boy with a restless spirit, the kind tough to tame.

Young Arnold was a thrill-seeker who yearned for excitement and activities which provided immediate gratification. Although possessed of superior intelligence and an outstanding aptitude for mathematics, he was bored. Arnold flunked out of high school to devote his attentions to his father's real estate and other businesses. Arnold immediately converted his math skills into the ability to make money. He did just that at anything he tried. Arnold's interest in business expanded, but his interests were not his father's. His father's business began to feel suffocating in a relatively short period of time.

He became drawn into the underworld of gambling. Passion for the quick strike became an addiction. Arnold drew increasingly deeper into a world much different from his Orthodox Jewish upbringing. He spent most of his time and money gambling, his bank account and confidence growing with his unending streak of success. Finally his beginner's luck ran out in 1910, when he lost $200,000 on a single roll of the dice and another $100,000 on the turn of a card, busting in a game of twenty-one. Nearly broke and embarrassed by the events, Arnold Rothstein figured out that 'for anyone to make money out of gambling, he had to be on the right side of the fence. I was on the wrong end of the games tonight.' No longer wanting to leave anything to chance, Rothstein set out to take control of all the variables.

In his late 20's, he sought out the help of one of New York's most sinister underground figures, 'the Bottler.' Rothstein needed to borrow enough money to open his own gambling parlor. He had picked out the perfect spot, an abandoned ground floor shop on Bleeker Street, where poor immigrants provided the perfect prey — dumb, and desperate bettors.

Baniti Sadar arrived in New York from Cairo. The Egyptian was described as 'round, inoffensive, well-dressed and affable.' He led a well-guarded, secretive life. Although from the Middle East, his olive complexion enabled him to blend in with the influx of Mediterranean immigrants flooding Ellis Island from Italy, Greece and Spain. The Bottler ran the most successful of all the gambling houses in lower Manhattan. His methods of cheating were so clever that, although many suspected his games were not on the up-and-up, no one ever proved otherwise. Even more important, no one challenged the outcomes of those games. As the gambling empire of the Bottler expanded, so did his association with unsavory characters. Five Points gang leaders Maxwell Zwerbach 'Kid Twist' and Harris Stahl 'Kid Dahl' not only provided the protection he needed, they then muscled their way into his operation. Kid Dahl got so deeply involved, in fact, that soon he began siphoning most of his profits in excess of his agreed-to take. Surprisingly, neither the Bottler nor Twist seemed to notice. More likely, since Dahl's gang was the largest in Manhattan, they noticed but elected not to rock the boat.

Unhappy with the three-way split of the profits he did not steal, Dahl decided to further alter the terms of the relationship. He brought a local enforcer called Nailer and his accompaniment, a small army of goons, to intimidate the Bottler and the absent Kid Twist from any further connection to the Suffolk Street stuss parlor. Stuss is a card game similar to faro but played with fewer cards, a quicker pace and with much less strategy — an ideal game for the simple-minded.

Not wanting to be driven from the business he had built, the Bottler faced a dilemma. With his street protection now turning against him, he considered going to the police. Deciding instead to make a stand against Dahl, he decided to lock Dahl out and wait for Twist to return. While barricading the casino's front doors and windows prevented Dahl's team of thugs from entering, the Bottler's several attempts to get a message delivered to Twist each proved unsuccessful, unpleasantly derailed by the Nailer's henchman. The Bottler, with front doors barred and windows secured, remained hunkered down in his betting establishment for two days, awaiting the cavalry. Kid Twist and the anticipated reinforcements from the Eastman Gang never arrived.

In what proved to be an unwise decision, The Bottler, thinking there was safety in numbers, decided to reopen for business. Within a few hours, the regular clients returned, manning their normal positions at the stuss tables in the main parlor. The casino remained packed the entire day, giving the Bottler a sense of security. Shortly before 11PM, an angry stranger, with deep brown eyes, black wavy hair and a thick black beard entered the stuss parlor, sought out the Bottler and accused him of cheating. Although the Bottler did not know the man, there was a sense of familiarity. Perhaps this man was from his homeland. This was not an unusual scene, although usually it was the result of an embarrassed dock worker having lost his paycheck and returning only after a rash of venom from an unhappy spouse. Naturally denying the accusation, the Bottler realized things were anything but typical. Visible to the Bottler, the stranger now held a small revolver in his right hand and a scimitar in his left. Without another word, he pulled the trigger. Two bullets ripped through the Bottler's torso, small blackened circles, the slightest of smoke rings emanating, marking the entry wound. Leaning over the fallen Egyptian, using the slim curved knife with the ease of a surgeon, the stranger sliced through the Bottler's shallowly heaving chest, struggling to capture the

Bottler's final breaths. Tucking the smoldering gun in his pocket, the stranger reached down into the cavity and yanked out the Bottler's heart, placing the bloody organ on the now-still corpse.

Chico Eckstein, a corrupt, half-Mexican, half-Jewish New York City detective, conducted an inquest. His style of interrogation was to put the suspects and witnesses at ease through casual conversation, followed by intense questioning. He failed in this circumstance, as none of the twenty-five or so eyewitness patrons caved into providing any details of the slaying. Kid Dahl, who repeatedly threatened the life of the Bottler whenever he visited the stuss parlor, was fined $5.00. Kid Twist, however, was held at the Delancy Street detention center for twenty-one days. Sometime later, Twist and his bodyguard were gunned down in a Coney Island dancehall by another unidentified assailant.

Rothstein absorbed all of the knowledge the Bottler would share as quickly as it was offered. Rothstein's stuss parlor was so successful he paid back every dollar within a few months. This pleased Rothstein, since he feared indebtedness to someone with a life as shady as the Bottler, and felt it could not be good for his long-term health.

From the financial success of the stuss parlor, Rothstein graduated to a full-scale casino with faro, roulette and craps. Carolyn Greene, his erstwhile platinum blonde, head-turning actress wife, convinced him that he needed to play to the desires of the very rich. Rothstein immediately recognized the magnitude of this financial opportunity. He decided to relocate his gambling operation from the lower east side to Park Avenue West and 72nd Street. This area was among the wealthiest, most affluent neighborhoods in New York City. Rothstein took advantage of what he termed 'snob appeal' for his gambling den. "People like to think they're better than other people," Rothstein once told Damon Runyon. "As long as they're willing to pay to prove it, I'm willing to let them." For three years he allowed them to pay, to the tune of profits in excess of a million dollars. The casino, a postcard for decadence, was decorated to attract a high caliber of patron. Greeting customers at the front door were bellmen dressed in tuxedos, complete with top hats and white gloves. As the patrons entered the main betting parlor, they were handed a glass of champagne in blue-tinted crystal. Rothstein wanted his guests to feel safe and relaxed so that these extremely wealthy high rollers would not only bet wildly, as much as ten thousand at a time, but feel satisfaction in doing so. He followed his formula for success, 'they bet dumb.'

Rothstein finally decided to close up shop because it had become too well-known. In 1916, he opened a new casino in Hewlett, Long Island, where the cost of 'protection' was not nearly as high as in Manhattan. Both the building and the land the gambling house occupied were owned by a state senator who was recognized as a major political figure in the area. The casino was lavishly furnished and provided the gamblers, who arrived by invitation only, with the best in food and drink. All of the casino's employees were required to dress in appropriate eveningwear. Local police and politicians became too greedy, wanting a bigger piece of the pie for 'protection,' so he closed that club in 1919. Rothstein did not remain out of the casino business for long. Racetrack owners approached him about bankrolling a gambling house at Saratoga, which he did.

Eventually, not wanting partners, Rothstein opened his own place in Saratoga, which he named "The Brook". The combination cabaret, gambling casino, nightclub and restaurant was described as one of the grandest of its kind. The Brook drew the wealthiest gamblers in the country. Rothstein wanted only the best and most recognizable people as customers, although he shied away from mingling with them. Rothstein's sole measure of 'best' was in terms of money. If you had wealth, you were good; if you did not, then you were no good. Not to him, anyway. To him, 'best' and 'wealthiest' were synonymous. In the interim, Rothstein expanded beyond the casino. Services now included bookmaking, loansharking and very selective companionship services, provided by up-and-coming actresses with beauty equal to that of Mrs. Rothstein. Loansharking proved very lucrative as he continued to finance others' illegal schemes at exorbitant interest rates. Rothstein channeled most of his profits into legal businesses such as real estate, racetrack operations and bail bond services. Rothstein ingratiated himself masterfully with New York's corrupt Tammany Hall political establishment, earning protection for his operations. He also took equity positions in several racetracks including Belmont, Havre de Grace and Saratoga.

By age thirty, Rothstein controlled the variables so well that he amassed millions doing so with very little, if any risk.

Rothstein's magic with numbers cultivated a new angle in bookmaking, and by 1914, Rothstein was already the go-to guy for layoff betting in the gambling industry. Across the country, Americans have had a love affair with horse racing, and of course, wagering on those races as well. Rothstein figured out a way to capitalize without risking a nickel of his own. He worked to organize all the various bookmakers and convinced them to look at betting one huge pool. He then created a system of balancing out all of the bookmakers' accounts; this became known as the layoff bet. This is the process of evening out a bookie's slate when one horse or team has so much money riding on it that the results can break the bookie's bank. He simply bets the other way with someone using enough money to handle the bet, and the two then split the winning percentage from the bets placed. Bookmakers were happy, and Rothstein was the happiest, since he collected a percentage from both sides. By 1915, Rothstein's ever-growing bankroll allowed him to set all the terms for any layoff bet. Rothstein was known from coast to coast as the man who could handle any layoff bet. Assembling a loyal group of men who worked around the clock for their master, Rothstein's ability to take care of this type of betting would last until his death.

Meanwhile, as the country moved through the second decade of the 1900's, Rothstein's gambling rivals and contemporaries in New York fell by the wayside, generally in the same manner as the Bottler. As his empire expanded, Rothstein grew less and less comfortable with the limelight and sought to lessen any personal attention or notoriety. He began to implement the same management principles in his casino operations as he used in his legal business operations. He implemented an organizational structure with a chain of command and a hierarchy which distanced him from any direct orders or commands. Law enforcement, news reporters, crime syndicate figures and street-level gamblers kept a careful eye on the moves made by Arnold Rothstein, knowing the odds were always long in his favor. Rothstein, recoiling further and further from the public eye and day-to-day activities, became somewhat of a recluse.

"Now, Dandy, who is it that is coming to see me?" Arnold Rothstein asked his most trusted associate, Phil Castel.

Reviewing ledger sheets with his bi-spectacled, pointy-nosed accountant, Rothstein drifted in and out of the attention required for the boring financial figures and details. Sol Schwartz, in an incredibly soporific, nasally monotone drone, oblivious to his surroundings, dragged on through the numbers. Rothstein was sure that financially, all was well, but he was equally uncomfortable about the upcoming meeting. He had only agreed to the meeting as a favor to and out of friendship with the Italians, specifically the rising power broker Frank Costello, at the behest of his somewhat unrefined underling, Charles Luciano. Rothstein understood that Sullivan had a proposal which he would find extremely advantageous.

"Just a two-bit gambler from Boston, Joe Sullivan, and a no-name malcontent baseball player, I think with the White Sox, Arnold Gandil. This Sullivan has made a decent living betting baseball games. He's a big fish in a small pond," Castel replied.

"Is this Gandil a Jew?"

"Not sure, I don't know. Sullivan's a dumb Irishman who controls the local gambling action."

"Sol, let's finish this later. I have some things I need to go over with Dandy. What do they want with me?"

"I am not sure, something about the making a lot of money in the upcoming baseball series."

Gambling had become like shooting fish in a barrel — find someone dumber than you and take their money. By 1916, Rothstein had begun to think of scams with even bigger thrills, fixes with a greater rush. The larger the fix in any sport the more people that were needed. This created too many loose ends for Rothsteins comfort. If Rothstein's involvement were ever uncovered, the exposure would be devastating on his personal life. Even if people simply thought he was involved the takings were no longer easy.

Beginning in 1903, rumors abounded throughout baseball about Sullivan and his hand in the outcome of several very questionable World Series. He accumulated a fair amount of wealth, betting on games in Fenway and on teams with little chance of success; including the coronation of the miracle Braves over the mighty Athletics in 1914, a contributing factor in Connie Mack's purge of the team.

Joseph J. 'Sport' Sullivan was a known gambler in the Boston area, who met Honus Wagner and other disgruntled Pirate players before the 1903 World Series began. He was purported to have had a hand in the cancellation of the 1904 series, betting against the prevailing belief that in spite of McGraw's protests, the series league officials would exert enough pressure to force the Giants to play. In the next few years, he became brazen in his illegal gambling, so much so that he was arrested for betting on baseball in 1907.

In 1916, Sullivan was living in the Boston suburb of Sharon, Massachusetts. In September, 1916, Sullivan met with the Cleveland Indians' first baseman Charles Arnold 'Chick' Gandil at Boston's Hotel Buckminster and conspired with Gandil to perpetrate a fix of the 1916 World Series. At Sullivan's suggestion, Gandil recruited another Red Sox player, Speaker's long-time friend and supporter, Hooper, in the plot to intentionally lose the series games. Sullivan wanted this to be his big score, so he decided that a meeting with a noted New York City organized crime boss was in order. He wanted Rothstein to bankroll their plan to determine the outcome of the series.

Tapping lightly on the heavy oak door, Angie Magenelli, the gum-smacking, wisecracking, big-haired twenty-something office assistant with an acidic vocabulary as deadly as some of the Nailer's assassins and a body even deadlier, poked her head into the cavernous office. From humble beginnings, Rothstein had transformed himself smoothly into picture-perfect elegance. The first impression was that Angie was misplaced in Rothstein's immediate surroundings.

"Guests are here, Arnie dear," spoken in her deep, lower eastside accent. "What is it you would like me to do with them?" The final two words of the sentence came out as 'wid dem.'

"Phil, have you met Angela? She likes to be called Angie. Angie, this is Phil, a very old friend and quite eligible."

"No, I have not had the pleasure," Dandy responded, probing her interest with his best salacious look, his wide-open eyes fixed on the voluptuous vixen as he was finally able to take a full look at her.

Angie, although not one to miss the opportunity to flaunt her assets, shot out one of her pat responses, "Take a picture next time, mister, it'll last longer."

"Now, Angie, be nice."

"Well," she said, tapping her foot impatiently while waiting for a response to her initial question.

"Have them wait ten minutes, then bring them in, thank you."

"Sure, sure, sure, what ever you say."

Her hips swaying, Dandy watched the saunter of her sultry exit. "What gives with your new secretary?"

"Loyal as the day is long, and she'll do most anything I ask." Understanding the nuance, both men chuckled.

In 1920, Angie provided unsubstantiated testimony to the baseball commission concerning September, 1919 meetings in Milwaukee and Chicago attended by Joe Jackson, Lefty Williams and certain known gamblers, none of whom were named Rothstein. At these meetings, Jackson and Williams were paid several thousand dollars each to not play their best in baseball games. Sometime after providing her convincing testimony and affidavit, effectively sheltering Rothstein from any involvement, Angie and her family moved from their dingy, noisy, fifth-floor four-room New York City tenement to a lavish apartment in Miami Beach, taking a similar role managing the office affairs of Hyman Roth.

Hands folded underneath his chin, Rothstein listened to the proposition outlined by his two visitors. Rothstein stated on many an occasion that he would 'bet on most anything but the weather, because he had no way of ever controlling the elements.' Putting together a fix of this magnitude took a great deal of planning and coordination, so although Rothstein was somewhat intrigued, he also hesitated. He couldn't be certain that this unlikely pair had the requisite ability to tidy up all the loose ends.

"Mr. Rothstein, Speaker and Dutch Leonard have been fixing games since last year. Speaker says Leonard, Foster and Mays are in. The Red Sox are heavy favorites. We can make a bundle."

"The games they've been fixing are penny-ante crap. As far as fixing the series, I'm not sure it can be done without attracting attention. The World Series has gained popularity and it's tougher now than it was a decade ago. How certain are you that the players will cooperate?" Rothstein said, sitting on the edge of his high-back chair and leaning forward as he addressed the men.

"Look, Mr. Rothstein, Speaker is hotter than a Louisiana tin roof in the summer. Lannin sent him packing for no good reason, and he's still mad. That's all you need, one or two players angry about their treatment by miserly owners. Look how easy it was just two years ago," Sullivan responded.

The four-game sweep of the powerful and heavily-favored Philadelphia Athletics by the Boston Braves in the 1914 World Series stunned the baseball world. The general public suspected that the Athletics were angry at their notoriously stingy owner, Connie Mack, and that the Athletics players did not give the Series their best effort in return for compensation they felt was justified. The losing players picked up $2,000 as their share, a meager $800 less than that of the winning team, plus nearly five grand apiece in gambling winnings. Mack, apparently furious with the thought that it was at least a strong possibility that his players were less than loyal and participated in this travesty of competition, traded or sold all of the stars away shortly after the series, including his trusted scout Chief Bender. Bender, sporting a 17-3 record and an earned run average of 2.26 for the season, inexplicably surrendered seven runs in a performance best categorized as disgraceful. The powerful Athletics lineup, featuring Eddie Collins, Home Run Baker and Stuffy McInnis, led the inept performance at the plate against a somewhat average Boston staff. Unfortunately for the decimated A's, within two years, they slumped to the worst season record in modern history (36-117 .235), and it was years before the franchise recovered.

"What about the kid, Ruth. Can he be bought?"

"No, but Carrigan still does not like him a whole lot. Carrigan will listen and bench him, just like he did against the Athletics. Sport just needs to give Carrigan the word."

"Mr. Sullivan, there are things going on in baseball I don't think you know about. Ban Johnson has pledged to clean up the Fenway situation. What did he call it, Dandy, 'a cesspool of gamblers built on a cesspool of land?' He's set on getting the gamblers out of baseball. You and the others up there have been sticking it in his face by betting right out there in the open, with player involvement."

"It's not exactly like that."

"You make Johnson out to be the fool and he's angry. So angry he is going to move the series away from Fenway. The timing is not right, gentleman, there's too much attention."

"Mr. Rothstein, Johnson ain't doing anything of the sort. We'll be…"

Visually irritated, Rothstein jumped out of his throne-like chair, "That response tells me you're even more ill-informed than I thought and certainly not a real player in this type of business. I can't say this is the type of business in which I seek involvement. Even so, boys, without Ruth this is a no-go. From everything I hear about him, he can win the series alone, as hot as he is. If Carrigan were to bench Ruth without justification, he would draw a great deal of attention to himself. That, gentleman, creates too much risk. Good luck to you and goodbye."

Now alone with Dandy, he said, "That is not a very good man. If we ever do anything with him, we'll need to be careful." Dandy knew exactly what he meant.

Rothstein had an ability to compartmentalize business subjects. He had already put the discussion behind him and moved onto the next topic.

"Dandy, is everything set with the fight Friday?" Rothstein inquired of Castel. The monthly boxing card was set with a rising local middleweight, Maxwell Baker, squaring off against the number 3 contender, Jimmy Dolan. Dolan was a heavy favorite, but a lot of local money was beginning to come in for Baker. "Maybe the locals think they know something. Put $25,000 on Baker to win, and then lay off $100,000 on Dolan in Newark. Make sure the Irish cop gets word to Dolan he's not to be standing past the third round."

"What do you make of those two guys?"

"Small time; they're looking for the score of a lifetime. I like the idea of fixing a series, but only after Johnson thinks he cleaned up the game and lowers the heat. Under no circumstances can Boston have any involvement; Johnson has that slimy town in his crosshairs. Maybe in a few years it could be pulled off. I think you need to have two Midwest cities in the series. Maybe then, it might be ok, when there's less attention."

For the disappointed duo, the train ride back to Boston seemed much longer than the journey down.

"That didn't go well," a perplexed Sullivan probed Gandil, "no big score this year."

"Not unless we can get Ruth."

"Leonard says Ruth is unapproachable. He plays with the vigor and simplicity of a child. He wouldn't throw a game of checkers against your grandmother if you asked him."

"You're right. Leonard couldn't even get him to give up a homer in a meaningless situation. Told Dutch if he asked one more time he'd break Dutch's nose."

"Chick, let's salvage what we can out of it. Brooklyn shouldn't win a game; let's get game three. Work it out with Carrigan and Mays."

The National League pennant winner in 1916 was the rebuilt Brooklyn Baseball Club, another franchise with a history of fluid nicknames. In 1914, the club owner appointed Wilbert Robinson field manager, and within two years, he had brought the struggling club back to respectability. The beat writers following the team adopted 'Robins' as the nickname, after the popular and well-beloved manager, 'Uncle Robbie.' The Robins had made a remarkable stretch run to edge out the Grover Cleveland Alexander-led Philadelphia Phillies and capture the pennant. The World Series newcomers managed to make their way into the series with solid hitting by Zack Wheat and standout pitching from the arm of Jeff Pfeffer, a twenty-five game winner, and veterans Rube Marquard and Jack Coombs. Brooklyn manager Robinson believed that starting two lefthanders could give his team an upper hand.

The strength of the Red Sox pitching staff proved an insurmountable obstacle for the Robins. Ruth, whose pitching down the stretch was pure magic, mowing down opponent after opponent, was expected to start game one. Carrigan, announcing his rotation, elected to start the series using Ernie Shore, while Ruth, his most dominant hurler down the stretch, was relegated for the second game, Carl Mays for game three and Dutch Leonard in game four. Experts anticipated the Red Sox would sweep their way into their fourth series title on the strength of their more-than-capable staff.

Johnson had enough of the gambling threat; he would take action to nip the problem in the bud. The gamblers had ruled the roost at Fenway for far too long. Braves Field provided better security. Additionally, from the American League office, Johnson had circulated a list of spectators not welcome in attendance. Heading the 'unwelcomed' list was none other than Sport Sullivan. His mind was made up, regardless of any opinion to the contrary by the Red Sox owner.

In a meeting with Lannin, Johnson expressed his frustration over the unresolved gambling problem. He said that he felt Lannin had done nothing to seriously curtail the rampant betting. It took several hours for Johnson to finally convince Lannin of the merits of switching venues for the series. Lannin fell into line only after Johnson spelled out he would rule a Red Sox forfeiture of the series. This would have had severe financial consequneces on the owner and the players.

Lannin had agreed to a similar switch in 1915, but only after Johnson promised him that if they won the pennant in 1916, the games would be played in Fenway.

Braves Field was largest of the concrete-and-steel ballparks built between 1909 and 1915. Owner James Gaffney built a wide-open ballpark. He had a personal affection for the inside-the-park home run, believing it to be the most exciting play in baseball. A covered single-deck grandstand seating 18,000 wrapped around the diamond, past first and third bases halfway to the foul poles in both left and right fields. From there, uncovered pavilions extended on both sides of the field. Each seating 10,000, they went from the end of the grandstand to a point just past the foul poles. A section of bleacher seats located in right field, called 'The jury box' after a sportswriter noticed during a game that only 12 spectators were sitting in that section, seated 2,000. Counting standing room only, over 45,000 spectators could squeeze into Braves Field. Fenway topped out at 35,000. Johnson claimed the difference was just meaningful enough to justify the change in order to satisfy the Bostonians.

In game one, the Red Sox held a commanding lead into the final frame. Laboring, Shore nearly squandered all of a five-run lead in the ninth. Carrigan brought in Mays to set down the Robin uprising. Game two was also tighter than most expected. Ruth, pitching after an unexplained lengthy layoff at Carrigan's hands, stymied the Robins over 14 innings, the final thirteen holding them without a run. Matching Ruth pitch for pitch was another youthful lefthander, Sherry Smith. Backed by the weight of New York City's powerful and plentiful newspapers, Smith was thought to be coming of age and ready to challenge the younger Ruth as the best lefty in the game. Smith continued on an insufferable path to sub-mediocrity, finishing his fourteen-year career in 1927 with 114 wins and 118 losses. That was the very year Ruth delivered the greatest accomplishment ever witnessed in baseball.

Eighteen-game winner Carl Mays took his 2.35 ERA to the mound in game 3. He quickly surrendered four runs as the Robins captured their first win. Games 4 and 5 were each more one-sided, with Leonard and Shore throwing complete game victories.

Lannin was unhappy with Johnson's Machiavellian approach to the gambling problem at Fenway, as well as the fact that his profits were reduced because of the 'rent' he paid Gaffney.

Sullivan was unhappy. He failed to find a way to attend the games, but he did find a way to make money, just not as much as he might have with Rothstein's help.

Johnson was unhappy. Betting on the game by players was more prevalent in the sport than ever. His efforts to rid baseball of gambling and the influence of gamblers were failing. A frustrated Johnson knew the sport needed to be cleaned up before the game suffered a black mark so profound it might not recover.

The Red Sox players were unhappy. Lannin cut the winners' shares by an amount equal to what he paid for the use of Braves Field. The players were clearly responsible, and he blamed the players for the problem. The winners' purse was a mere pittance of $200.00.

Ruth was extremely unhappy. Carrigan reneged on his promise to pitch Ruth more. He pitched in just a single World Series game when he could have pitched and won three games. Promised to play more in the outfield and hit, Carrigan did play him twenty-five times in the outfield. Certainly he played more than he had in 1915, but not nearly enough to please the anxious twenty-one year old. Walter Johnson was right; Carrigan was denying him a chance at immortality.

Rothstein was happy. Watching the betting flow out of Boston, particularly with the large amount bet on the Robins in game three, he made $100,000 by simply laying off the bets to unsuspecting gamblers. Rothstein had mastered the elimination of betting risks.

Chapter 21

As 1916 drew to a close, the troubled water surrounding baseball continued. Johnson's personal war against gambling and gamblers' influence over baseball proved ineffective. So long as the owners held all the purse strings and treated the players as mere property, gamblers would keep their unwelcome place in the game. The players justified their involvement as a necessary means to get the extra money they needed to feed their families. America braced as the deep, turbulent skies over war-torn Europe moved closer to the United States involvement. An increasingly aggressive, antagonistic Germany, in a bold move, proposed an alliance with Mexico and resumed its unrestricted submarine warfare on shipping lanes in the western Atlantic, sinking dozens of unarmed, unprotected United States merchant ships without warning or provocation. This forced the neutral hand of President Wilson and his campaign vow 'to keep the US out of war.' In the months before Congress issued the declaration of war on April 6, 1917, the country readied for the inevitable. Spring training locations resembled base training camps, with Army sergeants assigned to each team. Players were put through rigorous drills in preparation for their being called to duty. Proceeds from Sunday games were to be donated by the owners for war dependents.

Baseball was in a golden age of growth across the country. Local radio stations were in their infancy but they were popping up all across the states, with game recaps and, in rare instances, live play-by-play of games. Newspaper coverage also expanded. In the larger cities like New York, with over a dozen daily rags, there was fierce competition for the scoop; each and every newspaper assigned a writer to attend games, travel with the team and find an angle no one else thought about. All in all, the familiarity of not only the hometown players, but all the stars of the professional teams grew.

Byron Bancroft 'Ban' Johnson, completely fed up with the antics at Fenway Park, decided to take matters into his own hands and get control of the situation. Johnson would arrange an immediate visit with Joe Lannin shortly after the conclusion of the 1916 series. If Lannin did not deal with and eliminate the criminal elements at the ballpark, Johnson decided he would deal with it directly, even if it meant forcing Lannin to sell his interest in the Red Sox.

Within three days of the close of the series, Lannin would have an unplanned and rather unpleasant meeting.

On October 16, festering over his treatment during the season and through the series, Ruth, too, decided to bypass Carrigan, going directly to Lannin to plead his case. Ruth needed to take control of his career and guide his own destiny as best he could. Ruth decided to go unannounced to Lannin's office and see him, one way or another.

"Look at the numbers, Lannin, just look at the numbers," Ruth urged. "I knocked three homers out in just 150 times at bat. It took Pipp over 600 times. I'm a natural hitter, Mr. Lannin. The more times I get to bat, the sharper my batting eye will be. Hell, if I were in the field every day, I may knock forty over the fences. You know I can outhit every one of the fellas playing in the field."

"Tell you what, Ruth. I'll talk to Carrigan to get you into the field more. You're all too valuable on the mound, but I can see your point about batting. I'll see you get your chance. You can rely on my word, you'll get your chance to play in the field more," Lannin responded, simply hoping to defuse the situation and end the hostile encounter.

"Thank you, Mr. Lannin. I will take you at your word." Ruth left, politely tipping his bowler to the woman hiding in the shadows of the far corner of Lannin's office. "Thank you, ma'am, for seeing me in."

"Miss Leslie, never let that big lummox into my office again," Lannin belted out at his secretary after Ruth had gone. "Never, or you'll be out in the street."

"Sorry, sir, it won't happen again. Would you like me to telephone Mr. Johnson back? He is anxious to speak with you."

In a bit of irony, Lannin requested a meeting with Johnson at the Metropole Hotel in New York City, located in the Tenderloin area, a seedy entertainment and lowlife section of Manhattan, just west of Longacre Square on 43rd Street. The meeting was set for October 29, 1916. Lannin's hotel holdings continued to mount. At the insistence of a prominent New York City figure, Lannin invested about $75,000, with a commitment for further investment of $100,000, in exchange for a small equity stake in a new casino and hotel venture in Saratoga, New York.

The Metropole Hotel earned a place in New York City history on two fronts. The Metropole was the first hotel built in New York City to include running water to each guest room. The second source of notoriety occurred on the hot and sticky summer night of July 15, 1912.

The east coast was in the middle of a weeklong heat wave, complete with smothering humidity from dawn until the wee hours of the morning. Throughout the city, windows were open and people were sleeping on fire escapes, praying for any reprieve in the form of the cool nightly breeze that sometimes wafts across the island of Manhattan.

The area was still lively, with the after-show crowds coming and going to the restaurants and gambling joints. Hotel Metropole had a few loungers drinking and discussing the latest gossip. The major topics for the big city were the most recent disclosure in the newspapers of the extensive corruption within the city's law enforcement units and the widening grip of the gambling industry on the general populace.

The dapper but natty Jewish hoodlum, Herman Rosenthal, nicknamed 'Beansie,' as was the case for most nights, was at the Metropole. Waiting for a reporter turned confidant, he grew nervous and impatient. A familiar face, Clive 'the Rat' Straub, entered and asked him to come outside for a moment. Unsuspecting, he got up to leave, slapped down a dollar to cover an eighty-cent tab and walked to the door, still smoking his cigar. The bright light of Broadway temporarily blurred his vision, denying him the opportunity to grasp the imminent peril present in the several approaching gunmen. Five shots rang out, only one missing the mark. One cut through his neck, one nearly severed his nose, and two plowed through the side of the head. Dead immediately, he hit the concrete sidewalk, blocking the entrance to the bar. The shooters quickly got into a 1909 slate-colored seven-passenger Packard and sped off at the thundering speed of 35 miles per hour. This was the first killing in American history that included a getaway car. More importantly, the other investors with Lannin in the Brook Hotel venture had ties to Beansie.

Lannin decided to have his dear old friend and business acquaintance, Harry Frazee, accompany him to the meeting with Johnson. This would prove to be the seminal moment in a period that would bring the baseball world to its knees and simultaneously create a baseball icon of mythical proportion.

'Handsome' Harry Frazee was born in Peoria, Illinois, to William Byron and Margaret A. Frazee on June 29, 1880. Frazee loved baseball, playing third base for his local high school team, and spending a great deal of time with the manager and players of Peoria's entrant in the Western League. At 16, he found his way into the theater, taking a job at the Peoria Theater, mostly doing the menial chores no one else cared to. At 17, he was an advance man for a touring production and two years later he enjoyed his first theatrical success, making $14,000 on a show called *Mahoney's Wedding*. Over the next several years, he produced a string of hits, including *Madame Sherry* in 1910, a successful musical that netted him $250,000, breaking most of the Midwest theater house records. Leveraging his financial success, he built the Cort Theater in Chicago in 1907. With additional hits in 1912, *The Kissing Girl* and *Ready Money*, Frazee showed the knack for turning previous failures into financial successes. Eugene Walter had written a play that was originally called *Fads and Frills*, and then was renamed *Homeward Bound*, but it had failed at the box office both times. Frazee met Walter on a train ride from Chicago to New York. "He was the bluest and most melancholy playwright you ever saw," recalled Frazee. By the time the train reached its destination, Walter had convinced Frazee that the rewritten play, now called *Fine Feathers*, was the best play he'd ever written. Frazee offered the playwright a contract and a royalty check with the stipulation that Walter would allow Frazee to do things his way, which included hiring a star cast. When the revamped show opened in New York in 1913, it garnered rave reviews. Frazee had realized how to bring a script alive with music.

In 1913, Frazee sufficiently excited had secured enough investment money to build the French Neo-classic Longacre Theater, a 1400-seat theater designed to accommodate the demanding acoustics of the Frazee musical productions. Another Frazee venture was the building of Boston's Arlington Theater, also in 1913. At the opening night of *Adele*, he met Lannin. Frazee was an innovator who adopted the custom of 'flying matinees,' a popular practice in London that had yet to catch on in the United States. Frazee's productions would play in cities close enough to New York that they could be performed during the day in places such as New Rochelle, Mount Vernon, Stamford and Yonkers and then again at night in New York. Frazee also held the reputation that he was a 'producer of the old school—buy cheap, sell dear, and screw the world.' Frazee was a heavy drinker and philanderer. Some of the playwrights and songwriters wondered, not so softly, if, 'Harry Frazee never drew a sober breath in his life, but he was a hell of a producer. He made more sense drunk than most men do sober.' Maybe Frazee needed to be sober when Lannin convinced him to buy the Red Sox. Frazee's success bred within him a deeply arrogant confidence, convinced he had the Midas touch and could turn the darkest of situations into gold.

"Good afternoon Joe, this is Garry Herrmann, National Baseball Commission president," Johnson said to Lannin as he sat. "I didn't know you were bringing anyone. Who's your friend?" Lannin stood a more than half a foot taller than Herrmann, but the men dressed nearly identically. Each had on a deep charcoal three piece wool suit, with the three jacket buttons buttoned. White shirts, both with gold-and- diamond stick pins accenting loud ties, and completing the ensemble, each had French cuffs holding gold cuff links with diamond studs. White carnations adorned both men's left lapels. Each man parted his hair nearly in the middle of his scalp. Deepening cheek lines began to carve the cheek of their developing jowls; only Herrmann's brushy moustache and height marked real any difference.   "Ban, I would like you to meet the new owner of the Red Sox, Harry Frazee. We will complete the transaction very quickly."   Johnson had ruled the American League with an iron fist. Every transaction and player movement had his stamp of approval, the owners' sometimes just pawns in his master chess game. Stunned, his deeply crimson face resembling a fully ripe beet, Johnson was filled with silent rage by the unexpected announcement. Johnson did little more than glare contemptuously at Lannin and Frazee, partially outstretched hand trembling from his inner anger.

Herrmann, sensing his close friend Johnson might unleash an unnecessary tirade, interceded, "I'm Garry Herrmann, pleaseed to meet you, Harry. I've heard a lot about you. I think I have attended one of your shows. It was great entertainment. Let's have lunch. Waiter, please bring over some of that good German sausage and a few steins of beer for us." Herrmann, quickly taking hold of the awkward situation, got Johnson to cool off a bit so the foursome could engage in a more fruitful and civil discussion about the future of the Red Sox.

Frazee went into the details of his background and his financial wherewithal, sufficient enough to run a professional baseball team. More important to Johnson, however, was his vision of the game and its growing place in Americana. Johnson believed the game should be played with simplistic honor. He sought to eliminate the players' rowdy behavior that marred the game. He vowed to give umpires his full support, something they'd never had. Johnson wrote that "rowdyism ran amuck on the professional baseball diamond of those days" and that it was his determination to "pattern baseball along the lines of scholastic contests, to make ability, brains and clean, honorable play, not the swinging of clenched fists, coarse oaths, riots and assaults upon the umpires decide each issue. Nor will I have outside influences that erode the morals of players, decide the outcome of baseball games."

Johnson did not possess the power to prevent the sale of the Red Sox, and it may have been a blessing anyway, since Lannin had not demonstrated any real intention of ridding Fenway of the gamblers and politicians. Johnson was also relieved that the rumored sale to Joseph P. Kennedy was out. He thought about the personal gratification in delivering the news to the powerful political leader 'Honey Fitz' that his son-in-law would not get the team. He also considered that although preventing the sale to Frazee was not possible, Johnson would control him in other ways.
After the November 1, ratification meeting held in the Italian Gardens overlooking Vanderbilt Avenue, at the New York Biltmore Hotel on New York's 42nd Street, Johnson set out to convince the seven

other professional baseball owners of the American League only to cooperate with Frazee with his express approval on every issue. Colonel Ruppert and Colonel Huston, co-owners of the Yankees, and Charles Comiskey, owner of Chicago's White Sox were growing tired of Johnson's heavy-handed control and balked, preventing unanimity. The other owners blindly implemented Johnson's personal embargo against Frazee, which would limit player sales or trades between Boston and the White Sox or Yankees only, thus cementing a path for baseball events and the course of its dramatic history. Detroit's Frank Navin, Washington's Clark Griffith, Cleveland's Jim Dunn, St. Louis' Phil Ball, and Connie Mack in Philadelphia sided with Johnson and were dubbed the 'Loyal Five.' The American League owners, less than two decades removed from their uniting to fight the rival National League, had now split into two groups and were poised to fight each other. The press dubbed the triumvirate of Boston's Harry Frazee, Chicago's Charles Comiskey, and New York's Jacob Ruppert he "Insurrectos."

"Mr. Frazee, with all due respect, spending one year managing the Peoria Canaries when you were, what, sixteen?, does not qualify you to manage the vigorous daily matters of a professional baseball organization," Johnson said, responding at the conclusion of Frazee's abbreviated history.

"I assure you, Mr. Johnson, that the challenges of coordinating all elements of a theatrical performance are equally as complex and difficult."

"Mr. Frazee, this is the big leagues, not some two-bit show hall in Peoria!"

"This is Broadway, the biggest stage in the world. Performances require perfection each day!"

"Well, here's the deal, then," Johnson replied, thinking on the spot that he was upping Frazee's ante to enter the game. Maybe, just maybe, a bit of extra investment would make him skittish, perhaps even enough so to back out. "In addition to what you're paying Lannin, you will pay the league an additional $150,000 immediately upon the sale, and another $300,000 over the next three years. During that time, the league will take a lien on Fenway. Think of it as a mortgage. Is it a deal?"

The prideful Frazee did not flinch, and without a bit of reluctance, he agreed.

"New Owner for the Red Sox – Lannin Quits Baseball"

The headline for the Boston Globe on November 2, 1916, mesmerized every baseball fan in the city. The article continued.

"Joseph J. Lannin, owner of the two-time defending world's champion Red Sox and controlling owner of the Buffalo Bison, suddenly sold his interests to Broadway producer Harry Frazee. He declared he was leaving with regret but finds it impossible to devote the necessary time, due to his growing real estate and hotel interests. Harry Frazee is a prominent producer of theatrical musicals and fan of the sport. The terms of the deal are undisclosed, but estimates put the price tag at nearly $1,000,000."

The fourteen-story concrete building stood at the intersection of Charles and Baltimore Streets in Baltimore, as proud against the downtown landscape as Gulliver among the Lilliputians. The crown design ribbing the top floor resembled a short tiara on a long head. From the south-facing side, there was a view of Baltimore's busy harbor and railroad yards; the west-facing view was somewhat more alluring with the hustle of the red-light district. Remaining devoted to the beliefs of its founder Arunah Abell; the Baltimore Sun Company brought readers the news that matters most to them for over 75 years. The lead story in the first issue of The Sun dealt with actions of the Baltimore City Council, which affected the lives of the citizens. None of the other half-dozen papers in the city found it important enough to report. Because of Baltimore's proximity to Washington, D.C., events in the nation's capital were regarded with particular interest; and on June 13, 1837, less than a month after it was founded, The Sun carried its first account by a Washington correspondent writing specifically for Sun readers. Through the years, that coverage was expanded and a formal Washington Bureau was established. Matching the growth of the game's popularity and interest, the Sun also established a sports bureau to report on baseball happenings throughout the year. The Sun's national and local news coverage became one of the most complete in the country.

Bursting through the front doors into Ruth's tavern on Camden Street, 'Sunshine' Alice Sonserrento, the pleasantly plump, slightly out-of-shape, delightful thirteen-year-old had a smile which lit up any room she entered. Despite her gorgeous feminine features, Alice was a bit of a tomboy who preferred climbing a tree to learning to bake. Babe had taken a fancy to the young girl, teaching her how to throw, catch and take mighty cuts at the baseball. Sunshine loved the Babe, imitating his batting stance and his trot around the base path when she poked a ball over his head during batting practice. With her hands on her knees, Sunshine took some very much-needed deep breaths after the short seven block sprint. She yelled out for Babe. Not hearing a response, she scanned the room.

Ruth and Helen had taken residence in the apartment above the tavern. In exchange for Babe's tending bar and Helen's serving customers, the newlywed couple received free rent. George Sr. and Babe had reconciled their differences, and while the younger Ruth made his way through the ranks of professional baseball, he had a home close to his father for a very fair price.

"Over here, dear," said Helen, recognizing Alice in her dirty overalls that she wore along with a stained and tattered dark navy woolen sweater, an obvious hand me down. *Pretty face, she'll break more hearts than bones when she gets a bit older and gussies up a bit*, Helen thought.

Sunshine finally spotted the Babe standing behind the bar, a white apron tightly cinched around his waist. In his left hand he held a white towel with which he was wiping the messy bar while chatting with a few of the regulars.

"Well, hello, there, Sunshine, what's the fuss?" Babe asked.

"Babe, have you seen the news in the Sun today?"

"What is it about, those nasty Germans, kiddo? There's a war a-brewing."

"No, Babe, about baseball."

"There's no baseball news, the season is over."

"Did you read all of the news in the paper or just the back page?"

"Ok, what're you getting at there, kid?"

Alice reaches around and from the waistband of her denim overalls she slams a copy of the November 3rd edition of the Sun onto the freshly-cleaned glass covering the bar.

"Look there, Sunshine, they're writing about college football. Army, Ohio State, Colgate still undefeated. I think Colgate will lose to Yale tomorrow."

"Why, Babe, you're so darn stinkin' lazy!' Alice said as she flipped the newspaper open to page seven. 'Right there, see! You're such a silly goose!"

On the column closest to the center fold, two-thirds of the way down the page, in a spot generally reserved for only the dullest of news stories, the paper read - **Red Sox Position Pleases Owner.**

"Okay, so… we're expected to win the pennant again."

"Babe, you are as thick-headed as the day is long. Read down the article."

Harry Frazee expressed his confidence in the returning pitching staff which had dominated the league and the returning position players which provided significant punch ....

"Who the hell is this Frazee character? What the hell does he know about baseball? Lannin's in charge, anyway."

"Read further down, you lunkhead. He purchased the club over a month ago. He's your new boss!"

"Helen, pack clothes for me in an overnight bag, I'm catching the next train to Boston."

"Why, for goodness' sake, are we going back to Boston now?"

"Not we, just me."

"No, sir, I'm going with you."

"Then, Helen, let's just get a move on. We're going to have a conversation with Mr. Lannin."

Ruth's promise of moving into the field and seeing more at-bats was dashed by one simple phrase; *"Confidence in the existing pitching staff."* Ruth understood the implications that Helen did not.

Exiting onto Dartmouth Street, the Ruths were rudely greeted by the chill wind blowing in off Massachusetts Bay. Holding onto the brim of her hat, Helen tilted her head and asked her husband, "Which way?"

"You OK for a brisk walk? Lannin's office is in the Lennox Hotel. Wind is at our back."

"Ok, but let's hurry."

"I'll check us in and you can get warm in the room."

"No! I want to hear what Lannin has to say."

The couple covered the brief distance in less than five minutes, exposed skin quickly becoming bright red from the biting gusts and the sub-freezing temperatures.

The hotel's red and white terracotta brick exterior and lavishly decorated interior were unmatched in the city during the early part of the century, and at the time it opened, the hotel was the tallest building in Boston and could be easily seen from Gloucester. The Lenox served as a home-away-from-home for luminaries in politics, entertainment, business, sports and the arts, and it came to occupy a prominent and cherished role in the circle of Boston society.

"Is Mr. Lannin expecting you?" the demure Leslie McKnight in her nearly undecipherable Irish brogue questioned Ruth.She thrust both hands out toward his massive chest, palms facing him in a gesture similar to a third base coach signaling a runner to halt. "I shall announce you, SIR,"she said firmly.

"Get out of the way, sweetheart, before you get yourself run over. No need for announcing anything, he knows Ruth is here."

"Please be careful there dear. Babe, it ain't her fault, you don't want to accidently hurt her. Sorry, little lady, he is very upset."

"I can see that. But if he goes in there unannounced, Mr. Lannin will have my head."

Hearing the commotion, Lannin peeked out just in time to see the devastation an enraged Ruth could unleash. With one swift kick of his left boot,

Ruth splintered the door, twisting the brass hinges and splintering the wooden panel. Pieces of wood flew past Lannin, who had risen and was stepping backwards toward the window sill, six feet behind where he had been seated in the chair of his desk. Sharp pains in his chest limited his breathing. Lannin thought he might suffocate from the fear. With his heart throbbing, breathing shallow, brain pounding, faced with the spector of fright, Lannin felt like he was floating above his body. His uninvited guest, Ruth, vaulted through the newly-created opening, neck veins bulging, arms swinging, charging with the intensity of an angry rhinoceros fending off any opponent. Subconsciously, Ruth built an emotionally-charged anger directed at a man to whom he entrusted his well-being, who in the end used and then abandoned him. Lannin, desperately wanting to escape, remained hypnotically frozen.

"You dirty son of a bitch. What's going on? You sell the team and don't tell me? You haven't lived up to one stinking promise!"
Lannin yelped ahead of an anticipated brutal assault. Reaching over the width of Lannin's oak desk, Ruth clutched the lapel of Lannin's black Italian wool jacket just before backing away far enough. Ruth shook Lannin violently, and then pulled him forward. Stabbing pains shot from Lannin's legs as his shins forcefully hit the edge of his desk. *This kid is powerful*, he thought, as Ruth continued his vicious tug-of-war on Lannin unsuccessfully. As the young assailant tightened his grip, two buttons popped from Lannin's once

crisp, neatly-ironed shirt. Each button hit the parquet floor with a soft tick. Lannin was no match for Ruth's strength. Lannin's brilliantly-shined shoes screeched across the surface of the desk, leaving long, deep scratches in the once pristine surface as Lannin desperately tried to gain traction by digging his toes in. Another forceful yank brought him precipitously closer to Ruth with no ability to avoid a powerful blow. Ruth was now nose-to-nose with his cowering former boss, so close that Lannin inhaled the deep, exhaled snorts rushing from Ruth's flaring nostrils. Curling his right fist in a tight ball, Ruth was ready to smash the club-like fist into Lannin's unprotected mouth. Helen, worried for Ruth's future in baseball, let go a high-pitched screech with all the force she could muster.

"No, Babe, STOP! Please stop! You're going to hurt him bad. Think about your career!"

"He's a liar. I trusted him, he gave me his word."

"Ruth, what promise to you didn't I keep? Stop and let me explain about the sale. Just calm down before you do something you may regret. I'll explain everything," Lannin begged, realizing that the out-of-control behemoth could easily inflict a crippling assault.

"You shut up, creep. You're just another liar who casts me aside at the drop of a hat. I am going to smash you," Babe retorted, pulling his fist back to his ear, ready to unleash a strike.

"Babe, dear, please stop. Let's listen to him. Give him a chance. Stop before you do something you'll live to regret. Do it for me." the calming voice of Helen pleaded.

"Okay, Helen, for you." Ruth released Lannin, dropping him with a thud to the top of the desk.

Nearly ninety minutes later, the trio emerged from Lannin's office, all smiles — except for the splintered door frame and the crooked tie, shirt with torn collar and missing buttons on the normally-fastidious Lannin. Other than those items, an onlooker could easily believe a civil meeting had just concluded. Lannin explained that it was Carrigan who held Ruth back from playing more games in the outfield and that he also held the young pitching star back because of his intolerance for left-handers throwing in Fenway, so he limited Ruth's pitching.

"Our new manager, Jack Barry, is committed to putting you on the field more than Carrigan ever would have," Lannin told the intently-listening Ruth.

"I've heard that before. Why would I believe it'll happen?"

"Well, Babe, the game is changing, its popularity is growing. Spectators want to see more hitting. Fans are energized when they see a ball disappear over the fences. The more that happens, the more fans will come to the games and fill the parks."

Lannin convinced Ruth not to fear that Lannin was abandoning him. Although he had sold most of his interest in the team, Frazee did not have all of the cash, so he mortgaged Fenway park to

Lannin and the American League, which left Lannin with a great deal of control and say in how the team was run, at least until all the debt was paid off. By that time, he expected Ruth, who'd be in his late twenties, would have become a man with a family of his own and would be making enough money to easily take care of himself.

Mollified by Helen's encouragement, Ruth apologized for his childlike temper tantrum, promising to pay for any damage. He threw his arms around Lannin's neck and, like a petulant offspring, planted a big buss on his cheek. Lannin told Ruth he would instruct the accountant to deduct the damage from his next paycheck. They all laughed, but January's paycheck was several hundred dollars lighter to cover the damages.

In spite of all the promises about an increase in the games in which he would pitch and play in the outfield, not much materialized. Ruth finished 1917 with a 24-13 record, a stellar ERA of 2.01, 35 complete games and 326 innings pitched while yielding only 2 home runs. Each of these statistics ranked him among the best in the league. In the ten games he played in the outfield, plus his 42 games as a pitcher, he batted .325 with 2 home runs, just one shy of Hooper's team high. Ruth was 22 years old and had already compiled 67 wins in his short career.

As the season wound down, Ruth's frustrations mounted. The White Sox were running away with the American League pennant. The season did not go as planned, nor was it without challenges for Ruth. The Red Sox finished second in the league, nine games back of Chicago and just in front of the Indians. Ruth played fewer games in 1917 than in 1916. Adding to his disappointment, in 1917, there would be no World Series money. Ruth liked to spend money and his lifestyle was changing quickly. He succumbed to the carnal temptations that went along with having that bit of extra cash. Ruth, the consummate competitor, remained unapproachable when it came to playing the game any other way than to win.

Ruth remained perplexed by the effort of some of his Red Sox teammates at times; he thought there were games where not every player gave his best every day. During one particular late September game against the Indians, player manager Jack Barry unexpectedly called upon Ruth to substitute for the scheduled pitcher, Carl Mays. Earlier in the day Carl Mays began complaining to Barry about not feeling well. Mays said he felt a tad weak due to the flu, but added he would be better by game time. Mays was setting up his alibi for the poor performance he was about to deliver. Mays never imagined Barry would pull him out of the game. Had the Red Sox been in closer contention, or had any probability to overtake the White Sox, Barry might have thought differently and started his ace, Mays, anyway. A nine-game deficit was too much to overcome, so resting the ill Mays just made more sense. Barry held his position to start Ruth, ignoring Mays' miraculous pre-game recovery and frantic plea.

Boston held a slim, one-run lead through the last of the fourth on a stubborn Indian team. As the

Indians came to bat, the winds picked up to signal the start of a routine late-day summer storm. The thunderheads raced across the nearby bay, bearing down on Boston and threatening to deliver a deluge onto Fenway within minutes. Ruth, determined to finish off the Indians, hurried his pace, retiring Cleveland's first two hitters on six pitches. By getting the last out in the top of the fifth, the game was official and Boston would have a victory if the game was called due to rain. Batting third in the frame was the exiled Ruth nemesis, Tris Speaker. Drizzle quickly became pelting rain. Each time Ruth stood ready to deliver a pitch, Speaker stepped out of the batter's box. Jocko Snider, the home plate umpire, granted him time. Speaker did everything possible to extend the game, hoping the umpires would stop the contest. After several long, frustrating minutes of this cat-and-mouse game with Ruth, Snider had had enough.

"Speaker, what is your problem today?" the crusty veteran umpire barked at Speaker, "Get in the box and get yourself ready to hit." With water streaming now from each bar of the face mask, Snider pointed to the mound and ordered Ruth to deliver a pitch. The ball missed the plate wide by two feet. Snider called strike one and pumped his right fist up and in the direction of Speaker with emphasis. Openly irritated, Speaker turned his ire on the man in black behind the plate.

"I can barely grip the bat, my hands are so wet, Jocko. I need a towel," Speaker insisted.

Snider would have none of this argument. Once again the umpire took his position behind home plate and instructed the Red Sox catcher to do likewise. Speaker stepped toward the Indians' dugout and wiped his hands with a towel retrieved from the batboy, doing so without any appearance of urgency. The uniforms for the players on each team were now noticeably darker as the rain continued seeping into the wool.

"Speaker, get yourself in the box, now!"

"Hold your horses, ump. You should really call this game. I can't even see the mound, the rain is so heavy."

"I've had enough of your delays, Tris. Play ball!"

Snider once again gave instruction to Ruth, who delivered a straight, but softly-tossed ball right down the middle.

"Strike two!" yelled Snider.

The disbelieving Speaker, hearing the call, raced to confront Snider. Water spraying from his shaking head, waving his arms, Speaker threw his bat down into a puddle at the back of the batter's box in an effort to force Snider into a fracas. Mud decorated Snider's pants.

"What the hell is wrong with you? I ain't been in the box and you've called two strikes. I can hardly hold the bat and he cannot throw the ball harder than an egg toss. Call this thing before someone gets hurt."

"Get in the box, Speaker," Snider said, again pointing at Ruth to play.

"Hold on, I need to dry me hands, again."

"Speaker, get into the box, now!"

Ruth leaned back, beginning the routine of his full windup. His hands were wet, the ball slippery. He threw the ball as hard as he could. He had tightened the grip on the ball a tad too much in an effort to get a little more speed on the pitch, and the result was a ball wildly inside. Speaker, seeing the wet projectile racing toward his unprotected chin, stumbled backwards, towel flying, just as the ball whizzed harmlessly past him, narrowly avoiding catching the brunt of the pitch on his face.

"God damn you, Ruth, you did that on purpose," Speaker yelled, directing his rant now towards Ruth, who, realizing the situation could get out of control, hurriedly began walking to the shelter of the dugout.

The ball landed in the pocket of Sam Agnew's awaiting mitt. Whump! "Strike three. You're out." Delivering a more animated pump, Snider accentuated the last out of the inning and game. Speaker, stunned, turned to Snider just as he was finishing his signal for game's end. Snider crossed his hands left over right in the air and quickly, in a waving motion, brought each arm back to his side. "Game called — rain."

Smartly Agnew, the Red Sox catcher, stepped in front of Speaker, who was still holding the bat. He had to be restrained from attacking Snider.

Speaker, irate, held personally Snider and Ruth each responsible for the $500 taken out of his pocket. He knew Sport Sullivan would come calling, and quickly, to collect on the bet, shortly after the game's conclusion. Speaker had wagered that Cleveland would prevail in the game. That had been before Barry changed the plan.

"Tough luck, there, Tris, so much for that sure thing of yours. Sometimes sure things just aren't that sure at all. You can't control the weather," Sullivan said, half-laughing, as he grabbed the loot.

"Nor that bastard, Ruth," responded Speaker.

Players respected that Ruth played every game to win without letup, even though Barry did not live up to the assurances given by Lannin. Barry penciled him into the lineup sparingly, a mere fourteen times more than the games he pitched. Ruth's anger within built, but his integrity towards the game was never compromised. Whenever Sullivan asked about Ruth, even just to walk a few batters, the stern response was "unapproachable." When Sport begged to push the issue directly with the Babe, he got an even sterner warning. "Don't do it. Just don't."

Chapter 22

The cruel New England March winds whistled in from across Massachusetts Bay. Seated in the warmth of Nuf Ced's pub were baseball players Dutch Leonard, Carl Mays, Rube Foster, Chick Gandil and the gambler, Kid Becker. The group was listening to Chick Gandil's latest get-rich-quick harebrained proposition.

Henry 'the Kid' Becker was a gambler from St Louis. Although known as 'The King of Gamblers' to the gateway city crowd, Becker was little-respected by the east coast gambling heavyweights, who viewed him as 'all sizzle and no steak.' In a recent gambling escapade involving a couple of local St. Louis boxers, Becker narrowly dodged assassination after a botched scheme to bilk bettors on both sides of the aisle. Becker spread the word that the bout was not on the level and that the veteran boxer of over 100 fights, who had served as a punching bag in most of them, would emerge the winner through a decision. He bet the other way when the odds changed, and Becker himself cleaned up. Enraged gamblers plotted to get even with Becker. Arnold Rothstein mercifully stepped in to bail him out of trouble. This was not the first time Rothstein had done so, but he did assure the Kid that it would be the last.

"Here are your beers, boys, and drink up. I don't know for how much longer, though," McGreevy commented, "Prohibition is coming."

"Honey Fitz says it's not happening," Gandil casually chimed in.

"I hear him say that, but there are winds of change about. Dries are outnumbering the wets and gaining strength. Plus, with us at war with the Krauts, support is building every day for prohibition."

Wet (those supporting the continuation of serving alcohol) versus dry (those in favor of prohibition) was the description of the position of the political candidates on the issue of prohibition. In the November 1916 elections, candidates supporting the dry initiative were overwhelmingly swept into office by a nearly three-to-one margin.

Placing the five pints of beers on the round table, McGreevy shook his head and tugged at his handlebar moustache before returning to his customary spot behind the bar. As he walked, he mumbled just loudly enough for the gang of five to hear him, "What does Honey Fitz know? Enough said."

Gandil leading the conversation continued, "Dutch, you, Cobb and Tris have been throwing games for card game ante money. The White Sox are considerable favorites to win the pennant as much as twenty-five to one. If the White Sox just happen to finish two games back, a ten thousand dollar wager can become a two hundred and fifty thousand dollar grand slam. Of course for your parts in helping assure the scales are tipped, there'd be a twenty-five thousand dollar bonus. What do you think?"

"I think you guys are all nuts. That is what I think. It's hard enough keeping wraps on tanking a few games here and there just to make some extra dough. This is big. Something this big could bring suspicion and draw an investigation. But then again, throwing away an entire season, just might work. It's so bizarre no one would believe it. I'm in under the right circumstances. Do we have the right players from Boston? And Chick, you're thinking a bit too small for the real money players. A hundred thousand dollars can get you two and a half million," Kid Becker, flashing pensive glances at the group. "But this needs to be kept quiet."

"That's a fair amount of money. Where do we get it?"Gandil asked.

"I'll take care of those details; someone I owe big time will go for this, if there are assurances from the few key players needed. Losing games here and there over an entire season, you've already proved you can do that. Now it just needs to be at the most crucial points of time. This just may work. We'll need to know who on the White Sox we can count on."

Several days later, the back page headline for the Chicago Tribune read:

"Two More Players Join Lawsuit against Comiskey"

Scandal erupted once again inside of baseball, this time threatening the core of baseball's existence. Four players of the 1917 pennant-winning Chicago White Sox led a lawsuit against team ownership and management, alleging collusion with the Tigers to throw the four games played between the teams, essentially locking up the pennant for Chicago. George 'Buck' Weaver and Oscar 'Happy' Felsch joined a lawsuit already filed on behalf of Charles 'Swede' Risberg and 'Shoeless' Joe Jackson. The American League club ownership received summonses based upon the substantive evidence, testimony and materials provided by Weaver and Felsch. Through his lawyer, George C. Hudnall, Charles Comiskey vowed to fight these baseless accusations and challenge them to the bitter end. He would not submit to any attempt to drag him into court to testify or be submitted to any extensive examination.

The war of words escalated as Raymond Cannon, attorney for the plaintiffs, was quoted in the Tribune, saying "We have not revealed all we know. Our evidence will shake the very foundation of the organized baseball leagues and reveal the depths of corruption within the sport at every level. Owners, players, stars, no one is exempt. "

Unfortunately the suit was filed in Wisconsin; Hudnall, in his first legal maneuver, successfully challenged the venue. Since the alleged crimes were said to have taken place in Chicago and the team was domiciled in Chicago, he won easily. Cannon refiled on behalf of the plaintiffs in the Chicago Federal District Court within 72 hours.

Hudnall filed a motion for summary dismissal, claiming a lack of *prima facie* facts. A single affidavit was presented, that of Clarence Rowland, team manager. The affidavit was among the briefest ever filed in a Federal lawsuit. "I have no knowledge of any 'fixed' games played by the White Sox as charged by Happy Felsch and the others. As far as I know, no one connected with the White Sox organization conspired with any Detroit pitchers. Weaver, Jackson, Felsch and Risberg are each a disgrace to the club, ungrateful for the generosity of Mr. Comiskey and are certainly not credible witnesses."

"Your honor, we can show the trail of the money back to Tiger players from known gamblers acting as go-betweens with White Sox management and players." Cannon valiantly argued, "The evidence is even more substantive than the claim."

"Mr. Cannon, Do you have any corroborating evidence from any Detroit pitcher? Or any evidence other than hearsay to show the involvement of any Tiger player and their connection to the White Sox ownership or management?"

"Not directly, but we can show Your Honor how players from both teams received money from gamblers for betraying their respective teams and the integrity of baseball."

"Unfortunately your suit is not against the game of baseball, but against Mr. Comiskey, Mr. Rowland and other gentlemen with pristine reputations. Although baseball may be a dirty game, the problem, quite honestly, does not rest in the ownership. I will pray on the facts argued and render an opinion shortly. Court is in recess." The morning session ended with the abrupt slam of the gavel at 9:45 AM.

At 10:25 AM the bailiff informed the attorneys that the judge would resume the hearing in 5 minutes.

The presiding judge in the case ruled with incredible speed. So quickly, in fact, that one could question whether there had been any deep thought, consideration of the facts or serious deliberation given to the matter. Some in attendance thought the judge may have had his mind made up before he had entered the courtroom at the outset of the morning arguments, or if not, then certainly at the adjournment. As Cannon lowered himself into his seat, Hundall arose, eager to present his counterarguments to the claim outlined by the plaintiffs' advocate. The judge summarily waved Cannon back down from the bench.

"They'll be no need to hear from you, Mr. Hundall. I do not see any reason to take action in this matter or allow the lawsuit to proceed. The story presented by the plaintiffs is just that, an undocumented tale. If money was exchanged, it was not for players to throw a game but to serve as reward for extra effort. The alleged $400 payoff given by Chick Gandil and Eddie Collins to Detroit pitchers Daus, James and Mitchell and catcher Stanage cannot be shown to have any criminal basis. I find the actions of these plaintiffs against their employer to be utterly reprehensible. If I were the employer of these ungrateful men, given the opportunity, I would see to it they never worked for me or anyone else in the business again! Case dismissed," so ordered Judge Landis.

Judge Kenesaw Mountain Landis was relishing the afternoon solitude when he heard the gentle tapping on his chamber door. Renee Castalino, the brown-eyed twenty-something who served as his assistant, aspired to someday attend law school. Although the daughter of immigrant parents, she had rallied for women's rights and the cause of women to serve in judicial capacities. After two years with Landis, her knock had become familiar to him. Not expecting any visitors, since he always set this time aside to prepare for the scheduled hearings, he fully expected the interruption was so Renee could vent about the tokenism women faced to appease the mounting female movement, or a recent breathtaking ruling or opinion rendered by Catherine McCulloch up on the North Shore. In the past year, Renee's outspokenness on feminism had increased, as had Landis's discomfort with her.

Maybe shipping Renee to Evanston for assignment with the female judge might be an option, he thought.

She poked her head in, "Sorry, your honor, but Mr. Comiskey is here to see you."

Having just ruled in favor of the White Sox owner the previous day, he was startled by the surprise visit. Placing the brief he had been holding on the desk, he said, "Charlie, what the hell are you doing here? You got your decision and this visit is anything but appropriate."

"I'll only take only a few minutes of your time. I think the decision was one step short of our agreement."

"Okay, Charlie, you need to stop right there. There is no basis for what you suggest as a punishment for the players who brought the suit. It is their right to sue. Neither you nor anyone else can prevent them from playing baseball. For me to rule that way would have been seen as punitive. That is, at least, for now. Fix baseball leadership so you rid the sport of the filth infiltrating it to the core and then we'll talk. But it seems to me that the owners have as much to lose as the players, so long as the public is none the wiser. Americans believe the game to be honest, so naturally there's no reason to clean up the game until that opinion changes. Only at that point will you and the other owners be in danger of losing gate revenue. Until that time, everyone wins, right, Charles? After all, it's virtually impossible to fix a game, isn't it? Now I've got work to do. Renee will show you out. Oh, Renee, after you're done, please come back in. We need to discuss your future."

By the start of the 1918 season, the United States had been engaged in World War I for nearly a year. The national pastime had carried on, carefree, but the citizens at large began to take notice. The minor leagues had been shut down since the spring of 1917. Only a handful of players had enlisted to serve their country. The on-field "military-style training drills," once thought of as a show of support for the US troops engaged in the savagery of trench warfare, were now looked upon with disdain by spectators. The owners united in an attempted show of support, vowed to pledge a portion of the gate receipts to the war effort and cut players' salaries to defer some of the costs. Spring training was reduced in half.

Pressure was building on baseball from both the general public and the White House to end the easy life lived by ballplayers. Most believed they needed to face the same real-life sacrifices as other Americans during this time of war. The most outspoken critic of baseball was the Provost Marshal of the Army, Enoch Cowder. One month into the 1917 season, he issued an edict ending baseball's exemption from the draft as an essential full-time occupation and decreeing that, "by July 1, 1918, all men must apply for work that benefitted the war effort directly. They must end working in non-essential activities. This includes baseball players. Failure to do so is to gamble for selection into active military service."

Crowder, a military veteran with over 41 years of decorated service to his country, was a primary driving force in the efforts of the reintroduction of the draft and mandatory service in the Army for young men. In April, 1917, the fruits of his labor ripened as Congress passed the Selective Service Act, requiring all men between the ages of 18-30 to register for service in the Armed Forces.

As Provost of the Army, he oversaw the enrollment, classification and induction of over 2.8 million men into active duty. Raised in the tiny Missouri farming town of Edinburg, his domineering father put him to work in the fields, without success. His small, waifish frame failed him during the endless rigors of farm life. Believing he could turn around the life of his young son, his father arranged an appointment for Enoch to the United States Military Academy at West Point.

The years at the Academy were anything but pleasant. His diminutive stature persisted, even with the daily training routines and better diet. Coupled with his lack of athleticism, Crowder became reclusive rather than face endless ridicule. Burying himself in legal books, he became focused on the military justice system. Even with spending the majority of time alone in his dorm room, he remained the target to regular, tormenting harassment from other cadets. One autumn afternoon, while casually strolling across the commons, a plush grassy quadrangle in the campus center, to the library, Crowder was confronted by several larger, more muscular students. "We heard you don't care much for baseball or ballplayers," John Shannon asked him. "I think that's because you're a runt. I've got a cure." Raising the arm in which he held a rusted watering can, Shannon poured water over Crowder's head to the rising chant of those cadets gathered around, "Grow, Crowder, grow!" Crowder lashed out, pushing Shannon with both hands and attempting to punch the much larger cadet. Shannon stepped aside and Crowder stumbled past him. As Crowder turned to resume his attack, Shannon's knuckles found the soft tissue above his eyebrow, splitting the skin immediately. A second punch also found a welcoming target, the left side of Crowder's nose, just under the eye. A sickening crack signaled a crushing of the tender cartilage. Several blows later, Crowder lay on the ground in a ruby pool of his own blood, nose broken and forehead split. After two days in the infirmary, Crowder was released. This intensified the indelible ill-feelings towards baseball that Crowder carried within him throughout his life.

Shortly after his graduation from West Point, Crowder gained admission to the bar, his focus military justice. Crowder experienced the horrors of war firsthand. While in the Philippines, three men of his company died in his arms. During his stint in the Spanish-American War, he established the system of military law in the Philippines, then governed by Arthur MacArthur, father of Douglas MacArthur.

In 1912, he created the system for the legal education of all officers in the military, with particular concentration on the abuse of soldiers during training practice and the inhuman treatment of prisoners. Crowder concluded, after staring at the destruction of war from three different campaigns, that apathy and complacency brings down nations faster than conflict does. He believed every male citizen had an obligation to serve their country, during peacetime and most especially in wartime.

As World War I broke out and escalated, the United States remained neutral while much of the rest of the world was engaged in battle. The Germans took misinterpreted neutrality as a signal of American complacency. That began to turn when German U-boats sunk an unsuspecting unarmed cargo ship, the William P. Frye, the first American merchant vessel lost. The incident sparked the indignation of many Americans. President Wilson demanded reparations. The German government issued a shallow apology. Americans remained angry. Outrage boiled over when the Germans sank the British-owned ocean liner *Lusitania* a few months later killing more than 1,000 people, including 128 Americans. President Woodrow Wilson, demanded Germany end all attacks on unarmed passenger and merchant ships. The German chancellor gave his assurance the attacks would cease, but they continued In February 1917, Germany announced the resumption of its submarine warfare. This action served as the final straw to break America's neutrality. The U.S. broke off all diplomatic relations, thrust into a war it did not want. Crowder took on a personal agenda to see to it that every able-bodied adult man who was a US citizen served his country. Begrudgingly, under congressional pressure, when the Selective Service Act was passed, he granted major league baseball an exemption. The lack of flow of baseball players to the ranks of the military had gone on long enough. It was time for an ultimatum. In a letter to the National and American League Presidents, he laid down the law: "players shall begin reporting for service in one of the Military service branches on July 1, 1918." These were just grown men playing a boy's game. The sport required a purging anyway. It was filled with lascivious, skirt-chasing low-life drunks, not possessed of any moral character, at the beck and call of gamblers and unscrupulous owners. The best thing that could happen to baseball would be for it to shut down for a few years. Maybe then the public would come to its senses about this game. After the United States became involved in the war, Cowder led a campaign for baseball to cut the season to 140 games to accommodate the timeline of the "work or fight" draft initiative set out in the Selective Service Act of 1917. Baseball had gained an exemption which set July 1 as a deadline for either having full-time employment in a job considered essential to the war needs or run the risk of being drafted into military service.

Some of the professional players, anticipating no escape and as retaliation for the owners' reducing their pay, enlisted for duty just before the start of the season. The defending World Series Champions were on the edge of devastation by the threatened departures of several players who had been keys to their success. Uneasy about the prospects of going to war, Swede Risburg, Joe Jackson, Eddie Collins, Happy Flesch and Red Faber decided they would enlist for active duty well before the deadline.

"The World Champion White Sox are about to come undone, not that Comiskey does not deserve the treatment. Ban, if the draft continues, we'll lose all momentum for the sport. Baseball will be destroyed," said John K. Tener, National League President, speaking to his counterpart, "We can do more for the war effort playing baseball then by sending ill-trained, unprepared players into harm's way. We can donate more gate receipts, we can send over more equipment."

"John, if we try to stop players from serving, I beleive we'll be viewed as un-American. This is a dilemma."

"Let's us get a Senator to get an audience with someone who can help steer us through this minefield."

"Who would you suggest?"

"I think maybe Honey Fitz can get to Henry Cabot Lodge."

"That pair does not particularly get along."

"Maybe not, but Lodge is powerful. He chairs the armed services committee. That's the best way to get to Crowder's superior. He's no pacifist, but I've heard he's a big baseball fan."

"Like most politicians, John, he'll want something in return."

"I thought of that. Let me handle that aspect and maybe we can deliver some excitement to the state in the fall."

Henry Cabot Lodge was, early on, associated with the conservative faction of the Republican Party, a staunch supporter of the gold standard, and an even stronger supporter of the expansionist elements of the US government. Lodge called for the U.S. intervention in Cuba in 1898, arguing that it was the moral responsibility of the United States to do so. Following the American victory in the Spanish-American War, Lodge came to represent the imperialist faction of the Senate, those who called for the annexation of the Philippines. Lodge maintained that the United States needed to have a strong navy and be more involved in foreign affairs. He was a staunch advocate of entering World War I on the side of the Allied Powers, attacking President Woodrow Wilson's lack of military preparedness and accusing pacifists of undermining American patriotism. Even after the

United States entered the war, Lodge continued to attack Wilson as hopelessly idealistic. He further assailed Wilson's Fourteen Point Platform as unrealistic and weak. He contended that Germany needed to be militarily and economically crushed and saddled with harsh penalties so that it could never again be a threat to the stability of Europe.

Johnson and Tener got their wish, and on April 30, 1918, a meeting was convened in Lodge's Washington DC office. Lodge invited from the cabinet Newton D. Baker, the Secretary of War, and the Provost Marshal of the Army, Enoch Cowder. Baseball was represented by several owners, including Colonel Ruppert, Connie Mack, Charles Comiskey, and newcomer Harry Frazee. Also invited to the meeting was Honey Fitzgerald. Passionately each owner presented his plea for their players and the game. Secretary Baker and Marshal Cowder listened, allowing the remarks to flow without interruption.

After the owners had been heard, Baker delivered his response. "In all honesty, I have listened to your pleas in the past two hours for leniency, here. However, I do not believe for a minute that baseball has endeared itself to the American public. Many women have sent their husbands and sons off to war. Wives have said goodbye to their husbands. Their children view ballplayers as idols and heroes, while able young men in the military, the true heroes, lose their lives for our freedom. Those not in the military trudge through their daily routines, 12-14 hours in a factory every day, waiting for the news they hope does not come their way, that a loved one has met their fate. I must agree with Crowder. Baseball players are in a non-essential job. They will and are expected to serve their country. Although you've had more than a year to prepare, you've done very little to do so. However, I do not wish to see an entire season thrown into chaos. So I will grant an additional two-month extension, to September 1. Have your regular season done. For those teams participating in the World Series, we'll begin to call those players into service on October 1," Baker decided. "Now I have more urgent national matters needing my attention, gentleman. As you know, the nation is at war. Good day."

Baker arose and Crowder followed, frustrated at having to take this step. They left in a huff. Lodge broke the silence after the departure of the pair. Baker, a true diplomat, supported Crowder and forced the issue about baseball players and the draft to a conclusion, but had found a compromise for baseball to save the season. Crowder, although not completely happy, succeeded in the point that ball players are subject to the draft. The deal was simple. If drafted, Crowder assured Lodge the baseball players would experience, firsthand, the stark horror and brutality of war through assignment to the front lines, testing every measure of true bravery and heroism. If the players elected to enlist before September 1st, their assignments would then be limited to essential but noncombatant duties.

"Well, gentleman, it seems each of us has sold a bit of our soul to the devil today," Lodge offered, providing his personal assessment of the agreement reached.

Baseball did not go completely unscathed. Fearing a military assignment where the odds favored the players suffering debilitating injury or worse, many of the teams had begun losing those players prior to the start of the season. Players would rather enlist for 'essential' military service jobs and avoid seeing action on the Western Front. Red Sox player manager Jack Barry left before the start of the season, followed by Duffy Lewis, their best everyday player since Tris Speaker. The Giants and Cubs had nearly all of their regular pitching staffs leave. The early defections of Jackson, Risburg, Flesch and Collins were done more to serve notice to Comiskey because of his malicious treatment of the players than out of any sense of patriotic duty. Gandil was made to look like a soothsayer as the White Sox plummeted from contention, finishing 17 games behind the pennant-winning Red Sox. From the start of the race, there was never any doubt about the White Sox not winning the pennant.

Kid Becker, considerably upset, had not been able to reach Gandil for several days.

"Chick, none of the bets are going to be paid off. All bets were off after the decision about the ballplayers." Becker tried to explain to Gandil. "Plus, each bookie is keeping their percentage, so we're all losing money.... I don't know how I'm going to square this with AR. I'm going to have a problem, a big problem. Is there a series play here?"

"No," Gandil replied. He thought to himself, *not so long as Ruth is playing for the heavily-favored Red Sox.*

Ruth completed his finest overall season to date, showcasing his talent in the field and on the mound. In twenty games Ruth played as a pitcher, he compiled a win-loss record of 13 and 7, with an astounding earned run average for a lefthander of 2.22, yielding just a single home run. Spectators lucky enough to attend the games caught a glimpse of Babe's tremendous strength and abilities when he muscled three long home runs in consecutive games on May 5th, 6th and 7th, tying the major league mark. For the year, Ruth batted exactly .300, hit 11 homers and knocked in 66 runs. The homer mark tied him for the league lead with Tilly Walker that year, although he played in nearly twenty fewer games.

On September 2, 1918, Kid Becker sat alone at a table in the back of a smoky uptown Chicago tavern. The Green Mill Jazz Club on North Broadway had become the host of rising young jazz headliners, many bringing New Orleans-style sounds to the north. With the approach of the 20's, the club was often frequented by seediest of the figures from the Chicago underworld. Brass lanterns hanging from the walls created the dim ambience. Tonight the patrons listened to hot and sweet sounds of a talented Negro band playing *Just Crazy*. The Stetson-wearing, cigar-smoking pianist whipped marvelous chords from the ivories and charmed the crowd into a rhythmic sway.

Becker owed nearly $25,000, growing each day from interest, to various bookmakers ranging from St. Louis to Boston. He had bought a grace period of thirty days. Becker thought about running, but there was no place to hide. His only road to salvation was to somehow come up with a big score and in a hurry. Becker, involuntarily tapping to the beat, impatiently waited for the one person who perhaps could provide that path.

"Kid, how are you? I hear things are a mess for you right now."

"Sit down, Hal, let's talk."

"Prince Hal," as the sports pundits referred to him, was considered the best-fielding first baseman ever to set foot on the diamond in 1918. The smooth-as-silk fielder had a range far beyond that of the brawny, typical first baseman. Chase made the difficult plays look routine and the routine look stylish, whether ranging far to his right or charging a ball for a bare-handed pickup. The professional career of Harold Homer Chase began with the New York Highlanders. Playing nearly every game from the time he was a rookie, he quickly began constructing his legacy as the consummate player, resulting from the combination of his flawless fielding, timely hitting and game knowledge. At the same time, managers and teammates alike sensed that there something about Hal that just wasn't right. Murmurs of corruption swirled around young Hal as early as 1905, his first year with New York. Somehow the novice ballplayer led a more luxurious style than his meager salary would support. Clark Griffith, the

Highlanders manager, approached Chase during a late summer road trip and questioned whether Hal had given it his all. Griffith was intimating politely that Chase had laid down on the team.

"Four errors, Hal, three in one inning," Griffith chastised the rookie.

"Mishaps happen. People, bad hops, bad luck, that's all," a defensive Chase lashed back.

"Your fielding lapses hurt the team. Eventually dissension will escalate and cause friction with your teammates. Son, you are going down a dangerous slope here. You can decide to either have a stellar career or one tarnished with distrust and suspicion," the manager continued.

"Let me tell you something, Mr. Griffith. You know I come from a very poor area of California. I left there with a dream to play baseball and make enough money to relieve the poverty of my family. Come to find out the owners pay us less than the field hands working the farms in Southern California. The owners say there's a limit on what they can pay ballplayers. You know, Mr. Griffith, there are no limits on bets you can place."

"Chase, you just keep your nose clean or you'll not only be run out of my club, but from this city and from the game itself. That's if your teammates don't take matters into their own hands first. If you continue to lay down in the games, I'll run you out myself."

In the off season between 1905 and 1906, Chase, using the name Childs Schultz, played in several Western League games to pick up some extra cash. The Wichita Jobbers travelled across the heartland states of Kansas, Nebraska, and Oklahoma and into California. Chase used this time to hone his skills on manipulating the outcome of baseball games. With a sparse amount of talent on these low-level minor league teams, the pickings were easy. As the season wound down, Chase began betting more heavily. The game against a weak San Diego team was to be his finale for the Jobbers; it was time to return to New York. Chase became exasperated when his teammates refused to yield the game that day. Unfortunately, Hank Gehring was pitching that day. He was attempting to win his 33rd game of the year for the Wichita team in what would be the finest season of a dull and undistinguished professional league career.

"Time," Chase called his instruction to the home plate umpire as he strolled to the pitcher. "Look in my glove, Hank. This Grant ($50) is yours. Let these guys score a couple. Get your win next time out."

Gehring, an imposing figure whose shadow threw a blanket over Chase, simply cast a disdaining glare. The owners, knowing that Gehring finished every game he started, instructed the more-than-likely idle other pitchers to remain home that day, saving the per-game compensation the players received. Since three of the pitchers also served as reserve field players, this left the Jobbers with no available bench players. Chase, understanding the implication of Hank's look and sensing no good outcome to the brewing confrontation, not only walked back towards first but he kept right on going, into the dugout, through the lockers and out of the stadium, abandoning his perplexed teammates. The business proposition was simple, $5 to play or collect on a $3,000 wager. Without enough players on the field, the win was awarded to San Diego.

Chase returned to New York, where Griffith rewarded him with a $4,000 contract.

"I selected him last year to play for us and we'll stick with him. He's a natural ballplayer, fast as greased lightning, easy, confident, and brainy. He's the counterpart of Fred Tenney in the way he goes after grounders, wide-thrown balls and bunts," Griffith crowed to the press. He hoped that Chase, with a considerable salary increase, would stay clear of the gambling temptations that haunted him. This leopard's spots were not to change throughout the next decade, though, and speculation about Chase mounted. The tempest of distrust boiled over in 1910 when he was confronted by George Stallings, the Highlander, for feigning injury. During a crucial game in Philadelphia, the pair came to blows in the dugout. Ownership backed their star player, assigning the ethically-bankrupt Chase to serve out the season as manager. He remained in that post through 1911, dooming the Highlanders to sub-mediocrity. At the start of 1912, ownership removed the 'star player' from the position of player manager, but the Highlanders struggled for two more years. Chase was not only an artist with his glove and bat, but also with his effort to put forth enough to raise an eyebrow but not enough to put it beyond reproach. Griffith, having finally seen enough, shipped Chase into the waiting arms of

Charles Comiskey in 1913. After a year in the Federal League, Chase returned to the National League to the Cincinnati Reds. Old habits were hard to change, and Chase continued gambling on games. During a mid-season game, Chase offered John Ring a 'Grant' to throw the game. Christy Mathewson, the Reds manager, who had no tolerance for corruption in baseball, heard of this in the dugout and immediately suspended Chase for the remainder of the 1918 season.

By midnight, the Green Mill smoky haze increased in density as the beats from the invisible stage amplified. The emcee for the evening belted out, "Please welcome tonight, in a surprise appearance, Mr. Vonn Freeman." The thunderous applause drowned any conversation in the room.

"Look, Kid, let me talk to Magee. Not sure what I can do with all eyes watching me, but I will let you know." Chase rose and left with the same aplomb as he entered.

Becker hoped the seed was planted. That was all he could do.

The World Series was scheduled to open on Thursday, September 1, 1918, at the expansive ballpark on Chicago's south side, the recently renamed Comiskey Park. The game was moved from the Cubs' normal home location, Weegham Park, in order to capitalize on a larger attendance. Several days prior to the opening game, an unsubstantiated report was leaked that the Red Sox's and Cubs' owners were reducing the players' shares of the gate receipts. Upon hearing the rumor, Cubs and Rex Sox players together approached the owners, threatening not to take the field unless they were paid the amounts that had been promised. Comiskey, not without selfish interests, i.e. his negotiated share of the revenues, intervened as a moderator. He convinced the players that they stood to lose more in the public relations battle, with the war still raging. Boys were losing their lives in Europe, so they would be viewed as not only refusing to play soldier, but now refusing to play a game as well. Disgruntled Cubs players Max Flack, Hippo Vaughn and Phil Douglas convinced the other players that due to public sentiment, a boycott would backfire. The players relented.

Fred Thomas, the Red Sox third baseman and, in the offseason, a Great Lakes commercial sailor, led a local civilian marching band onto the diamond in the crisp late summer air. Ban Johnson insisted on a show of patriotism at this difficult time for the country. Thomas commanded everyone on the field to stand, remove their hats and place them over their hearts. Fans stood in conformity, most rendering the requested salute. The Star Spangled Banner was flawlessly delivered to every corner of the park. None of the 35,000 in the throng had sat back down. The crowd, overwhelmed with emotion and pride, continued to applaud and wildly cheer the eighteen-piece band. In response, the band gave an encore, performing the more upbeat, easy tune "Yankee Doodle Dandy."

Hippo Vaughn and Babe Ruth squared off in the contest, each being asked to dull the attack of the opposition. Vaughn retired the Sox easily in the top of the inning. Max Flack, hitting third for the

Cubs, with two outs, drove a ball into the right centerfield alley, but his listless base-running effort managed only a single from what should have been an easy double.

Ruth, placing his left foot aside the pitching rubber, took the stretch position. As a left-handed pitcher, he had a full view of first base and its occupant, Flack. Ruth couldn't believe what he was witnessing. Flack, with seventeen stolen bases to his credit, not speedy but known as a savvy player, was casually increasing his distance from the base. Patiently, Ruth watched until Flack was beyond the point of no return. Ruth flipped the ball over to the first baseman, catching Flack off-base for the final out of the inning.

"Max, did you come to play today? You're acting like a horse's ass!" Ruth teased him.

Flack winked at Ruth, and then picked his glove up as he took his outfield position.

The series ended on Wednesday, September 11, in Boston. Lefty Tyler was on the hill for the Cubs. Tyler had bested Bullet Joe Bush in game two, holding the Red Sox to a single run. If Tyler could shut them down, the Cubs would have a chance with Hippo Vaughn, their best hurler, ready to go in game 7. In the pivotal third inning, with two runners on, Babe Ruth strode to the plate. Tyler looked toward Flack, who inexplicably moved several steps closer to the infield.

"Max," Tyler yelled to get the attention of the outfielder. Flack nodded in acknowledgement.

Motioning with his glove to retreat, Flack tipped his cap. Both players repeated the ritual before Tyler, frustrated, turned his attention to Ruth. The Babe promptly deposited the first pitch well over Flack's head. Hurrying to retrieve the ball, Flack kept Ruth from completing the inside-the-park homerun, stopping him at third. But the damage was done, the decisive runs delivered. The Cubs, with the best record in baseball, outhit, outscored and out-pitched the Red Sox, only to lose the series 4-2.

Two days later, Frank Bustellano, who worked for a well-known Boston gambler, delivered a sealed package to Becker at the Green Mill.

"Costello says hello. There's enough here, Kid, to get you out of trouble. But you owe the boss. Next year he's looking for a bigger score, much bigger."

Becker had dodged the bullet, at least for now. With enough to cover his debts, he was relieved, but now he was in debt again in a different way, much deeper and with much more at stake than he realized.

Shortly after the series end, Ruth and Helen retreated to the Sudbury, MA farm they rented. Ruminating about the series, Babe, leaning against the stone mantel, addressed Helen, "You know, something wasn't right about what was going on. Some of guys just didn't seem to be playing their best."

"Oh, Babe, how could someone not try their best during the series?"

"No, Helen, something just wasn't right. The whole year was strange."

"Maybe it's the war, Babe."

Babe turned and walked from fireplace carrying the wrought iron poker, pausing to look aimlessly out the windows of back door as he thought silently, *Nah, Helen, it's something else. It's something else.*

Chapter 23

By March of 1919 the mood of the country had changed. There was a sense of relief in most Americans. Peace had progressed positively; each dawn brought increased hope of world peace and an end to more than four years of the bloody hostilities of World War I. A formal end to the war would be announced soon. Families were excited that young American men were to be reunited with their families and other loved ones. Baseball players were being dismissed from duty and flocked back to their teams, just in time for the start of spring training. Baseball had withstood the effects of the war. Its popularity across the country exploded. Most attributed the latest spike in interest to the patriotic unification of the crowds at the recent World Series, which came from the playing of the soon-to-be-named national anthem during each game of the past September, with resplendent refrains in the 7th innings. All present stood and sang while the band played.

Others attributed the growth and development of baseball to the expansion of the newspaper industry. Newspapers reported baseball information to more Americans and at a fast pace. Reporters, through their accounts, fictionalized the heroic feats of baseball players. Baseball was now the national pastime, distracting many from the everyday pressures and fears which war had brought. Leagues spawned across the country, providing a level of play for most anyone with even a bit of talent. Led by New York, many states initiated and approved referenda allowing baseball for pay on Sundays. This opened the door for many more family outings to witness games, only now to professional stadiums. Owners, anxiously anticipating a wonderful summer of baseball in 1919, had invested heavily in recent years to modernize and expand their stadiums. Nearly a quarter of a million spectators witnessed the six games between the Boston and Chicago teams the previous fall. Expecting a full schedule and the return of its stars, attendance would skyrocket and franchise values would vault through the $1,000,000 mark. The owners had a near-license to print money. They had control over the players for life, with friendly judges squashing the threat of competition regularly and a near-limitless audience. Nothing could possibly slow this train down.

The White Sox, with the core of the 1917 pennant-winning club back in the fold, stood ready to reclaim the top spot in the American League.

Finally honoring his word, Ed Barrow made Ruth an everyday player, sacrificing his role as a pitcher in the process. Ruth believed Barrow would stay committed and still put him out on the hill. He and Carl Mays both missed the ill-fated team cruise from Boston Harbor to Miami to begin spring training. Ruth had held out during spring training, asking for more money. Barrow and Frazee reluctantly met the Babe's demand for a thousand dollar increase to $10,000, but chose to limit one of his loves, pitching.

During the second game of a Sunday doubleheader on September 24, 1919, Bob Shawkey, ace of the New York Yankee staff, was protecting a slim one-run lead into the ninth. He had held the Red Sox in check, except for the powerful Ruth who had hit two balls well over four hundred and fifty feet. The first turned out to be nothing but a long out, as Chick Fewster made a sensational over-the-head catch after a long run. The second escaped the outfielders for what turned out to be a harmless triple, as Ruth was declared out by umpire Tommy Connelly for missing third on his attempt for an inside-the-park home run.

Ruth stood on his spindle legs awaiting the Shawkey delivery, but he froze as the Yankee hurler threw a tantalizing slow curve which broke into the strike zone.

Ruth whistled toward the pitcher, "Shawkey, you got the guts to throw that again?"

Across from Brush Stadium (the Polo Grounds), beyond the right field stand, stood Manhattan Field. This was a popular spot for many upper west side New York families to picnic and watch the local men and youngsters play casual baseball games. Maureen Smith was just finishing her preparation of the Sunday spread for her children when she glanced for a moment to see her husband Tommy, who was participating with several members of his family against another Irish clan for the pride of Highbridge, the primarily Irish immigrant neighborhood hugging the Harlem River from Coogan's Bluff to 173rd Street.

Looking down as she resumed her preparation of the meal, the pitcher of milk had been knocked over, spilling its contents all over the picnic cloth.

"For Chrissakes, Jimmy, you've made a mess," Maureen said, addressing her ire at the oldest of six children, her nine-year-old son.

"No, I didn't, mommy."

"Don't you sass me, young man; you'll get double the punishment if you lie. You'll feel the back of your daddy's hand."

"I didn't do it. The ball came rolling over. I think someone hit it from the stadium."

"James, hush, now, you're digging yourself in deeper and the fib is just getting bigger. You were playing with a ball we brung with us and knocked the milk over. That park is too far way, no one can hit a ball that far. No one, just admit what you done."

"Mommy, dad and the other men are playing with the ball we brung."

Maureen looked as her son, then turned to her mate, "Tom, do you have the ball we brung with us?"

"Of course, woman, we're playing, aren't we?"Tom responded.

"Tom, can a man hit a ball from the stadium to here?"

"MAUREEN, we're playing here. No man can hit a ball this far. At least not no mortal man. Now hush, I'm trying to play."

The mighty contact from Ruth's swing unleashed a glorious drive that rose spectacularly, at a rate never seen before and went sailing over the forty-five foot façade, four hundred and fifty-two feet from home plate. The ball cleared the imposing facade with room to spare. Shawkey had indeed taken up Ruth's challenge, hoping to fool him by throwing the same slow ball. The Boston mauler uncurled all of his strength on the pitch. Shawkey and his teammates watched in quiet admiration. The ball continued to sail, passing over a narrow strip of weeds and finally landing on the soft grass of the adjacent field, where it rolled until it collided with the pitcher.

Although the Yankees rallied to win the game in the 13th inning, everyone was talking about the shot.

Ed Cicotte, several days later, read the wire report to Joe Jackson before their scheduled game. The White Sox star outfielder remarked, "I hit a ball about a good as I possibly could and it barely made it to the roof top. It ain't so, he ain't human, and that's all there is."

The New York Times on September 27th, reported that, after detailed research, it was determined that Ruth had surpassed Ned Williamson's record of twenty-seven home runs in a season, a mark which had stood for thirty-seven years. The paper further commented that modern parks were significantly bigger than those in which Williamson played, making Ruth's feat that much more colossal.

At season's end, Ruth's home run total stood at 29.

The Chicago Tribune headline on September 26th proclaimed the following:

"Comiskey's Black Sox Clinch Pennant"

Gate receipts had unexpectedly dipped during the 1919 season. Comiskey had kept the players' salaries the same or had reduced them, promising bigger bonuses if the team made to the Series, and he decided to shave costs wherever he could. Players started sharing berths on train rides, two players in a hotel room became three. In a last desperate move to squeeze out every penny he could in profits, as the summer began, Comiskey made it the responsibility of the players to launder their own uniforms. Unanimously, the players responded that none would wash their uniforms. So it began, from July 4th until the end of the season, game upon game, each player pulled on the same pants and shirt that were carrying dirt and grime from each of the previous games. Home whites became beige, then tan, brown and finally ebony. Dirty to filthy, filthy to foul, foul to fetid. The sports writers picked up the plight of the players and began to call them the Black Sox.

Ban Johnson sent a telegram to Comiskey on the evening they clinched the pennant.

"Charles, sentiment is currently not in favor of the owners. Americans believe owners have enslaved the players and pay substandard wages, certainly below their worth to the franchise. Clean up your team in preparation for this national event, otherwise I shall instruct the National Committee that you have forfeited the series and award the title to Cincinnati. In addition, you will be assessed a fine in an amount equal to the share due the Redleg ownership, Ban"

On the morning of September 28[th,] 1919, Comiskey once again went calling on his friend, Judge Landis.

"Charlie, I am uncertain what you think I can do about this. Your players are the walking disgrace of baseball. They look other than professional. And to be quite honest here, Charlie, you look like something of a tightwad."

"Judge, I cannot help it they don't want to pay for…"

"Stop it, Charlie; do you think me a fool? You drove them to this. You cut their pay, make them travel under Spartan conditions, give them less to eat and drink. Charlie, *you* are driving their disloyalty. Rightfully so, I might add. You are making them easy prey for the gamblers and yourself an easier target for criticism. Wash the damn uniforms; pay them what they're worth. You barely escaped last year with the franchise intact. One more scandal and you could lose your team altogether. Charlie, no one is above the rules of ethics. That includes you."

"Judge, you do not realize how much money I have lost the last two years with the war and all."

"Charlie, I am certain you've found ways to recover your losses. Now go get your team ready for the series and get those players cleaned up."

Detectives Jim Vasey and Elias Hoagland were carrying out surveillance on the evening of

September 28, 1919. They both had been on many uneventful stakeouts in St. Louis. This particular night took them to an upscale section of the city. As they approached the twelve-story Jefferson Hotel in downtown St. Louis, they saw something unusual. The grand structure had been built to cater to wealthy patrons. The four-hundred-room hotel opened on May 1, 1904 in anticipation of the World's Fair. The lobby featured marble columns, a sculpted ceiling with designs and had been painted deep hunter green, providing guests with the feel and visualization of a surrounding forest. There were also gilded mirrors and rosewood furniture. The hotel served as home to the 1916 Democratic National Convention. The Jefferson was about as distant in location and clientele as one could get from the seedier haunts of St. Louis.

"Elias, look over there. Isn't that Nate Evans?" Vasey asked his partner.

"Sure looks like him, Jim, but what the heck is he doing on this side of town? Plus, look at his company. They're not from around these parts." Hoagland answered. "I say we watch for a while and see what happens."

"Maybe they're just helping Mr. Breadon build the still and speakeasy he's been talking about in anticipation of prohibition."

"Jim, let's not be obvious. We'll circle the block a few times and just watch and see."

In May, 1918, the St. Louis police department took delivery of four new Model "T" Ford wagons at a cost of $550 each. Across the nation, city law enforcement agencies were adding retro-fitted multi-seat vehicles to their fleets. With the imminent passage of the Volstead Act, officials were anticipating increased raids and arrests from raids. The "T" was widely used and popular because of its reliability, durability, ruggedness, easy maintenance and repair. The automobile could withstand the heavy punishment and neglect inherent in police activity. Its modern two-speed forward transmission operated without a clutch, making for easier driving than standard clutch and stick. Five body styles made it adaptable to different uses, from police sedans to ambulances.

Two paddy wagons and four sedans rolled down Tucker Boulevard, quietly pulling to a halt at the ornate entrance of the Jefferson. The detectives had witnessed nearly a dozen known gamblers entering the hotel during their impromptu stakeout.

A force of 15 uniformed patrolmen and 8 detectives stormed the front entrance, marching to a private dining room where a concierge had indicated that the law enforcement officials would find their prey. Inside the makeshift dining area, a motley crew had assembled.

All those present at the meeting were caught off-guard. Each of the more than a dozen there were loaded into the paddy wagons and hauled down to central police headquarters for questioning. Their deafening silences and vague responses provided nothing substantive to the frustrated police and prosecutors. They were readied for release. There was no reason to detain or file charges against them.

Addressing Detectives Vasey and Hoagland, Lieutenant Hollihan blasted the red-faced pair.

"Dammit, you two, this is an embarrassment. We've wasted a lot of time and money. If I had my way, I'd bust you back down to uniforms. They weren't doing anything illegal. There's no wire, no money, no nothing."

"Lieutenant, there's something going on. Look at these scraps of paper with notes all over them: Kerr poison, Rausch poison Jackson dumb, Williams in, HF in, Cicotte bag, Weaver X, Gleason no, Sallee no, Groh no. Then there are what look like betting slips with some large amounts: AR $350K, KB $25K, RB $15K. Something is going on, even if I'm not sure what," Hoagland responded

"Unless you can unlock that mystery in five minutes, they're all walking. Now get out of my sight and take your semi-intelligent partner with you."

As the sun began to peek out above the Mississippi River, Rachie Brown, whose real name was Abraham Braunstein (he used the name of the female bookkeeper for Arnold Rothstein as an alias), Nate Evans and Joe Sullivan walked out through the entry doors and down the concrete steps of the downtown precinct. Evans, a polished and personable character, served as a partner of Arnold Rothstein in several legitimate casino and racing ventures. The two were also partners in a succession of Manhattan and Long Island gaming places. Although he had a deep involvement in the Rothstein legal ventures, he made his position clear, that he wished no involvement in certain seedy businesses, including smuggling, fencing, drugs and prostitution.

Unhappy about the detainment, Evans spoke, "This thing may be getting out of hand. If we cannot keep a lid on it, AR will pull out."

Sullivan responded, "Don't worry. We've pulled fixes like this off before."

"Sport, you're living in the past. There are a lot more eyes watching baseball nowadays. I do worry and so does AR. Neither of us likes it when things are upset. Think about a few fall guys, just in case this situation ever does blow up. We've also got a few calls to make, to the guys in Des Moines, Chicago and Cincy. Things are just getting out of hand, AR, no one will like this."

Although baseball's post-season competition had been taken place every year now since 1905, Americans eagerly awaited the 1919 series, looking on it as a most joyous event. The popularity of baseball soared, propelling the World Series into an event with national notoriety. Americans continued to stream home, the horrors of the bloody warfare of WWI behind them as peace spread around the world. The timelessness of the game of baseball provided a promise of tranquility to men and women across the country. The 1919 series pitted the American League champion Chicago White Sox against the National League champion Cincinnati Reds. The league commissioners, Ban Johnson and Garry Herrmann, owner of the Reds, decided on a best of nine series through 1921.

There were the usual rumors of gamblers trying to extract inside information from players and managers. Pat Moran had complained to Herrmann about gamblers keeping several of his young pitchers out through the night prior to start of the series, but he had stepped in and put an end to it.

The opening two games were to take place on the home field of the National League champions, Redland Field. Constructed on the same site as their former home, the Palace of the Fans, Redland Field was completed for the start of the 1912 season. The Reds played their first game there on May 18, 1912, against the Chicago Cubs, to a capacity crowd of 22,000 faithful fans. The lower deck of the ballpark extended from home plate to the right and left field foul poles while the magnificent upper deck grandstand extended from behind home plate past both the first and third base dugouts. The cerise-painted seats in the grandstands matched the caps and stockings worn by the home team. Bleachers were located in right field and came to a point in right center field. This area became known as the sun deck. Outside, the ballpark had a red brick facade. The park's most unique feature was the terrace in front of the left field fence. It was an incline that started 20 feet from the left field wall and gradually increased until it reached a point four feet below the terrace.

Redland Field underwent many changes for the World Series in 1919. The street behind left field was blocked off and temporary stands were built to accommodate a few thousand more fans. Portable seats were added in front of the lower deck and then converted to permanent box seats in 1926. The same year, the distances were shortened again as the diamond was repositioned closer to the outfield. When all was said and done, over 35,000 fans would pile into Redlands for game one.

Entering from Findlay Street, strolling down the aisleway arm in arm, Mr. and Mrs. Babe Ruth worked their way through the lively throng in the lower grandstand of Redlands Field just after 1:10PM on Wednesday, October 1, 1919. Red, white and blue bunting adorned the railings of the upper deck.

Babe pointed towards seats three rows down, "There, Helen, there they are."

Already present in the box were Christy Mathewson, Tom 'Titanic' Thompson, Hugh Fullerton, Colonel Jacob Ruppert, Garry Herrmann and Cy Young. Tensions among this unlikely gang of six were thick enough to cut with a knife. The American League President and Harry Frazee had yet to arrive.

Johnson and Ruppert had ganged up, applying pressure to get Herrmann to step down as commissioner for the length of the series; assuring him they had the support of many of the owners. Ruppert believed that baseball would be exposed to criticism if the commissioner was from the pennant-winning team. Angry words passed until Herrmann, finally having had enough, shouted aloud, "What on earth could go wrong to necessitate a commissioner independent of any financial or emotional attachment?"

Spotting the game's emerging star slugger, ever the consummate gentleman, Cy Young arose from his seat and extended his hand toward the pair.

"Well, gents, enough of the frivolity of intrigue. Let's focus on the picture of beauty," he quipped, temporarily dousing the flames of the heated conversation.

"Good afternoon, Ruth. Such a lovely bride, how did you ever persuade her to marry you? I am so very pleased to meet you, Mrs. Ruth." Young introduced himself first and then proceeded to introduce the other men present.

"Well, Cy Young, I did not think you even knew who I am," Ruth bellowed "Helen, I didn't even think he liked me."

"Ruth, I had you wrong, I will admit. Thought you to be a braggart, but you do back your words. Plus, Ruth you are the talk of baseball with all the home runs you're knocking out. That story about the blast over the roof last week has mesmerized all of America. Children are idolizing you, men are jealous and the women . . . well, Helen, don't take your eye off of him. Ruth, you and your bride come sit right here next to me."

Helen and Babe settled into the wooden chairs, the attentive husband wrapping a brown wool blanket around her legs. "Let's keep the chill off of you, dear."

"Thank you darling. You are so kind, Mr. Young."

"Just call me Cy, please."

"Ruth, I think your pitching talents are being wasted. You have more wins than I did at your age. You can pitch for a long time, maybe even long enough to get close to my win count of five hundred and eleven," Young offered Ruth.

"Young, you're out of touch. Fans want to see the long ball. They want to see runs, runs and long home runs! I'll break the hitting records."

"Maybe home runs, but for batting average, Cobb and Wagner and Hornsby are out of your reach. And pitching, you can never reach my total wins."

"Young, I could break your record. I could break every record, hitting and batting! That is, if I got the chance. Owners believe that more fans will come to see me in the field every day, knocking the ball out of the park."

"Those are big words, maybe too big for one's own britches. Let me tell you a thing..."

Mathewson interjected, bringing a new line of thought as he sensed the conversation was becoming too heated. "Babe, what have you heard about the series?"

"Christy, the White Sox'll win in a walk. They're too strong at every position. The Reds have a pretty good team with outstanding pitching. The Sox have a great line up, and that Jackson, he can hit. Nearly as good as me, you know. That's *nearly*. Writers who think they know the sport say pitchers can stop the hitters. I've never seen a pitcher can stop me. Well, not for long, anyway. "

"Ruth, I didn't ask for your prediction for the outcome. I asked what you're hearing about the series."

"You're not asking me who I think will win."

Titanic Thompson jumped in, "Ruth, you ain't changed since we met in Hot Springs, still a baby and wet behind the ears."

Ruth and Thompson crossed paths in 1915, during the Red Sox spring training in Arkansas as Titanic was making one of his legendary cross-country gambling treks. Born in the squalor of a log cabin deep in the Ozark Mountains, the uneducated Alvin 'Titanic' Thompson made his way through life on the quickness of his wit and the speed of his hands. He had become known as a bold gambler, a man who would bet on literally anything, but his unsuspecting prey did not know he gambled most heavily when the odds were aligned in his favor. In spite of his lack of formal education, Titanic had a gift for mathematics. He studied diligently and quickly developed an understanding of the odds in throwing dice or playing cards. He knew the probabilities of throwing a seven or the numbers in craps, or drawing to an inside straight at the poker table. But understanding the odds was not enough. Titanic was in fact a con man at heart and left nothing to chance. He became a master of slipping in mercury-laced dice and marked cards. His understanding of statistics also meant awareness of the chance that he could lose, so in every play he sought to eliminate that possibility. Yes, Titanic was a man with a reputation for betting on anything, at least whatever was a sure thing.

Titanic shined when it came to finding a sucker to bet on a long odds situation when the outcome would be heavily tilted in his favor. One such occasion arose during an early December fishing trip to a lodge in northern Minnesota. The facility included an 18 hole golf course. Titanic bragged that he could hit a golf ball over 400 yards. This claim belied his stature. Although he stood about 5' 10" tall, his frame was rather less than muscular, as he tipped the scale a shade shy of 160 pounds fully clothed. Travelling with his hired bodyguard at the time, Dick Wade, the brazen Thompson cajoled $40,000 in wagers from the business men, golf professionals and gamblers all in residence at the lodge. If Thompson was to lose the bet, the services of Wade would have become quite necessary as Titanic was $39,000 short of being able to cover the bet. The defining moment of the braggadocio came when he proclaimed he could prove himself correct here at the lodge and would need one swing.

The next morning, two dozen confident spectators accompanied Titanic to the first tee box. The elevated tee created a beautiful vista of the long wide fairway of this picturesque, long par five. Two forces of nature would work against this braggart: the sub-freezing temperature, which would limit the ball's flight, and the residue of a recent six-inch snowfall, which was sure to halt the white sphere when it landed.

Titanic, readying himself, peered over the fairway, commenting to golf pro Herman Keiser, "You don't think this can be done; do you?"

"Impossible, Ti, impossible." Marshall Clemens, the 75-year-old grey-headed proprietor of the lodge was standing to Thompson's right.

"Mr. Clemens, how far you think it is to the other side of the lake?"

"Exactly a quarter mile across," Clemens answered.

Ti adjusted his stance and took dead aim.

"A quarter mile, four hundred and forty yards, well, that'll make measuring pretty easy, boys."

What Ti lacked in stature, he more than made up for with his hand-eye coordination. A smooth elegant downswing resulted in the club face striking squarely on the ball at the precise time his weight shifted forward. The ball arced into the air and fell onto the snowless surface of the frozen pond nearly two hundred and twenty yards from where it was struck, the initial hops quickly added sixty yards and the dimpled ball skidded the balance of the distance, nestling against pale reeds bent over at the shore line, a quarter of a mile away. Ti easily cleared the distance and collected his winnings, including an extra $5,000, courtesy of a last-minute wager by Mr. Keiser.

The crowd was so shocked at what they had seen that no one thought to ask why the surface of the lake was so pristine. The night before, Ti paid one of the resort's groundskeepers $1,000 to clear a path about seventy-five yards wide of any snow, and to ensure the man gave it extra effort, offered $1,500 more as a bonus that would be earned the next day if Ti did, in fact, win his bet.

Ruth was about to fall victim to Ti's con scheme in Hot Springs. Titanic had just been separating several of the locals from a few hundred bucks at the country club. He had boasted that he could whip them all left-handed. Titanic had spent most of the previous day with them playing cards. He did everything with his right hand — dealt cards, poured drinks. He took the deception to the point of wearing his watch on his left hand and put his wallet in his left rear pocket. He beat the best of the locals by a single stroke. During the match conversation in the locker room, he heard about the brash young fireballing left-hander with a big arm and a bigger ego. Ti now had a mark, so he sought out Ruth. There were only a few hotels in the town, so it would not prove to be very difficult to find the bar where the Red Sox players were gathered. The lobby of the Hot Spring Hotel proved to be that location. Before he even spotted Ruth, he could hear the lefty boasting of a prank he had pulled off earlier in the day. Several teammates were gathered around. Helen had long since retired for the night. Ruth was every bit Ti's match in touting his skills, but he turned out to be far less savvy when it came to understanding the traps and cons of real life.

Ti sidled up to the bar, integrating himself into the crowd. After a brief introduction, Ti turned to Ruth and the setup was underway. "Hey, big boy, everyone says you have an arm stronger than anyone has ever seen. I say it's all crap."

Ruth fell into the web more easily than a fly into a sugar-coated jar, "Yes, that's the case, I will say."

"Well, Ruth, let's test that theory. I say I can throw a peanut further than you."

After a belly roar, Ruth responded, "Mr. Thompson, not for nothing, a scrawny fella like you ain't going to outthrow me."

"How much you got to back up your words, a thousand?"

After nearly a half minute of more hearty laughter and several goads by his teammates and Thompson, Ruth sheepishly took Ti up on his challenge. "Sure." Ruth commented he was a little embarrassed to take the challenge from this slender stranger.

Neither one knew the other did not have enough cash to cover the bet. Thompson was sure he wasn't going to lose, as was Ruth.

Players from the Red Sox and St. Louis Browns and Athletics quickly gathered in the street to watch this ad hoc event.

Thompson handed Ruth a peanut pulled from his pocket, letting Ruth have the honor of the first throw. Ruth took a mighty windup and threw. The peanut hit the sidewalk on the other side of the street, just in front of the Arlington Hotel, a distance of 100 feet.

Thompson drew back his arm and released the peanut in an easy motion. Stunned players and other onlookers watched in silence as the peanut ascended above the second-floor windows of the hotel, landing on its rooftop. There, Ti's partner quickly switched a buckshot- laden peanut with one which had not been altered and left the roof, with no one the wiser. Ruth borrowed money from several teammates to make good on his losses.

Unknown to the others in attendance, Ban Johnson had arranged for Mathewson and Hugh Fullerton to sit in the box together. Fullerton had predicted in recent newspaper articles that Chicago would rout the Cincinnati team and would need no more than six games to finish off their rivals. The league president was reacting to rumblings that gamblers had gotten to certain members of the White Sox and the series was not going to be played on the level. He instructed Mathewson and Fullerton to observe the White Sox players during the course of the game, looking for suspect plays, and then compare notes at the conclusion. Neither highlighted a single suspicious play during the game.

"Mr. Mathewson is asking if you hear anything about the series not being on the level. I guess we just need to spell it out for the big guy," Ti, leaning back, let go a series of hearty laughs, "Ain't that right?"

"Well, Mr. Thompson, "Mathewson stammered.

"Let me see if I can make the point clearer. A week ago the Sox were very heavily favored. If you bet on the Reds to win you could make three bucks back for every buck you bet. Today you basically make fifty cents on the same buck. So, Babe, he's asking if you think there's any good reason the betting should change and the odds should drop."

Hugh Fullerton, writing pre-series commentary and analysis for the Chicago Herald, commented, "If either of you had read my article today, you would see clearly where I stand. Stay away from wagering on the series, as there are ugly rumors afoot."

"Excuse me, gents. Why, no self-respecting ballplayer is going to intentionally throw any ball game this big. Why, if I found out a teammate of mine was not playing on the up and up, I'd sock him one right on the snoot. Mr. Thompson, this series is more on the level than the peanut you tossed back in Arkansas. I heard you filled it with shot. Maybe you should give me back the thousand I lost."

"Don't carry any sour grapes there, Ruth, it'll eat you up. I can help you make your money back, put everything you own on the Reds."

"Do you think their pitching will stop Chicago?" Ruth continued, still focused on the baseball aspect.

"No, you dope, I think they're going to win the same way I knew I could toss my peanut the furthest. Tell you what, Ruth; I'll give you a chance not only to get even but to make twice your money back. I'll bet you $2,000 that Cicotte hits the first batter."

Without hesitation, Ruth took the bet, quipping, "Who's the dope now? Cicotte hardly walks anyone, and he ain't hit a batter in two years. You're on."

"Ruth, you are forever the innocent and gullible child. Cicotte's streak will end shortly."

At 1:45 an announcement was made to the crowd that President Woodrow Wilson had taken ill suddenly at the White House and would not be in attendance. The crowd stood, in respect for President, and silently prayed as instructed.

The first pitch of the game was made at exactly 1:52 PM, a called strike. At 1:53PM Morrie Rath headed to first base, having been plunked in the back by Cicotte on his third pitch.

"Damn it, Thompson, dumb luck," Ruth proclaimed.

"When you roll dice which ain't loaded, that's dumb luck. Ruth, ain't you figured out I don't bet when that kind of luck is involved?"

Not discouraged by losing the bet, Ruth feverishly worked at recovering his losses, continuing to wager with Thompson. At game's end, his losses were substantial, amounting to well over $10,000. To the delight of the 31,000 in attendance, game one of the 1919 World Series ended with the White Sox on the wrong end of a 9-1 decision.

"Ruth, listen to me, make your money back betting on the Reds." Thompson wrapped his left hand around the back of Babe's head and pulled his ear to near to his lips and whispered so none of the others could hear, "Bet on the Reds, but go the other way in game three. Be smart, now, and listen to me."

Thompson bid farewell to everyone in attendance and set out on another of his adventures. Ruth slumped back in his seat, worn out from the troubling day; he wondered what would drive a man to not do his best, especially on a big stage like the World Series.

Cincinnati completed its conquest of the White Sox in eight games, losing games three, six and seven. Thompson went on to win $75,000 betting on the series. Two days after the end of the series, murmurs of a fix and scandal began to surface in Chicago and Cincinnati. Within two weeks, the swirling news of the Big Fix was gaining national attention, rapidly.

Back in his Massachusetts home, Ruth read the October 31, 1919 headlines of the evening edition of the Boston American,

"Comiskey offers $20,000 reward for Fix Evidence"

Ruth walked from the fireplace and stared pensively through the glass panes of the rear door. Autumn now in full swing, he stared silently west as the sun retreated beyond the nearly barren trees, a few still sprinkled with ecru leaves not yet fallen from their branches. The placid lake, water shimmering from a soft breeze, soothed Babe's ire.

He was digesting the story of the White Sox owner putting out a bounty for anyone who could produce an ounce of evidence to support the accusation that his players did not play their best during the World Series. The story had commented that the White Sox owner had placed an ad in newspapers in every major city across the country. Charles Comiskey tried to discourage talk of a fix that had been brought on by his team's dismal performance in the Series. He had told reporters, "I believe my boys fought the battle of the recent World Series on the level, as they have always done. And I would be the first to want information to the contrary — if there be any. I would give $20,000 to anyone unearthing information to that effect." The report also claimed that Comiskey had hired a private detective to investigate the finances of every player on the White Sox and the Reds.

Ruth knew that during the regular season, certain players, to make a few extra dollars, would toss a game, but this was on a national scale. Ruth had an abject disdain for the practice. Throwing a World Series like this was beyond his comprehension. How many players were involved? If a travelling con man like Alvin Thompson knew about the fix, how many more were aware as well? Ruth feared that this, if true, would destroy baseball, not only from the inside, but also the American public would walk away from this sport as they had boxing and horseracing. Because the gamblers infiltrated those sports, the average Joe didn't know if any venue were on the level. Nor was he sure who to trust.

The game, which had become Ruth's life, needed to change or fail. Americans returned to the sport in large numbers. If gamblers continued to make the game unsavory, the fans would leave just as easily. Ruth vowed he would do everything in his power to keep spectators from abandoning the game he loved.

Helen stepped up next to him, "What is it, Babe?"

Without moving his eyes from the lake, he handed Helen the folded newspaper, headline facing her.

"Oh my, can this be true?" a simple involuntary response, "What now, Babe, what now?"

Ruth did not react immediately to Helen's question. Suddenly shrouded in a deep sense of loss, akin to the death of a best friend, he thought about the Sox players. How did they become involved in such a conspiracy? His belief that every man played the game as he did, giving his best all the time, slipped away, crushed under the weight of the headline. He had looked up to the players older than he with a great deal of respect. The implication of this gut-wrenching revelation started eating at him from the inside.

"Just more disappointment from the people I most trusted," Ruth answered. Not yet 25, a litany of abandonment had already crowned his life. He wondered if there was anyone who could be trusted. Ruth questioned his own resolve.

Chapter 24

Ban Johnson paced the length of his Cleveland office in the company of his longtime friends Charles Somers and Jimmy McAleer. The trio, along with Charles Comiskey, had lured talent from the rival leagues to jumpstart the American League. Johnson had slammed the Cleveland Press on his desk, prominently displaying the same headline as that of the paper Helen Ruth had held in her hand just the day before. McAleer and Somers were seated around a coffee table. Ban Johnson, usually neat and pristine, was clothed in a wrinkled suit, one which he was wearing for a second day. His starched white shirt was disheveled, with a hint of a light brown patch outlining his armpits. The contant rubbing of his furrowed brow was a clear indication of his worry. The effect of his long battle with Comiskey over control of the American League was now beginning to extract its toll. For years, Johnson had been working tirelessly to end the stranglehold gamblers held on the baseball. He sought to drive the gamblers from the parks, taking players out of easy reach. Each and every effort at player and owner discipline was trumped by the unholy triumvirate of the Red Sox, White Sox and Yankee ownership.

"What the hell does Charlie think he is doing?" Johnson remarked. "Does he think anyone will believe this crap? This is akin to a stone-cold killer putting a reward out to find the murderer of the bodies he stood over, to serve as a distraction."

"Ban, he is trying to stay above the fray and present an image of being clean. One rogue reporter, this Hugh Fullerton, just will not let the story die." Somers responded. "Plus, there is talk that Fullerton is trying to unite newspapers across the country to limit reporting of baseball to just scores, to thwart information that gamblers may have. Ban that is potentially a death knell for the sport. Scandal and silence is a powerful combination for disaster. Charlie is desperately making an effort to give the appearance that he is keeping his house in order."

"Does anyone sense Comiskey is clean in all of this?" rhetorically Johnson asked. "Personally, I don't believe so. I received a letter from Joe Jackson's wife, alleging that Joe had gone to Charles before the start of the series, asking that he step in and tell Gleason not to play him. Comiskey dismissed the notion that his players would not play on the level."

Somers added, "I can't say for certain. There are conflicting stories on the street. It is hard to tell if Old Roman is covering for himself or his players. My sources downstate agree that Jackson tried to beg off playing. He had gone to Comiskey before game one, telling him things were not right. Both Comiskey and Gleason ignored Jackson. Makes you wonder why. Now Comiskey is offering an eye-catching reward for evidence when it was right there in front of him. My sense is that Charlie will protect his own interests and sell everyone else out, including his players. He believes the players cost him a bundle last year, so he's seeking revenge. This stinks to high heaven, Ban."

Interjecting his thoughts, McAleer added, "Frazee and Ruppert are all spun up over the Mays issue." (Johnson had blocked the sale of Carl Mays from the Red Sox to the Yankees, seeking disciplinary action against the pitcher for his role in game-fixing activities, angering owners of the Yankees and the Red Sox) "He wants nothing more than to position you as a weak commissioner. Comiskey is working to convince Frazee and Ruppert to threaten to jump to the National League with the White Sox. This would cripple the American League and dismantle the commission. They want this runaway racist judge, Landis, to be appointed as a lone commissioner, with full authority over both leagues. The best way for them to get you is with a full frontal assault, a scandal of such magnitude that only the leader can take the fall."

"We need get Frazee, Ruppert and Comiskey all in here, and quickly. Of course, that grampus judge from Chicago needs to be here as well. This group may ultimately get me out, but they'll ruin baseball in the process, unless I take action first. If any of the owners had knowledge of a fix, the sport will crumble before our eyes. We need a path to redemption before the final curtain on the scandal falls," Johnson summed his intentions. Within a few minutes his assistant was in motion, putting together the details of the meeting which would save baseball.

Chapter 25

"Excuse me, your Honor," a demure secretary whispered, more in fear than out of any reverence for Landis, "Mr. Ban Johnson is calling on you."

Sitting on the corner of his desk, Landis roared, "What the HELL does that impotent SOB want now?"

Sheepishly, inquisitively, Charles Comiskey looked up from his chair at Landis and turned his palms up in an 'I don't know' expression.

"Tell him I'm busy and I'll return his call."

"Your honor, you don't understand. He isn't on the telephone; he's in the ante-room." Almost before she got the words out, Johnson barged into Landis's office, followed by Colonel Ruppert and Harry Frazee.

"Look, gentlemen, the soon all-powerful and brave baseball commissioner is looking to duck me. You pompous SOB!" the visibly annoyed Johnson railed at Landis.

"Come on in, Ban, what insignificant issue is on your little mind?" The anger between the pair was coming to a boiling point amidst the speculation that Landis, in assuming the throne of National Baseball Commissioner, essentially neutered any and all of Johnson's authority.

Landis promised to the owners and preached to the newspapers that if her were named commissioner, he would deal a heavy blow to baseball, barring any member of the Chicago White Sox, or any other team, for that matter, from ever playing in major league baseball for life, if it were believed they had bet on baseball or had guilty knowledge of any player, manager or owner who did and chose to do nothing with the information. This seminal action in and of itself created a tacit admission that the sport of baseball was in fact under the influence, if not the full control of hoodlums and gamblers. Landis believed this step was an absolute necessity, since baseball had been elevated to national prominence to the point that it was now referred to as the national pastime. Sunday outings for families became trips to the stadium to watch a doubleheader that would last most of a summer's afternoon. Ballparks were now the norm, replacing picnics in the open fields and parks. Children followed and idolized the stars of the times. Newspapers responded to the public's demands and changed their view on how to report about baseball; skimpy box scores were replaced with full stories and analysis. Editors dedicated journalists to follow and write about each team and file homey stories about the star players.

"Look, I'm not here because I like you, JUDGE, or need something. But we need to restore the public's faith in the game. You and your puppet over there are dragging your feet about doing something. There's the potential for a financial disaster here. Charlie, how are you bracing for the loss of fans? Or do you think everyone will continue to go to games when a few of their heroes have been driven from the game, even if there's no evidence of their guilt?"

"Ban, we have plenty of other baseball players who will replace the lost heroes . Fans will flock to other great players," Comiskey interceded.

"Charley, you're missing the point, as usual. Your players may have, in fact, just been caught throwing a world series. Maybe they did, maybe they didn't. News travels fast these days, so does speculation. Some people are beginning to think that owners were involved." Ban continued, "Yes, Charlie, you're off base. You couldn't read the tea leaves if they spoke to you. Gentlemen, the time for more heroes has passed. We need to take a bold step before ultimate punishments are doled out. Baseball needs a legend. Heroes are remembered: Legends never die!"

"What in God's sakes are you babbling about?" Landis asked

"We need a real hero, and he needs to be on the biggest stage in the world, New York City."

Comiskey chimes in, "Assuming you're correct, who would be this mythical figure, is there even such a player?"

"Yes, there is! That kid Ruth who's buried in Boston! I believe he may be the greatest baseball player we'll ever see. He can do it all. Pitch, hit, hit for power, run..."

Johnson glared at Comiskey as the righteous White Sox owner interjected his thought rudely.

"Come on, Cobb is a better hitter."

"Better as a hitter is like beauty, it's in the eye of the beholder. Ruth will get on nearly as often and if he wasn't so fixated on the long ball, most likely more. Cobb doesn't hit with the sheer ferociousness and power of Ruth."

"There are others catching up to his power. Power is a fad. Baseball fans like the art of base running, moving players bag to bag. Not one swing and it's over. It's a thinking man's game of perpetual positioning."

"Charlie, times are changing, the game is evolving. Fans are awakening to the thrill of the moment. Their skyward eyes tracking deep majestic blasts; their ears welcoming the thunderous crack of the bat as baseballs are forcefully driven out of sight. The thrill of this raw strength is heightened by the elements of the game you mention. But Charlie, even those players with an ability to hit home runs, well, they are not dominating pitchers like this kid is. No, this Ruth has it all. Given the chance, he can break all the records. Given a fair chance, that is! On the proper stage, in the limelight, he can save our game and restore it to its prestige. Yes, gentlemen, we have a legend of Biblical magnitude within our grasp. Yes, right here in front of us. The game needs a mythical figure, a legend for the ages! The game needs Babe Ruth!"

Johnson anticipated that investigation processes would carry on for very long time. Cook County, Illinois had already convened a grand jury and was compiling a list of witnesses ranging from every White Sox player, manager and the owner to known gamblers from all corners of the country. Johnson was sure it would take a year at least, maybe longer for this scandal to play out. At the conclusion, a handful of players, maybe a star or two would end up taking the fall. Some would be barred from the sport they loved. They would be unable to making a living, courtesy of the inflexible former judge. Crooked owners would be spared. Gamblers and their influence would still lurk in the bowels of the game and keep their relationships with dishonest players less out in the open. That a self-righteous, iron-fisted, narrow-minded man like Mountain Landis would become the Czar of the sport was an affront to Ban. Such a man should not have the sole responsibility for this great American institution; Johnson would diligently work to prevent that from happening.

On deck for Ban: get a meeting in New York City with Ruth and the owners of the Red Sox and Yankees.

Chapter 26

During World War I, Curtiss Aeroplane and Motor Company manufactured a significant number of Curtiss JN-4s (called *Jennys*) for the U.S. government's war effort. Nearly every U.S. airman learned to fly using this plane. At the conclusion of the war, the U.S. and the manufacturer, due to cancellation of contracts, each held a significant surplus of the *Jennys*. For a fraction of the plane's original $5,000 purchase price, Jennys were secured by ambitious servicemen, already familiar with the operation and capabilities of the biplane. Although some worked alone, many of the former servicemen pooled their resources to form small flying circus teams as the barnstorming industry emerged.

Typically, a pilot or a group would buzz (fly low) over a rural town and attract the attention of the community. Using a local farm as a landing strip (hence the name "barnstorming") they would negotiate with the farmer for the use of one of his fields as a temporary runway to stage their air show. The locals would be treated to a display of daredevilry, death dives, barrel rolls, loop-the-loop and other aerial stunts. Aerial acrobats thrilled the crowds with their wing-walking, stunt parachuting and mid-air plane transfers. The bravest of the locals would fork over the $1.00 fee for a plane ride. Many locals who had never seen an airplane up close were thrilled with the experience. When the barnstormers arrived, word would quickly spread and the town's businesses would close so that people could purchase plane rides and watch the show. Within a decade, flying circuses and aerial barnstorming would decline as quickly as they arose as safety regulations were introduced.

The post-war years brought a rebirth of baseball's popularity. Barnstorming helped drive the meteoric rise of baseball in rural America where exposure to major league games did not exist. Professional baseball players seized on the opportunity to make more than twice the season salary earned from their respective clubs. They were paid for playing 154 games, and when the season ended, players, led by the stars, organized, forming several different travelling teams. Johnson feared that the travelling players would use the extra money to neutralize the leverage that the owners held on them. Ban needed players to sign on again for the 1920 season, and he needed them bound to the owners for life. Seeing this as a threat to the death-grip the owners had on the players, Johnson issued a warning that suspensions would be placed on any player participating in barnstorming tours. The warning went largely ignored as players set out on their tours.

Ruth was included on a team with several Red Sox and White Sox players, including the now-troubled Joe Jackson. This team traveled through the southwest corner of the states, ending in Southern California. Except for St. Louis, major league baseball had not yet crossed west of the Mississippi.

At each every rail stop, the players were met by jubilant throngs. Most folks who had heard tales of the Babe rushed the slowing train, hoping to get a glimpse, or, if really lucky, a shake of Babe's mammoth hand. Legends of his massive blasts made Ruth the primary drawing card of his troupe. The professionals played games against teams comprised of town locals. This was done less to please the locals than to take their money.

Ruth relished the part of drawing card with arrogant showmanship. Not one to leave the fans wanting, he would hit at least one ball further than anyone in that county could remember seeing. As soon as a long fly had left the ballpark, Ruth was mobbed by spectators. Young boys and girls would wrap their arms and legs around the legs of Ruth, or clutch at his belt. No one cared about the score. The fans got what they wanted, a long homerun or two and autographs of the players. At their final whistle stop, in San Luis Obispo, playing on a makeshift diamond at the mission, Ruth launched a ball up into the afternoon sun that carried past the end of the field, over the side and bounding down the hill into the creek. Fans young and old stormed the field, latching onto Ruth. Waddling like a penguin, he attempted to encircle the bases, only to be yanked to the ground under the weight of idolizing youngsters. Teammates rolled with laughter.

In a gesture of graciousness and excitement for the throngs of fans, Ruth always ensured that one local pitcher struck him out.

The players made extra cash by pooling their money to entice the church league pitching *legends* to challenge the big guy in an at-bat. The players gave odds for the each local hero to strike out the Babe. Minimum bet was $100. When the odds got long enough, they would bet the other way. Of course, Ruth conformed. A violent and mighty whiff at the ball, often followed by a fake tumble thrilled the locals even though their pockets had been picked. By the time the barnstorming troupe rolled into the Santa Barbara Train Station on December 16th, the players, thanks to Babe, had each made more than $20,000.

Christy Walsh, a lawyer by training, enjoyed the high life of New York City: the all-night soirees, the fashion, and the opportunity. He held jobs in the newspaper industry and advertising. Fired from both jobs, he decided it was time to move to another field, so he switched to ghost writing for radio shows. The erupting popularity of professional sports drew his attention and when he realized the anguish and unfair treatment athletes faced when dealing with unscrupulous owners. He concluded that the players needed someone to represent their interest. All he had to do was land a marquee player to get the ball rolling. Cobb, Speaker and others were too distrustful, so he set his sights on the Babe, whom he had heard was still a bit wet behind the ears.

Walsh was a pit bull, stalking Ruth across the country on his 1919 barnstorming tour. Along the way, he staked out Ruth's hotels, hoping for a chance to corner Babe and get a few minutes of his time alone. Hanging out in the palatial lobby of the Belvedere Hotel (recently sold and renamed from the Potter Hotel), his fortune began to change when he overheard a Western Union courier explaining to the desk clerk he had a telegram for Mr. Ruth. Presenting a convincing story that he was the brother of Ruth's lovely wife Helen, the courier entrusted the telegram for delivery to Walsh. Now how to get the telegram to Ruth?

The 390 room Potter Hotel was Milo Potter's greatest achievement. The finished product was six-and-a-half stories high with sun shaded and with glassed-in porches gracing the front. Guests could enjoy a breath-taking view of the Pacific and the near shore islands from the roof gardens. When looking east, the mountains could be seen and to the north, the city. The grounds were elaborately landscaped and included tennis courts, a zoo, a palm and fernery building, cactus gardens and tranquil pathways.

"Helen, this is one beautiful hotel. Look at those palm trees. And the sun, Helen, doesn't it feel great?" Ruth exclaimed to his wife as they casually strolled back to the hotel.

Helen, exhausted from not only the daily grind of each stop which now had been going on for 60 days straight, but also the cruel deceptions and the growing nightly antics of her husband, did not respond. The time alone she had once treasured with Babe was now more of a chore. She knew his attentiveness to her became fleeting as soon as something more exciting came along. The allure of a wilder, carefree life had begun to consume Ruth, and she sensed it could not be stopped.

"Helen, let's have some chow out on the terrace," Ruth barked aloud.

Helen debated letting him eat dinner alone, until she glanced in the vicinity of the only unoccupied table which was in the far corner of the outdoor dining area. Several of the players were seated at the tables to either side. Some of the guys already had women, probably selling their wares, adorning their once-vacant arms. Helen was leery of another escapade by Ruth. The pain of the stopover in Denver was still a fresh wound in her heart. She did not want to go through a reenactment. Returning to the train after a brief shopping spree, she walked into their private pullman to find Ruth nestled with several coeds in the soaking tub. The only thing which prevented her from storming out was that Ruth, although thoroughly soused, had remained fully clothed, unlike the other occupants. But he had pushed her patience to the limit. He begged forgiveness and swore nothing like that would happen again. Now, not wanting to test his resolve with temptation or explain her disdain for his new-found habits, she acquiesced, quietly walking to the dining table with him.

Walsh spotted the young couple just as they sat down at the table. *Of all the luck*, he thought. *Ruth just dropped into my arms. The heck with chicanery; I'll just go at this head-on; this is probably my best chance at talking to him.*

"Good afternoon, Mr. Ruth, let me introduce myself. I'm Christy Walsh, sports agent."

"Sir, do I know you? Can't you see I'm at dinner with my wife? And what the heck is a sports agent?"

"I'll get to that in moment. But I have a telegram here for you from New York City."

"Then hand it over. Say, how did you come on it, anyway?"

Before Ruth had a chance to rip open the envelope, Stuffy McInnis made his way to the table, barging into the conversation.

"Hey, ain't you the guy who been pestering some of players about needing representation with the owners? Yeah, this is the guy, I think Speaker wanted to pop him one, he was so pushy," McInnis interjected.

Ruth said, "Hold off, let me hear what he's got to say. After all, he paid his own way to come out here. I think I'll show him some courtesy. Okay, mister, you got five minutes to catch my interest. If you have not done that the conversation will end and I will enjoy a meal with my bride. If you persist, then I'll pop you one myself."

Walsh squared up with Ruth, telling him of his failures in life and his recent success, but most of all, his idea of players having someone who can vigorously fight on their behalf with owners. Ruth was fascinated.

Ruth had demanded that the Red Sox increase his pay to $25,000 for the upcoming season, which simply matched an offer from yet another upstart league. He had balked at meeting with Frazee and Johnson until the Red Sox owner had agreed to the pay increase. In addition to his share of the gambling winnings, Ruth collected $500 per game on the tour. Over a 152-game schedule, this came to $75,000. Ruth's opinion was that even with the increase in pay he had requested; he was a bargain.

Twenty minutes later, Ruth was hooked. Leaning back in his chair, which creaked loudly beneath Ruth's shifting weight, he thought, *finally someone who understands and can take my argument up with the owners, now this is a proposition with merit.*

"Helen, what do you think of what Mr. Walsh, here, is saying? I like it."

"I think the smartest advice he gave was for you to stop spending money like water! You do need someone to help you with managing our money." Helen had carefully listened to Walsh as he reminded Ruth that there is no stopping Father Time. He was in the prime of his life, but if he was lucky, his skills would not fade appreciably for maybe seven more years, and then Father Time would see to it that the decline would begin. Too many athletes fall victim to the belief that they are above mortality. Walsh was aware of Babe's carefree attitude about money and said he could help Ruth become financially secure as he aged.

"Oh Helen, don't worry about money. I'll make more moolah than anyone has ever imagined possible in this sport. Plus, once I can no longer play, I'll become a manager," Ruth laughed with a roar coming from deep inside his belly. Ruth had completely forgotten about the telegram. "Helen, let's enjoy our lunch. Thank you, Mister Walsh, and have a good day. Come look me up in Boston in the spring."

At noon on December 23, 1919, Ban Johnson left the small New York office he kept. Johnson's favorite dining spot in the city, Madeline's, was located at the Knickerbocker Hotel.

Vincent Astor, who had taken over management of the hotels built by his father, named the restaurant after his father's second wife.

John Jacob Astor IV, along with other family members, built a string of high-class hotels in New York City and in California. As an anniversary gift to his wife, John had booked passage aboard a luxurious cruise liner to New York City. The ship, the largest and most technologically advanced in her class, departed on her maiden voyage from Southampton, England on April 10, 1912. After a collision with an iceberg in the North Atlantic five days later, she was struggling to stay afloat. John, fighting the mayhem on board the listing ship during its last desperate moments, had managed to secure a seat aboard a lifeboat for his much younger and pregnant second wife. Madeline survived. John's fate was the same as fifteen hundred and thirteen others, lost as the Titanic went down to an icy grave.

A shining star in the Astor–Waldorf Hotel Empire, the Knickerbocker Hotel stood proudly at the corner of 42nd street and Broadway. Shifting winds suddenly covered the city in a driving cold drizzle. Without an overcoat, Johnson decided against his customary walk, descending the stairs into the subway and took the Times Square shuttle the one stop. Debarking from the most forward train car, he headed towards the door with the simple white-lettered dark blue sign on the lintel, Knickerbocker. Although protected from the fierce elements of nature, the fastidious Johnson disliked walking through the grimy underground tunnels toward his destination. Jogging up the final two flights of stairs, he ascended from the bowels of the underground New York into the lobby. *No way for a gentleman to travel*, he thought. Johnson rather enjoyed walking through the ornate doors of the red terracotta building that housed over five hundred rooms. He enjoyed the casual hellos to celebrities and the other highbrows that flocked to the restaurant. Among his favorites was Enrique Caruso, who charmed the daylights out of New Yorkers just a little over a year earlier, on Armistice Day. From a balcony, Caruso excited the throng gathered to celebrate war's end with versions of the Star Spangled Banner in three languages. Entering from the subway just did not have the same feel. Johnson expected that the bartender, an Italian immigrant named Mr. diTaggia, to have the faddish drink concoction ready for him. A combination of dry vermouth and gin, demand had swept swiftly across Wall Street to become the drink of choice of the millionaire stockbrokers.

As Johnson entered the restaurant, "Buongiorno, Mr. Johnson," a familiar voice called, "Your drink will be at your table before you finish saying ciao to your guests."

"Thank you, Martini," Johnson responded, proceeding to his table.

Walking across the room to his table, he paused momentarily to absorb a mural painted by Frederic Remington, 'US Calvary Charge.' Uniformed soldiers with guns drawn, sat atop their steeds. Every horse in the scene was in a full gallop, their destiny to secure a portion of the plains for the unseen citizens. Here comes the cavalry to save baseball from self-ruination. Ruth had better be up for the charge.

For weeks now, Ruth had been the toughest of the participants to corral for this meeting. He had avoided all requests by the commissioner for a meeting. Threats of suspension fell on the deaf ears of Ruth. Those damn barnstorming trips, Johnson thought, I have got to find a way to put an end to them. Finally Johnson pinned down the indomitable Ruth and the other participants needed. The meeting, to take place shortly, Johnson considered central to the survival of baseball. Concerned about Ruth's reaction to the discussions, Johnson thought a casual lunch meeting in a public location would serve to keep the waters calm.

Johnson arrived exactly 12:30PM, and waiting for him at the table were the owners of the Yankees and Red Sox.

Ruth strolled into the Hotel Knickerbocker through the glass doors on the 42nd Street entrance. Four days ago he had left the warm California sunshine. His travels east included only a single stop in St. Louis to change trains for Pennsylvania Station in New York City. Not worrying about cost, Ruth had booked the most expensive of Pullman cars so he could be well-rested for his rendezvous with his new destiny. Glancing down at the Western Union telegram clutched tightly in his left fist, Ruth rechecked the time and place for the meeting. The frigid winds from the northeast Atlantic swept into Manhattan. Winter had taken hold. Shaking off the cold air and rain, Ruth unbuttoned his grey woolen top coat and scanned the hotel lobby for the restaurant.

Mumbling as he read the message to himself, *Mr. Ruth, Mr. Dempsey has agreed to honor your request for a boxing exhibition to take place February 6, 1920. The bout is to be held at Madison Square Garden, so long as parties can agree. Please join Mr. Dempsey, Jack Kearns and myself at the Knickerbocker Hotel in New York City on December 23 at 12:30 PM. Sincerely, Tex Rickard.*

George Lewis 'Tex' Rickard's star as a boxing promoter had recently skyrocketed. New York City journalists referred to him as the P.T. Barnum of the sports world. Tex, travelling across the country with his partner, Jess McMahon, in a strike of marketing ingenuity, brought concerts, boxing and wrestling to the same venues, creating a surge of interest in a re-excited fan base. This aroused and provoked media attention, which in turn fostered even more public interest. The pair had carved a path for the resurgence in the boxing industry, which was reeling from the daily barrage of newspaper attacks due to its associations with gamblers and criminal elements. Every fight seemed to be tarnished with common descriptions such as 'fixed' and 'cheating.' Even Dempsey was not immune to such accusations. No longer did any fights appear to be on the level. Rickard realized that although the world was changing, Americans had not when it came to watching to men beat their brains out in the ring, nor had their passion in rooting on the underdog waned; but they needed a new reason to come to the show. Holding out the promise of 'clean' fights and live entertainment was a winning combination.

In a coup, Rickard secured the exclusive rights to promote live events at Madison Square Garden, a move which further demonstrated his business savvy. A new, more modern Madison Square Garden was scheduled to be built and opened in 1925. Rickard had secured a 20-year contract to serve as the Garden's exclusive promoter. Until 1940, every event held at the Garden took place under his watch.

Ruth, giddy throughout his trip, still could not believe his good fortune. He may in fact get a chance to square off against the heavyweight champion of the world. And to top it off, on his birthday! This was something Ruth had wanted to do for some time. Big, strong and athletic, with an ego equal to the task, Ruth believed he could hold his own in the ring. Hell, he was bigger than Dempsey. As excited as he was, Ruth did need to make certain of the ground rules. He did not wish to have his baseball career placed in complete jeopardy.

Ruth had baited the champ regularly, ever since running into Dempsey in a late-night speakeasy just after the series ended. He bragged he could knock the champ out quickly. Dempsey was good-natured about it, not giving Ruth much credibility. Ruth told him all he needed to do was train at Gleason's Gym for two weeks, and he would be ready. Any tutelage he needed would be provided by local boxer–manager Kid McCoy. Kid's stab at glory was a sore point with Dempsey. McCoy had trained Fireman Flynn, an underachieving boxer whose right uppercut in the first round sent Dempsey into dreamland two years earlier. Dempsey was not one to forget such things.

Fighting an angry Dempsey may not have been the best of ideas, but Ruth needed to show the owners he was prepared to leave baseball if they did not agree to his monetary demands. Of course, a good outing with scores of fans attending would certainly drive his point home. Ruth felt sure he was in the driver's seat.

Jack Dempsey, known as the 'Manassa Mauler,' in 1919 immediately found his way into the hearts of sports fans upon capturing the heavyweight crown on July 4 from Willard. His rags-to-riches story captivated imagination. While Ruth was playing ball in the big yard at St. Mary's, Dempsey was living in hobo camps and fighting for meals in dusty saloons across Utah and Colorado. The considerably larger Dempsey knocked Willard down seven times in the first round. Standing over Willard, Dempsey repeatedly hit him as soon both knees were lifted from the canvas. Suffering a broken jaw, broken ribs, several broken teeth, deep lacerations and facial fractures, Willard was unable to continue in the 4th round. Dempsey had inflicted so much damage that boxing experts were suspicious that Dempsey had cheated. Doctoring his gloves, plaster of Paris tape or using brass knuckles were the common accusations. Fans simply ignored the musings, attributing the devastation of Willard to Dempsey's savagery and brute strength.

Ruth asked the restaurant's majordomo to take him to Mr. Dempsey's table.

"Follow me, Mr. Ruth, right this way."

Striding confidently behind the maitre'd, Ruth was led to a table occupied by Johnson, Ruppert, Huston and Frazee.

"Enjoy your lunch, Mr. Ruth."

"Sir, this isn't the right table. I need the table of Mr. Jack Dempsey. You know, the heavyweight champion of the world." Ruth was thinking that there was some kind of error.

Johnson greeted Ruth gruffly, "Sit down and do not make a scene."

"I'm here to meet the heavyweight king. I've decided to change careers, give up professional baseball and pursue my first love, boxing," Ruth asserted in his thundering voice.

"Ruth, there is no meeting with Dempsey. You need to sit and hear what I have to say."

"Sit down, Ruth," Frazee chided, "You may be king of the world on your little bandwagon, but outside of it, you are naïve beyond imagination."

Johnson continued, "Ruth, there is no boxing match, no meeting with Dempsey or his agent. We're here to talk about the future of baseball and what you mean to the sport."

Stunned that he been duped, Ruth glanced at the group around the table. Slowly lowering himself into his chair; Ruth failed to acknowledge anyone's presence.

Ban Johnson got on a roll, explaining every sordid detail about player corruption and games being thrown at the behest of gamblers. If the stranglehold on baseball became known, the outcome of every series since 1903 would be thrown into question and the sport could crumble. Johnson held nothing back. The gambling was bad enough, but he also spoke of the unknown feuds and schisms amongst American League team owners, surprising his unsuspecting rivals. Boston's Harry Frazee, Chicago's Charles Comiskey and New York's Jacob Ruppert and Cap Huston were united in their stand against Johnson's leadership, referred to by the press corps as the Insurrectos, Detroit's Frank Navin, Washington's Clark Griffith, Cleveland's Jim Dunn, St. Louis' Phil Ball and Connie Mack (the money behind the team the Shibes) in Philadelphia remained steadfast behind Johnson (called the Loyal Five.) and his attempts to keep the sport clean. Where once the American League owners had banded together to fight the rival National League, they had now split into groups and were fighting each other. Johnson admitted to Ruth his grave concern that baseball would eventually crumble if the gamblers continued to run over roughshod over players. The mood within the country had changed. All eyes at the table were affixed on Ruth as he absorbed the proposal Johnson put before him. Baseball needed a real American legend without the remotest threat of a stain from his relationship with gamblers or underworld figures. Not only did baseball need a hero, but they needed that hero performing in the biggest stage of all, New York City!

Ruth, absorbing all of the information and the litany of the baseball's hidden secrets of corruption which had stained the sport for decades, sat stone faced. He could offer no immediate response other than, "Can I get some beers and a few steak sandwiches?"

Chapter 27

The Volstead Act passed the Congress on October 28, 1919. This law set forth rules for the enforcement of the ban of alcoholic beverages in the United States. The 18th Amendment to the Constitution, which had been passed by Congress two years earlier, was finally gaining steam in the state ratification process. This amendment made the manufacture, transportation and sale of alcohol illegal. The country expected that ratification imminently. Private ownership and consumption of alcohol was not made illegal. Public opinion of the law was equally split. Irish Catholics and other immigrants saw this as an intrusion of their everyday life. Effective enforcement of the alcohol ban proved difficult and led to widespread disregard. Without consensus for the law, the result would turn out to be a rise in illegal activities and corruption. This more lucrative new business acted as a magnet, drawing the criminal element away from betting on baseball.

After watching Ruth gulp several more beers, followed by a massive belch, Ruppert spoke, "You certainly expressed your enjoyment, Mr. Ruth. Pretty soon that beverage will be a rarity, so take pleasure while you can."

Ruth had not yet digested what he had eaten and drunk and even less of what he had heard. Helen loved their farm, as did Ruth. Babe didn't know much about New York City, but what he had heard was that it was a city which could swallow the naïve faster than he had the third steak sandwich. His stomach twisted into a knot, thinking that Frazee was throwing him to the wolves. He did not know Ruppert or Huston and each looked stiff and highbrow. To them baseball was a business, while for Ruth it was a game. Ruth believed they would have little tolerance for his carefree attitude to life . Frazee had to know this, and, he had to know this was not necessarily a good match for Ruth. All that aside, Ruth sensed he truly had the upper hand.

"Well, Colonel, it did hit the spot. Gents, this is certainly nothing like what I had in mind when I walked through the doors. Thirty minutes ago, I thought I was here to negotiate a donnybrook with the heavyweight champ." Ruth emphasized the point with a slow motion jab with his clenched right fist. "I thought that a stunt like fighting the heavyweight champion would put the fear of God into you and that I just might leave baseball and make a living in another sport. Now I come to find out that you need me more than I need you. But I don't like being fooled the way you got me here. Why not just level with me? Hear this, boys. Unless I get my terms, and by that I mean all of my terms, I will not be willing to leave Boston. Now that you've told me how important I am to the future of the game, I'll hold out for what I've asked. I should ask for more. But unlike you clowns; my word is my bond. There are two things I want. First, I want the opportunity to break every all-time record. Then, when this body of mine can't do it any more and my playing days are over, I want to manage a team. I know this game better than anyone. I want to be known not only as the best player of all time but the greatest manager. Heck, Helen likes Boston, we have a farm. That's our home; we really don't want to leave. Make it worthwhile for us to leave."

Ruth abruptly pushed his chair away from the table and shot up from his chair. Sliding his arms into his coat and pulling the fur collar around his neck, he announced that he was returning to the warmer pastures of Los Angeles to finish out his barnstorming commitment with the guys and play golf, lots of it.

"By the way, gents, since I am apparently not devious or smart enough to deal with you, I have enlisted help to deal with you on my behalf. This someone will represent all my interests in the talks with you. His name is Mr. Christy Walsh. Oh, and I expect his fee will be paid directly by you all."

As soon as the broad-shouldered Ruth exited, Ruppert began, "Ban, this is highway robbery. He wants $40,000 to play baseball. Harry, you may just be stuck with him. I am on the verge of walking away from this mess and leaving Ruth to you all. He's a crude, arrogant sort and may turn out to be nothing but problems."

Johnson stepped in to calm the waters; he wanted everyone to focus on the most important matter at hand, getting Ruth to play for New York.

On New Year's Day 1920 the headline in "The Sporting News" read:

"Ruth to New York deal dead. Frazee wants starters for rising young player"

Ruth's sale or transfer to the Yankees was in considerable doubt. Frazee did not wish to give away a player with such ability without adding strength to the Red Sox. Boston's owner stated, "The team would not consider any deal for Ruth that did not include five quality players in the exchange. The Red Sox wish to remain competitive." This roadblock all but guaranteed that Ruth would remain in Boston. No club would strip their cupboards bare, not even for a player with the electrifying power of Ruth. Frazee continued in his statement, "The club wouldn't give in to Ruth's outrageous salary demands, either. If the rising star wanted to play ball in 1920 with Boston to help the Red Sox make another pennant run, he would do so at the salary offered. He has been offered a fair compensation."

What was unknown to the general public was the meeting which had taken place twelve days earlier. Harry Frazee and the Yankee Colonels remained at the table with Ban Johnson holding the negotiations together, hammering out an agreement in principal which cemented the deal that would deliver Boston's young slugger into the largest entertainment market west of Paris. Frazee agreed to sever Ruth from the Red Sox in exchange for an immediate cash payment of $25,000 and three more like payments annually at six percent interest; each of the installments becoming due on the first day of November, 1920 through 1922.

The down payment was far short of the capital Frazee needed to navigate through his financial crisis. There was a second separate agreement made around the table that day, one which also remained absent from view of the public for another ten months. Frazee secured the substantial financial resources he needed for his other business interests, but not without a heavy price.

"Colonel Ruppert, you're asking for a mortgage on Fenway Park! That's outrageous," Frazee argued, "but I'm afraid I am left with no alternatives."

Jacob Ruppert was a street-smart businessman. He was commonly referred to as 'Colonel' although he had only served briefly in the National Guard. After serving four terms in Congress, he returned to work in the family brewery and was named its president in 1914; the references to him as Colonel started shortly thereafter. The rank carried with it a sense of maturity, leadership and intellect and Jacob saw the potential advantage. If people wished to call him Colonel, then he wouldn't deny them the honor.

"Harry, from my view, you got yourself overextended with all of your show biz ventures. We'll make this arrangement separate from the Ruth trade. This will be a personal transaction, just between us."

"Cap", Ruppert said referring to Huston by his popular nickname, "let's say we write the agreement this way. We offer to loan or cause to be loaned to Frazee $300,000. The loan, until paid in full, will be secured by a first mortgage on the land now used as a baseball playing field by the Boston American League Baseball Club. Failure to pay such loan on the maturity will result in the transfer of the title to such land to pass to Mr. Ruppert and Huston. See, no direct mention of the ballpark. By the way Harry, my wife and I like musicals. We'll be sure to come see our investment. What's the name of the play, *My Lady Friends*? That's if you get it finished. Harry, could you imagine how Boston fans would react if they knew the Yankees not only got the game's best player but we could, in fact, end up owning Fenway as well? Brr, just that thought will send shivers up the fans' spines. Of course, someone will speculate that with all those witches up in Salem, an angry Boston fan visited them and, for a fee, got a hundred-year curse on your ball team. Can you imagine the great Boston team not winning a pennant for century?"

Nothing was final, as the trade was contingent on the Yankees getting Ruth to agree to a new contract. The mortgage on Fenway, though, would go forward, regardless of whether Ruth becomes the property of the Yankees or not. The daily rags across the country splashing headlines about the ballplayer making outlandish salary demands gave Ruth a quick rise to celebrity status. Speculations popped up in communities that he had demanded twice the salary of the President of the United States.

On the West Coast, Ruth had become a barroom orator, boasting he would never tolerate a trade and that he'd only play for the Red Sox.

"Hell, I'll retire from baseball altogether before I play for another team. They can give me a king's ransom, but I ain't playing anywhere but in Boston," Ruth stated as often as anyone would listen.

The Sporting News called Ruth's public stance "'a pathetic plea for attention' by a selfish and crude brute who is only out for the money."

Ruth continued his barnstorming and increased his carousing in California, unaware that the deal to send him to New York had already been struck.

The *Washington Post* reported on January 3 that Ruth was the leader of a 'host of baseball holdouts' who had put their own interests above those of the national pastime. The columnists speculated that he and his renegade road warriors might just start their own league.

After playing a game in San Diego, Ruth announced that playing with the coloreds was neither out of the question nor a challenge he would shy from.

In Boston, Frazee remained firm, not yet willing to concede to the slugger's increasingly outrageous demands.

Walsh, now operating as Ruth's agent, continued putting pressure on Frazee and Johnson by increasing his monetary demands on a daily basis. Walsh included in Ruth's contract terms calling for bonuses based not only for certain levels of on-field performance but also on ballpark attendance. "I'm the one who put the butts in the seats, so let baseball pay me for that," Ruth crowed, "The owners can afford it!" The Colonels prepared themselves for a protracted salary negotiation, which was all but inevitable given the monetary success Ruth was having with his west coast travelling baseball circus.

Johnson was losing his grip on the owners loyal to him. This was a last-ditch effort to save his role as the American League president. Since he had the most to lose, he needed for this deal to become a reality quickly. Cleverly, the Colonels continued to squeeze Frazee and Johnson. Monetary penalties were included in the agreement, just in case Ruth made good on his threats to abandon the American League. The Colonels demanded that if Ruth didn't report to the Yankees by March 1, the Colonels could call the loans to Frazee. Frazee then would be left with no wiggle room. He would be required to return the cash. The additional three notes would be voided and Frazee would incur a 20% penalty to boot. The ball club would then be the property of the Yankee owners. Any salary increase for Ruth above the $15,000 that the Yankees agreed to pay, the Red Sox or the league would have to cover. The agreement with Frazee had additional financial landmines. The final clause required that if the slugger demanded a bonus, the Yankees would pay the first $10,000, but Boston or the League would have to pay anything above and beyond that.

"Colonel, this must be important. It's New Year's Day, for Christ's sake," barked the diminutive man with chiseled features and steely gray eyes greeting Ruppert as he walked into Ruppert's office at the Bronx brewery.

Ruppert had summoned the Yankee manager in to discuss the potential acquisition of Ruth. He had prayed on the Ruth matter most of the morning. Ruppert was not interested in the money. No, he wanted Ruth playing for the Yankees. He wanted to build a team of destiny that would be remembered for all time, and Ruth was the fellow to lead that effort.

Miller Huggins, although a scrawny man, a shade under 5 feet 5 inches, was blessed with agility, quickness, high intellect and a great deal of strength on his wiry frame. At the University of Cincinnati, he studied law and served as captain of the baseball team. Huggins realized that his earning power was greater in baseball than in law, so he scrapped thoughts of entering the legal profession. Huggins had an astute business mind and invested a significant portion of his salary in real estate across Florida. In 1917, while serving as the manager of the St. Louis Cardinals, he cobbled together a group of investors and made a bid to purchase the club. The offer was rejected out of hand with no explanation. This was Miller's second failed attempt to buy the struggling franchise. Huggins was so insulted that he promptly presented his resignation as the Cardinals' manager. Ban Johnson had developed an affinity for Huggins. He called the Colonels and told them to grab Huggins and install him as the manager of the Yankees, which they did. The no-nonsense manager was a guru for developing talent. In 1915, he changed the grip and batting stance of one of the Cardinals' youngest players, Rogers Hornsby, resulting in an improvement in Hornsby's batting average. With the Yankees, his managerial style became more demanding. With the support of Ed Barrow, the team's general manager, he demanded the players look, act and conduct themselves as the professionals they were. He prohibited facial hair. Carousing was especially not looked upon kindly. Staying out late, drinking and whoring would lead to player suspensions without pay. Barrow told the players that the Yankees name was the business. He was the custodian and the players were the assets. He expected that they were to represent the Yankee name a certain way when in public. If anyone veered too far from the norm, he would personally see to it that they ended up playing in some Podunk town.

Miller Huggins took a train to Los Angeles and found Ruth playing golf at Griffith Park. When the Yankee manager told Ruth he'd been traded, the slugger immediately launched into his salary demands and that Huggins needed to go talk to Walsh. As the caddy began to hand Ruth his driver to tee off at the fifteenth hole, Huggins stepped between them. Nearly ten inches shorter and seventy pounds lighter, Huggins, not the least bit intimidated, grabbed Ruth by the collar.

"See here, you big oaf. This is an opportunity which never comes along. But you need to behave yourself. If you do, the Colonels would be willing to offer you a rich deal. I'll do everything in my power to see that you are regarded as the greatest player there's ever been. If you don't, I'll cut your testicles off myself."

At that moment, Ruth gained a great deal of respect for this mighty mite. Agreeing to meet the next day, the men hammered out an agreement. Ruth would honor his current contract and get a $10,000 a year bonus for the next two years. Ruth would also earn a series of several other bonuses, from performance to increased attendance that would bring his earnings potential to a figure in excess of $100,000. This was substantially more than what he would have earned in Boston. If nothing else, the Sultan of Swat was consistent. Clearly his love for money was stronger than his love for the Red Sox.

The news story broke finally on January 6, 1920, as nearly every city newspaper displayed the identical headline:

"Ruth Sold to the Yankees for $100,000"

Cash-strapped Harry Frazee, owner of Boston's baseball franchise and Broadway producer, has agreed to ship one of baseball's brightest stars, outfielder George Herman Ruth, to the New York Yankees for $100,000. Frazee, suffering from a recent string of Broadway failures, needs money to continue production of several entertainment projects in various states of production. It is rumored he has a major musical *planned for a Broadway release in 1922. Owners of the Yankees agree to pay the 24-year-old Ruth $40,000 to play baseball.*

Chapter 28

"Hurry, Helen," Ruth shouted. "We've got to get to track 3."

Arriving from their farm just outside Boston, Helen and Babe walked briskly to meet up with the rest of the Yankee team in Pennsylvania Station on February 28. The plan had been to arrive two hours ahead of the scheduled departure, but their train from Boston had been delayed. The Ruths had arrived a scant 15 minutes before the train was set to depart for Jacksonville, Florida. Their bags had already been taken to their sleeper car.

As the couple scurried toward the train, the Yankee center fielder, Frank 'Ping' Bodie, who was generally regarded as the friendliest player on the team, leaned out of the car and waved encouragement as the couple approached. Hearing a bit of commotion from the opposite end of the tracks, he raked his hands back through his thick curly hair in a sign of amazement.

Yelling into the rail car where many of the players had settled into card games, Bodie exclaimed, "Fellas, you're not going to believe this."

Hundreds of fans raced onto the platform, making a beeline toward Ruth and Helen. Within moments, Ruth was besieged by what was then an uncommon sight away from the ballpark, a horde of fans begging for handshakes and autographs.

Most ballplayers looked down on this task, thinking it an undesirable chore. Ruth received more requests than anyone, yet few were as generous with their time or as naturally warm toward fans as he. He seemed to have a constant urge to see others happy, perhaps stemming from his own neglected, unsatisfying upbringing. Often he stayed for hours after the end of a game to talk with the fans.

Warmth ran through Ruth as he set down the bag of golf clubs he'd been lugging. Happy and somewhat surprised, Ruth lit up with an ear-to-ear grin and immediately obliged. The New York fans were accepting him as if he were family. This moment marked the beginning of the end of any privacy Ruth would have when out in public. He was no longer in control of his own time.

Within a few minutes, the teeming crowd threatened to spill onto the tracks. A few venturesome youngsters had latched on to the handholds of the engine where they engaged in conversations with the chief engineer. This served as a distraction.

The head dispatcher, Genarro Volipecello, fought his way through the crowd to inquire the cause of the delay from the engineer.

"Steve, what's going on?"

Steve Wilson, a 20 year veteran of the rails and who grew up on the tough streets of Bay Ridge in Brooklyn, wisecracked, "What going on? Ain't you seeing so good no more?" he chortled.

"Blow your horn, get those kids off the engine and get this train out of here. I got inbounds backed up to Trenton!"

The crowd continued to greet Ruth with genuine openness and caring, wishing him good luck.

"Helen, New York loves us," Ruth shouted. Although Helen stood just a few feet away, she barely made out what he had said. In this moment, Ruth had forgotten all about his life of emotional abandonment; for now, it seemed as if the entire city loved him. For the rest of his career, especially while in New York, Babe would have to grow used to living under the scrutiny of his adoring admirers. Even so, he would never come to understand how fickle their love was and how quickly the "what have you done for me lately" fans would disappear.

Ruth picked up several small children, giving them each a big hug. He found sharing his broad smile was sometimes all the young fans wanted. Children always received the most attention.

"Helen, we have to make one of these," Ruth roared as the chubby little girl he had just picked up giggled and squirmed while he held her.

The engineer pulled the whistle in two long bursts and released a bit of the brake to shake things up. The teens jumped off the engine and back onto the platform.

Another long whistle and a small jump forward forced more of the crowd backwards.

A conductor several cars back yelled, "All aboard!"

"Babe, they've been holding the train for almost thirty minutes now. We had better get going or they'll leave without us."

"OK, let's go."

Ruth grabbed his clubs as he and Helen made for the slow-moving train. Helen got alongside the Pullman first. Bodie caught her arm, pulling her safely aboard.

"My word, what is your husband doing?" Bodie asked her

Ruth had stopped to hug a pair of toddlers and sign one last autograph for a ten-year-old who was walking with a cane, thanks to a bout with polio.

The train was picking up speed, Ruth was in frantic pursuit. He handed his golf bag to a porter, telling him to hold them until his return. Catching hold of the caboose just fifteen feet before the end of the platform, he swung himself up onto the rear platform, narrowly clipping a column. He stood on the platform, absorbing what had just happened. He continued waving to the adoring crowd, now too far in the distance to see him. The train roared into the tunnel for the long journey south and Ruth's inaugural spring training with the New York Yankees.

Walking through the cars, Babe was handed $5 for expenses and meal money from the team's business manager.

"Okay, boys, where's the card game, I've got my ante! Plus a present for all you, courtesy of Boston," Ruth, showing no shyness, quickly urged his new mates into a game of poker. Babe had invested in a Boston-based cigar factory that produced the 'Babe Ruth Cigar.' From his inside coat pocket, he grabbed nearly a dozen, handing them to those around him.

"Don't worry, boys, I've got plenty more in my suitcase. I hear this is a long trip."

The Yankee players greeted Ruth much differently than the cold, combative manner of the Sox six years earlier. For Ruth, this was refreshing, the city and his teammates bringing a sense of warmth and family to him. Even the gruff Huggins, who never had children, took a sincere interest in this uncontrollable force.

Barrs Field served as the spring home for Brooklyn and the Yankees in 1920. The field was built on property once owned by a Union officer, abutting the Jacksonville Fairgrounds.

Neither team had drawn much attention from the press in the past, especially the Yankees, who owned no pennants to their name. The arrival of Ruth changed all that. Reporters from fifteen different dailies lined the field's perimeter, when in the past, two or three reporters, tops, covered the teams.

Ruth, carrying on with the boyish appeal and mischievous imp persona, stepped right into the role of clown on day one, but the response of his teammates was much different this time around.

Huggins had ordered Ruth to throw in the outfield to strengthen his arm. Ruth, his thoughts a bit different than Huggins, decided to try his hand at playing a little third base. Cutting in front of Bodie, who was now his roommate, Ruth fielded the ball only to launch consecutive throws beyond the reach of the first baseman into the stands. Bodie had a plan of his own. On the next grounder, he cut quickly in front of the unsuspecting Ruth, feinting to pick the ball. He let it pass under his glove, where it struck Ruth squarely on the shin.

Bodie and the Yankee infielders burst out laughing while Ruth, hopping on one leg, yelled, "You little bastard!"

Ruth grabbed Bodie around the waist, lifted him over his head, carried over to the fence line beyond third and deposited him into a fresh pile of soft cow manure recently deposited there by a local farmer.

Unlike the animosity and fisticuffs he had encountered as a rookie with the Red Sox, Bodie and the team laughed even harder at this.

Huggins, walking over to view the commotion, said, "Well, if you don't get back to playing ball, you'll *all* be on the dung heap!"

The press did not see this as amusement, but more as a chance to launch a campaign of unrelenting criticism. Babe, because of the money he had demanded, had a bull's-eye on his back. Before the first game of the season was even in the books, renowned writers Fred Lieb, Damon Runyon and Sid Mercer were cranking out articles such as 'Ruth Complains of Indigestion After Overindulgence,' 'Ruth's Big Bat and Bigger Appetite Arrive in Camp,' and 'Ruth Stinks on Links; Smashes Several Clubs.' The details of every meal made news somewhere.

Jacksonville loved the notoriety. Thousands of people found their way down to this sleepy town from New York, just to get close to Ruth. Seizing on the opportunity, the Jacksonville Chamber of Commerce began publicizing each Yankee exhibition game throughout Florida as a chance for fans to see baseball's great new star. With Ruth as the draw, the club performed before record crowds throughout the spring.

Tourism boomed and every hotel sold out through the end of March.

Ruth started slowly. Pitching against the Dodgers, he failed to record a single out while yielding seven first inning runs before Huggins removed him. Adding to the pain, Ruth struck out three times. Although his mates supported him as he struggled, Ruth was bothered by something. It was unclear whether it was the acidic comments and headlines in the newspapers back north, the venom spewed from the Dodger hopeful who did not like the Yankees drawing the spotlight, or Ruth's notoriety bringing hordes of fans into the now-crowded Jacksonville.

Bodie, not to miss a trick, stuck the NY Times under Ruth's nose at the breakfast table one morning.,

"There is Some Rotten Cheese in Florida."

"Hey, Babe, I think they're talking about you."

Criticism and acrimony were directed at Ruth through camp. Ruppert, concerned about reports that Ruth was spending too many late nights at the hotel bars, sent Huston down to check in on their investment.

After another futile day, this time against the Cubs, Huston invited Ruth to dinner.

Addressing his star, "Babe, Huggins tells me that Bodie has become roommates with your suitcase. You know he wants a tight ship."

Babe seemed intent on doing everything Yankees manager Miller Huggins had warned against during their first meeting. Ruth's reputation for late night mischief was growing as fast as his popularity. Protecting Ruth, Bodie took the responsibility of both his own suitcase and Babe's to their hotel room whenever the Yankees traveled from Jacksonville. For Ruth, the town did not matter; he was determined to find the best the city had to offer in entertainment.

"Well, Colonel, I think I just need to relax a bit, I'll get going when the games matter, and don't you worry. Some of the boys are meeting me down in Ruby Town."

The Colonel, sensing an opportunity to see Ruth's transgressions first hand, decided to go with him.

Ruby Town was the hottest section of Jacksonville, emerging from the backdrop of an area once occupied primarily with tents, where several new restaurants and clubs lured jazz acts from New York. Celebrities followed, flocking to this hidden gem.

Several hours later it was the babysitter needing assistance, as three Yankees carried the inebriated Huston to his room.

"Let's get Huston to his room before Huggins sees any of this," said Bodie, instructing the three Yankees who were carrying the Colonel what to do. "Huggins expects everyone at the field in three hours, so we need to hustle."

Huston was out for the count, having consumed much more alcohol than he had expected. Ruth was not much better off. He asked Huggins not to play him in right field, that he felt as though his reflexes were a bit off. Huggins, of course, denied the request. Pursuing a ball into the right field corner, Ruth ran directly into a palm tree. Knocked out cold, it took fifteen minutes for him to come to. Staring directly at Huggins, Ruth said, "Told you my reflexes were off."

With just days left before the close of camp and the return north, Ruth was yet to emerge from his slump. Fans, frustrated at traveling so far, had expectations of seeing greatness, not failure.

The riding became so consistent and personal that Ruth finally was pushed to the brink and snapped. In the seventh inning, he charged into the stands towards a fan that had been cascading relentless insults. As the enraged Ruth approached, the man simply pulled out a long knife. Ruth braked abruptly to a stop, although harsh words were still being exchanged. Two spectators intervened before damage was done.

The morning headline on the local newspaper sent a wakeup call through Ruth:

"Ruth Turns on Blatant Fan Who Calls Him a Useless Piece of Crap"

Hurt that fans would think he could turn on them shocked Babe. He longed for their adoration and attention; he needed them to *like* him. "Bodie, I'm straightening things out, starting today."

Arriving at Barrs Field, he was greeted by an unhappy Huggins with a copy of the paper clenched tightly in his fist.

"Ruth, you need to sit still until we get north. We cannot have you going after the fans. We need you bring them in, not chase them away."

"Skipper, I'm ready to play. No more shenanigans."

On April 1, 1920, in his first at-bat, Ruth launched a 570 foot homer and proceeded with three other hits that day. Pitching seven strong innings against the Dodgers, retiring fifteen straight at one point, Ruth showed little rust from his year away from the mound.

The hot streak for Ruth remained as spring training drew to a conclusion, and he did not slow down with the start of the 1920 season. As play got deeper into the summer, though, Ruth grew frustrated, boiling inside, because while he managed to win twelve of the games he started, Ruth was only being used occasionally as a spot starter.

Several times he had approached Huggins to question why he was not being used more as he was promised.

"Hug, I think you misled me when you came to visit. You promised me a shot at all the records. I expect you to pitch me more."

"Ruth, look, I'll manage the team. Maybe you'll pitch more if you follow the team rules. You eat to excess and stay out past curfew. Follow the rules and I will then keep my promise."

"That ain't the deal!"

"Ruth, you go back to the field or you'll see less of the outfield."

Carl Mays was Ruth's Boston teammate from 1915 until he was traded to the Yankees during the 1919 season. His underhanded-style throwing motions earned him the nickname, 'Sub.' Carl Mays was a consistent winner throughout his career. His calling card was challenging hitters who crowded the plate by pitching them high and inside. As a result, he was consistently at the top of the list for plunking batters, earning him a reputation as a headhunter, a baseball term not of endearment but of disdain. Players respected the pitcher who gave you the polite plunk in the back. A headhunter was something else. A pitcher gunning for the cranium with a wee bit of wildness could ruin a man's career; take away his livelihood or worse. One particular game in his rookie year started Mays on a path of acrimony with several veterans. Already having been hit three times, Ty Cobb strode to the plate, jawing at the young pitcher.

"Try it again, rook, go ahead, try it again," Cobb barked as he took a position even closer to the inside corner of the plate than before. Tension filled the air. Cobb spit out his wad of chewing tobacco. He was on edge. Staring at Mays, Cobb dropped his hands to his waist, holding the bat tightly as he readied his hands for the first pitch.

Pinch Thomas, the Red Sox catcher, sensing what was about to unfold, tried to calm Cobb, "Ty, don't do anything stupid, he's just a rookie."

"Well, he's just dumb enough to learn a valuable lesson."

Not deterred, Mays wound up and buzzed the first pitch directly under Cobb's chin.

"Aw, crap," was all Thomas could mutter.

Expecting the close shave, Cobb let the ball pass within inches of his face. Incensed by the defiance of the rookie, Cobb rushed the mound as he uncoiled violently, hauling his bat at the legs of Mays. As Mays skipped to avoid the lumber, Cobb slid at him spikes high. He caught Mays right ankle and left thigh, cutting his sock and pant leg and Mays' tender skin, drawing blood.

Cobb yelled, "You're a no-good SOB coward." It took several minutes for order to be restored.

"Hang over the plate again, you yellow dog, and see what you get."

Cobb took his stance in the batter's box, inching as close to the plate as the umpire allowed. He delivered a menacing stare over his right shoulder, daring Mays in this duel of wills. Cobb had hopefully gotten the message across with the delivery of a three inch gash to the thigh and ankle.

"You got the boy bleeding, Ty," Thomas commented.

"He should count his lucky stars I didn't cut his leg off. This boy is playing with fire."

Mays glanced at his aching leg to see the red patch spreading. As he readied himself for the next pitch, Thomas, hoping to avoid further problems, held his glove hand to the third base side of the plate, low and away from Cobb. Mays delivered the next pitch more side armed across his body. Mays ignored Thomas's hint. The ball whistled directly towards Cobb's head. Cobb threw his hands up for defense, but the ball struck his right wrist as he used it to guard his eye. All hell broke loose. Players stormed the field as a wild melee ensured. Some fans decided to get in on the action. It took the Boston police over an hour to restore order. The umpires, deciding that was enough for one day, halted the contest, awarding the Tigers the win.

*****

At 11:30 AM on August 16, 1920, an ambulance raced from the Polo Grounds to St. Lawrence Hospital, carrying the listless body of the Cleveland Indian shortstop. At 4:40 PM, the chief of the surgical unit, Dr. T.M. Merrigan, announced that the 29-year-old Ray Chapman had fought gallantly, but the procedure, which lasted just over an hour, had failed. The surgeons removed pieces of the skull which had lodged in the brain. The compression and trauma were just too much for anyone to overcome.

Chapman had strolled to the plate in the top of the fifth inning with the Indians ahead. In his two previous at-bats, he had weakly popped to first and sacrificed a runner to second. The umpire had just tossed a new ball to Mays. As was usual, Mays began the pitchers ritual of dirtying the new ball. Deciding he wanted the ball to move a bit more, Mays added a combination of tobacco and licorice juice to the dirt and just one little nick for good measure. The Yanks and Indians were locked in a dogfight for the pennant, and Mays needed to protect the lead. The unsuspecting Chapman leaned over the plate for the first pitch. Rearing his arm back just a tad more, Mays let it fly from below. The combination of elements created a spit ball with nasty late movement. The ball careened from Chapman's head with such a thud, most thought the ball was struck on a swing. Mays caught the ball on one bounce tossing it to Wally Pipp at first for what he assumed was an out. Chapman staggered as he attempted to leave the batter's box and fell. Unsteadily he arose, only to fall once again. Hitting the ground hard, Chapman twitched. His eyelids, descending slowly, closed for the final time.

Huggins and Tris Speaker, now the Indians manager, returned to the Yankee clubhouse where they found a disconsolate Mays sitting alone in the far corner, the only break in the darkness the light provided by a flickering incandescent bulb. The headhunter had finally done what Cobb had warned five years earlier. There were a few pats on the back from teammates, but not a single empathetic word was offered. As he sat weeping, as he had since a medical team carried Chapman off the field nearly eight hours earlier, Mays was ostracized. A player was in a battle for his life, and it was all his responsibility.

Tris, sliding his arm around May's shoulders, addressed him first, "This is not your fault, Carl."

Huggins voiced an unconvincing agreement to that.

"Is he gone?" Mays asked.

"Yes."

"Guys," Mays spoke in a quivering voice, burying his face within his trembling hands, "I am done. I cannot do this. I killed a man. My days as a player are over; this was my fault, all my fault." That made him a killer. The label 'headhunter' was no longer without meaning. He had caused the death of person, brought anguish to his family. A man is dead and *for what? It's just a silly game*, he thought solemly

Huggins, seeing the despair in Mays, ordered him to go home and take a week or more off if he needed it. Nodding his head in agreement, Mays gathered his belongings from his locker, and departed, not looking back, resolved never to return.

Ruth, upon hearing the news that Carl Mays had left the team; sought out Huggins before the next Yankee game.

"Hug, I need to talk to you."

"What now? I'm busy. I need to find someone to fill in for Mays down the stretch. He was pretty well shaken."

"I can do it. I can pitch more games. I think I can start 50-60 games a year."

"Babe, pitchers just aren't pitching as many games as before. Not with the livelier ball."

"Hug, I can do it, give me a shot. Hell, I am never tired, nor I am sore after pitching. Let me have a crack at it. You promised me a chance and now you're barely pitching me."

Huggins, fearing he might come to regret his decision, hesitantly agreed.

The Yankees finished the 1920 season in third place, their best finish in a number of years and just three games behind the Indians, who captured the American League title.

Ruth completed the season having pounded out 54 home runs, batting .376 and driving 137 runs across the place. His mark on baseball was beginning to take shape again. In the last six weeks of the season, picking up for Mays in the Yankee rotation as well as his own starts; he started twenty-two games, winning eighteen of them. His career win total stood at 121.

Chapter 29

Mount Morris is a plateau created by the abrupt rise in the solid rock formation on the near north end of Manhattan. Here the boundary river turns north, carving the island's needle-shaped peninsula that extends several miles to where the Harlem River unites with the Hudson River. This is among the highest points in New York City, and it boasts views that extend east into Long Island Sound and west across the Hudson to the palisades of New Jersey. Looking southward one could see Harlem; following the sight lines through the emerald expanse of Central Park onward past the skyscrapers to the Bowery and finally locate Lady Liberty, the tribute to American freedom and prosperity from France, confidently standing alone in New York Harbor. Although the calendar had turned to April, the roaring winds of March had not left New York City; on this rise their full force was felt.

Atop the promontory stands a Palladian style manor, the oldest home in New York City, which, because of the strategic location, served as the colonial headquarters during the American Revolution, the Morris-Jumel Mansion. Patiently waiting, in a high backed rocker, on the newly-painted white portico between the Tuscan pillars, was Jacob Ruppert. He enjoyed the serenity the surroundings of the estate provided, absorbing the moments of reflection.

Huffing as he climbed the last few yards of Edgecombe Avenue's steep escarpment, Ruth spotted Ruppert as he turned into entrance. Waving, Ruth asked, "Colonel, why the hell did you drag me all the way up here?"

"Welcome, Ruth. Come up here and have a look. Perspective, Ruth, just want to provide a little view of the future for you."

The Colonel stood, and placing his arm across Ruth's broad shoulders, turned him to the east, extended his left arm and pointed across the Harlem River.

Ruppert's natural passion for baseball began so early in his life that he was probably born with it. His family was among the wealthier residents of the Little Germany section of New York City. As a result, at age fourteen he took the initiative to finance a team of neighborhood urchins, buying the equipment and uniforms needed to play. The nattily-dressed team gained notoriety not only for their sharp appearance but also for their abilities on the field. Emerging as legends of the sandlots, they surgically disposed of the top Manhattan teams routinely. Soon they stretched the reach of their wrath, fairly effortlessly wrecking the pro baseball dreams of teams in Brooklyn and the towns of New Jersey. Ruppert was the evangelist leading the charge that they would take on serious challengers only. Ruppert recognized that the more success a team achieves, the easier it was to raise money to fund their costs. He managed the team with a relentless inner drive for success. As the team accomplishments grew, better ballplayers were attracted. Ruppert understood the vicious cycle of success. Success attracts money and talent.

Conversely, he knew failure would start a death spiral: the loss of financial support and exodus of good players. When Ruppert reached eighteen years old, his father instructed him that playtime was over. He was thrust headlong into the family brewing business. He demonstrated the same initiative. Quickly he rose from barrel washer to company vice president. Inside, though, the desire to own a baseball club never waned. As early as 1903, Ruppert began making overtures into the potential purchase of the New York Giants. Rebuffed by the league on each occasion, Ruppert shook up the comfortable New York City balance by threatening to bring in a team from a rival league. In an attempt to defuse Ruppert's attempts, league president Henry Clay Pulliam, offered the Chicago Cubs. Ruppert had one other strong passion — the night life of Broadway. The allure of the stars, the lights and excitement of an intricate musical production pulled his inner magnet. Ruppert spent weeks mulling the prospect of finally owning a team. After lengthy consideration, he declined. Chicago was just too far from the neon lights. Instead, he decided to make another run at the Giants, but again he was trumped by their refusal to sell to him.

    With each failure of Ruppert's attempts to acquire the Giants, his animosity towards their ownership deepened. Between 1903 and 1914, he made seven unsuccessful bids to acquire the team. Frustrated but not wanting to leave New York City, he was left with few choices. Brooklyn was out of the question. The only viable option left open to him to purchase the other New York City team, the inept and floundering Yankees.

The Yankees' roots were the Baltimore Orioles. Just in time for the 1903 season, their inaugural season in New York City, a couple of unscrupulous characters purchased the team. One owner, "Big Bill" Devery, was a former New York City police captain. Devery's lack of discretion in his collection of graft from the petty hustlers and street walkers made him fair game for critics. Amid a sensational scandal, he was reassigned to the position of the first police chief of New York. The position was created solely to relegate him to an administrative role. The move backfired. The very affable Devery became even more brazen in his collection of monies for protection services while serving as New York's top cop. He survived legislative moves to eliminate the position. At the time of the purchase, Big Bill was arguably New York City's most corrupt cop.

Frank Farrell, his co-investor, was a well-to-do owner of several saloons. Before the turn of the century, he controlled most of the pool halls and betting parlors in New York City. He and Devery had met years earlier, while he was tending bar at one of his saloons. Farrell mentioned he needed some help in dealing with a shakedown from some local thugs. Devery guaranteed that for modest monthly 'insurance' payments, he could assure Farrell that his establishment would remain safe and his horse stables insulated from any 'accidents.' Thus the relationship and long-term friendship began. Farrell's money smarts and Devery's political clout made for a perfect match. Devery and Farrell were able to orchestrate the successful transition of the second professional baseball team to New York City.

Andrew Freedman, the owner of the Giants, had successfully blocked every attempt by Ban Johnson to secure land for an American League Park, necessary to bring any American League team to the city, claiming that each parcel proposed was necessary for the Interborough Rapid Transit System, the sweeping underground subway labyrinth under construction.

In December 1901, Johnson believed he had struck an agreement to acquire a piece of land between 142nd and 145th streets and bordered by Lennox Avenue and the Harlem River, an ideal location. The newly constructed IRT station was nearby, providing fans easy and inexpensive transportation to the ball park. He had convinced IRT founder and financier August Belmont, along with one of its directors, James McDonald, to lease the land he had identified to the American League. Freedman, still fuming over Johnson's continued raids of National League players, which included several Giants this time in the defections to the rival league, swore he'd see to it that city leaders would block the process permanently. The thirteen IRT directors declined the proposal, with Freedman casting the final vote in the 7-6 no decision. Adding insult to injury, the New York city council issued a directive to Johnson that they would not undertake any applications by the American League nor Johnson to bring a franchise to New York unless he demonstrated the financial wherewithal, including investors and approved plans for the construction of the park.

Johnson, thwarted again and now with considerable roadblocks thrust in front of him, decided he needed help. The Midwesterner decided the best approach was to get a few Tammany Hall insiders in his pocket.

Freedman boasted of his string of victories over Johnson and the American League every chance he could. While drinking at one of Farrell's downtown watering holes in late January, he bragged to the pub owner, "Someone of significant influence must be stringing those poor American League bastards along. They've got no chance of ever getting a team in my city."

"Ever, now that's a mighty long time. Something I'd be willing to make wager on," Farrell offered, speaking in a thick Irish brogue.

"You're on for $50!"

"That kind of money, I hear tell, is more of a woman's bet. Tell you what. $25,000 says Johnson gets the land for a park within six months."

"Never happen. You got a deal." Freedman extended a hand, the wager sealed as the men shook.

News traveled quickly within the political circles of New York. Self-made coal broker Joe Gordon had sought an appointment with Ban Johnson for several days, finally getting in to see him on February 3rd. Gordon, a younger man, had dreams of bringing a major league team to the city. After years of financial setbacks and maneuvers to prevent his team from being successful, he folded his semi-pro club, the New York Mets, before the turn of the century. Unlike most of the investors in his club, Gordon did not suffer a crippling financial setback when the team dissolved.

"Ban, let me start off by expressing my admiration of your efforts and sympathy since you've had no success. That hasn't been for the lack of trying. As you may or may not know, I suffered the same fate. But I do believe that with some assistance, the time may be right. I have friends who can arrange for you to get the piece of land you need and have a ballpark built in time to open in the spring of 1903," Gordon stated, cutting right to the quick.

"Even if I had the site tomorrow, there is no conceivable way the ballpark could get finished in time for the season. The city will just tie me up in a lot of red…"

"Look, I need to stop you there. All I can say is that with friends in the right places and the right amount of resources, things in this city can happen fast," Gordon said, interrupting Johnson in mid-thought.

"Say I'm intrigued. What will it take and what's in it for you?"

"I require a $25,000 introduction fee. You'll meet the two gentlemen who will shepherd this through the political maze to get you the needed property. I'll provide the construction services to build the park. My friends charge a transaction fee of $75,000. You agree to have a franchise sold to them. Do we have a deal?" Gordon asked.

"Can I think about it for a few days?"

"No. The window for getting this done is small. If you're serious about moving forward, the time is now."

"You're asking me to get the owners to agree to sell a franchise, sight unseen, to some unnamed individuals. Potential owners need to go through an evaluation process and..."

Again Gordon abruptly halting Johnson's words, "Hold off, here! Let me be perfectly clear, as this may very well be your last chance to put an American League team in New York City for a very long time. The American League needs a team here in the city. If you try the normal process the Giants and Brooklyn will slow your efforts for at least a decade. You already know that. So I need to know your answer, now."

Johnson needed a moment to evaluate the situation. *'Who was this guy, why is he so willing to help?'* He had little bargaining power. Johnson was anxious. A team in New York City assuredly cemented the future success of the American League.

Johnson stood up, extended his hand and agreed to Gordon's conditions. *The owners would agree with his decision to move the Baltimore team. There was no choice.*

The next morning, Farrell and Devery arrived at Johnson's office precisely at the pre-arranged time of 10:00AM. After Johnson's reply, Gordon proceeded to provide the names and background of his two associates and how the meeting would unfold.

Johnson, generally a composed man, was clearly uncomfortable with the rapidly unfolding situation. After years of battling the New York City political machine, was it possible that three complete strangers could bring the jewel he coveted for his nascent league?

"Mr. Johnson, let's get right to business," Farrell began. "My partner here is William Devery; he is currently the chief of police. You may have heard of him. My name is Frank Farrell; I am just a simple saloon keeper."

"Gentlemen, I may be a newcomer to New York, but I'm far from wet behind the ears. You, Mister Farrell, are quite a bit more than just a simple saloon owner. And Mr. Devery, here, wields a far bigger stick than his position would suggest."

"Mr. Johnson, let's discard the niceties. We all know why we're here. Do you have something for us?"

Johnson handed over the payment for $100,000. In return, the pair submitted a check to secure the franchise. Johnson had already had the paperwork drawn, with Devery shown as the lone owner and Joe Gordon installed as the president. This was a relief for Johnson, as he had been concerned by Farrell's shady associations.

The more the Tammany Hall politicians tried to curb the activities of Devery, the more determined he became. Although the city council controlled the real estate landscape tightly, Devery was determined to beat them at their own game. Thanks to Devery, the pieces were falling into place.

The estate of Josephine L. Peyton, after seven years of finally-resolved legal challenges by her second husband, was to be sold at auction on February 18th. Josephine believed her husband to be somewhat of a lout and skirt chaser, which was not the proper conduct of a high society husband. Citing estrangement, she completely cut William K. Peyton from the will, revoked his trust fund and removed him as executor. Through several codicils, she made her favorite charities, churches and close friends her heirs and beneficiaries. The substantial real property holdings of the estate, spread across much of Manhattan and into Hoboken, New Jersey, had risen sharply in value since the time of her death in November, 1894, and were now drawing the attention of investors and speculators.

John J. Byrne, a nephew of Devery and a political operative in Manhattan's ninth district, was dispatched by Big Bill to secure the eleven parcels in Morningside Heights and Manhattanville. For the modest sum of nearly four hundred thousand dollars, the auctioneer threw in an unusable and miserable piece of land in Hamilton Heights.

Devery's ability to outfox the city council had paid off for Johnson, who finally secured the land he needed. The Baltimore franchise was sold. The team's relocation to the near north end of Manhattan marked the end of the Orioles. The advent of the franchise destined to become the Yankees had been set in motion for a mere $18,000. American League Park (Hilltop), a too-quickly constructed ballpark, located at 165th St. and Broadway, served as the home of the Highlanders from 1903 to 1912. Unfortunately the new owners failed to deliver 'payments' to city officials quick enough, workers abandoned the project weeks before the first game. The park opened with a grassless infield, a bog-like outfield and an incomplete clubhouse. The Senators and the Yankees had to get ready for the game without a locker room, dressing across the street in a hotel. But New York City had its second baseball franchise, the Highlanders.

While serving as police chief, Devery appropriated the design of a commendation called the New York Police Department Medal for Valor. The badge featured a distinctive emblem with a unique interlocking N and Y supporting it. Devery decided to 'borrow' this logo for his new team until something one with greater distinction could be developed.

After just a decade of use, Hilltop was in shambles along with the franchise. On October 5, 1912, the city condemned the ballpark for safety concerns and scheduled its demolition. Rechristened the Yankees, the woefully hapless and now homeless franchise became a tenant of the Giants in the Polo Grounds. Devery, a decade removed from any real influence with the city and Farrell, tired of pouring more and more of his money into the sinking ship, put the Yankees up for sale in 1914. Ruppert had his team.

The novelty of simply owning a team wore thin very quickly. By early 1915, Ruppert, being second fiddle to the Giants had already worn thin. For him, success was to see the Yankees as the preeminent team, not only in New York, but in all of baseball. He could not do that without owning his team's own home. In a letter to Ban Johnson on July 16, 1915, Huston wrote:

"We have canvassed the feasibility of the 42nd Street site for a ballpark," Col. Ruppert and I will be with the club when it reaches Chicago, and we will be glad to discuss the subject with you then ...."*

In a meeting in Johnson's Chicago office several days later, Ruppert outlined his case for the Yankees.

"Ban, you have a chance to make the American League much more than the junior league it is currently thought of. We will build a stadium in a premier location, dead square in the middle of New York City, attract a few more of the better players. The league will evolve into something special," Ruppert pleaded.

"Colonel, the league owns Chicago and Boston. Stripping those franchises of talent to satisfy your needs is not something I can support at this time, "Johnson responded

"Ban, the location of the ballpark is unprecedented, Forty-Second Street and Broadway!"

"Before you go any further in your endeavors, please read this letter."

As the color drained from his face, he handed the document to Huston. The final paragraph was emblazoned in his mind as he closed his eyes, the upset Ruppert thought. *"Mr. Johnson, I realize that as much as the city of New York might enjoy being the home to three professional baseball teams, baseball is a luxury, not a necessity for the citizens. Easy and affordable transportation is of most importance. To be blunt, the site chosen by Mr. Ruppert for his ballpark project has*

been DISAPPROVED. The council will DENY
application at any future sites other than those explicitly
identified on the fringe of the city. Yours very sincerely,
John Purroy Mitchel, Mayor."

        Despondent, Ruppert apologized for wasting Johnson's time. The situation was very uncomfortable. For the first time in his life, he was not in control. He just needed to wait until the right time. The team continued to struggle in its efforts to draw fans. The Giants were immensely popular and financially successful; as the top dog within New York's baseball community, no team or owner had the ability to present any real threat to their dominance.

        In 1920, with the acquisition of Ruth, all that began to change. Driven by fascination with a man possessed of Bunyanesque strength, someone who could drive a ball far from sight and could also shut down opponents with the prowess of his arm brought fans out to the park in Coogan's Hollow in droves. Attendance for Yankees exploded, eclipsing the 1,250,000 mark. The main attraction, Ruth, did his part on the field, winning games as the Yankees ascended the standings. Off the field, the tales of his late-night boozing and carousing multiplied. Tabloid stories appeared almost daily of him going directly to the ball park for a game after a night of wild partying and womanizing. While not impacting his play on the field, an enormous strain was placed on his relationship with Helen. He managed to pitch in sixty-three games and accounted for half of the Yankee win total in the 1921 season. At the plate, fifty-nine balls left the ballpark from the swing of his bat, breaking the record he had set just one year earlier. His forty-nine wins for a pitcher placed him fourth on the all-time list. The Yankees won their first pennant.

Tensions between Yankee and Giant ownership boiled throughout the season. Stoneham resented the Yankees' recent success. The Giants were losing steam as the city's premier baseball attraction. After the Giants had captured the 1921 National League title, seething over facing his much more popular tenant, Stoneham decided make the Yankees' life at the Polo Grounds miserable. For the World Series, the Giants owner declared that for each of the games played at the Polo Grounds, the Giants would don the home team uniform. Stoneham refused to concede any of the customary allowances for the Yankees during their designated 'home team' games. Under no circumstance would the Giants ever be considered the visitors.

Stoneham stated regularly, "For all I care, the Yankees can arrange to play their series home games on some dirt field in Queens. The Yankees are a very unwelcome tenant and will not displace the Giants in their home."

Just prior to the start of game one, he closed half of the visitors' dressing room for construction, moving their equipment and uniforms outside and unprotected, further fueling the acrimony.

Babe Ruth, as his stature grew, was granted some latitude with the club that the other players did not have. Discouraged by the loss to the Browns, Babe and Helen decided to travel ahead of the team to Philadelphia. Accompanying them were

Fred Hoffman, a light hitting backup catcher and coach Charlie O'Leary. On September 30, 1921 the New Star- Eagle reported,

"Ruth and Teammate Die in Tragic Accident"

"Travelling at unsafe speeds along US Highway 1, the vehicle driven by the New York Yankee star pitcher spun out of control, flipping twice as it rolled down an embankment before coming to a stop. Two passengers survived the accident. Helen Ruth, wife of Mr. Ruth and Fred Hoffman, a Yankee teammate...."

When Ruth entered the dressing room at the Polo Grounds for a game against Philadelphia, every one of the Yankees stared in surprise.

"Good afternoon, boys," Ruth bellowed.

Huggins, startled spoke first, "Well, I will be damned. We were getting ready to decide whether to play or not. You and O'Leary are reported dead."

"No big deal, a scratch on my elbow. Everyone else has a few bumps and bruises. Sorry we're late. It took a while for us to get a cab from Jersey."

"Let the trainer examine that arm. It looks nasty."

Ruth's arm was not good; an infection developed and spread quickly. Ruppert tracked down Carl Mays and coerced him to rejoin the Yankees in time for the start of series.

Fans swarmed the bleachers of the Polo Grounds as the New Yorkers readied for the start of a long-anticipated matchup, eighteen years in the making, between the intra-city rivals. Dignitaries, politicians and stars of the stage and screen all sought high priced tickets. Scalpers could garner an unheard-of $10 for a box seat.

The Yankees took the first two games from their landlord, thanks to successful but daring base running. Without Ruth's big bat, their offense stalled. After the Giants captured game three, Huggins tapped Mays to start game four, but because of his extended absence from baseball, any likelihood of success was a longshot.

Ruth, idle from the injury, stood next to the dugout, peering into the stands. He was never shy about mixing with other famous Americans. He had managed to spot his old pal Al Jolson seated behind third base, before game one. Today he managed to spot Nathan Miller, the governor of New York State, whom he had met before game one, the baseball commissioner, and a third man whom Ruth did not know but would come to find out later was the Attorney General of the United States, Harry Micajah Daugherty. Daugherty was eventually forced to resign under questionable circumstances. Rounding out the unlikely quartet was the indomitable Arnold Rothstein. *What the hell is the baseball commissioner doing with someone like that?* Ruth thought, referencing the rumors about Rothstein's background.

Finally he spotted the person he'd been looking for, Helen. "Excuse me Hug, I have to go say hi to my gal. She wants something." Helen was waving her arm signaling him to come over.

"Yes, babe, who's the gal sitting next to you?"

"This is Carl May's wife, Marjorie. Did you see Carl talking to the baseball commissioner? He's been worried. Landis gave him some encouragement."

"Well, pleased to meet you, sis. Don't worry, he'll do fine."

"Let's pray there is not another incident. He has never recovered, emotionally. His nerves are shattered. Carl will need a lot of help from above," responded a worried Marjorie.

"The game is getting ready to start and Huggins wants me to take the lineup card out to the umpires. I have to get used to doing stuff like that if I am going to manage someday." Ruth headed back to the dugout.

Mays breezed through seven innings, keeping the Giants' batters in check. The Yankees had squeezed out only a single run. Mays was extremely sharp, far from a player who'd been away from the game. Mays was all over the strike zone once again, as he'd been in game one. Up to this point in the game, he had not come close to issuing a walk to any hitter. Mays was cruising along so smoothly it appeared he would have enough to make the lone Yankee run stand up.

With his warm-up routine completed, Mays looked over toward the third base box seats. He spotted his wife standing. She waved at him. Inching her way past the knees of the seated spectators, she made her way to the aisle. She turned and briskly walked up the stairs.

Apprehensively she'd make her way to the subway. Once home, the uneasy feeling that put a knot in her stomach would pass.

Marjorie paid no mind to the handsome blue-eyed teenager she passed as she scurried from the grandstands to the dank corridors leading to the ball park exit. The grey fedora, matching the color of his Italian woolen suit, was pulled down firmly on his head, hiding his steel-blue eyes. Coming all the way from his home in the Greenburg section of Brooklyn, this was an unusual request from his boss. Benjamin demonstrated skills in bringing different ethnic groups together to enhance New York City's bootlegging operations and gambling operations. He had a plan and that involved working his way up in the organization with his brain, quickly. Growing up as part of as part of a poverty-ravished immigrant family, before reaching puberty he was determined to make better life for himself. If he had to use his muscle to accomplish that, he would. But taking out a lady, well, as distasteful as it appeared, he would do what was asked. She was a decent looker, he rather would have wooed and seduced her and not have stuck a knife into the left side of her rib cage, piercing her heart. Luckily, she did what she was supposed to and the dilemma was avoided.

Benjamin found a pay phone in a small boarding house after descending the steps down to Edgecombe Avenue toward the subway. He dialed a number which rang in a social club located on Lafayette Street in the Jewish section of lower Manhattan.

"This is Benjamin. Everything is good. She and her husband did as told. I'm heading back to Brooklyn now. Moe, just let Meyer know. Okay." Benjamin Siegel, unnoticed, boarded the subway, bound for Brooklyn.

Mays tipped his cap to his wife before returning to the task of getting the final six men out. Four walks and three hits later, the Yankees were down two.

"Hug, you need to go out a settle the pitcher down," Ruth said to his manager. "All of a sudden this guy has lost control. That ain't right."

"If you're so worried, you go talk to him."

"I hope for your sake he isn't doing anything stupid."

"Time," Ruth erupting from the dugout, yelling to the umpires.

When he reached the mound, he confronted Mays. "What the hell is going on? You ain't been this wild all day."

"Don't know. I just seem to have lost it."

"What's up with the misses?"

"Mind your own beeswax, Ruth."

"I saw your wife signal you. She rushed kind of quick there. What was in the envelope she was carrying?"

"Shut up, Ruth, go sit down."

"Well, I'll just go over and see Landis."

"Go right ahead, Ruth. Landis ain't doing nothing. You see who's sitting with him. Go ahead, make a fool of yourself," Mays chuckled. "Get back to the bench."

"Just get the next guy out."

Ruth felt certain there was more to the unexpected collapse than Mays was letting on. He buried his thoughts of rushing over to the new commissioner who was tasked with cleaning up the game, which is what Mays was implying when he said Landis would not take action. Ruth tucked his chin down as would a scolded child and walked sullenly back to the dugout.

"What'd he say, Babe?" Huggins asked

"Say's he's okay. Let's see what he does with the next hitter."

The Yankees dropped game three and did not recover, losing the series in eight games. Ruth never forgot the conversation from that day, unsure whom to trust.

For Huston and Ruppert, that was the last straw. At the conclusion of series, they began to explore possible locations for a new home. Stoneham, with the City Council in his pocket, had ideas of his own. The Giants had failed to surpass the million attendance mark. He blamed this squarely on the immense popularity of the Yankees. With the interests of his team in mind and the press on his side, he created doubt about the ability of the city to support three baseball teams. City Council leadership under Fiorello LaGuardia offered The Colonel two sites at no cost. One was on the far west side in Manhattan, between 136th and 138th streets and Amsterdam Avenue, part of an abandoned railroad yard. The second location was a marshy plot of land situated on the southeast side of Jamaica Bay. South Ozone Park was a community of low-cost housing, as far south as you can get on

Queens before hitting the Atlantic. The stadium, when done, would be neatly tucked in between a horse racing track and Idlewild Golf Course. Stoneham had carefully steered the city council in the direction of either location; each was fraught with problems. Twenty-six miles from the heart of the city, with limited transportation ability, access for fans would be difficult. Stoneham hoped this would stunt popularity and attendance growth and bring folks back into the Giants' fold. The latter selection, Stoneham considered a stroke of personal genius. He ruminated, "The mosquitos and bugs from the marsh and the proximity to gamblers, prostitutes and low life element — let's see how the Yankees' popularity survives."

Ruppert realized the situation at the Polo Grounds was untenable. Ruth had become the largest drawing card in American sports in just two short years, and now was the time to capitalize on the phenomenon. He also set himself on a path to beat Stoneham at his own game. He needed to build the Yankees into a formidable franchise that would endure for decades after Ruth was gone from the game. Yankee fans and their association to the club would steepen with sustained success.

"Look down there, Ruth, what do you see?" Ruppert began.

"The Polo Grounds, why?"

"Yes, from here we see Coogan's Hollow. Look across the river over there."

"It looks like a beat-up lumberyard, a pretty big one at that."

"Ruth, I will tell you what I see. I see progress. I see the Germans in Manhattan moving to there in the Bronx, a new Kleindeutschland. Music gardens, a transportation center, houses built to accommodate the influx of people coming to the states. I see a town square where people congregate. I see German schools, sports clubs and theaters. All that, right there. If Stoneham had his way, he would move the Yankees as far from here as possible. He's even gotten the mayor and the city council to offer us land out somewhere in Queens. He wants to make it difficult for Yankee fans to get to games. I'm not going to take that bait. No, Ruth, over there is where the Yankees will plant their roots. Huston and I will announce soon that we have purchased that lumberyard, and we will build a ballpark. Not just an ordinary ballpark, but a huge park, with several tiers that will seat seventy thousand. Can you imagine, Ruth, seventy thousand screaming fans coming to see you? The park will have an enormous, cavernous left field and centerfield. The architects think there is enough for outfield walls in left and center to extend nearly 500 feet away from home plate. In right field the walls will be closer. We are going to build the park to your strengths as a left handed pitcher and batter. You'll win more games here than anywhere else. You'll pitch more games because you just need to have them hit a fly to left or center. Ruth, you'll dominate baseball for another decade. Ruth, the Yankees are moving to the Bronx and building that field for you! Ruth, we plan for this ballpark and the Yankees to survive the Giants in New York City."

Ruppert had just completed the acquisition of the crumbling, abandoned lot from the estate of William Waldorf Astor, a longtime friend. Ground breaking was unceremoniously scheduled for May 5th, 1922. The plans and dimensions disclosed for the new playground of the Yankees stunned many by its breath-taking size and the enormity of the outfield. The ballpark in the Bronx was designed with three tiers and a seating capacity in excess of 70,000 fans. The shape, together with a six-foot red clay warning area before the fence line, created the appearance of arenas where Olympiads of old had taken place. The New York newspapers, reporting on the progress of the construction, began referring to the park as a stadium.

Babe, although captivated by the soliloquy, struggled to absorb the enormity and simple complexity of what Ruppert was telling him.

"I just bought that piece of property. We are going to break ground next month and open in time for the season next year. Ruth, you're an important part of the equation, but the way you're acting, you're going to throw it all away. The drinking, the pandering, staying out until all hours — you may be able to keep it up for a short while, but not for very long. You eat like you're a man on death row. Excess, your life has become about excess. Ruth, you're on a path to a very unhealthy situation. I take up the fight for you with Landis and Huggins nearly every day. Each of them wants you suspended or gone. Look at you, you're already starting to put on weight, and in the wrong spots."

"Colonel, I'm fine. I can pitch and still bang out long ones."

"Ruth, it isn't that simple. You keep flaunting a 'bigger-than-the-game' attitude. Understand that Landis is vindictive when it comes to challenges to his authority. Look at what happened to those poor SOB's in Chicago. He is serious about the barnstorming ultimatum."

"The man's a tyrant, a bully. He can't keep the fellows from making a little extra dough."

"Ruth, I had to pay your series share to the league as a fine."

"So what? I'll make ten times that, barnstorming in California this winter. I'll pay you back."

"It's not just the money."

"Look, Colonel, he's a bigot. He's more upset that we play against the coloreds."

"Yes, he is very upset about that. Look, Ruth, Landis does not think it's good for the game."

"Well he'd better wake up. Some of those boys can play."

"And the cavorting! You can't keep that pace, Ruth, since you have already passed Connor in home runs. Huggins thinks you'll wear down faster playing in the field, so he wants to keep you focused on pitching."

"Hogwash, Colonel, I ain't slowed a bit."

"You're fooling yourself; I could hear you huffing all the way up the final few steps up here. You need to keep yourself clean and healthy, or I will give Huggins his way."

The Yankees finished out 1922 at the Polo Grounds, managing to earn a second straight pennant. But they had to battle a resilient St. Louis Browns club down to the wire.

Leading by a slim half game, the Yankees visited Sportsmans Park for a three-game series in mid-September. Browns fans had mixed emotions as they left the ballpark after the first game of the series. George Sisler, the Brown's biggest star, hit in his 40th consecutive game to tie Ty Cobb's modern record, but the Yank's Bob Shawkey beat Urban Shocker 2-1, for the victory. An ugly incident marred the game. In the ninth inning, one of the 30,000 fans in attendance threw a bottle that hit Yankees center fielder Whitey Witt in his forehead and left a gash down to the bone. Witt and Yankee right fielder Bob Meusel raced into the gap when Witt was hit. Meusel made the running catch as Witt fell to the ground. Mounted police galloped over as thousands of fans ran onto the field. Order was finally restored and Witt was treated. The injury, while bad, was fortunately less severe than first believed. Witt did not miss a game.   The Yankees lead now stood at one and one-half games. The Browns had to win the next day or face a deficit perhaps too deep to overcome during the remaining games of the season. Ruth, buoyed by his performance during the recent three seasons, was considered the top left-handed pitcher in the game. He would oppose the Browns in second game of the series. Ruth took the hill for the game in less than peak condition. Heeding neither Ruppert's advice nor Huggins' rules, Babe discovered the 3:00 AM bars and jazz clubs on the St. Louis waterfront. Ruth developed a strong camaraderie with many of the Negro League players and their music; he found their exotic women a temptation far too appealing. Any resistance Ruth might have mustered was crushed by the allure. When he walked into the clubhouse a mere hour before game time, Huggins exploded.

Planting a pointed finger in the middle of Ruth's barrel chest, a red-faced Huggins shouted in a voice so loud it shook the walls, "Dammit, Ruth, don't bother dressing. Just stay put, you're not playing."

"Hold on, Huggins, Ruppert would not like you benching Ruth and neither would I."

"Huston, what the hell are you doing? I thought you were going to keep Ruth on the straight and narrow, not become his drinking buddy! Five minutes longer and his name would have been erased from the lineup and his ass gone for the season."

"Relax, you shrimp, I'm fine. If you were a foot taller, we'd be nose to nose and I'd pop you one. Go back to doing back to do what it is you usually do — nothing!"

Unsteadily, Ruth took the mound and managed to keep the Browns at bay until the sixth inning. Sisler, the Browns' hitting machine, singled in the sixth inning and leapfrogged the consecutive-game hitting streak set by Ty Cobb. Ken Williams smacked a long two-run home run. The Browns kept their hopes alive with a 5-1 victory. Ruth went hitless, striking out three times.

Enraged, Huggins cornered Ruth with three of the other Yankees at the game's end as he relaxed in a vat of ice with a wet towel draped over his face.

"Look at you! You're turning into a broke-down old war horse and you ain't yet thirty!" Huggins let loose on Ruth.

Peering with one eye, Ruth responded, "Pipe down, you squirt, or I'll pop you like a pimple. Hey, look, guys, now we're face to face, but I'm in this tub," Ruth said to his teammates in a more deferential tone.

"If Ruppert weren't investing so much in you and you didn't have that other idiot protecting you, I'd have you gone. Count your blessings if you're in the lineup card tomorrow."

After a night to think about things, Huggins decided that discretion was the better part of valor. Huston was back on a train east immediately after the final out of the game. Ruth managed a quiet night and recovered from his overindulgences very quickly.

Ruth was at Sportsman Park well in advance of the start time the next day. Browns fans gasped in unison as he knocked seventeen consecutive batting practice pitches deep over the right field fence.

Staying true to what he did in pregame, Ruth broke a scoreless tie with a solo home run off Browns starter Hub Pruett in the sixth. The Browns refused to throw up the white flag as they touched Waite Hoyt for a two-spot in their half of the inning, not quite enough to win.

The Yankees won the final game 3-2, as Whitey Witt drove in the decisive run. Lee Fohl, the Browns manager, pulled every move he could, but using both previous starters and Pruett and his ace Shocker in relief, he could not stem the rally.

Safely in front of the Browns, the Yankees coasted down the stretch, readying for a rematch from the previous season.

The feud between Yankee and Giant management escalated with Ruppert's announcement that he was going to build the big ball park in the Bronx. News reporters lauded the design as a wonder of modern engineering. The three-tier all-concrete structure, the enormity of the playing field and the ground-breaking use of a red clay track around the wall to prevent an outfielder from having a devastating destiny with the outfield wall were incessantly touted in the media. The New York Evening News said the ball park brought back visions of ancient Rome and Greece. The triple tiers of the Coliseum melded with the stadium of Olympia. The new home of the Yankees was a perfect combination of old and new, capable of seating over 70,000 fans. The Polo Grounds would sit in the shadows of this new majestic park. Construction on the park was well ahead of schedule. As the series was set to open on October 4th, White Construction had remarkably transformed the undefinable skeletal piers into the vision which would become the home for the Yankees. No less than ten temporary construction buildings were on the grounds. Ezekiel Schmidt, the construction supervisor, orchestrated hundreds of workers broken into dozens of crews, each working on different aspects of the project. His diligence kept the project on target for a June 1923 grand opening.

"Hey Zeke, the Colonel is here to speak with you," shouted the foreman working to grade the infield grounds.

"Tell Ruppert to meet me in the main construction building. I'm on my way," Schmidt said. He then mumbled under his breath, "What does he want now?" *I've gotten the damn Irish to stop drinking and those I-talians to stop stealing.* He kept those thoughts to himself.

The main building was located on River Avenue and 161st street, abutting the building abandoned by Osborne Construction of Cleveland. Ruppert had had his fill of the Giants and the stress of the relationship was weighing heavily. He was investing heavily in the team, so they needed to produce. He did not want to have to answer more questions if there was a second straight series loss. Ruppert was facing south, staring in the direction of the 155th Street Bridge, when Schmidt approached him. "What brings you here today?"

"Well Schmidt, I understand you're on schedule. That's terrific, but not acceptable."

"Colonel, I don't understand. I'm pushing the men as hard as …."

"Let me finish. To be clear, I want the park ready for opening day, not the middle of the season. Find a way."

"With all due respect, that's not possible."

"Schmidt, anything is possible. What can be done?"

Schmidt paced, rubbing his hair with his gritty palms. "Well, Colonel, the two upper tiers have not yet been extended completely to the outfield. That could save six to eight weeks. We could finish those later."

"Good, we're settled, then. The park will open for the game on April 18th, 1923."

"Colonel, I have to verify that the structure is not compromised with this change."

"Schmidt, you'll figure it out. Two more things before I go. You had better be right about the city's planned height for the elevated train. The park needs to stand above the train. Second, the concrete exterior had better work. There's a reason no one else has built parks this way."

"Good luck tomorrow against the Giants."

The Colonel turned and walked slowly through the soft muddy grounds towards his automobile parked on a narrow strand of gravel, "And get rid of that goddamn Osborne sign. We need to make it perfectly clear to everyone. New Yorkers are building this stadium."

Ruppert was ready to explode if the Yankees had to spend a single second more than necessary as a tenant of Stoneham. Complaining of filth and rat excrement in the clubhouse for weeks, Stoneham responded with a certified letter that exterminators were arriving on Monday, October 2, in the evening at 7:00PM to accommodate the Yankee afternoon practice. Any gear remaining would be relocated to accommodate the exterminators' needs in ridding the clubhouse of unwanted vermin.

On Monday evening, October 2, 1922 a heavy thunderstorm began sweeping across the east coast, dumping anywhere from four to eight inches of rain on the cities in its path. Philadelphia, New York and Boston bore the brunt of fifty-mile-an-hour wind gusts and the driving downpour. The skies cleared as the morning sun peeked out from spotty cloud cover, just in time for Yankee players to make their way to the park for their final practice.

Uncharacteristically Ruth has arrived early. Standing on the top step of the dugout, Ruth stood motionless, his head bowed slightly and forehead resting against the intertwined knuckles of his hands, as if praying. Waite Hoyt bounced up the steps, "What gives, Babe? The clubhouse is locked."

Ruth inhaled with the tragic air of one who had just received news about losing a loved one. He raised his left arm slowly, his index finger pointing out onto the field.

Hoyt took three tentative steps before turning to look at Ruth.

"Does Huggins know about this?"

Ruth shrugged his shoulders, "No one else is here."

Hoyt flitted down the steps, disappearing into the shadows of the dugout as quietly as he had arrived, passing many of his arriving teammates as he sprinted toward the manager's office.

The ballpark was strewn with Yankee road grey uniforms, many settling in the placid puddles left from the storms of the night before. Bats, gloves, baseballs, towels — every piece of gear was completely soaked, most were unusable and all were sitting in near ruin.

Hoyt, pushing open the door which stood ajar to Huggins Spartan office, heard Huggins on the phone, "Okay, Colonel, I'll talk to Ebbets, we'll see if he can send equipment over. Understood we'll beat their fannies in the series. I agree this is the last straw."

"Yes, Waite?"

"I saw Ruth. He didn't think anyone else was here."

"Ruth was early, for a change, but no one beats me here, not no one. Tell the boys there'll be no practice today. We'll get some equipment from the Robins for tomorrow. Let's win the series and stick this right back at Stoneham and McGraw."

Walking back into their dugouts at the Polo Grounds for the final time, their heads down, the revenge was not to be. Ever so surgically, the stunned Yankees were swept from the Polo Grounds by their landlord, leaving a scar of the final painful memory. The Yankee offense was held in check not so much by McGraw's pitching staff but by the undersized bats sent over courtesy of their other National League rivals. The powerful Yankee lineup swung heavy lumber; Ruth's bat was the equivalent of a two-by-four. As it was, hampered by the tiny stick he had to use, he led the struggling lineup as he managed two hits and one RBI for the series.

The conspiracy of the vandalized equipment quickly became an afterthought with the controversy surrounding game two.

A laboring Shawkey enticed Frank Snyder, the Giants catcher, into an easy second to first ground out to end the Giant's half of the ninth. Ruth was the sixth batter due up in the inning. As the Yanks walked off the field, Huggins instructed Ruth to go to the bullpen. The game was deadlocked 3 -3.

"Ruth, we've got the bottom of the order hitting, so you need to be ready fast. You're going in if this goes to the eleventh. We need this game."

Huggins' instincts were correct; the Yankees, already down a game, would be in an unenviable position with a 0-2 deficit in a hostile environment.

After an Aaron Ward strikeout on a full count, Everett Scott drove a single to center. Huggins did not pinch-hit for Shawkey, never checking to see if Ruth might have been ready. Huggins inexplicably kept Shawkey in the game to bat. Huggins directed Shawkey to sacrifice bunt. A successful sacrifice would put the delivery of the potential winning run on the shoulders of Whitey Witt, who was hitless so far in the series. As Shawkey moved into position, squaring off to face the plate, Scott walking into a bigger lead took off. Shawkey, trying to place the ball up the first-base line, was handcuffed by the pitch and instead directed the ball right back to a charging Barnes. With a cat-like turn, Scott was forced out at second base. Witt managed his first hit of the series, but the triumph was empty since Shawkey could advance no further than second. Dugan had reached base three times, and Ruth, hoping to get a chance to win the game, ran back to the dugout. The threat died as

Dugan fanned. Ruth would be the first batter to hit in the bottom of the tenth.

Trying to watch the action on the field, Ruth hurried through his warm-up, throwing harder sooner than usual. After his seventh pitch to backup catcher Al DeVormer, Ruth clutched for his left shoulder.

DeVormer yelled, "Babe, you OK?"

Wincing a bit while he flexed his left arm, he replied, "Nothing there, kid, I'll be okay. I'm ready. Let's get back to the dugout. If Dugan can get me a turn to hit, I will end the game."

DeVormer approached Huggins, advising him that Babe was not right. Ruth was trying to mask his arm stiffness down the stretch from the manager. Huggins, as always, was a step ahead of Ruth and used him sparingly in late September. Huggins stoically absorbed what DeVormer had told him without a response.

Huggins walked over to Ruth, who was slumped on the pale green bench of the dugout as he watched Dugan's futile last swing.

"How's the arm?"

"Fine. You manage the game. We should have already won this game." Ruth was visibly upset at Bob Shawkey's failure to move a runner into scoring position, denying Ruth an opportunity to win the game with a base hit in the ninth. "If Shawkey holds them down and I'll knock one out."

McGraw's strategy was clear early in this series; the Giants would not give the Yankee slugger any good pitches. McGraw believed Ruth would become anxious and swing at bad pitches.

After two weak ground outs to second, trying to pull low pitches away, Ruth finally coerced a walk. Then in the last of the eighth, he walloped a low outside fast ball to deep left center for a double. He became the tying run two batters later when Bob Meusel drove him home.

On Thursday, October 5, 1922, sunset would occur at approximately 5:03 PM.

At the conclusion of the Giant half of the tenth, McGraw sallied over to the box where Commissioner Landis sat. Landis leaned toward McGraw and nodded, in a manner not detectable to any but those closely observing, before returning to his erect position. It was 3:55 PM.

Both Shawkey and Barnes got through the opposing hitters quickly. Ruth and Meusel each popped out to the catcher on the first pitch from Barnes.

The time was now 4:07 PM.

Landis waved Bill Clem, the third base umpire, over to his box and gave him instructions no one else could hear. Clem and the home plate umpire, George Hildebrand, huddled for a few moments. Huggins was summoned to the meeting. Blocked from the view of most there, McGraw and his players had already begun their departure from the dugout to the lockers.

The Broadway betting commissioner took bets and laid odds on everything imaginable within the series. The wagers ranged from the score of each game to the number of balls and strikes of every at bat. Prior to the start of the 1922 series, the heaviest betting action centered on the pitching. As game two progressed into the late innings, the odds of Joe Bush and Waite Hoyt winning their next starts dropped. The odds against Babe Ruth pitching in the series increased. Huggins was generous in the days off he afforded Ruth down the stretch. Ruth had pitched every third game for the Yankees until the St Louis incident; he started just once after that. Many inside the gambling community sensed that Huggins did not think Ruth was reliable, and he may have worn down.

With the conclusion of the 4:15 PM announcement, a chorus of boos reverberated through the Polo Grounds as fans reacted to the news heard from the public address system, "Today's game is declared a tie due to darkness."

The sun in the western sky was still 45 minutes from dipping below the horizon.

"It is now been relayed to me that the umpire crew was alerted to a grey haze which had descended onto the field, making it impossible for the outfielders to clearly see the infield or to pick up the balls batted in their direction. From my vantage point, I can see the outfield perfectly fine. It's clear as a bell and the sun is just now sneaking behind the stands. I think there is a good forty-five minutes of daylight left. I just got the thirty-second warning from broadcast headquarters. Stay tuned to the full-length broadcast of the Mozart opera, Impresario. This is Tommy Cowan of WJZ radio, signing off from the Polo Grounds."

"Well, Arnold, this has become easier than taking candy from a baby." Kid Becker told a relaxed Arnold Rothstein in his suite at the

Knickerbocker, as he turned the dial to the 'off' position on the RCA Victor radio. "And no ball players are involved."

"You're right. We just play to the greed of the owners and the arrogance of a self-righteous commissioner. We can play Landis all day."

"Do you think Huggins will risk pitching Ruth in the series now?"

"Nope, the big man is tired. He will put himself into an early death at the pace he is going. Stoneham got what he wants, bigger gate receipts. We got we want, an easy payday."

On Sunday, October 15th, 1922, Robba Young had made her way back to their farm from the general store in Gilmore. Cy, relaxing on the porch, coffee cup in hand, could not understand what errand she had to run after Church. This was a day of rest from their farm chores and a day to spend with their families after breakfast.

"Coffee's brewed, dear. The bacon and biscuits are still warm. What was so important you could not walk back with me?"

"Oh Denton," she giggled in the caring manner she did each day of their married life, "You're so silly. Surprise!" she said, thrusting the newest edition of the Sporting Life in his direction.

He responded, "Well, I'll be! I forgot all about this."

"I know you did, so I got it for you! Took some work, too. Fellows down at the general store helped me out. And look, it's the baseball final edition. Tells you how all the players did."

The Sporting Life had ceased the publication after a thirty-four-year run, done in by competition from the Sporting News. . During the newspaper's hiatus from print, Francis Richter correctly believed that with the right inducement, he would recapture his readership. The inducement to the subscribers was a small rectangular card with the image of the player in the front and interesting facts about that player on the back. Readers would receive 10 random cards with each monthly edition. Quickly he hired correspondents to cover baseball within the major baseball cities and key smaller locales and convinced 40,000 loyal readers to pay for the annual subscription. The periodical re-emerged in 1922.

With the patience of a child unwrapping a gift on Christmas morning, Cy unrolled the newspaper, whereupon several cards fell to the ground near his feet. "What are these?"

"I think they're called baseball cards. I don't know for sure, but they didn't cost anything more. You can probably throw them out after you read them."

Cy scanned through the pile of cards, not spending much time with any one card before moving to the next. "I have never heard of some of these guys." He tossed the stack down, flipping through the newspaper to find the stories on the World Series. Robba glanced at the pile as a partially obscured card caught her attention. Brushing two cards aside she picked it up: George Herman Ruth – New York Yankees – Pitcher /Outfielder.

"Hey Denton, this guy sort of reminds me of you, with his boney legs and barrel chest. Plus, he is a pitcher. It says here at age 27, he has more wins than you did at that age."

"Let me see that."

Cy studied the image of Ruth and turned the card over to examine his statistics. "I've met this guy. He's a rebellious sort, drinks a lot, and stays out late whoring. A few more years and he'll fade from memory, fast as can be. Plus, he wants to hit more than pitch." Flipping the card back unto the small stack, Cy turned his attention back to reading the paper. He stared at the words as if absorbing every syllable, "Giants Sweep Tenants," but his deeper thoughts were on Ruth and his 191 wins.

Chapter 30

On April 18, 1923, New York City was abuzz. Less than a year after construction began, the big ball park in the Bronx was set to open. A stiff breeze from the southeast commanded the array of flags around the top of Yankee Stadium into a steady wave towards the Hudson River. Sixty feet above the main entrance at the home-place side, 'Yankee Stadium' was spelled in massive black block letters, on each side a seal of the United States, the emblem resplendent with the glorious bald eagle, its mighty wingspan and talons exposed, representing perseverance and vigilance. Above each insignia flew the stars and stripes. A flag of the Empire State stood dead center above Yankee Stadium on the roof, flanked by seven additional US flags on each side. Over one hundred thousand New Yorkers came out and stood in line, and twenty-two thousand of them would be turned away from the baptism of this great new ballpark. Not a single person complained of the 49 degree temperature or the dirt blown up onto their faces from the still unpaved roads leading to the stadium. This was a mixed crowd, some dressed in expensive heavy woolen overcoats, some in suits, others just in heavy sweaters, but everyone was excited. The line progressed slowly through the turnstiles past the ticket takers into the stadium. Each person paused and inhaled the exhilarating sight before them. A ball field in the shape of a giant horseshoe, the grass stretching as far as one could see and accented by the red clay marking the infield, three tiers of seats reaching upward over one hundred feet, and finally, gracing the top deck was a fifteen-foot copper façade. Those arriving on the elevated train were stalled in their descent, but enjoyed the view of the field from the platform.

Al Smith was seated in the box reserved for dignitaries with Kennesaw Landis, who was visibly uncomfortable. The Governor of New York State, at 3:25 PM, would have the proud and distinct honor of throwing out the first pitch. Out in the area of the stadium destined to become known as "Death Valley" were Ruppert, Huston, Harry Frazee and New York City Mayor John Hylan. The ceremonial dedication of the ballpark nearly finished, the Army reserve marching band pounded out a final march, John Phillip Sousa's 'Stars and Stripes Forever.' The band deftly switched to the Star Spangled Banner just before the start of the game. All spectators stood as a member of the color guard hoisted the American flag on the pole standing at attention, four hundred sixty feet from home plate. Cheers erupted with the raising of the 1922 American League pennant.

It took several minutes for the foursome to complete the long walk to their assigned box. Ruppert was the first to speak. "Mayor," Ruppert said, "What is your reaction to the Times' front page today?"

John McGraw never missed an opportunity to fuel of the animosity between the ball clubs. NY Times reporter interviewed McGraw the day before. The headline read, "Stadium in Goatville Set to Open, Says Giants' Skipper." McGraw told the reporter that the Bronx was filled with nothing but cow pastures, swamps and goat fields. "No serious New York City ball club should call anywhere but Manhattan Island home."

Ruppert was speaking tongue-in-cheek with the Mayor, hiding his fury within. He had spent a substantial amount of his own money, only to be slighted in the press because of the location, an effort spurred on, he believed, by McGraw. All of his life he had dreamed of owning a baseball club which he would build to great stature. Yankee Stadium was a testimony to his efforts, not far from where he first brought baseball to the Northside of the City.

He believed Stoneham was behind the article, trying to downplay the reality of the baseball stage he had created to overshadow the Giants. The owners were contending for top dog in the city and Ruppert had now surged ahead. The Yanks had consistently had greater attendance than the Giants; with a newer bigger ballpark, he expected the number by which the Yanks outdrew the Giants to grow considerably larger. If he could capture a World Series title, his team would own the city.

"The Bronx is the Bronx, Colonel. It's still full of cesspools, poor immigrants and a lot of livestock," said Hylan.

"All that is changing, though, Mr. Mayor, the immigrants are industrious. Look at the crowd, the immigrants next to blue bloods. The ballpark brings them all together."

"Colonel, if I were you, I'd worry more about Ruth. I hear he's still burning the candle at both ends. He still defies the barnstorming ban. When he becomes a complete disgrace to the game, I will step in and hard. I don't know how you tolerate his insolence. Seems like Huston, Ruth, and your boys like to mix with the . . . well, you know what I mean, certain dark elements of society," Landis said.

Ruth had been at odds with Landis since the end of the 1922 Series when Ruth announced a trip through the northwest corridor, playing his way through many of the small rural towns and concluding on November 1 in Buffalo. Ruth had put together a team of stars which included many of his Yankee teammates. Landis, in an attempt to limit the team's attractiveness on the road, issued a rule that members of the participating Series teams were prohibited from involvement in such tours. The threats did not dissuade Ruth.

Landis became irate over Ruth's steadfast refusal to cancel the tour and contacted Ruppert. He informed him that Ruth would be considered a detriment to the game, suspended for the season and considered for a lifetime ban by his office. "Colonel, if Ruth goes through with his plans, he will become the sorriest person on the planet when the consequences are doled out. The game needs Landis, the game does not need someone like Ruth," Landis ranted. Suspension was avoided only because Ruppert paid promoters to cancel the trip. None of the players, including Ruth, ever caught wind of what Ruppert had done. Landis continued to threaten Ruppert with a suspension for the Yankee star, which would be the ultimate slap in the face to Ruppert and the tens of thousands of New Yorkers ready to cheer the big man at the inaugural game. Six weeks earlier, Ruppert and Huston met with Landis at the Martinique Hotel in Manhattan. Landis, as expected, announced that although the barnstorming had been cancelled, Ruth was to be suspended for the first six weeks of the 1923 season. Ruppert realized that this was as much due to his stance as a loyalist to Johnson as it was for the actions of Ruth. Ruppert successfully trumped several efforts by Landis to block Ruppert's stockpiling of talent on the Yankee roster. The meeting, which included Harry Frazee, another loyalist, was contentious from the outset. Ruppert, in a very direct manner, opened the meeting.

"Judge, here is the situation. Harry has informed Huston and me he cannot make the required payment on the mortgage for Fenway. Come April 1, we will have served notice to the Red Sox of immediate eviction. I have a buyer for the property and postponing the action would jeopardize the transaction. Unless Harry can find an alternative location, the Red Sox will have no place to call home. Now that would be a real curse to the franchise, I would think."

"Damn you all! This is not at all about Fenway. This is about Ruth and your precious new park."

"Why, Judge, is there a solution to this mess that you are suggesting to us?"

"Harry, you're helping these two thieves who are stripping your franchise blind," said

Landis, making reference to the Yankee recent acquisition of Herb Pennock from the Red Sox.

"No, Judge, they've been a big part of helping me through my financial difficulty."

"What is it you want then, Colonel?"

"I'll make it easy for you. Opening day at Yankee Stadium will be spectacular with all my boys there playing."

The judge stormed from the hotel without a handshake, backed into a corner without options. Ruppert knew he won this battle, but he just hoped this war would end and the Yankees would not be on the losing end.

"He's full of confidence; I'll give you that, judge. Ruth is ready to put on a big show for the grand opening of the stadium," said Ruppert.

"Confidence! No, just arrogance, hidden behind that guarded juvenile charisma. Look at his comment in the Times article. Essentially he stated that ban or no ban, he will continue to barnstorm and bring recognition of the baseball talent possessed by the Negros," a visibly agitated Landis added, "He's making a bad mistake in thumbing his nose at my authority."

Ruth disclosed a deep desire to that same reporter. "I would give my life to win the first game at the Stadium and knock one out of the park in doing so." The child within Ruth fantasized about hitting the winning home run, just as many youngsters began doing the same thing with their hometown heroes. He went on, "If I did that, many young boys would feel good. When I travel across the country, within the negro communities, their boys have the same admiration for stars like Biz Mackey and Oscar Charleston. Well, it was un-American for Commissioner Landis to keep them out of professional baseball."

Landis added in a callous tone, "Ruth believes he's above the rules of the game as I set them. I would not tolerate his behavior if I were you. Colonel, if I believe for one second he becomes more of a detriment to the game, I will see to it he's gone for good. He'll join Joe Jackson and the others back in the sandlots. His association with baseball will end more swiftly than his rise to fame."

"Kennesaw, we are watching Ruth closely. With Pennock joining the club, we have another lefty workhorse, so Huggins can keep the carrot dangled in front of Ruth."

Ruth, carrying a glass case trimmed in fine mahogany, walked with several other Yankees toward the box.

"Judge, it is my pleasure to present to you a memento of today's dedication," said Ruth.

He handed the case to Landis. Enclosed was an oversized bat with the inscription, *April 18, 1923 — Yankee Stadium Dedication, A Home Built for Champions*

Wally Schang, a few moments later, deftly caught, on a short hop, the inaugural pitch, delivered courtesy of Governor Smith. He ran to the governor and shook his hand.

In the background, home plate umpire Tommy Connolly let loose with a shout familiar to many, "Let's play ball!" Bob Shawkey took the hill and the game was underway.

The Yankees broke through a scoreless tie in the last of the third when Dugan delivered on a single to center that scored Shawkey. The Yankees had opened the frame with consecutive singles to left by Shawkey and Witt. Ruth now came to bat. In the first inning, facing Ruth, Howard Emhke nibbled on the corners of the strike zone. Generally impatient, Ruth took the walk. With two men on in the third, Emhke was forced to pitch to Ruth. Babe, in his second at bat, came to the plate ready. Hoping to catch Ruth off his stride, Emhke floated a slow curve towards the inner half of the plate. Ruth, hands back, waited until the perfect moment, and the savagery of his swing drove the ball deep into the right center field bleachers for the first homer hit at the new park.

Completing his circle of the bases, Ruth headed towards the dugout, where just before he entered, he tipped his cap in the direction of Landis, "That one's for you, commissioner."

Day two into long season dealt the Yankees a setback which Ruth capitalized upon. Herb Pennock had been a teammate of Ruth ever since they both emerged as left-handed starters from the minor leagues to become members of the Boston Red Sox. Pennock did not have nearly the success of Ruth, so he viewed this as protection against Ruth getting another tired arm in September. He was disappointed when he saw Pennock penciled in as the game two starting pitcher. During the pre-game warm-up, Ruth asked Huggins when he would be in line for a start.

"Ruth, you keep yourself clean and worry about your own business. I will handle the team. "

"Huggins, you know little about me and less about baseball."

"Mind your mouth or you'll be sitting."

"If you're still worried about my arm…"

"No, ya big oaf, I'm worried about your belly and your legs!"

"I knocked one out yesterday. Is that not enough for you?"

"No, winning the whole thing is. You know, the series, for starters. And me not havin' to worry about where you are all night is another."

In the top of the second inning, Joe Harris, the Red Sox outfielder, had lifted a routine fly to right field that Ruth misplayed into a two-base error. Huggins came to the top step, showering obscenities at Ruth. Ruth pointed at the sky, gave the indication that he could not see the ball and casually shrugged his shoulders, further infuriating Huggins. Huggins looked to Ruppert in his now-usual box and waved his hand in disgust as he descended the dugout steps. Ruppert panned the overcast sky from the left to right field pole. Realizing there was little possibility the ball could be lost in the sun, he chuckled, "What I am going to do with this kid?"

Pennock settled into his stretch, peering over his left shoulder in an effort to keep Harris close to the bag.

"Hey, Pennock, instead of dancing around with me, you should be worried about the oaf in right."

Pennock stepped off the mound, trying to maintain his composure. He wiped the sweat from his brow. He looked at at Wally Schang, the catcher, and shook off each sign calling for a heater. Burn was a notorious fastball hitter; Schang probably thought they could catch him napping with a fastball on the first pitch. Pennock once again settled into his stretch, but no sooner had he delivered the ball than the wicked line drive came back against his right shin before he had a chance to react. The second crack heard by the standing-room-only crowd was louder than the first, which had been the ball striking the bat. Pennock was hurt, badly.

Schang was the first to get to him, "You OK?"

"I don't think so, Wally, I think my leg is broke."

Ruth started throwing on the sidelines well before Pennock was carted from the field on a stretcher.

Huggins instructed the umpire on the changes — Elmer Smith to right field, Ruth pitching.

Before heading into the dugout, Huggins approached the Babe. "Ruth, you son of a bitch, you're about as a lucky a man as there is. Someone up there is watching out for you. You had better keep your nose clean and win some ball games."

The Yankees never looked back; finishing 1923 with the same command they started. Their closest rivals finished 16 ½ games behind. Over one million fans enjoyed baseball in the Bronx. Once again, only McGraw's Giants stood between Ruppert and a Yankees championship, but this time they met on a level playing field.

Ruppert's prognostication about the big ball park in the Bronx playing to the Ruth's strengths was as expected. He batted nearly .400, led the league in several offensive categories, including home runs with 41, 131 runs driven in, a remarkable 170 walks and 151 runs scored. Ruth played in all 152 games.

The baseball world, mesmerized by Ruth's staggering offensive production, managed to overlook his efforts on the mound. His easy delivery aided by the deep valley of left and center field afforded him the luxury when pitching at home to let hitters put the ball in play. Ruth delivered twenty-six wins, dropping just three road decisions.

The move by the Yankees across the Harlem River had done nothing to quell the acrimony between players and owners.

Fuming from his office at the brewery, Ruppert instructed his assistant, "Marjorie, please get the operator to connect to Landis in Chicago. See if they can connect immediately."

Late in the season, the Yankees called up a little-known player to fill in for an injury to their solid first baseman, Wally Pipp. Late-season additions required the approval of the league commissioner for player eligibility on the series roster as well as of the opposing team's owner. Requests were routinely granted. Landis had approved the request but Colonel Ruppert ran into a problem.

"Judge, I've spoken to Stoneham. He told me that he's okay with the change, but McGraw is dead set against it." Imploring Landis to intervene, Ruppert continues. "This rookie is a marginal fielder who is slow afoot."

"Colonel, let me stop you there. McGraw is upset that you blocked his two rookies from being added."

"Certainly not the same instance. His two guys played five games between them and he needs fresh legs and wants more pop in the lineup."

"Colonel, your guy has hit over four hundred since joining the Yanks. He's hotter than a hornet that's been stepped on. Sorry, Rup, there is nothing I can do. Gehrig is not eligible."

Fate had brought the intra-city rivals to battle again. The teams were ready to square off, and this time the Yankees would serve as hosts. Due the proximity of the ball parks, Landis had made another decision which would fuel the flames of hostility.

"Colonel, one more thing, I have decided that the games will alternate between locations."

"I know."

"No, Colonel, it's a little bit different. Each game will alternate location. So games one, three, five and seven will be in your place."

Although Ruppert was perplexed as to the rationale and saw no detriment, the departure from the traditional format angered him.

The teams battled evenly through the first four games. The Giants had won two games by one run each, their weak-hitting outfielder, Charles Dillon 'Casey' Stengel providing the game-winning four-bagger in each of the victories.

After game three, Charles Stoneham was in a foul mood. His team had come home to the Polo Grounds with a one-game advantage and one of his steadiest pitchers of the year was on the hill. The Yankees hammered Jack Scott from the game before he managed three outs in the second inning, coasting to an 8-4 victory.

The pivotal game five was scheduled for Yankee Stadium on Sunday, October 14, 1923.

Relaxing in the lobby of the Plaza Hotel, Stoneham and McGraw were chatting about the pitchers for game five. Stoneham decided to stay in midtown to be as far away from the Bronx as he could, at least for the night. McGraw decided on his fifth different pitcher in the series, Jack Bentley.

A concierge approached Stoneham, toting the familiar Western Union envelope in his grip.

"Mr. Stoneham, sorry to interrupt, this is marked urgent."

After reading the correspondence, Stoneham steamed as his neck tightened, the veins bulging blue and cheeks reddened.

"What's wrong?"

Stoneham placed the telegram on the table and waved for McGraw to pick it up.

"Okay, I get the part about the visitor's lockers being flooded. That's a dirty trick. But what does he mean 'are you up on your French novelists?' "

"He is referring to Joseph Eugene Sue and a line from the Memoirs of Matilda. '*La vengeance se mange très-bien froide*'; 'revenge is very good eaten cold.'"

"Charlie, let's turn this around on that SOB. I have an idea. I've got to go talk to the fellows. We'll meet at the Polo Grounds."

John McGraw, a man of fifty, never found the time to learn to drive. In New York, he easily got around using taxis, his chauffer, or the subway. On mild days, by far his favorite was to walk. At 11:15 AM on October 14, he emerged from the Polo Ground door on the 8th Avenue and 155th street side. He adjusted his cap, stared into the morning sun and waited as his charges assembled behind him.

"Let's go kick the ass of those brazen Yankees!"

Thirty-four players, coaches and others in and out of uniform cheered.

"We're with you, Mr. McGraw!"

Behind them were several horse-drawn carriages with musicians and singers. One flatbed carriage held a jazz band that was blasting out Ellington's *Take the A Train*.

Strutting like a conquering general, McGraw led the contingent west toward Sugar Hill. Descending to the Harlem Speedway, an overcrowded stretch of highway designed for horse-drawn carriages, McGraw thrust his arm high into the air, signaling all to stop. Staring across the Harlem River, McGraw readied his troops to cross the 155th bridge into the Bronx. Ahead lay the imposing concrete arena.

"There, look there," McGraw ordered, "that is where we'll meet our enemy. The Yankees want a fight, so let's give 'em one!"

The crowd was in complete hysteria! The throng began the march across the steel span that traversed the very narrow section of river. On cue, McGraw and entourage crossed the eighth-mile bridge as the band blared out a sassy rendition of *When the Saints Come Marching In*.

McGraw and company inched through the thousands of boisterous fans lined up to get tickets. Twelve minutes later, they arrived at the doorstep of Yankee Stadium, raring to go. McGraw proclaimed that the Giants would prevail and avenge this atrocity.

The game began at 1:00 PM, and one hundred and fifteen minutes after the first pitch, the music for the Giants was over, the light of the day was fading to a gloomy shade of gray, and the Giants faced a very long walk back; silenced in the 8-1 pummeling. Now the Giants were on the brink of elimination.

The next day the Yankees completed the capture of their first World Series title by winning the sixth game.

Ruth had catapulted the Yankees to their first championship by his remarkable season. In spite of the not-so-silent protestations of Landis, he was unanimously selected as the league MVP for 1923.

At the award ceremony, Ruth extracted a small measure of personal satisfaction. In 1922, Landis had issued a proclamation that if the American League baseball writers ever chose Ruth for the MVP award, he, Landis, would personally vacate the selection. With all the exuberance of an adolescent eating his first ice cream cone, Ruth proudly caressed the plaque. Flashing his customary ear-to-ear grin, he proudly thrust both arms into the air in a triumphant display. The audience of writers and teammates, sensing his jubilance, cheered wildly. Addressing the crowd, Ruth bellowed in his deep voice, with a now-increasing amount of rasp which was ever so familiar.

"Here, this is for all of you, you chickenshits. I earned this last year and you knew it. Not one of you was man enough to trump that old bastard and self-professed king. He wants to call all of the shots in our sport, and you're all pawns for this tyrant of baseball. Landis, you can take this and stick it…"

Stunned by the words all eyes watched as Ruth forcibly hurled the plaque to the ground, splintering it into several pieces. Most at the celebration did not believe Ruth capable of holding a grudge.

"Now you have plenty to write about. Add this note to the dear commissioner: you are invited to the Ruth all-star baseball show. We will be playing twenty games against the best of the Eastern Colored League. The first game takes place in

Chicago three days from now. That's right in your back yard, Judge Landis!"

Ruth had elevated the stakes, making the hidden feud between the bigger-than-life player and the headstrong commissioner front and center in the news.

Landis, already seething when he received the news of the 1923 vote by the eight writers, realized the magnitude of 'the Babe' and how his popularity was growing like an avalanche. Now that overgrown, immature bastard was flaunting the award and his disdain for rules which Landis, as commissioner, had set down. When not in control of a situation, Landis tended to lash out in a capricious manner.

He decided to call on his old friend, Charles Comiskey.

"What happened? Are my words falling on deaf ears to the sportswriters? I'll bar them from the clubhouse."

"Calm down, Judge. There was no way the reporters could avoid voting for Ruth after what he did this year. Fans across the country would have been up in arms, claiming foul. They were already upset after last year."

"This Ruth is getting too big for his britches. He's becoming real trouble. If he had his way, we'd be bringing the coloreds into the game. We don't need a makeshift team of professional players playing across this country or in Cuba against coloreds. He cannot be bigger than the game. I will suspend him for the season. Maybe I will ban him for life."

"Calm down, Judge. You'll have a full-scale rebellion if you do that."

"I've got to get him into line."

"I have an idea, Judge, now hear me out. This will cure at least one of your problems with Ruth."

Two weeks later, Landis, in a letter to the owners, using the broad powers granted him, issued another proclamation in an effort to maintain his iron grip on the game.

"In the best interests of baseball and in an effort to maintain maximum fan interest, and to ensure that players from every team have a fair chance of winning baseball's most prestigious awards, I have decided to limit eligibility. The American and National League most valuable player awards can only be given to a player once in their career."

This was a very unpopular decision among owners, writers and fans. The commissioner's office was flooded with thousands of letter expressing protestation every month. The Landis – Ruth feud was now front and center, out in the open for all to see.

Under intense pressure from owners, writers and fans, Landis finally rescinded this capricious ruling in 1929, but unfortunately Ruth, with his best days in the past by then, would never again receive such recognition.

Chapter 31

The end of the 1926 season culminated a rocky six-year stretch marking the beginning of Landis' regime. The period after his appointment as commissioner, with unquestioned absolute power, was not smooth. Ban Johnson fought the idea and cautioned the owners not to consolidate so much power over the game, finally losing his battle in the fall of 1920. On November 8th, Colonel Ruppert convinced Johnson to concede rather than see the American League crumble and get swallowed into a large National League. The owners supporting full consolidation of power came up two votes short of giving Landis total control over the game. As an olive branch to those owners who supported Johnson, each league would keep its own president, with limited operational duties. Landis was charged with the responsibility for the overall affairs of baseball. His decisions were deemed final and not subject to any appeal. Ruppert believed and convinced other American League owners that Landis was there to help to clean up the game's image. Once the news about the 1919 World Series died down, hopefully within a few short years, the need for Landis and his active role would lessen.

Landis, unaware of Ruppert's gambit, did not share this view. Landis came out with guns blazing and a quick trigger finger for suspension or banishment of players. His avowed stance against gambling was so firm that in some cases he banned players based simply on an accusation of their association with gamblers.

Landis believed players, particularly the stars, with their growing popularity, would evolve into role models. He demanded two things from every professional baseball player: their unquestioned dedication to the league and their ability to remain above any suspicion from any outside influences.

The office of baseball commissioner had no authority over exhibition games. Landis believed that gambling elements were at play in many of the barnstorming tours. Throngs of regular red-blooded Americans flocked into small town whistle stops where cow pastures were turned into makeshift diamonds to watch professional players. Losing their hard earned money was one thing, but if they sensed games were not in the level, that was another. Ultimately, the fans' view of the players would become tainted by suspicion, hurting the game.

Landis, almost immediately upon assuming office, was at odds with the young president of the St. Louis Cardinals. Branch Rickey, the newly appointed executive, had helped the Cardinals build a strong development program for young players through their minor leagues, some of which included coloreds. The commissioner stepped in with an order that required minor league independence from American and National league teams.

Many of the coloreds were identified as possessing major league talent during Ruth's and Hornsby's barnstorming swings through the south.

Landis, the hypocritical tyrant, as Rickey viewed him, was shutting that avenue down. Rickey, along with the five American League owners, persisted in keeping heavy pressure on Landis. The owners were divided; a small majority supported the newly crowned baseball czar. Rickey had broken ranks with the other National League owners. He and the American League owners maintained 'informal' relationships with minor league teams.

Barnstorming, led by the American League stars of the game, remained rampant. Although less overt, Landis failed to eliminate wagering at the ball parks. Babe Ruth, the biggest star of the game, remained an incorrigible and immature pain in his rear. Despite threats too numerous to count, for the sake of his popularity, Landis and the owners of the Yankees always found a way not to suspend Ruth, especially with the Yankees earning their way into the World Series after a two-year absence.

Bowing to fan popularity, Landis was overtly softer on the likeable and more popular players. Except for the eight White Sox players, none of the banishments were household names or a drawing card with fans. Mumblings were afoot that the punishments of Landis were arbitrary and vindictive. Dickie Kerr, a member of the 1919 White Sox, had won both of his starts in the fabled series. Initially implicated, he was exonerated from any involvement in the fix. Landis believed otherwise. Kerr decided to participate with several of his former teammates in a barnstorming game held in Des Moines, Iowa against members of the Cincinnati Reds and the St Louis Cardinals. In a letter to Kerr, Landis had warned this would violate the prohibition of fraternizing with known gamblers, although no specifics were provided. Kerr ignored the warning. Kerr was the lone player singled out; he received a lifetime ban. Landis' ruling was final and all appeals were blocked. Newspapers soon reported that Landis was not evenhanded; rather, he was downright biased in dealing out punishment. Landis, with no owner daring to challenge his authority, ignored the complaints. Baseball would be run his way. At times, Landis did find mercy in his rulings, but only if doing so served his own best interests.

In October 1926, a broad betting scandal once again rocked baseball to the core. Ty Cobb of the Detroit Tigers and Tris Speaker of the Cleveland Indians announced their resignations, shocking fans. Each had chosen to retire rather than face a lifetime ban, oddly at the direction of Johnson. Although Landis knew of their indiscretions a year earlier, he had failed to deliver any ruling. Landis generally liked both players, especially the Georgia-born Cobb.

Reviewing the accusations, Johnson realized that Landis had made an attempt to keep the information about Cobb and Speaker quiet. Johnson was not going to let this go away. He did not seek the approval of Landis. If Landis fought against his ruling, the owners would see first-hand the extent of his bias.

Seething, Landis invited Cobb and Speaker to his office in Chicago, feeling that he needed to provide the duo with a small bit of legal guidance.

In November, Speaker and Cobb filed a lawsuit naming the American League and Ban Johnson as plaintiffs.

Landis called on an old bench friend for a favor. Despite a crowded court calendar and the upcoming holiday recess, somehow time was made for a preliminary hearing on Friday, December 17th, 10:00AM at the United States District Court for Northern Illinois.

The scandal first came to the fore late in the 1925 season. Dutch Leonard was out for revenge against Cobb. Explaining to Smokey Joe Wood that knowing, and not disclosing to the Commissioner, information about players fixing a game could get him suspended, Leonard got him to join in. Ty Cobb and Tris Speaker were then accused of consistently betting on and fixing the outcomes of baseball games that had occurred for a half dozen years, including several games of the forever-marred 1919 World Series. Leonard had kept detailed notes in a handwritten diary. He meticulously logged dates, games, scores, names of gamblers and the sums of money which changed hands. Wood corroborated Leonard's accusations. Separately, Wood kept a ledger of his own in a grade school notebook that included the dates and locations of meetings which were held between Cobb, Speaker and certain of the St Louis gamblers linked to the 1919 Series.

Leonard told Landis he possessed two letters documenting what had taken place. One was written to him by Wood, the other by the great Cobb himself. Landis asked to see the letters. Leonard held them at his California house for safekeeping, but he could retrieve them if needed.

Landis told him not to bother getting the letters. He dismissed the allegations as he challenged the veracity of the story.

"Gambling is in baseball's past. I've made a point of seeing to that. Nobody is going to believe any of what you've said, especially if it was seven years ago," Landis scolded.

Then he added, "Cobb is one of the biggest stars; he's played in the league for nearly a quarter century. He has more hits than anyone and one of the highest lifetime averages. Unless you have some real proof, don't bother me. From what I understand, this is a personal vendetta for you. Just remain retired, stay quiet, go back to California and grow your grapes."

Leonard went looking for another option, so he decided to pay a visit to Ban Johnson.

A few minutes into the conversation with Leonard, Johnson realized what was at stake: a showdown with Landis and control of baseball. His fate as American League chief would hang in the balance, suddenly dependent on the flawed character of one Hubert Benjamin "Dutch" Leonard.

In his capacity, Johnson conducted an investigation into the allegations. He held a closed door meeting to review all the evidence. At its conclusion he was satisfied that the facts as Leonard presented were accurate. He decided to confronted Cobb and Speaker. Johnson was firm as he offered them an ultimatum: retire or face suspension. Without any resistance both agreed to leave the game.

On December 16th Johnson checked into the Palmer House Hotel. Before heading to his room, he made a stop at the concierge. 6:00PM dinner at the Walnut Room provided sufficient time for a quick review and good night's rest. Two hours after cancelled dinner plans, Johnson became increasingly uneasy. He had already checked several times with the front desk to confirm the arrival of Leonard and Wood. By 11:00 PM, neither had checked in. They were most likely delayed in their travels, not unusual for Chicago this time of year. The pair certainly would arrive shortly, Johnson thought. Tomorrow was a big day; everyone needed to be at their sharpest. With two witnesses and more documentation than the 1919 scandal which had buried eight players, he was certain this nuisance lawsuit would be dismissed, with it the suspensions upheld. Then he'd have Landis in a corner.

Convincing himself not to worry, Johnson finally went in and out of a restless series of naps. The loyalist owners were starting to realize that Landis had a role in the player lawsuit. Neither Cobb nor Speaker was smart enough to think of this response. A victory in court would knock Landis down a peg or two further, serve to reduce the reach of his authority, and, given his pride, hopefully get him to resign.

"Dutch" Leonard was born on April 16, 1892, in Birmingham, Ohio, the youngest of six surviving children of David and Ella Hershey Leonard. While attending St. Mary's College, the nickname 'Dutch' was hung on him by teammates, based on his appearance, not his bloodline. Blessed with a vibrant left arm but void of intestinal fortitude, the promise of a great career was curtailed by his inherent distrust of others and them in him. The entire span of his career would be clouded in controversy.

Signed by the Philadelphia Athletics in 1911, Leonard did not have a great start, reporting late to training camp. Upon arriving, he found the competition fierce for a spot on the club. Suddenly sporting a lame arm, Leonard left the club. The competitive Connie Mack had no use for a player without heart, so Leonard was cut. He signed with Boston the following year. Rusty from a year out of baseball, he was shelled in each of the preseason outings. Boston sold his contract to Worcester. Rather than report to a minor league team, he abandoned the team. A brief insubordination suspension followed. Leonard had a strong season with Denver, of the Western League. Between 1912 and 1919, his career alternated between short stints of brilliance that included two no-hitters and longer bouts of suspensions and injury.

Leonard avoided the 1918 draft order by bolting from the majors and joining the Fore River (MA) Shipyard team, enhancing his reputation for lacking a spine. Upon returning to the major league, many of the veterans, especially those who lost friends and family in the war, were not shy in labeling him a draft dodger.

In 1919, Leonard was traded to the New York Yankees along with Ernie Shore and Duffy Lewis. His tenure with the Yankees did not survive the honeymoon. Leonard demanded that his salary for the entire 1919 season be deposited before the season was to begin. Ruppert responded pointedly, "No man who does not trust me at my word will play for the Yankees." During Leonard's short walk to his hotel, his trade to the Tigers was completed. Landis suspended him in 1922 for violating the reserve clause provision of his contract when he signed a contract with a rival baseball league. He was reinstated two years later.

Cobb distrusted Leonard from their first meeting, and during his years with Detroit, the acrimony intensified.

The veteran told him, "Boy, I do not like you or what you've done. But as Tigers we look out for each other. I'll have your back so long as you have your teammates'."

Leonard's disdain for Cobb began years earlier. Leonard repeatedly dusted Cobb with pitches up near his chin. Cobb refused to give ground and back off the plate. Cobb, a magician with the bat, cleverly pulled a swinging bunt up slightly to the right of first. In order to make the out, Leonard needed cover the bag and take the throw from the first baseman. Cobb scurried up to first, not hustling. He could have easily beat Leonard to the bag for a hit. Cobb timed his run to arrive at the precise moment as the unsuspecting pitcher.

Leonard casually reached with his right hand to grab the toss and record an easy out. Cobb leapt toward the base, faking an attempt to beat the throw. For most watching, it simply looked like any other hustle play. Cobb planted the toes of his left foot directly on Leonard's shin. Fists flew, benches emptied, but Cobb got his point across. Leonard was left with a scar as a permanent reminder. Leonard, now pitching for his nemesis, refused to follow retaliation orders from Cobb, who was now serving as the field manager. In 1925, the situation was brought to a head when three Tiger players had been hit intentionally. A clubhouse confrontation escalated, and the brawling players were separated only after Cobb split Leonard's left eyebrow.

"Now you'll have two scars, you yellowbelly," Cobb said, pouring more fuel on the fire.

The manager marched directly to the owner's office, kicking the door open, "Damn it, Mr. Navin. Leonard has got to go. He is a coward and a disgrace to the club. Hell, he's a disgrace to the game."

"Settle down, Ty," Frank Navin responded.

Cobb and Navin conversed for nearly an hour. Navin supported Cobb and suspended Leonard for sixty days, citing conduct detrimental to the team and insubordination. Leonard did not argue.

Returning to the club in late June, Cobb immediately inserted Leonard in the pitching rotation and pitched him every three days. Although Leonard struggled, Cobb offered no relief help for

Leonard. Forced to finish each game he started; surprisingly he did so as a winner. On July 13, under a cloudless sky and with temperatures hovering in the middle90's, he completed nine innings, beating the Athletics' 6-5.

The next morning, Leonard casually strolled into the club house at Navin Field, anticipating a much-needed day of rest. The weather forecast called for an even hotter day. Leonard planted himself on the small grey couch on the far side of the locker area, away from where the rest of players dressed. Curling up and using his uniform shirt as a makeshift pillow, he somehow found just enough comfort and dozed off.

Johnny Bassler, the Tiger catcher, gently tapped the napping Leonard on the shoulder and spoke when he saw the pitchers eyes open, "Jesus, Mary and Joseph! Cobb's been looking for you. Let's go, Dutch. It's time to get you loose. You're starting today."

"What? Quit breaking my chops," Leonard responded, thinking it was a bad joke.

"No joke, Cobb wants you ready."

"What are you talking about? I can't go again. Maybe tomorrow, look my arm is dead tired."

"Look, this isn't my choice. He'll take a piece out of my hide if you don't get ready. Hell, he's threatened to cut me," pleaded the catcher, now begging Leonard to begin his warm-up routine.

"Dammit, Johnny, I'll get loose, but my arm is so tired I can't throw that many."

The Philadelphia Athletics lineup featured the first six players hitting over .300, including the mighty Al Simmons. Cobb, to the surprise of everyone, penciled Leonard in to start on only one day of rest.

Leonard was no match for the Athletics. Jimmy Dyke led the game with a hard-hit single. Frank O'Rourke limited the scoring by nabbing three hard balls to third. As they walked in from the field he told Leonard, "If they keep hitting the ball at me like that, I am going to end up with a broke hand."

"Don't worry, Frank. Once they figure I ain't got nothing, they'll be pounding the ball into the outfield, so you'll be safe."

"I sure hope so for your sake, Dutch."

Using every piece of artistry in his craft, Leonard had escaped trouble in the first few innings. By the middle part of the game, the Athletics' timing caught up as they drilled the ball at will, piling up 20 hits in the process. Cobb was cruel, but this was, perhaps, the crowning moment in his career. Leonard was mercilessly punished, yielding twenty hits. He completed the game, facing forty-six batters. The Athletics won the game 12-4 but demonstrated compassion in their last two at-bats. After the completion of the visitor's half of the seventh inning, Connie Mack, the opposing manager, called for a meeting with the umpires and Cobb. He pleaded Cobb to take Leonard out of the game, "You're killing that boy." Cobb scoffed at the suggestion and told Mack to just mind his own business. Mack turned for help from the umpire in chief. Bill McGowan agreed with Mack. Cobb became enraged at the challenge to his authority. "Connie, you manage your team. I will manage mine. So long as he is a Tiger, I will handle him as I see fit," Cobb screamed and kicked dirt in the direction of Mack.

McGowan sensed that he needed to end this discussion quickly. He stepped between the pair and motioned Cobb to return to the Tiger dugout. As Cobb walked away, he turned and addressed Mack, "Connie, you're a class act. Always have been. Unfortunately I cannot say the same about others, but my hands are tied."

"Thanks. I'll handle the situation." The final six Athletics went down in order on weak grounders, inflicting no further damage.

At the end of the July, Cobb placed Leonard on waivers. Before doing so, he made calls to every team to assure that no other team claimed him. These included a call to Connie Mack, whose response to Cobb was simple, "You're a bastard." Cobb joyfully let Leonard know that he personally put an end to his career.

Leonard, having burned too many bridges along the way in his career, was in disbelief that every major league manager passed on him. After Leonard had cleared waivers, Cobb, with the Tigers still holding his rights, traded him to Vernon, a third-rate team in the Pacific Coast League, in northern California. Leonard refused to report; his professional baseball career had been brought to an ignominious end.

December 17th was a rare day, only a few small clouds dotted the Chicago sky. The morning rays warmed the rather large 11th-story corner office of Judge George Carpenter. The forecast was holding true, full sunshine and temperatures in the low teens. Landis paced in short quick steps across the floor. Located in the courthouse for the District Court of Northern Illinois, the location afforded Landis a spectacular view of Lake Michigan and the Chicago skyline. Occupying the center area of the oak floor was a hand-woven Dilmaghani rug, complete with a resplendent floral pattern accented by deep harmonious blood-red markings. Marching from the east-facing windows to the large bookcase overcrowded with reference books, Landis showed his consternation. He was outwardly nervous.

Pausing, Landis admired the view. He ran his long, bony fingers through his curly black hair, feverishly rubbing his scalp with his fingertips before turning to resume his march back to the other side.

"Kenesaw, sit and relax. You've been parading back and forth for over two hours. You're going to wear a path in the carpet," Carpenter exclaimed.

The ridges in Landis' face had deepened in the scant years since he assumed ultimate control over major league baseball. The more he tried to impose the power of his office onto players and owners, the deeper the resistance against him. His single-minded effort to rid baseball of the gamblers and influences of unsavory underworld characters, after six years, was on the verge of coming apart at the seams. His battle with the game's larger-than-life star helped turn the tide of fan support against him.

"Tell you what, George, this is one beautiful city. I don't like this one at all. Ban just continues to try and usurp my authority. I just cannot believe he took it upon himself to issue those suspensions without checking with me."

"Come on, Landis, he's following your lead. You can't play favorites when it comes to meting out justice. Have you forgotten the blindfolded Lady Justice?"

Landis and Judge Carpenter had waited patiently. The two key witnesses in support of the Johnson ruling, Dutch Leonard and Smokey Joe Wood, were no-shows.

"Kenesaw, looks like you may have gotten lucky. Without witnesses to support Johnson, the motion to vacate the suspension will stand. I'll set the hearing on the calendar for January 5th to issue the final ruling in open court, rather than behind closed doors."

"George, there are times one makes his own luck." *Leonard darn well better enjoy those new acres, damn grape farmer, Landis thought.*

After a hearty chuckle by both men, Carpenter's next comment was sobering to Landis. "Your bigger problem is still with the fans."

"What do you mean?"

"Come on, the reinstatement of two players with a long history of betting, coming off the heels of another unlikely series outcome? The biggest star of the game financially distressed, now under heavy scrutiny. Many will look at today and say the stars can still throw a game without repercussion."

"Ruth never does not play to win."

"You and I both know that, but the fans see guys like Cobb saying what they think. This year had better be one for the ages, or you'll lose the fans, Landis."

Landis needed to pull a rabbit out of a hat. Restlessness in the fans across the country was affecting attendance, and the fans were distrustful that games were on the level.

The start of the 1927 season was a few short months away.

Chapter 32

At the start of the 1926 World Series, the Cardinals were thought to have no chance of defeating the mighty Yankees; the betting odds reflected their stature as the prohibitive underdogs. It took seven games, but the Cardinals beat the mighty Yanks. The final out of 1926 championship contest came on a base-running blunder by none other than Ruth. A two-out free pass put Ruth on as the tying run in the bottom of the ninth. Bob Meusel came to bat with Grover Cleveland Alexander, the Cardinal ace, on the hill. Alexander had pitched a complete game the day before, but Rogers Hornsby, the Cardinal's manager, decided he had one out left in him. The only bright spots for the Yankees the previous day against Alexander were a double and triple off the bat of Meusel.

"Hey, Grove," Ruth baited the Cardinal hurler, "you can't have much left in the tank after what you and I drank last night. Plus you're a bit of a lightweight." Ruth had decided to show Alexander some of the late-night watering holes of midtown New York City. Alexander agreed, believing he would not pitch again in the series. "If you don't bear down, Meusel will pop one outta the park."

Alexander stared Ruth down; the left edge of his lips pulled up in a bit of a smirk, but offered no retort. Ruth inched his way slowly, casually, off first, edging into a sizeable lead. Ruth was a pretty good base runner but swiped a base very infrequently. On the delivery, Ruth took off to the surprise of everyone at the stadium. A shocked Huggins jumped to the top step, yelling, 'Oh no!"

The pitch was a foot off the plate to the third-base side. Bob O'Farrell, smoothly extending his mitt, caught the pitch, set his feet, and delivered the ball to the front edge of second base. Hornsby, covering the bag, allowed the strong throw to settle into his grounded mitt. Squeezing the leather, he held it there watching the less than graceful Ruth slide in for the easy tag out. The ball beat Ruth to the bag by over ten feet. The drama of the series abruptly over, a deep and eerie hush drew over Yankee Stadium.

"Dammit," Huggins lamented softly, kicking the dirt with his left foot.

Landis watching from his customary spot wondered, *what motivated Ruth to attempt such an ill-timed high-risk move? If he had been successful, baseball strategy would dictate the bat be taken out of a hot hitters hand with an intentional walk. Might Ruth have finally succumbed to the temptation of the gamblers?*

Ruth was his own worst enemy when it came to Landis and Ruppert. Prior to the start of the 1925 season, his weight ballooned to nearly 260 pounds. Numerous times during the Yankee Spring training, Huggins had to have players return Ruth to his hotel, often too inebriated to participate; one time Huggins even removed him from the batting practice, when a thrown ball narrowly missed hitting him in the head.

Worries about the status of Ruth's health escalated. Missing in action from an exhibition game, he was found unconscious on his hotel bathroom floor. When teammates tried to revive him, he went into convulsions. Diagnosed as a case of influenza, Ruth, against the advice of the physician, traveled with the team to Asheville, North Carolina. Ruth was determined to play in the final pre-season ending series against the Dodgers. He was the draw and felt a strong obligation not to let the fans in this small town down. Even with the flu, he delivered excitement to the fans with home runs and several innings of shutout ball in Chattanooga and Knoxville.

Each year, Yankee players complained about this trip across western North Carolina. The up and down through the hills and the poor condition of the tracks caused even those with the most resilient stomachs varying degrees of motion sickness when healthy. Babe, already suffering from the flu and overindulgence, was no match for the trek through the Smokies. On the train ride, Ruth began to complain to Paul Krichell, the team's lead scout, about not feeling well. "Hell, Babe, what do you expect, the way you pounded down hot dogs and soda on the train ride here? How many? A dozen? Two dozen? I lost count."

Ruth, on unsteady legs, needed help leaving the train. A large crowd greeted the team, cheering wildly as Ruth came into view. Steve O'Neill rushed over to Ruth, gingerly maneuvering through the welcoming throng.

After assuring O'Neill that he was fine, Ruth began, very tentatively, to walk into the hotel lobby. Nearing the front desk, the Babe collapsed in a heap. Krichell, keeping an eye on Ruth, reacted with a desperate stab, and managed to grab his coat collar. His quick thinking prevented the Babe's head from hitting the floor. The desk clerk froze, not sure what he had just witnessed. Huggins took charge and barked him back into the moment. 'Son, get your wits about you and call a doctor, immediately!"

Several Yankees assisted in carrying Ruth to his room. Doctor James Hartman, a local GP, addressed Huggins after a less-than-thorough examination.

"He'll be all right, he just needs rest. I don't think he was over the flu yet. But you should get him to New York. He'll need better treatment than we can offer here."

Concerned with the well-being of his star, Huggins reluctantly agreed with the doctor. The Yankees made plans to ship Ruth to New York along with Paul Krichell. Although the Yankees attempted to keep the status of Ruth quiet, news of his illness cluttered the airwaves. Fans far and wide sat patiently near their radios, waiting for updates of Ruth's reportedly grave malady. A premature obituary published in one of the New York newspapers raised the stakes.

While alone in his Battery Park hotel room, Ruth collapsed again and was found unconscious by Helen. Suffering from more convulsions, an ambulance whisked Ruth to a small private hospital in the Northwest Bronx in the hopes of avoiding any public circus. Admitted while unconscious, Ruth was placed directly into the intensive care unit. Nurses, hospital staff and Helen formed an around-the-clock watch, not leaving the stricken star alone in the room for the next five days. Cards, letters and flowers flooded Montefiore Hospital. Sympathy and popularity for the Babe abounded; NYPD needed to set up barriers along 210th street to keep the emergency entrance clear from the adoring fans, who were now gathering outside the hospital by the hundreds.

While the public showed its concern and worry, Stoneham and Landis were appalled. Charles Stoneham was burned, not only by the unexpected loss to the Walter Johnson-led Senators in the 1924 World Series, but also that, even though the Giants had just appeared in their fourth consecutive championship series, his franchise was losing the popularity battle.

"What the hell is the attraction to this guy?" Stoneham asked Landis, speaking loudly into his phone. Although the connection was scratchy, he needed to have this conversation with the commissioner.

"Charles, we agree that Ruth's veneer needs to be stained some." Landis was referring to the band of owners he considered loyalists. "He's brash and highly popular, but he's not an invincible god. What can you tell me about that sportswriter? How can he help us with this matter?"

W. O. McGeehan, one of the best known sportswriters in America, had the magical ability to translate sports activities into silver-worded descriptions. McGeehan proved his skills not only with the pen but also during live broadcasts.

Providing the play-by-play commentary for the large New York radio audience during the 1924 series, he mesmerized audiences with captivating phrases and descriptions. McGeehan, a staunch Giant supporter, possessed a bit of a mean spirit, particularly towards the rival Yankees. The Giants were the heart and soul of baseball in New York City, not these ragtag upstarts from the Bronx. He would use every ounce of energy he had to see to it that McGraw and company regained their supremacy in the bright lights of the city.

Ruth progressed back to health quickly and, within a week, was released. He would be back with his team in time for the first game of the season. Helen, now caring for the Babe back in their residence, made every effort to get life into a normal routine. The crowds of adoring fans stationed outside had abated. Yankee team officials were readying for opening day. Life finally quieted some. Babe was resting peacefully in bed. Knowing Babe liked to scan the newspaper headlines in the morning, Helen went to see if the morning Herald had been delivered.

"Oh, my!" Helen squawked a tad too loudly. As soon as she saw the sub-headline on the front page she froze for several minutes: 'The Yankees Big Bellyache.' page 12.

From behind came the familiar voice of her husband. "What is it, Helen?"

She held open the newspaper to page 12. The date was April 13th, 1925; the New York Herald printed an elegant editorial, courtesy of McGeehan:

The Bellyache Heard Around the World

...lacking any medical evidence of a serious medical affliction, the illness which has knocked the Babe out of action is simply indigestion, caused by reckless over-indulgence, excessive eating, and uncontrolled alcohol consumption, nothing more, nothing less. Without a care, even after all this caught up with Ruth and knocked him on his back a few weeks ago, Ruth has continued to binge. He gorges not just on hot dogs and soda pop, but on alcohol and cigars and, of course, taking a woman or two at a time. He has little regard for baseball or his team, as he is often found before games at the local hot dog stand. The mystery is how those in the Yankee organization are calling the cause of his ailment. Even those very close to him are echoing this diagnosis. The only mystery to this writer is what medical school could have granted those caring for this boor a degree. To this reporter, this is just a child in a man's body with little respect for the game we love. He is no hero, just an out-of-control bad boy. His skills will fade soon and his popularity along with it, as the intelligent New Yorkers will eventually become fed up with these juvenile antics. Parents will keep their kids from him, realizing that this man they call the Babe is no role model, just a disgraceful stain to our national pastime.

The words tore Ruth up at a gut level. Ruth, personality flaws aside, had given all he could to the game. He loved playing baseball; he loved bringing joy to every fan, especially the youngsters. Being called a disgraceful stain cut deeply, and he could not understand how someone could write so ill of him.

"Helen, help me back to the bedroom."

The Yankees' fortunes sunk in lockstep with the malaise of Ruth, finishing ahead of just one team for the basement, and they were absent from the series for the second consecutive year.

The anguish affected him so much that Huggins placed him in the lineup for just 98 games, Ruppert fining Ruth half of his salary.

Not having money when growing up, Ruth lacked both an understanding of the significance of having money and the self-discipline to make smart decisions for himself. Poor judgment led to entanglement in several money-making schemes, including a Cuban cigar scam. Financial woes crept rapidly into Ruth's life as he lost another $40,000 in investments.

He became even more reckless, several times spending a night in jail when caught racing his Stutz Bearcat on Riverside Drive. His overnight stays in a precinct cell became so common that the desk sergeant kept a clean Yankee uniform in a closet.

Even in the games he played, Ruth found difficulty in maintaining focus and compiled his worst season as a Yankee. Batting, he managed a paltry .290 average and 25 home runs, while on the mound he won just thirteen times. For the only time in his career, he would lose more times than he won. Together with the 27 wins in 1924, he had amassed 254 wins at age thirty. Along with his 309 home runs, it was Ruth who everyone came to see.

Ruth could not let go of the McGeehan missive. Fans proved fickle as boos replaced the cheers. Ruth, although churning inside, outwardly remained gregarious. His cash had run out, and he and Helen were living off IOU's and handouts. After a crash put an end to the life of the Stutz, a local car dealer gave Ruth an Essex to drive at no cost. Finally, in late October, a concerned Ruppert came knocking with Christy Walsh in tow. The fortunes of the Yankees would mirror the success of Ruth, so for at least the time being, he had to get his star straightened out. Gehrig, somewhat Ruth's equal, did not pitch and his personality was cold by comparison. Nobody would ever come just to see Gehrig.

"Babe, you remember Christy. I'm sure you do. Let me get to the point. Christy will be your financial manager. No Christy, no contract."

"Hi, Babe," Christy said welcoming the Babe as he would an old friend, his right hand extended.

Ruppert continued, "He will not only manage your money, he will make you a budget and put you on an allowance, so to speak. Look, for your own good; you'll need to be on a tighter rein."

Babe rose, getting ready to speak, when Helen interceded, "George Herman Ruth, sit back down. This is how it is going to be."
Ruppert went on. "I'm giving you five months to shed the baggage and get ready to play. You have a chance to be the best there ever was, in every aspect of the game. You're 30, for Chrissakes. Start taking responsibility or you'll lose it all."

There was a series of knocks on the door.

"What is this, Grand Central station?" barked an annoyed Ruth.

Helen opened the door, immediately throwing her welcoming arms around the surprise guest. Their hug lasted a few too many seconds, freezing the others in the room.

"Thank you so much for coming," Helen said as she eased out of the prolonged squeeze.

The newcomer turned to Ruth. "Look at you, you fat SOB. If I didn't know who you were, I wouldn't have recognized you. "

"Well, you're still a skinny bastard. Good to see you, Asa," Ruth said, walking over to his old friend. Ruth's bear hug was not nearly as gentle as Helen's. He lifted the small man off the floor; Asa winced a bit as Ruth's powerful arms clamped around his lean frame and shook him in joy.

"It's good to see you."

"Put me down before you break my back. You're the size of my house in Hempstead! By the way the name is now Al, Al Jolson. There's still a great deal of bias against Jews. Now that we're all here, let's talk. We're all here to help."

Ruth and Jolson reminisced about their brief time together at St. Mary's. Although many years had passed, the pair spoke of their experiences as if they had just occurred, and as if this were the continuation of a conversation that had taken place the day before.

"Ruth, everyone at St. Mary's thought you'd amount to nothing. But you showed them, you were the second-best singer in the choir. Sorry, but I have to take top billing. The best shirt maker and you could kick the crap out of anyone in baseball. Brother Matthias made sure you didn't feel sorry for yourself. Now it's time for you to step up to the plate and become an adult. We all want you to succeed."

Ruth cutting him off before his next sentence could begin. "Except that bastard Landis, he would rather see me go away."

"Look Babe, let Ruppert deal with Landis. You have the support of the fans. If I could fill the house like you do, I'd be the Jewish Errol Flynn."

The emotional support from Jolson was just the medicine Ruth needed. Ruppert would handle the league and Walsh his financial matters. Jolson told Ruth when he was back in New York he would arrange dinner with a few of his Brooklyn friends with "connections" who could help with investment ideas.

Ruth just needed to take care of business on the field and everything would fall into place. After all the goodbyes, when the rooms were empty, Ruth grabbed Helen around the shoulders,

"Pack the bags. We're heading to Hot Springs tomorrow. I want to get a jump on spring training."

Six months later, as the Yankees and Dodgers once again made their way back through the mountains of the Tennessee and North Carolina, all realized Ruth was back in top form. He had emerged from his funk, shed thirty pounds, and was fit and ready for the season. In the finishing spring games, he duplicated an accomplishment from early in his career by holding the Dodgers without a run in three consecutive games.

As Ruth rebounded, so did the Yankees, until Hornsby's tag put a bitter end onto an otherwise sweet season. The season that fans and experts thought majestic, Ruth's win total matched his home run count of 47. Baseball had never seen the likes of Ruth.

Chapter 33

Ruth Fractures Wrist in Car Crash

Every east coast paper had the same headline and story on November 2, 1926.

"Babe Ruth took the day to visit orphaned boys at St. Joseph Catholic Home and the Minnesota Gopher football team. He spent the early evening at the Pantages Theatre, thrilling patrons with a vaudeville routine with old friends Al Jolson, Stan Laurel and Oliver Hardy. Renowned female mentalist Anna Eva Fay was coaxed out of retirement for a final show. Ruth agreed to act as her subject, and through somnolence she would touch the spirit world, giving Ruth a view into his future. We guess that three hours later was not far enough into the future, as Ruth, driving well above the speed limit, slammed into a tree navigating a turn. An unidentified female passenger in the vehicle did not survive the accident.

X-rays revealed a fracture to the wrist of his non-throwing hand. Ruth had a similar injury to this hand in 1925 when he met a brick wall at Griffith Stadium while chasing a fly ball.

This was an unlucky break for the Yankees and for Ruth."

"Huggins, what can we do to control Ruth?" said Ruppert rhetorically. Huggins had been hastily summoned to Ruppert's Bronx office upon learning the news.

"I don't know if anything can be done. A second serious injury on the same wrist, that's not good. Not sure the power will ever be the same."

"The fans were just getting over the 1925 nonsense before his stunt last month, now this. I am not certain he can regain their support. Landis is worried. I've invested a lot of money in this team. The Yankees need to win and keep on winning."

"Maybe we can build sympathy as a fallen star with just bad luck. Right now, he's the only player with 300 homers and 300 wins as a pitcher."

"That's good, but not good enough. First, we've got to quell any doubts about his finances. Pay him twenty thousand more than he is asking for. Next, get specialists in to get the wrist healed and strong, whatever it takes. Get him ready for the season."

In fact, Ruth was very lucky in some respects. The fracture was smaller and further above the joint then when the wrist was hurt in 1925. Then, with Joe Judge at the plate, Ruth was shaded a bit towards the right field foul line. Judge hit a ball high in the air, but with enough spin to curve away from Ruth towards the stands. Ruth took off full tilt, believing he could get the ball before it completed its flight. He had not broken stride when he met the Griffith Stadium wall full force, and crumpling to the ground unconscious. Ruth continued to play, hiding the extent of his injury for several weeks

After the wreck, Ruth was rushed to Columbia University Medical Center, built, ironically enough, on the abandoned location of

Hilltop Park. This was the leading center in orthopedic research and treatment. Within twelve weeks Ruth was healthy, and with intensive rehabilitation and strengthening, he was primed for the start of the season.

Unlike 1925, fans did not flock to the north Bronx in support of the fallen star. Helen's patience had expired. Fleeing New York, she returned to their Massachusetts farm.

Ruth was alone and isolated during his recovery. Friends and family were in limited supply. Once again Ruth would return to Hot Springs, this time several weeks earlier than his team. This time his escape to Arkansas was to avoid the daily criticism that challenged his integrity, dedication and devotion to the game. Ruth loved this children's game and the children who played it. He was deeply hurt; those he had played for had now abandoned him. He needed time alone.

Chapter 34
1960 Ohio

"Look Pepe, the Williams shift! I have never seen anyone play defense like this against anyone, not Ott, or Gehrig or any of the great hitters," Tonio yelled to Pepe.

"With first base open, and two out, papa, they will not pitch to him," his young son responded.

"Hey, kid, you got some pretty good baseball sense, but not enough experience. They'll pitch to Williams, all right. They think they can get him out. Also, neither team has anything to play for," said the old man, giving his uninvited opinion.

Pepe looked out over the field to see what was happening. The shortstop had moved from his usual position midway between second and third base to the first base side of second, about ten steps towards first. The second baseman was situated in short right field. Pepe exclaimed in octaves higher than his pre-pubescent voice, "Papa, you and the ol' guy are right."

"That's 'cause all he is is a dead pull hitter. Cy Williams was a big strong lefty hitter, back in the twenties. Managers started to play defense the same way. Boy, Cy could drive the ball to left field and when he did, it was usually an inside the parker. You know what that is, kid? Of course you do. Drive the ball every direction, that's hitting."

Barry Latman was still on the hill. Williams drilled his second pitch a towering fly, twenty-seven rows deep into the bleachers.

Seven thousand, seven hundred eighty-seven spectators erupted, shaking the stadium. They had witnessed history as only Foxx with his 534 homers stood between Williams and the all-time record.

Pepe, unable to contain his joy, was wildly jumping up and down on the wooden seat. He pushed the old man wearing a broad grin on the shoulder, gloating, "Or you hit it past them! What do you have to say now, pops?"

Tonio, scolding Pepe, said, "Mind your manners."

"Sorry for his disrespect, he is just excited," Tonio relayed, "Maybe Williams will play next year and go for the record."

The old man slyly smiled, demonstrating that he understood that children spoke honestly whatever came into their head. In many ways, it reminded him of the long-gone days of his youth. Pepe's comments did not derail him from getting back to his tale, but deep in the recesses of his mind he thought, *most of all it's the cheers I miss.*

Chapter 35

Charles Gardner Radbourn was born in 1854 in Rochester, New York. Searching for work, his father led the family to Bloomington Grove, Illinois, where they settled. His father, Charles senior, was a butcher. Beginning at age ten until just after his 23rd birthday, junior worked alongside his father for sixteen hours a day at the slaughterhouse. This was his formal education. He learned how to knock the life from steers, dozens a day, first wielding a twelve-pound sledge. Sometimes it took two or three whacks with the lighter truncheon. Within a few years, Charlie graduated to a twenty-five pound hammer and had grown plenty strong enough to deliver a mortal blow with one swift swing. The daily routine, which drove his muscles to the point of exhaustion, physically matured him quickly. The teen years saw his shoulders broaden and his arms grow thick. At eighteen, he was plenty strong enough to lug hundred and fifty pound slabs of beef and pork the three hundred feet from the ice house to the butcher shop.

In his community, no one had a fortunate life. Most were doomed to decades of relentless grueling labor, barely keeping a family with a roof over their heads, clothes on their backs and food on the table. All that changed for Charlie when his rollercoaster with lady lucky began its run.

In August, 1878, Charlie did what most folks in rural America did, spending the lazy, sweltering summer Sunday afternoon with a female companion, in his case a young lady named Carrie. She was Charlie's most recent conquest. Carrie had made Charlie's acquaintance just twenty-four hours earlier, and the couple had intended to relax away the previous night of hard drinking and harder lovemaking by watching the Cincinnati Reds in a barnstorming exhibition game. Their opponents were a team comprised of local men from Bloomington Grove. During the pregame warm-ups, the Reds' right fielder was chasing a soft fly arcing up the first base foul line. The ball, as is typical of a shot off the bat of a right-handed hitter when driving the ball in that direction, gently curved away from the Reds' player. He lengthened his stride, making every effort to attempt the catch. Suddenly he flipped head over heels, and chilling screams followed. Families readying food for their picnics stood up and turned to see the cause of the commotion. Pesky Smith had stepped into a gopher hole. For an instant his left foot was trapped while his body angled right. Smith rolled several feet, and then clutched at his injured leg in agony.

Team members sprinted to the side of their fallen mate. Their wily manager and third baseman, Cal McVey, had seen this before when playing in these cow pastures with annoying varmint holes, and he knew immediately that his player was finished, not only for the day, but almost certainly for a few months and most likely for much longer.

"It snapped, I heard it snap," Pesky affirmed, whispering through the pain, "How bad is it? It sure hurts like hell."

The eyes of all those standing around were magnetically drawn to his foot, which was lying in an abnormal, grotesque position. Everyone knew it was bad. Unfortunately for the Reds team, neither King Kelly, a regular outfielder, nor his replacement, Buttercup Dickerson, was on the tour.

Cal McVey knelt next to his fallen teammate, comforting him. "Son, you stepped in a gopher hole. It's not too bad. We'll see to it you get to the doctor." McVey withheld the truth, knowing the boy would be lucky to ever walk straight again. Right now, though, McVey was short a player.

McVey scanned the onlookers. Radbourn was sitting just a few steps from where Smith completed his tumble, and McVey, spotting the muscular young gentleman, briskly walked over.

"Son, do you play? I'd pick one of the older men from your town, but I'm not sure they would play to win. They'd take my money and then bet against me. You sitting here with your pretty young wife, well, you just look honest and wholesome," McVey said to the relaxing Radbourn. "To make it interesting, I'll pay you a fin if we lose and four sawbucks if we win. Agreed?"

Radbourn got to his feet in a flash, "Yes, I pitch some, and you got a deal. Her name is Carrie, we ain't married. She's not married to me, anyway. Heck, I barely know her. Thanks, the name's Charles Radbourn."

"Is that a relation of yours playing third for the hometown boys? I don't want any shenanigans. I hear he's a cheat."

"Yes, that's my cousin, Henry. Don't worry about anything like that. Forty bucks is a lot of money."

A little over two hours later, the game ended, and McVey was back at Radbourn's blanket, counting out the payment, "Thirty-eight, thirty-nine, and forty. Not bad, kid. I must tell you, after you walked the first two batters, I was somewhat worried, I tell ya. Then you coax a ground ball out, a double play, and then fifteen straight outs; that was some performance. On top of that you smash two doubles, knocking three runners around. I am going to recommend we make you a Red." Two days later, the principal organizer of the independent professional baseball player's league, William Morgan, had inked Radbourn to a services agreement.

After a very brief stint with the Peoria Reds, Radbourn arrived in the majors. He was assigned the duty of a change pitcher. Baseball rules at the time did not allow for any substitutions, but one player was designated as replacement for the pitcher who began the game, when and if it became necessary. Radbourn was well suited for this role, as he could field, hit and warm up at the drop of a hat. It didn't take long for Radbourn to ascend to the top spot in the Providence Grays' rotation, winning 106 games in three years.

In 1884 a twenty-one-year-old hotshot erupted onto the scene. Charles Sweeney struggled through the prior year, managing to lose as many games as he won. By mid-May, Sweeney was clearly the more effective of the two pitching stalwarts on the team. Sweeney, an Irishmen with fiery red hair, had a temper to match. Teammates regarded him as a fierce competitor on the field and in the pubs. Sweeney was not shy about his intentions to push the old man aside and become the team's main hurler. Radbourn was not so willing to concede his role. Tempers regularly flared between the two.

The more the manager called on Sweeney, the more visibly agitated and threatening Radbourn became. Sweeney was so effective that the manager called on him to bail Radbourn out of early-game jams and had Sweeney starting in Radbourn's place several times. On June 7th, Sweeney mowed down the Boston batters, striking out nineteen of them.

On July 20th, Sweeney had breezed through six innings. In the top of the 7th, Sweeney felt a twinge in his elbow during his warm-up tosses. The pitch he had developed at the start of the season, which contributed to his success, he called the fade-away. Right-handed throwers, in snapping the wrist sharply down, create rotation which makes a ball curve from right to left. Sweeney forced the motion of his wrist outward, causing the ball to move towards right-handed batters rather than away. His arm ached more with each successive pitch, until finally Frank Bancroft confronted him after Sweeney loaded the bases with no outs recorded. Sweeney told him about the pain in his arm. Trying to protect his young star; Bancroft called on Radbourn over Sweeney's animated objection.

Sweeney was in line for the win, and with the Grays leading by six runs with three innings to play, the lead was relatively safe. Sweeney, a good hitter, headed to the outfield. For an old man at age 29, Radbourn still could cool the opposing team's bats with relative ease.

Hours after the game and late into the evening, many Grays were still licking the wounds of the 10-8 loss at a nearby ale house. Intoxicated and angry, Sweeney confronted Radbourn, accusing him of throwing the game to intentionally just make Sweeney look bad. Radbourn shot back it was Sweeney who failed to catch two soft fly balls into the outfield and his errant throw allowed the go-ahead runs to score. The words escalated. Radbourn, slightly shorter than the younger man, had been trying to ignore Sweeney's abuse until he questioned the marital integrity of Radbourn's current woman sidekick. That was it. Radbourn lashed out and a full barroom brawl followed.

The town sheriff was called in. Although things calmed very quickly, there was several hundred dollars of damage done to the pub. Sweeney and Radbourn each accused the other of starting the melee. The owner of the Grays, C.T. Gardner, believing Sweeney and unhappy with Radbourn's performance, suspended him without pay as restitution on the spot.

Sweeney did not go home after the brawl, deciding to celebrate the banishment of his rival Radbourn. Throwing salt on the wound, he apologized to the woman he insulted earlier and somehow convinced her to share the rest of the night and wee morning hours with him.

The next day, Sweeney made his way to the field from two towns over after realizing the time. He was still inebriated from the drinking which had continued into the mid-morning hours. Bancroft and Gardner discussed the situation but decided to pitch Sweeney anyway. Sweeney was roughed up through the first six innings. In the 7th inning, the right fielder misplayed a sinking line drive into a triple. Sweeney ran out to right field, confronting the teammate guilty of the mistake. The Grays were down nine runs at this point. Sweeney took off his cap and delivered a backhand slap across the cheek of his teammate. Sweeney slurred and delivered every word with a generous supply of spittle, his face contorted, long mane flying and arms flailing. As suddenly as the switch was turned on, it was turned off. Quietly Sweeney turned away and headed back to the pitcher's box. He managed to walk thirty feet when he abruptly became unsteady and wobbled for a few seconds. His legs buckled suddenly and he lurched forward and went face-first into the ground. Out cold. The Grays, not having a change pitcher, forfeited the game.

Radbourn approached Gray's manager Frank Bancroft with a proposition, "Pitch me the rest of the season, every game, and every inning."

"Charlie, come on now, don't you think you'll get tired?"

"Frank, I worked in a slaughterhouse hammering animals with a twenty-five pound sledge from four in the morning until six or seven at night, seven days a week. How tired can I possibly get throwing a two ounce baseball a few hours a day?"

With forty games left in the season, this was a tall order, but Bancroft had little choice except to agree. Radbourn won 36 of the remaining 40 games he started, failing to play in just three. The Providence Grays were crowned National League Champions, distancing themselves from the pack by ten games. Radbourn had established a league record 59 wins and competed 678 and 2/3 innings, just short of Sweeny's record of 680 innings.

"Congratulations," said the nattily-dressed slimly-built man in the tightly checked dark suit to Radbourn, as he hoisted another whiskey. The team had settled into a small, noisy, over-crowded Boston pub to celebrate their accomplishment and Radbourn's unprecedented number of victories.

"Well I'll be," said Bancroft, stepping in front of Day as he approached his pitcher, "This here is the owner of the Mets, Mr. Day."

"So you know who I am. This is some horse you have here."

"Yeah he's like, well, the reliable ol' work hoss."

"He runs more like a broken-down warhorse. You think he's got anything left?"

"'Nuff' to beat the stuffin out of your guys."

Radbourn, rising up from his bar stool, piped in, "I'll drink to that!"

"Tell your owner I have a proposition for him. Best three of five games, American Association rules, all games played in New York. Winner keeps 100% of gate money with a guaranteed minimum of $50,000, plus another $50,000 as a side bet. Tell Mr. Gardner I'll be at my regular hotel until tomorrow noon. Games will begin in two days."

The Metropolitans of the American Association filled a void left by the expulsion of New York City's Mutuals from the National League in 1876. Declining an immediate invitation to replace the Mutuals in the league, the Mets had a great deal more flexibility in scheduling contests with an eastern rival of their choosing. The Mets soon became wildly popular, beating the competition regularly. Propelled by their popularity, both professional leagues extended invitations after the 1882 season for the Mets to join.

John B. Day, the self-educated business entrepreneur-founder, and Jim Mutrie, his streetwise equal, agreed that joining professional baseball was in the best interest of their club. Both league's presidents knew that to assure success of their league, a New York City franchise was needed. Day wrote a letter to each owner of both leagues of his decision.

October 16, 1882

"The New York Metropolitan Baseball club thanks you for your gracious offer to become a team associated with your professional baseball league. Due to the sustained success as an independent professional team, this is a very difficult decision.

New York City needs a baseball team recognized as a legitimate professional team. Accordingly we are proud to accept your invitation and the New York Metropolitan Baseball club will provide a team to the league effective immediately.

Our only requirement is that home games continue at the Polo Grounds and that I determine the home schedule for my team and any and all exhibition games are to be played in our home park.

Sincerely,

John B. Day, owner

Unanimous consent to the agreement was returned quickly by each league president. Day, with the help of Mutrie, had pulled off the coup of a lifetime. He owned a New York City team in each league. To fulfill his commitments, he had to get his plan in motion quickly. Day purchased the idle Troy, New York franchise. He relocated the team and changed their name to the New York Gothams. The Polo Grounds was situated with a second diamond, separated by twenty feet of landfill, so both teams could play at the same time. Day owned baseball in New York; soon he would *be* baseball in New York.

Gardner responded affirmatively to Day's offer. Day was close to a second coup, after which he could claim his teams had supremacy over all of baseball.

The teams assembled in the Polo Grounds the early afternoon of October 23rd. Day was confident that his team of handpicked, well-rested stars would win handily. The American Association had a few odd rules, one of which prohibited delivering a ball overhand. Radbourn, with an arm he could barely lift above his head, adapted to the restriction by throwing the ball side-arm. Three days later, the Mets were put down for the final time in an 11-2 loss. Radbourn completed all three games, holding the Mets to meager scores each time, only eleven men reaching base. In a very short period, he had mastered several different deliveries and angles of release, ranging from underhand to side-arm and was polished in making the ball sink or rise at will. Batters, who appeared off-balanced constantly, accused Radbourn of doctoring the ball, which he, of course, steadfastly denied.

Unfortunately for Day, there was not enough time to garner interest in the games within 48 hours. Day had to shell out nearly $45,000 to cover the gate receipt shortfall due to paltry attendance. He sold assets to make good on the side bet. In financial ruin, Day had no choice but to dismantle the Mets quickly after the last game. The Mets were exiled to a second-rate ballpark constructed between the smokestacks of several factories, on reclaimed land. The stink of the environment matched the stink on the field and within a year the Mets were gone and quickly forgotten.

Radbourn returned to the Bloomington slaughterhouse, back to pounding the life right out of half-ton steers, fourteen hours a day, every day. He had earned a well-needed rest from using one hand to hurl the two-ounce baseball for less than two hours a day.

While Radbourn's biggest passion was playing ball, consuming alcohol, carousing with women of loose moral standards and hunting followed closely. Trouble ultimately found him in each.

Six years after his retirement from baseball, Radbourn was on one of his protracted drinking sessions. LeRoy, a small town just fifteen miles outside of Bloomington, might just as well have been on the other side of the country. The town thrived on the shoulders of men who worked the rail yards and on the railway construction. Unless you were looking for trouble, no one came to this rundown dirty community. For the locals, Sparks Saloon and Billiards parlor was their oasis for relaxation after long hours pounding rail spikes and setting timbers. Charlie had befriended Willie Sparks, and since his retirement was pushing Willie to sell him an interest in the business, without any luck. Charlie nonetheless was now considered a local and he loved the isolated hideaway.

Radbourn, as usual, was in the company of a tall, buxom woman, both equally inebriated. The pair had, less than discreetly, shuttled back and forth between the bar and Radbourn's room at the flea-bitten motel. Georgiana, by twenty-three, had been married for six years. She left the house a week earlier, stopping by the out-of-the-way pub for conversation, light flirtations and a quick drink. Awaiting her return home in Bloomington was Jethro Flores and their four children, three of whom he had fathered.

Georgiana was no stranger to this behavior; in the past she always returned late the following mornings, even when she found herself comforted in another man's warmth. Jethro made his way to the fields not too much after sunup, where he worked a long day as a farmhand. She managed to avoid, at least temporarily, the inevitable confrontation.

This time was different, Georgiana melted into the allure of Radbourn's charm. Since taking up with Radbourn, she gave nary a thought to her family. When sober, she was passionate in her love for Jethro and four children. Jethro was prone to jealous rages over her infidelity. He suspected that

she was less than fully faithful, an accusation
Georgiana denied. Twice during heated arguments,
his punches caught her flush on the nose, the second
smashing the bridge so flat, Georgiana resembled a
prize fighter on the wrong end of one too many
battles. She hated him for stealing her beauty. Even
in fleeting moments of sobriety, she did not think of
leaving Radbourn to return home.

Henry Radbourn, Charles' older cousin,
aware of his dalliance, burst into the saloon.
Scanning the room, he spotted the couple nestled in
the corner.

"Charlie," he yelled, scampering over as a
startled Charlie looked up.

"This here is my cousin. He got none of the
family looks," the forever-vain Charlie said to his
gal pal.

"You've got to get out of here. I heard two
fellas yakking. Her husband is looking for her. He
suspects she's with somebody. Charlie, he's
carrying a shotgun."

"He'll never find us here."

"Charlie, he's already in this crap-hole town.
Someone must have told him you'd headed here."

"Don't say that too loud now, you'll get
yourself and me in some trouble."

"Charlie, you're already in deep shit."

"Henry, why don't you escort her out, I'll
just say here."

"I ain't leaving you here alone. Let's just
face the music," Georgianna said.

"Darling, it's time for you to go."

"Oh, Charles, I just don't want to go."

"Henry, just take her and go."

Finally, Henry grabbed her by the hand, yanking her from Charlie's lap. He provided just enough of a tug; the unsteady women flung her arms around Henry's neck grasping to retain her balance. Henry turned her towards the door, still Georgiana hanging on, clumsily. The couple moved in a slow waltz-like motion.

"So you're here!" Jethro exclaimed.

Willie Sparks looked over to the front door, as stillness came over the room. All eyes focused on the intruder who just entered. The four gents playing pool stopped. They wanted no part of an angry man with a loaded shotgun.

The walls suddenly reverberated as Jethro fired both barrels.

Jethro's worries about Georgiana ever stepping out on him abruptly ended. Her chest cavity was blown completely through as the force of the blast propelled her back unto Radbourn's vacant lap.

Henry caught the full force of the second shell in his left thigh.

Except for the bone shard from Georgiana hitting his left eye, Charles escaped unscathed. Within a few months, infection would set in, costing Radbourn his vision in the eye.

Jethro, seeing Henry was not mortally injured, began to reload. Georgiana was dead; her lover would suffer the same fate. Before his attempt to reload was complete, his head received the last of several blows to the head, the cue stick splintered. He stared at his wife's lifeless eyes for the final time as the room faded to dark.

"Thanks", Charles said to the pool player who'd struck down Jethro.

"Bastard disturbed my streak, cost me some money. Guess I need a new cue stick."

The hard-drinking and carefree carnal life ultimately took its toll. Within six years, Radbourn would pass away from effects of advanced syphilis on February 3rd, 1897.

Radbourn did not have an easy life by anyone's standard. Most of his friends considered him downright unlucky.

On February 7th, family and friends gathered at Evergreen Memorial Cemetery to say their farewells to Old Hoss.

As the minister began his prayers over the casket, a low hum became a chuckle, finally full laughter among all those celebrating Charlie's passing.

The headstone directly behind Minister Robertson displayed the following:

CHARLES GARDNER RADBOURNE

His reputation as being unlucky followed right to his grave, his name misspelled.

Chapter 36
1927 Arkansas

Landis did not savor the six-hundred-mile trip from Chicago to Hot Springs, but it was necessary. In his estimation, this meeting was crucial for the survival of baseball. News services across the country leveled attack after attack on baseball's leadership, with the commissioner the target.

Landis misjudged the backlash of Carpenter's hurried decision in a nearly empty courtroom. Despite having no witnesses, the attorney for Ban Johnson was more than credible in presentation of the facts. The characterization of Landis as biased and bigoted did not go unnoticed. Congressmen, in an unusual bipartisan move, were mustering support for a Department of Justice investigation into baseball operations. He did not take the situation lightly when words suggestive of criminal activity like racketeering and collusion were being tossed around. The owners were on edge, and all this was happening on his watch.

Travelling in late March, the weather was an uncertainty. Fortunately on this trip, Landis got lucky.

The meeting with Ruppert and Huggins was arranged at a time just past sunrise. No ballplayer would be up and about this early in the morning. Aptly, his legal assistant, Renee, drove home the importance and need to keep the meeting discreet to the other participants. After several years of clerking for a judge, she knew how to accomplish that.

Precisely at 6:30 AM, Colonel Ruppert, accompanied by the Yankee manager, knocked on the door to Landis's fifth-floor room. Coffee and breakfast were already set out on a table.

"Gentleman, please take a seat. We need to talk about all the *excitement* surrounding baseball."

"What's this about, Judge, more problems with Ruth?"

"No, not at all! We're here to talk about the business of baseball, putting millions of fans in the ballpark. We need to excite Americans and get them out to the parks. Have either of you ever heard of Charles Radbourn?"

"No."

"Well, he is a former player who's dead, and Ruth is about to go chasing his ghost."

Seventy minutes later the door to the suite swung open. The three gents were all smiles, shaking hands as they said their so-longs.

Walking to the stairs, the Colonel did not speak until he heard the click of the door closing behind them.

"Well, Hug, what do you make of all this?" addressing Miller Huggins, who'd been quiet.

"It's possible. It's already been a half-dozen years since he hit fifty–nine. The lineup has to be set so the pitchers give him some hittable balls. It's possible for him to knock out sixty. The other record though, that's going to be tougher, much tougher."

"But possible."

"I guess, but without any other player catching on." Huggins shook his head and glanced at his feet with an expression of doubt. "Why don't you just let Landis fry in his own juice?"

"That's a good question Hug. Perhaps he'll do us a favor and look at the Babe less contemptuously."

"Yeah, but you're saving that hypocrite's butt."

Ruppert grabbed Huggins by the shoulder and pulled him around so they were face to face, "We're not doing this to save Landis's ass. No, I want the New York Yankees to be as common a household phrase as bread and butter. We're known in the city, but isolated to the Bronx. The Giants have most of Manhattan. Damn Robins, or whatever they're called, seem to have captivated the attention in Brooklyn and Queens. When we go on the road, well, I want folks to know the Yankee name, to understand Yankee standards. We want them to come to see our players as professionals. Baseball is their business, not a game for drunken men with character flaws. I don't care if they root for or against us. That will all start this year. 1927, I want this to be a year that no one, fan or not, will ever forget ever!"

Chapter 37

Opening day of 1927 was more than Ruppert could have expected. Over seventy-two thousand fans filed into the Bronx cathedral as their anxious wait for the season to begin was over. Spectators returned to the ballpark for many reasons. Fanatics came to pay homage to their heroes. The *crankers*, nicknamed for their incessant jeering, came to serve notice on their adversaries. Others appreciated the respite from the drudgery of everyday life, desiring a simple afternoon of relaxation with the family.

The scene around the intersection of River Avenue and 161st was far cry from the pastoral setting for the initial opening of the Stadium in 1923. Horse-drawn carriages and couples casually strolling hand in hand with wicker picnic baskets were gone. Traffic in the streets was halted by the hundreds of Model T's and other autos snaking to the stadium from Harlem, New Jersey and Long Island. Aa*oogas* from the horns and clattering of the engines muffled any attempt at a conversation. A steady march of fans descended from the IRT's elevated platform and arose from the Independent underground subway toward the ticket booths and turnstiles leading inside.

The Yankees were facing formidable opponents, the Philadelphia Athletics. The team from the City of Brotherly Love, according to the bookmakers, was the odds-on favorite to win the pennant and ultimately the World Series. The Yankee ownership and players used this fact as a bit of motivation. After all, the Yankees were returning the same team, one that had come very close to winning it all the previous year.

Connie Mack, a clever baseball executive, rebuilt and remade the Athletics into a top team for a third time. He lured aging stars Ty Cobb, Zach Wheat and Ed Collins into joining an already powerful lineup, and the final piece of the puzzle for success, perhaps, was a little-known rookie named Jimmy Foxx.

At 3:27 PM on Friday, April 15, the four-game series ended. The Yankees had set the tone for the year. In three lopsided wins, the Yanks outscored the Athletics 24-10, and in the one game in which the Athletics were able to get to the Yankee hurlers to put up nine runs, the Yankees did likewise.

By the summer solstice, the Yankees had built a nine-game lead, and by Labor Day, the race was no longer in doubt. The Yankees carved their way through the American League, winning forty-three of their games by more than five runs. The landslide victories provided Huggins the latitude he needed to easily manage the season.

Ruth and Gehrig engaged in a furious battle for homerun supremacy. During the first twenty-nine days of September, Ruth hammered out sixteen homers. On Friday September 30, 1927, the Yankees were playing their 154th game of the season at home. The fans were back in full force, as the attendance at Yankee Stadium of nearly 1.2 million was twice the league average.

Unfortunately, on this day, only eight thousand fans were around to serve as witnesses.

Ruth, with his furious late season breakout, matched his previous career high of fifty–nine homers. He had two games left in which to surpass that mark. The Yankee run barrages enabled Huggins to use Ruth cleverly in his rotation and successfully insert him into short-relief situations where he could gain a win with limited innings thrown. With half the number of innings pitched as Radbourn, Ruth had caught him at fifty-nine as well.

To stem any controversy, Huggins started Ruth in game 154. He and Tom Zachary, for the Washington Senators, delivered a gem, dueling through seven innings, each hurler limiting the other team to two runs.

Ruth came to the plate in the last of the seventh, with Marty Koenig on third after a triple. Zachary's first pitch was high and inside, Ruth watched the ball casually sail under his chin. Strike one, called home plate umpire Bill Dineen. Eight thousand fans moaned in unison.

"Well, Bill, if you called that way all along, I think I would have already shut these guys out, " Ruth said to Dineen without the courtesy of a glance back.

The next pitch was nearly ten feet outside. There was a long pause; Ruth remained tense until the umpire's call came. Ball one.

"Took you long enough to make that call. That was a close one," Ruth said in sarcastic commentary.

Once again, Ruth took his batting stance, closed right foot, front shoulder turned towards third, hands held at the waist, fingers flexing around the bat handle. He was coiled and ready. The pitch came in, low and inside. Ruth swung with everything he had, golfing the ball off of his shoe tops.

The crack of the bat sounded so loud it was audible to fans in every part of the park. The ball landed halfway back in the grandstand, ten feet to the 'fair' side of the foul pole. Ruth trotted around the bases with a little less haste than his familiar trot. Fans showered the fields with straw hats and bits of confetti made from newspapers they'd shredded with their hands.

As he crossed home plate, Joe Dugan jumped onto Ruth's back. Before disappearing into the dugout, Ruth stopped, dumped Dugan, waved and tipped his cap.

The Yankees took their positions to start the eighth, all except Ruth.

"What's the matter, Ruth," a puzzled Huggins said. "Are you not feeling well?"

"Nope. Maybe one of the other guys should finish this?"

"Ruth, this is your day! You have a chance to do something ain't never been done and will likely never be done again. So go finish this thing."

Ruth set down the next five Senators in order. Walter Johnson was called to pinch-hit for Zachary with two outs in the ninth.

Johnson yelled out to Ruth, peering from under the bill of his cap, "Congrats on the season, Babe! This is some special team and year!"

"Walter, what the hell they have you hitting for?"

"Trying to get just a little a bit of payback, if I'm lucky."

Fans hurdled the three-and-a-half-foot concrete wall separating the seats from the field, too numerous for the police on foot and horseback to control. Dugan gracefully handled the tired grounder hit in his direction. In one easy motion he aimed his throw. The toss hung slowly in the air as it traveled across the diamond. The umpiring raised his fisted right hand. This signaled to all that Johnson was retired at first. Teammates grabbed Ruth and they all rushed to the quiet clubhouse. The wild celebration by the fans continued on the field for hours.

Babe could not be contained inside. He had reclaimed their allegiance and he would show his gratitude. Ruth greeted every spectator he possibly could. Grown men patted him on the back; women each got a giant bear hug, sometimes for a tad longer than was necessary. The youngsters expressed their adoration for Ruth. He told the concession stands to give the boys and girls whatever candy they wanted.

Harry Niles, a local sportswriter, finally caught up with Ruth after the celebration died down, for an interview.

"Babe, what thoughts went through your mind when the final out was made to end the game?"

"Well Harry, sixty wins and sixty homers, my thought's 'let some 'son of a bitch' break that!'"

The Yankees completed their assault on the American League, winning a record 110 games and in the process obliterating team historical offensive records. Ruth completed his conquest of the two most admired records in baseball for individual achievement, sixty wins for a pitcher and sixty homers as a slugger.

Ruth did not pitch in the series as the Yankees swept the Pirates.

Chapter 38

Ruth was anything but sad when the curtain came down on the 1930 season. Since the end of the magical 1927 season, much changed in his life, including finding someone to give him emotional support and eliminate his fears of abandonment. Claire Hodgson was the woman who would be at his side for the rest of his life.

At age 35, his body was thickening, his youthful athleticism was nearly gone, and the heavy toll of his carefree lifestyle relegated Ruth to the embarrassing role as a spot field player. A drunken tumble after a late-season game in which Ruth surrendered a 'safe' lead, a fall down the steps of a Manhattan night club, inflicted more damage to his surgically repaired wrist, stealing what little power remained from the once-lethal swing.

Ruth stared out the east-facing windows of his midtown apartment, eyes shut, letting the warmth shower his face. Silently he ached for the days when he was the heart of the feared Yankee teams. Now Gehrig was their cornerstone.

In 1930, he managed to knock out just eight home runs. Ruth had seventeen wins by July 4th, but his arm tired, and the relentless pain in his forearm just would not go away. Ruth took the brunt of the fan discontent for the Yankee fade, down the stretch. The Yankees finished with 83 wins, their lowest total since 1925.

Ruth seriously contemplated retirement. He told Claire of his plan to approach Ruppert on his longtime dream of becoming the Yankee manager.

Hell, there ain't nobody who knows the game as well as me, he thought. Back in 1926, the Colonel had promised that if Ruth would clean up his life, he could have a shot. He still liked the booze, a cigar and food, but after marrying Claire nearly two years ago, his antics of the past were kept well in check.

Ruth had met Claire Merritt Hodgson in the height of his halcyon days. Claire possessed a radiance of the kind that stopped conversations when she entered a room. Babe first saw her while she was attending a 1923 game in Washington D.C. While talking to Walter Johnson, before the afternoon contest was set to begin, Ruth fixated on the beautiful women sitting twenty rows behind the Senators' dugout.

Johnson, looking at Ruth, tapped him on the shoulder, "You all right, Ruth?"

Ruth, whose jaw was literally gaping open, wiped the sudden beads of sweat from his forehead. "Walter, who's the gal with the white sweater and hat with the black feather and black ribbon seated 'bout half way up the first section?" he asked.

"Babe, what are you talking about? I can't see that far."

"Come on, Walter, she's sitting right there on the aisle."

"I would have to go all the way over to our dugout to see who you're talking about. By the way, Babe, how is Helen doing? " Johnson asked, sending a not-so-subtle message to remind Ruth that he was married. Johnson respected Ruth as a competitor, but thought his moral compass was lacking direction. "You know, Babe, I hear she's circled the bases more than a few times, including with guys like Cobb."

"Helen, she's fine, she's a good woman, pure as the driven snow when I married her. She spends all of her time at the farm, does a good job of raising Dorothy. I've been around similar bases a few times, plenty, Walter. We all know Cobb doesn't swing a big bat." They both chuckled heartily.

Claire was a widow with a small child, and she was in D.C. with the road company for the Broadway musical comedy, *Dew Drop In*. She had a bit part, commensurate with her limited acting and singing skills, but nonetheless she attracted as much attention as the headliners. Since the death of her husband, she had had more than her fair share of male acquaintances and she was wise to the games men played.

Ruth managed an invitation to the closing night performance party for the cast, producers and their guests at the Mayflower Hotel. Holding court in his usual braggadocio manner, Ruth, with a young vixen on each arm, addressed Claire. She, also a center of attention, was surrounded by several men, all dreaming of passionate nights with the starlet. Ruth and Claire, both scarred emotionally, filled the void by surrounding themselves with members of the opposite sex.

"Hey, sister, come over and join my party," Ruth shouted.

Claire, Ruth's match in sarcastic wit, retorted; "Well, only if you could grow two more arms, one for me and one for Helen." That was an arrow straight through his heart.

"Suit yourself, sis." Ruth gave a guarded response.

"The name is Claire, and I'm not your sister. I'm Claire Hodgson, *fella*," she snapped.

Ruth had thrown the bait, but he failed to get a nibble. Claire deftly fought off her own urges, at least for the night. She was all too aware of Ruth's intentions, and knowing her own weaknesses, she would not give Ruth any encouragement to pursue her. Ultimately the deep physical and intimate attraction she felt would overwhelm her resistance.

Claire regretted many of her own affairs, which had led nowhere. Before jumping into any relationship with Ruth, she was insistent that he would forego other carnal relationships; otherwise she would be long gone. She would have to accept that the relationship might not lead to a marriage. Helen and Ruth were still married, although they had been separated for a few years. Very rarely did Ruth travel to his farm in Sudbury, Massachusetts, and when he did, it was to visit his daughter, Dorothy, whom whenever he was around, he showered with endless affection and adoration. Claire would not force Ruth into a divorce; as long as he toed the line, she would stand by his side. Claire recognized that there was an ache deep inside the Babe. It gnawed at him daily. Despite his carefree attitude, he missed Dorothy and believed he had let her down. He was not there as she grew, and in his heart, he wondered, "Have I done to her what was done to me all of my life?" Most days when his mind drifted to Dorothy, he felt sick to his stomach with fear. He was two hundred fifty miles away; he was not there for her. She was his daughter, his responsibility, and he had a need to protect her and let her know she was loved.

On the morning of January 12, 1929, Claire answered a knock at their Riverside Drive apartment door. Claire had been expecting a courier from Ruppert, who was to deliver the Babe's contract for the upcoming season. Spring training was less than a month away. At a private meeting with Ruppert, she finally convinced the Yankees to concede to her monetary demands and other considerations the Babe had wanted. Ruppert agreed to look the other way when it came to Babe's barnstorming, except against Negro teams. Landis remained adamant about not allowing Negroes to play against major league players; and Ruppert could only shelter Babe so far from the reach of Landis.

Ruppert also committed to Claire that Ruth would be provided a chance to manage, but that did not mean a promotion to that position for the Yankees. Claire tried her best to change his mind, but Ruppert maintained that Ruth was not trustworthy enough to manage his own life without her at his side, so how could he manage two dozen other men? Claire was raising a child in New York and could not travel. She had eased much of the tension between Ruth and Ruppert. She hoped that within a few years, and with the continued maturation of the Babe, he'd gain Ruppert's trust. Prove that he could handle the managerial responsibilities, Ruppert in turn would be open to Ruth's ambitions.

"Oh, may I help you?" Clair was startled to find a police sergeant and patrol officer at their door. Her first reaction was that Babe had gotten himself in some trouble that he neglected to tell her about.

"Sorry, Mrs. Hodgson, we have horrible news for Mr. Ruth about his farm," Officer O'Toole said in a barely audible whisper.

****

Strong gusts from a usual winter New England storm began pounding Boston in the early evening of January 11. Agnes, the housekeeper Ruth had hired four years earlier, was completing the pre-storm ritual. All the animals were secure in their inside pens or stalls. She checked that all the outside gates were tied closed, the barn doors locked. As she stepped onto the front porch, the side door of the barn slammed and then opened, only to slam again. She looked; the door was waving in the breeze, then caught again by the wind and catapulted violently closed. *The wind is going to rip the door from its hinges,* she thought. She placed the three items she was carrying on the porch, returning to the barn the situation. The latch had come loose; she needed to find a piece of rope to tie it shut. This should only time a minute. She found a small length of cord, hurridly fighting the wind; it took several tries until the door tied firmly.

As she turned to go back to the main house, something wasn't right. Instead the soft amber of the kerosene lamp, half the porch was lit up. *My God please help me*, she thought.

Old wooden frame homes with these conditions quickly became an inferno. The wind-whipped flames were already licking up to the second floor. She needed to warn Helen and Dorothy; they had little time. Screaming served no purpose, as the wind drowned out her voice. Fortunately Dorothy and Helen were in the far side of the house, cleaning dishes in the kitchen; their backs were to the side of the house that was ablaze. The fire was spreading quickly. Agnes started to panic as the flames charged in their direction. She had to get to the side door nearest the kitchen before the fire and smoke trapped them. She tripped headlong over the low stone wall five feet from the door. Gathering herself quickly, she had still lost valuable seconds. Ripping open the door, Agnes screamed, "You need to get out of the house immediately. Come on, quickly."

Dorothy, nine years old, yelled, "Mommy is upstairs!"

"Please, child, run to me. Get out now! I'll get your Mommy!"

Agnes had made sure the child was a safe distance from the house when a wall of flames engulfed the second story and a series of long, agonizing screams ended any further rescue attempts.

She turned just in time to grab hold of Dorothy, who had begun running back to the house. The cries of pain had ceased.

Clutching the trembling Dorothy firmly against her own body, Agnes's face streaked as tears rolled down her charred cheeks. The child, traumatized by what she had witnessed, tried unsuccessfully to speak. Agnes tried to comfort her. "Dear child, we cannot help your mommy."

****

In New York, Claire responded to the police officers, "I will get him."

"Mr. Ruth, I am Sergeant Muldoon. There has been a fire at your farm. We have some very bad news."

Babe's head spun, and his legs wobbled. He fell back into a nearby chair as all the blood drained suddenly from his face. Claire gasped, "Oh no!"

"There was a fire at your farm, Mr. Ruth." Muldoon continued. "We're very sorry to inform you that Helen Ruth did not survive."

Babe stared blankly. Shocked, he was trying to speak, but no words came forth.

Claire asked the question Babe feared the answer to, 'What about Dorothy?"

"Everyone else is fine."

Claire thanked the officers. "Babe, are you all right?"

He gathered himself and took a few deep breaths. "Claire, let's get packed. We have got to get up to Massachusetts."

Less than three months had passed since Helen's death. Babe was insisting he and Claire wed before the baseball season began, while the April air still held remnants of the long, harsh winter. Hundreds of onlookers crowded into the

Church of the Sacred Heart, located on Shakespeare Avenue, a few blocks north of Yankee Stadium. The normally quiet tree-lined street teemed with journalists, photographers, children and many others here to wish the newly-married couple well. When the couple emerged, they were immediately swarmed. Ruth was in his grey tweed overcoat with the black collar, and Claire, all smiles, was in a full-length mink coat with a soft beige turban hat pulled down around her ears, just a hint of her brown hair peeking out. The newlyweds stopped on the church step to greet adorers and answer questions. Each stood tall and smiled; neither acted ashamed of the previous six years. For nearly thirty minutes, the happy couple braved both the chilly temperature and the torrent of questions. The Babe indiscreetly whispered into the ear of his new bride, took his hand from his pocket and put it around her shoulders, winked to the crowed, gave a big wave and proclaimed, "It's time to honeymoon!" The crowd roared in approval.

****

Since the onset of their life together, Claire had reined the abhorrent behaviors in and, with the help of his financial manager, built wealth for the couple and their family. Now nearly two years into their marriage, she knew the child within Ruth would never be fully suppressed so long as he continued to play the young man's game; the bad boy inside him was always itching to escape. She also recognized Ruth's abandonment issues. When the game he loved, which had served as a surrogate family for him, no longer had use for him as a player, when his days of veneration from young fans waned, Ruth might very well be overcome with a devastating sense of loss. This happy-go-lucky man could very well decline quickly. His past was littered with people who had discarded him after they'd extracted their pound of flesh from him. Claire's devotion to Ruth was so intense that she would do everything she could not to permit baseball to do this to him. The best way she knew for Ruth to become a mature adult, since he would need acceptance as other than a player, would be letting him manage. Claire knew more than anyone how fully Babe understood the game. Her husband had no mediocrity in his blood. Given an opportunity, he'd quickly become one of, if not *the*, greatest manager of all time. She was his rock.

****

On September 15, 1929, Miller Huggins tapped a napping Doc Woods on the shoulder.

"Who's hurt?" a startled Woods asked as he jerked awake.

"No one. Try and stay awake, will you. My foot is getting no better. The swelling has gotten worse."

"Let's go to the clubhouse for some treatment. Hoyt has this game under control."

Woods' home remedy made matters worse for Huggins, spreading the infection within his foot. Finally the team doctor instructed Huggins to check into St Vincent's Hospital. With the Yankees playing in Boston, Ruppert and Barrow visited Huggins to cheer his spirits. Huggins did not like missing games.

"Hug, you'll be coming home soon," said Ruppert.

Myrtle Huggins, his sister, thanked Ruppert and Barrow as the pair left for lunch.

"Are you sure you don't want to come with us?" Ruppert asked. "He'll be okay." "You are so kind, but I will stay with Miller until he is fully recovered."

"Dammit," James Quinn, the Red Sox owner muttered, putting the phone back in its cradle, "Stella, please come in here."

"Yes, Mr. Quinn."

Quinn handed her a series of handwritten notes. "Please give these notes in the following order. The first goes to the third-base side grounds keeper, it's a note to the Yankee manager. The second is for the public address announcer, you know the man with the megaphone. The third goes to the scorekeeper in centerfield. Hurry, please."

As Boston recorded the final out in the top of the fifth, Art Fletcher noticed the flag in center field being lowered. "Let's get out their guys and hold them down." Not a player moved, Ruth had intercepted the note intended for the interim manager. His eyes were already swelling as he valiantly fought off a swell of emotion.

Fletcher grabbed the slip of paper from his hand, *'Huggins slipped into a coma and passed away a few minutes after twelve noon, condolences. JA"*

The sudden death of Huggins in September of 1929 had opened the door for Ruth. Art Fletcher decided, after just eleven games, that managing the

Yankees was not for him. Bob Shawkey, a long-time teammate of Ruth, in his opinion, 'had no depth to his understanding of the game.' Shawkey did not manage; he just let the guys play their game. During the season, he never offered advice to any of the veterans, especially Ruth. Ruth considered Shawkey a friend and would never think to undermine his position, but believed he would have managed the potent ball club to a better outcome in 1930.

Ruth ruminated over his feats as a player. He held the single-season record for two of the most prestigious individual records, for home runs and wins. He had participated in nine World Series, setting both pitching and batting records, a six-time champion. He held the career record for home runs, well ahead of his teammate, Gehrig. Ruth passed the Big Train, Walter Johnson, when he captured his 418th win. For his career, he was the only player with more than four hundred wins and four hundred home runs. Ruth was far above any other player.

The past three seasons were mediocre ones for the Yankees, which gnawed at Ruth, who had never been mediocre at anything. Ruth managed just twenty-three wins per year in this span, but he was looking for loftier numbers. Denton 'Cy' Young's win total of 511 now might be unconquerable. Most baseball fans considered Ruth the greatest baseball player of all time. Anywhere he went, Ruth was mobbed. Clearly he was the most recognized and celebrated athlete in the country. He was recognized around the globe. He thought he'd talk to Shawkey; maybe this would be the right time to become player manager. Maybe he could get a few more wins, knock a few more out of the park, and take several pennants. Ruth knew he would love to add to his resume 'the winningest manager of all time.'

"Claire, we need to go pay a visit to Ruppert, I want to change my contract this year to player-manager. I'm certainly better than anybody they're considering for the job. Hell, I bet you I can get us back to the series."

"Sit down, Babe. I need to talk to you about something."

Claire's recent meetings with Ruppert produced much the same result as those in the past few years: firm financial compensation, but no commitment for Babe's future in the Yankee organization after his playing days were over. Ruppert had told Claire the Yankees were bringing in a new manager. She hadn't the courage to endure the disappointment Babe would experience, but she also did not want him to explode into an uncontrollable rage with the Colonel, which would completely kill any chance he might have to manage.

"What! They're bringing a bush league outsider in? That S.O.B. Ruppert! Marse is the trashcan that got fired by the Cubs. Claire, I talked with Shawkey yesterday, while he was packing for the trip to Tennessee. Are you telling me Barrow and Ruppert have hired a new manager without having the guts to talk to Shawkey first?"

****

"Yankee Stars to Play Lookouts"

That was the headline for the Chattanooga News on April 1, 1931

"Joe McCarthy, the newly appointed Yankee manager, will lead his cast of sluggers with the adopted nickname of Murderer's Row to face the hometown Lookouts. Ten thousand are expected to attend the contest."

This was big news for the small, vibrant town considered very much the heartbeat of Dixie. Chattanooga was called home by several minor league clubs, including the Southern Association AA Nashville Lookouts. The Lookouts recently achieved notoriety by getting into the crosshairs of Mountain Landis. Their owner, Joe Engel, despite repeated warnings from baseball's dictatorial commissioner, inked a 17-year-old lefty pitching phenomenon. He now billed his team as featuring the only female playing professional baseball.

Landis, in a last-ditch attempt to prevent the young lady from playing, called Ruppert.

"Colonel, if you go through with the game, I will suspend all those involved."

"Commissioner, you have no authority over this game. There is no prohibition against women playing. Besides, Engel would be out of his mind to pitch her against my team. You attempt to suspend any of my players, and I'll have you in court so fast your head will spin. Plus, I have more than enough owners on my side to make your life miserable. Your stance on Negroes in the league and playing exhibition contests against Negro league teams is not sitting well. This is a traditional stop for the Yankees, we love coming to Chattanooga, and the fans give us a big welcome. This game is part of the baseball history of this town."

Furious, Landis slammed down the phone. "Damn it!"

Clyde Barfoot opened on the mound for the Lookouts. Two pitches later, Combs had scored, Sewell stood on second and Barfoot was writhing in agony, holding the battered leg pelted by the Sewell shot which had caromed all the way up the left field line.

Lookout manager Bert Neihoof gave the signal to the bullpen. Trotting in came the demure Jackie Mitchell, baggy pants flopping all the way. The 5' 4", 125-pound Mitchell appeared even smaller as she stood next to the six-foot husky frame of the Lookout catcher.

She peered in for the sign, curly brown hair peeking from under her cap. Coming to the plate was Babe Ruth, the first batter she'd face. Ruth looked at this imp on the mound and tipped his cap to her. Mitchell reached into her back pocket and added a bit of powder to her cheeks to dim the shine.

Awkwardly she began her windup, then rotating her left arm backwards twice, she delivered a ball outside. Ruth chuckled and yelled, "Come on, sister, get it over."

She repeated the deliver, this time throwing a tantalizing slow ball, Ruth focused on the pitch, swinging as hard as he could, trying to blow it out of the park. Just before making contact with the wood, the ball suddenly dropped as if coming off a table. Ruth tumbled.

Ten thousand fans jumped in delight.

"Okay, sister, you got me on that one."

Mitchell threw the next pitch from the exact same windup, same arm motion. The batter had the same awkward swing, and the same result; no contact with the ball.

This time an even more embarrassed Ruth pointed to center field. The crowd did not sit back down, but stood, wildly cheering.

This time the ball started high, sinking late into the strike zone, freezing Ruth. He saluted the youngster and walked away, taking a position against the fence behind home plate.

Gehrig and Bill Dickey went down in similar fashion. Jackie Mitchell had struck out three members of Murderer's Row on seven pitches. Mobbed by her teammates, she was carried back to the dugout. Her mind drifted and visions appeared in her head. She was in a St. Louis uniform, on the mound, the crowd loudly roaring with approval as she warned up. After today, yes, she had a shot to make it in the big leagues.

Ruth marveled how effortlessly she threw the ball. He would seek her out after the game. He was curious how she made the ball move so sharply; down, in, out almost any direction. When she tossed the ball, hitters were frozen, tantalized by the allure of pulverizing the ball that was seemingly suspended in flight. At the last minute, the ball darted away from danger.

"If only I could master one or two of her pitches, I could save my arm. Maybe I could pitch a few more seasons, just maybe." Ruth decided to invite her to dinner. She was delighted to join the legendary player. Ruth held the conversation strictly to baseball. She picked his brain on what she should do to increase her chances to make it to the major leagues. In return, Ruth got her to demonstrate how to throw all of her crazy pitches.

"Dazzy Vance, you must know him, Mr. Ruth? Well, he lived not too far from where I grew up. He told me to hold the ball like this, here, and put some pressure along the seams this way."

Mitchell showed Ruth each of her different grips. "Oh Mr. Ruth, I almost forgot the most important thing you'll need to do."

She bent her index finger and dug the fingernail into the seam. "When you do this the ball will..."

After dinner, the pair threw a ball back and forth, with Ruth practicing the easy throwing motion. He marveled at how quickly she adapted. Ruth bade her goodnight, placing her into a cab.

"Goodbye, sis, and good luck. You keep pitching like you do and you'll be in the bigs soon enough."

"Thanks for the dinner, Mr. Ruth. The team leaves for Nashville in the morning. They told me I'm in line for a start on Saturday, so I need to get my rest. The train leaves early tomorrow." Jackie was very upbeat; Ruth had given her a world of encouragement. After all, she had struck out three of the best the game had to offer.

As the taxi began to pull away, he whistled, bringing the car to a halt. He strolled over and gave her the sign to roll down window. He bellowed, "Hey, sis, would ya tell me what ya call this pitch?"

Jackie shook her head to hold her laughter as she snorted. She was fully expecting a thank you, or even a pass as she was familiar with Ruth's girl-chasing history, "Sure, Mr. Ruth, the knuckle curve."

The taxi sped off.

Two days after the game, Landis issued an order, "Women are not eligible to play professional baseball." Engel was forced to cancel Mitchell's contract. Landis had prevailed, crushing her dream and that of many women like her. Jackie Mitchell never stepped foot on a ballfield again.

Chapter 39

Joseph McCarthy was a marginal player who never graduated beyond the mid–level minor leagues. Whatever talent he lacked to play the game, though, he more than made up for in his understanding of the game.

While playing for the Louisville Colonels, McCarthy was told to give up baseball, since his ability would keep him mired in mediocrity and destined to eternal damnation in the hell of visiting Podunk towns. McCarthy responded that he had long ago set his sights on managing, not playing. His final day as a player came when he was roundly criticized for failing to haul in a tough throw from the Louisville first baseman. McCarthy tried to give his first sacker a bit of advice on where to put the ball in that situation. He was told in no uncertain terms where to stick the words of a .220 hitter like himself. McCarthy, promptly upon arriving in the dugout, announced to the owner his retirement as a player, triggering the clause in his contract to become the field manager. Before Jay Kirke, the player who had criticized him, could get to the dugout, McCarthy announced the first baseman's indefinite suspension.

At age 26, with a brilliant baseball mind evident, the promotion to manager was seamless. Over the next several seasons, his teams won the American Association title twice.

In 1925, the owner of the Cubs, William Wrigley, was desperate to have his team succeed. Aware of McCarthy's minor league resume, Bill

Wrigley knew he would be just the shot in the arm needed for his underperforming team. "This team has floundered in coal holes all too long. We need to change attitudes and perspectives," he told Chicago journalist James Campell. "We are going to take a chance on Joe McCarthy. He will lead the Cubs out of mediocrity!"

In his first team meeting, McCarthy informed his players that they would be treated as gentleman and professionals. Overnight the Cubs were transformed to relevancy in the league. His reputation for not tolerating nonsense or special treatment preceded him to Chicago. Everyone on the team had tasks before, during and after games. If you did not do what was expected, you were held accountable. McCarthy had a deep disdain for aging 'star' players.

At a Cubs pre-game meeting to review the situational aspects of a game, McCarthy began to explain, "When we have a runner on second …" Grover Cleveland Alexander, the team's star hurler, rudely interjected, speaking over McCarthy,

"We never have to worry about that with our offense."

McCarthy cut Alexander to shreds with his icy glare, "Mr. Alexander, I will deal with your problem after this meeting."

Twenty minutes after the meeting, McCarthy located Alexander in the dressing area.

"I've solved your problem with our hitting. We're shipping your things to St Louis. You've been sold."

The press immediately praised McCarthy for his courage to stand up to star players who expected special treatment. As the team gained success, the sports journalists in Chicago began referring to him as "Marse," the old English term for master; every player had a task in every conceivable situation. The Cubs completed their ascent out of the doldrums with a World Series appearance in 1929, only to suffer a four-games-to-one trouncing at the hands of the powerful Philadelphia Athletics. Wrigley and team president Bill Veeck held McCarthy solely responsible for the team's failure. Veeck and McCarthy had regularly disagreed on handling on field matters, including how to use the pitcher. McCarthy complained to Wrigley about Veeck to no avail.

"Until you bring a championship to the Cubs, Veeck will oversee with vigilance your decisions on the field," Wrigley told McCarthy after a heated discussion.

Disgusted with Veeck's interference and the situation with the Cubs, he acquiesced to many of the decisions, even those which he knew were flawed. His days in Chicago were numbered. Pennant hopes slipped from the Cubs by Labor Day.

When it was evident the Cubs would not earn a rematch with the Athletics, with the influence of Wrigley who held the sport writers in his pocket, news reports suddenly vilified McCarthy. The press used such terms as colorless, dull, lacking in imagination on the field, a naïve career bush-leaguer with no capacity for handling the game at the professional level.

On September 24, Wrigley had Veeck relieve McCarthy of his duties. McCarthy, taking the high road, packed his belongings quietly. He saw no sense in creating a fuss, as the vulture-like Veeck hovered about.

McCarthy walked to Veeck, hand extended, and said, "Thank you and Mr. Wrigley for the opportunity with the Cubs."

"What do you think you'll do now?" Veeck inquired.

"I'm heading to Boston to talk to Quinn about a spot with the Red Sox. He and I became acquainted in the American Association."

McCarthy began to leave when Veeck called out, "I'd cancel the train ticket and get my money back. Quinn called me to ask why your contract was not going to be renewed. Put it this way. Good luck finding a high school coaching job." Veeck took great pleasure in driving the stake deeper into McCarthy's heart.

Quinn and the Red Sox passed on the man who would rank as one of the greatest managers of all time.

Fortunately for the Yankees, Ruppert and Barrow had not.

McCarthy's first order of business upon the team's return to the Bronx after spring training was to pin his baseball mantra to the wall of the home team locker room.

COMMANDMENTS TO GOOD BASEBALL PLAYING

- Nobody ever becomes a ballplayer by walking after a ball.
- You can never hit .300 unless you take the bat off your shoulder.
- An outfielder who throws in back of a runner is locking the barn after the horse is stolen.
- Keep your head up and you may not have to keep it down.
- When you start to slide, SLIDE. He who changes his mind may have to change a good leg for a bad one.
- Do not alibi on bad hops. Anyone can field the good ones.
- Always run them out. You never can tell.
- Do not quit.
- Try not to find too much fault with the umpires. You cannot expect them to be as perfect as you are.

• A pitcher who hasn't control hasn't anything

Gehrig asked Ruth as the team began preparing for the start of the 1931 season, 'You get a look at these rules?"

"Sure, I thought they were just guidelines, like the other ten. You know, 'Thou shalt not... uhmmm... steal, kill!"

"By the way, McCarthy wants to see you."

"About what, do you know?"

"Nope, it's probably nothing."

****

Joseph Vincent McCarthy had the reputation as a no-nonsense manager. He was familiar with Ruth's antics. For the last decade, he had had the run of this team. *No more*, McCarthy thought. Ruth would play by McCarthy's rules or not at all. McCarthy knew how to handle guys like Ruth, especially one who was making $80,000 when the country was falling into a deepening depression.

Ruth suddenly burst open the door to McCarthy's office , startling the manager, declaring loudly so that all those present in the locker room looked up and began to listen, "You wanted to see me, Skip?"

"Ruth, this is a private matter, so shut the door. But know this, Ruth. From here on out, whenever you enter my office, you *knock*."

All ears were on the office. The heard the acerbic volleys back and forth, as both men were screaming. The conversation had begun with a pointed statement aimed directly at Ruth.

"Since 1929, the pitching has been crumbling. And you're a big reason why! Plus, as far as your outfield play, you're done. You won't see the light of day in the field again."

Ruth yelled back at him as they stood nose to nose. McCarthy, a husky 5'9" and 190 pounds, did not back down from the larger Ruth. His Irish face fully red, his nostrils flared, he would not put up with any of Ruth's shenanigans. Unexpectedly the room became quiet in the standoff of wills.

Ruth, in a calm voice, said, "I'll just see the Colonel. He pays me way too much not to play." Without changing out of his uniform, Ruth marched out of Yankee Stadium, heading for Ruppert's Manhattan office.

Twenty minutes later he walked into Ruppert's plush office, his metal spikes clicking on the highly polished hardwood.

"Dammit, Ruth! What are you doing here? AND take those goddamn baseball shoes off before you carve up my floor," Ruppert said, jumping out of his leather chair.

Ruth stopped as he noticed another person in the room.

"Darling, shouldn't you be at the park getting ready for opening day tomorrow?"

"Claire, what the hell is going on?"

"The Colonel and I were having a nice chat about your future."

"My future, my future! Colonel, that guy you just hired to manage said he ain't playing me. I have plenty left. I've been working on a couple of new pitches that'll be easier on my arm. Plus I know more about the game than that midget Irishman."

"Maybe you know more about the game, Ruth, but he knows how to lead men. He's a leader. Work with McCarthy over next few years. Learn how to handle men in the boy's game. Show me you can handle your own life and you'll have your chance to manage."

"He sucked all the enthusiasm from the Cubs! He doesn't know how to handle ballplayers!"

"Ruth, the decision is made."

"I want 43 starts unless I tell you I cannot do it anymore. You do that, if you make me that one promise, you'll get the best from me every day. I'll walk the straight and narrow. I do this and you promise me a shot to manage."

"OK, I'll talk to McCarthy. Now get back to the park. Yes, and you'll get your chance." Ruth said goodbye to Claire and headed for the door, satisfied.

"Hey Colonel, can I borrow twenty bucks I need to pay the cabbie? I left the park in a rush."

"Are you kidding, I pay you a king's ransom, and you don't have cab fare?" Ruppert shook his head and handed him the money.

Claire burst out in uncontrollable laughter and Ruth followed suit.

"Claire, this is the man who wants responsibility over twenty-four other men," Ruppert joined in the laughter. "Good luck tomorrow. I know you enjoy beating the Red Sox."

"I plan on being on the mound."

Ruth was satisfied. Ruppert sealed the deal with a handshake. He'd manage the Yankees in the near future.

"Colonel, there is no man more loyal and true to his word than Babe. Do not disappoint him, or you'll have made an enemy of me as well."

"Only time will tell, Mrs. Ruth. Now good day and be on your way," Ruppert said in a firm, dismissive voice.

Claire was insulted. *Ruppert will never change his mind about Babe. The die is already cast*, she thought. Claire proceeded to put on her own coat and hat, not waiting for or expecting any assistance. She sharply turned away from Ruppert, leaving with no further words exchanged. At that moment, she realized Ruppert was just going to bleed all he could out of Ruth and then abandon him, as had everyone else. She vowed to do all she could to protect him.

Chapter 40
Ohio 1931

    Cy Young had grown weary of the demands of travelling for baseball events. By the mid-1920's, he had elected to hunker down on the farm in Peoli, Ohio. It had taken several years, but he was deep into farming: growing potatoes, raising livestock, and breeding dogs.

    Since 1928, each spring, just before the start of the baseball season, Young opened his home to several sportswriters with whom he had kept fond relationships. He enjoyed being around them, but they asked the same questions each time they met. Which teams does he think has a chance to win the pennant or the World Series? Who does he think the best pitcher in the league is? Does he think anyone can win 500 games? What batter does he fear the most?

    He had given the reporters fairly consistent and bland answers, but they kept coming back. The group would sit around the fireplace and ask him about his mementos. A few days before their arrival, he toted out several boxes of trophies, medals, cups, baseballs, pictures and other reminders of his playing days' accomplishments. Cy made sure each piece was handled carefully, then he would tell a colorful story. Today, as he pulled the crystal trophy from the storage box, he stared at it for several minutes, and then held it tightly to his chest. Finally, he placed his most precious piece dead center on the mantel. The inscription read, "Denton Young — 500th Win, July

19th 1910", Young cherished this achievement. With Walter Johnson now retired and Ruth fading, Young felt secure that 500 wins, not to mention his record total of 511, were both secure. Cy Young, the only player ever to win 500 games, yes, that how he wanted to everyone to remember him.

To Cy it didn't seem so long ago, but two decades had passed since he had recorded his final out in a professional baseball game. His most recent two years, though, had been especially draining. His father, the person he considered his lifelong best friend, had passed away, as had Robba's parents. The farmhouse now carried a vast emptiness, with only him and the woman he'd loved faithfully for nearly forty years as the sole occupants.

Robba walked slowly into the parlor. The distance from the kitchen seemed interminable today. She was now tired all of the time as she tried to hide the uncontrollable twitching in her hands from Cy. The doctor simply told her she needed to eat more red meat and beets.

She asked Cy as she walked into the parlor, "Dear, are you almost done? I want to put some dinner on."

"Sure am. Are you having a good day?" He had become concerned about her recent bouts with severe headaches and general fatigue.

"I am doing fine, I think. Lately everything just seems to taste so odd."

He was not relieved. He knew Robba was not being honest. *I guess there are worse things than one's taste buds being off,* Young thought to himself.

"What time do you expect everyone?"

"Chief," Young said, referring to Chief Zimmer, "I expect will arrive first, about 9:00 AM. He's always early. He sure likes the way you make flapjacks. Everyone else will be here around noon. Of course, they'll be ready for lunch."

"That's fine. I'll bake some bread and roast a couple of chickens. I've already made a few pies."

Cy rationalized, *No wonder she's so tired.*

Robba returned to the kitchen, rubbing her temples with her thumbs. Damn headaches just won't go away. Saying goodbye to both parents was an experience that ripped her up from the inside. She was not at all prepared for the resulting anxiety and heartache. Cy filled with joy when his friends came for their annual visit. She loved to see him this way. He liked remembering the days when the game was played for the purity of the sport, not for money. With money came greed, treachery and temptation. Visits with his baseball friends put him back to a simpler time. The spatula slipped from her hands, clanging on the floor. "Darn it," she said as she took a dish rag and wiped the sweat from her hands, *I hope I am not getting the influenza,* unaware a disease was destroying her from the inside, slowly.

Chapter 41

From the end of World War I through the next decade, enthusiasm abounded in the United States. Industries within the country expanded. Citizens hoarding money in their mattresses, driven by confidence, discovered a new venue for investments, corporate stocks. As profits increased, Americans anxious to capitalize on this assured way of making it rich quickly moved even more money into the market, driving prices higher. There seemed to be no end in sight. Even if they were short on cash, Americans bought on margin, borrowing the money to buy, using the stock as collateral. Everything was great so long as the stock prices continued to rise. On Thursday, October 24, 1929, all this changed as the US markets fell dramatically, completing a remarkable retreat by the following Tuesday.

By early 1931, economic conditions across the United States and Europe had steadily worsened. Healthy American men were driven into unemployment as business failures multiplied at a dramatic rate and business productivity across all of the industrialized countries contracted. Consternation amongst owners mounted over the impact the economic conditions would have on the game of baseball.

The 1930 World Series players' share was in excess of $300,000, an eye-popping amount for the public. As poverty in the country grew, owners feared a backlash to the exorbitant pay, expecting fan attendance to plummet. In anticipation, teams began to cut their administrative expenses as well as their coaching staffs. Salaries for aging players dropped, and many became unwilling to ink new contracts when faced with acute salary reductions.

Ed Barrow, the Yankee general manager, agreed with a contrarian position offered by Barney Dreyfuss, the owner of the Pittsburgh Pirates.

"Listen to what I am saying," Dreyfuss addressing his fellow owners, "When people are working, they do not have the time or energy to attend weekday games. The loafers who refuse to find work will congregate at the ballpark to discuss their woes. The sportswriters will follow our lead. We'll tell them that Americans don't come to the ballpark to discuss their miseries, but to get a respite from them. Baseball has come through tough times before and it will again. "

Dreyfuss lacked compassion for any Americans not able to find work. An immigrant from Germany, Dreyfuss, a workaholic, drove tirelessly to make his whiskey business a success. For health reasons, he sold the distillery to focus on the business of baseball. His vision for professional baseball had become reality. He understood that competition would drive fans to the ball park and fans buying tickets would increase profits. He also foresaw that the more affluent would pay a higher price for better seats, service and accommodations.

"Fans do not want to see amateurs or broken-down old men playing. If you provide an inferior product, the fans will turn away from the game."

Barrow announced, "The Yankees will have no problem getting their players under contract. The offers will be generous, given the conditions in country."

Dreyfuss was proved right, at least for the moment, as opening-day crowds broke all previous attendance records as over a quarter-million fans piled into the ball parks.

The skies had finally brightened on April 14th, 1931. For nearly a full week, thick dark rain clouds had blanketed much of the east. Now, it was opening day of the baseball season, all teams were equal in the standing and hope sprang eternal. The hot-stove chatter and feisty discussions soon would play out on the ball fields, becoming reality. Still until the first pitch, youngsters across the country imitated swings and pitching windups of their favorite players. They'd extol their accomplishments, brag about what they'd do to their opponents and fully expected them to win the World Series.

Yankee Stadium was not different. The crowds scurried down River Avenue, full of excitement. A sea of red, white and blue bunting adorned every corner of the stadium.. The Yankees expected the standing room crowd to exceed 78,000 fans. Across the streets, hundreds more fans watched from the rooftops and windows of the tenement buildings.

There was a new manager in the Bronx. He brought hope to the Bronx faithful that their beloved bombers would return to glory. Disappointment had besieged the fans, in the form of their failures in the pennant chase the previous two seasons. Through the back pages of the newspapers, McCarthy was portrayed as tough, but the Yankee clubhouse was chaotic with the abrupt departure of Shawkey. Players were upset with the treatment of their former teammate. Ruth was the most outspoken among the players in his animosity towards McCarthy.

"Shawkey may not have been a good manager, but he's a person who gave fifteen dedicated years to the Yankees. He should have been treated with more dignity." Ruth boiled with frustration, helpless that Ruppert had shown so little regard for a person important to his Yankee family. 'Is there no man alive not capable of abandoning those around him?' He left, head hanging, trying to grasp his future once time completed its pillage of his physical abilities.

Ruppert and Barrow had paid a visit to McCarthy two days earlier, unaware of the festering storm. The pair was unaware that their botched handling of Shawkey had damaged their leadership of the Yankees.

"I will see him off to hell before I play that overgrown brat. He's fractured the clubhouse, which undermines my authority and hurts our chances for success. I may as well just quit now."

"Calm down, Joe," Barrow spoke, 'The fans come to see the big fella play, not a little guy manage. Having him on the field puts tooshies in the seats."

"Maybe you guys need someone else to manage your club!" McCarthy stated, reacting, feeling as though he was being boxed into a corner. He decided to push back and force Barrow's hand on who was in charge.

Ruppert interceded, "Joe, we hired you to lead this team back to the top. But when it comes to Ruth, you need to back off a bit. There are two things you two have in common. The most important thing for the Yankees is that you each hate to lose. So you'll pitch him according to the plan he and I discussed. Ed, let's go, we got a lot to do before opening day."

Ruppert turned to leave when McCarthy spoke, "What's the second thing, Colonel?"

Barrow laughed. To him, the answer was obvious.

"Why, Joe, when you look at Ruth, well, you see yourself. Not in stature, of course, but you're both thick-headed and want everything according to your own ground rules."

Ruppert had made good on his promise. McCarthy succumbed to the pressure and installed Ruth as the opening-day pitcher and made sure he was a regular fixture in the rotation.

"How's the arm feeling?" Bill Dickey asked Ruth during their pre-game ritual of tossing the ball back and forth for thirty minutes. The twenty-four-year old, now the Yankee regular catcher, had wisdom beyond his youth.

"Feeling good, kid, and very good." Ruth was amazed, "To think that a scrawny little broad could help me so much." There was no strain now in his left arm when he delivered a pitch. All the pain in his arm was gone, thanks to Jackie

Mitchell's tutelage. "Almost like I feel like I'm a kid like you again."

"Yeah, Babe, a kid again. Quite a crowd we have today."

"Let's not disappoint them."

The Yankees doubled up the Red Sox in a 6-3 win. Ruth went the distance, mesmerizing batters with his new array of pitches. He mixed in straight fast pitches and curves, but his new assortment possessed the elusiveness of June bugs as the balls floated, danced and darted on their way to the plate, tantalizing the hitters with promises of connecting squarely, then breaching those promises at the very last moments. The Red Sox did manage three runs, but sent many more weakly-hit balls into the field.

The Yankees performed much better in 1930, winning 94 games and scoring over a thousand runs, but in the end they were helpless to stop Philadelphia. The Athletics caught fire in May and never slowed down. The Connie Mack-led juggernaut pulled steadily away, winning the pennant over the frustrated and divided Yankee team that finished a distant second, thirteen games behind.

As spring grew closer to summer and the weather grew hotter, so did the tempers inside the Yankee club house. The veterans aligned solidly behind Ruth's lead, not supporting McCarthy on field moves, especially when they didn't work. McCarthy wondered if some players were giving their all in the execution of play. Twice in the last week, players missed a bunt attempt, causing the lead runner to be thrown out in an aborted stolen base attempt. Ruth openly questioned McCarthy's every move. He told anyone who would take the time to listen that McCarthy's smothering style would not let the best in players come out. Players just needed to go at it naturally.

Finally the pot boiled over. On May 23rd, young Dickey requested time off to return home to Louisiana to handle urgent family matters. Dickey was impressive in his handling pitchers and he'd become a steady bat in the middle of the lineup. The Yankees were preparing to start a crucial series against the first place Philadelphia team the next day. Ruppert, with the needs of the club as always placed above those of the individual, demanded McCarthy tell the youngster to stay put unless a death were to occur. McCarthy argued fiercely.

"These players are not chattel, not property, but *people*. Treat each of them with a bit a dignity." McCarthy assured Ruppert that Dickey would play better when he handled what he needed to handle and was ready to return. Veterans on the team, such as Lazzeri, Gehrig, Combs and Pennock, when learning about the intensity with which McCarthy had gone to bat for the youngster, softened their stance on the manager, deciding he deserved a chance. They were successful and persuaded the rest of the team to give the new skipper a chance.

Pennock speaking out in a clubhouse meeting, "This guy hates coming in second. You see how he is in a petty argument; imagine how he feels about baseball games."

The only remaining dissenter was Ruth. His resentment ran so deep that he vowed to himself he would never accept McCarthy as a Yankee manager. His teammates gradually lost tolerance with Ruth's immature rants about McCarthy's ineptitude as a manager. McCarthy's mature handling of the situation with Dickey had the unexpected side effect of driving a wedge between Ruth and his teammates. Looking at him in a different light, they saw him as a selfish man who'd hurt the team more than he'd helped. McCarthy saw Ruth as a spoiled oaf with declining skills and increasing waistline. Ruth, isolated, lost any chance the players would support him in the ouster of McCarthy. Fortunately, Ruth had Claire on his side. Husband and wife, every chance they got, continued their frontal assault on McCarthy.

Between May 24th and May 29th, during Dickey's absence, the Yankees lost five of the six games played against the Athletics, dropping out of serious contention for the pennant. Ruth and McCarthy survived only by ignoring each other; neither person was willing enough to give an inch.

As the 1931 season and the Yankee championship dreams slipped away, Ruth increased the ferocity of his criticism of McCarthy. During the final weeks of the season, Ruppert and Barrow told Ruth he was no longer welcome in their offices unless invited. They were exhausted by his relentless assault. Fed up, Barrow asked the Colonel, "Maybe it's time we shopped Ruth around."

"Not on your life. He's the one the fans come to see. Gehrig and Dickey are solid citizens and terrific players. Certainly they're gentleman:

professional, etc. etc. etc. But they are all so dull they just lack curb appeal. Ruth draws the common man. In him they see hope. They feel connected to someone bigger than a man. Not in a religious way. No, he's someone who, when he is around, gives them a sense of immortality. We'll keep Ruth until we have dragged every single dollar out of him. Not just for us either. The league needs him as a draw in the other cities."

The Yankees led the league in attendance, drawing nearly one million to the big park in the Bronx; the fans rallied around the team's core of lethal sluggers. Lou Gehrig was a rock; he had not sat out a game in several years. Lazzeri, Dickey, Combs, Chapman and Sewell could turn a close game into a rout very quickly.

The Yankees were fortunate to have two favorable factors which helped keep their attendance from falling. They had the most vibrant market in the country, New York City, and they had Babe Ruth.

Although Ruth's prowess as a hitter had faded, Ruth's new-found youth in pitching and the chance that he might hit a bomb out of the park drew the fans. Yankee Stadium was his home. Ruth performed more than adequately, finishing third in the league in victories, with 27. Hitting was different; he had a lingering pain in his right wrist that hurt the entire year. Whenever he swung and made contact with the ball, a deep stabbing sensation shot up through to his elbow. At times he could barely maintain a grip on the bat. No doctors or treatment helped. Ruth came to the slow realization the doctors had been right. He was not indestructible. He was experiencing the expected long-term effects of the repeated injuries: arthritis and nerve damage. Never again would he generate enough power to pop a ball out of the park with any regularity. Thousands flocked to him before and after each game, seeking a handshake, wave or acknowledgement from him. The scene was repeated at train stations, hotel lobbies, and ball parks in each city the Yankees visited. He was regarded at the greatest and most-feared batter the game had ever seen. He held the record of the most home runs in a season and in a career. He was inching closer to the pitching record of lifetime wins, already holding the single-season mark.

Dreyfuss had been only partially correct in his assessment of how the depression would impact baseball game attendance. People did go to ballparks as an escape from or a tonic for the reality of the deepening economic hardships, but this held true until their money ran out. For the teams in the smaller cities within the industrial belt, fans were less tolerant of men being paid 'ungodly' sums to play a game. Attendance waned quicker, except for the pennant-winning teams in St Louis and Philadelphia. Fans' enthusiasm matched their team's success. It was a glimmer of hope, a ray of happiness — temporary relief from the ills of life. In these cities, fans swarmed the parks in record numbers. At a game in Philadelphia, more fans were turned away than attended a late August contest at Shibe Park.

Barrow had invited McCarthy to his office to talk about the season and the schism in the clubhouse. McCarthy had a sense that Barrow was not fully on board with keeping Ruth, and maybe between the two of them, they would have success in convincing Ruppert that Ruth was preventing the team for reaching its full potential. Neither had judged Ruppert correctly.

"Second place, Joe, second place! Your approach isn't working. You'll have one more year. If there's still no championship in New York, I'll send you packing back in Class A ball in Louisville. Back where you started. Maybe you're a better fit with bush leaguers. That's if they'll have you! This is a championship team, not a second place club. You and Ruth need to find a way to play nice." Ruppert barked at McCarthy. "When I hired you I was well aware of the reputation you had of browbeating starters or driving them off. I'll have none of that. Maybe Mack will hire you; he's getting ready to dismantle his club again."

McCarthy clamped down on his jaws; he didn't want to say anything he might regret later. What team would want him if he were fired from the most prestigious managerial position in baseball?

Barrow spoke briefly, "Colonel, let's think about this in business terms. Ruth's value is going to decline, maybe."

"Shut up, Ed, Ruth is staying until he has no value and cannot hurt us any. So get used to him being around. Joe, you go win a series. Until you do, no further conversations about Ruth."

As the players packed their lockers at the end of the long campaign, Ruth addressed them, "Well, McCarthy was called to the Colonel's office. I imagine he's getting reamed right about now. He'll be gone by sundown." Very few turned to look at Ruth; they had had just about enough of the one-man war he waged.

"Are you proud of our finish to the season, Babe? None of us are satisfied. When times got bad, Marse stuck up for every one of us. The Colonel was ready to clean house, just like Mack does in Philly. But McCarthy told him he could win with this team, including you! You're dumber than a mud fence," Dickey said, speaking with an exaggerated Cajun drawl.

"Why, you little squirt, how dare you even talk back to me?" Ruth thrust forward, starting to rush the young catcher.

"Don't, Babe," Gehrig said as he and Lazzeri blocked his charge. "We got the kid's back. Go finish what you're doing and get out of our clubhouse."

"Hold on, there, fellas."

"No, *you* hold on. We have all the talent in the world on this squad, but Babe, you ain't been pulling the oars with the rest of us. Since '28, you've been sinking and you're dragging us with you. No more, Babe, we're behind the skipper."

These were Ruth's buddies, the guys he'd gotten drunk with, played cards with, caroused with; they all enthusiastically rallied to the youngster, patting him on the back. There was solidarity, not only in support of the manager, but in their disappointment with Ruth's antics. Dickey and Gehrig had secured the reins as the clubhouse leaders.

The scurrying to complete final preparations was done; Babe's teammates were ready to depart. So-longs and well-wishes were passed to each other. Most would not talk to each other over the winter. Only Gehrig, a man Ruth had not warmed to, came over to wish Ruth off. Amid the buzz of a noisy clubhouse, Ruth stood in silence, frozen in front of his locker. He held in his hands the bat he'd held so many times, but today the bat seemed heavier. He wondered if he really had let the Yankees down. Watching his buddies, one after another, depart, none gave any acknowledgment of him. Occasionally there was an uneasy look in his direction by a pair of darting eyes that moved away even more quickly. As the scene played out, Ruth softly closed his eyelids and held them; maybe it was just a dream. After several minutes, he opened his eyes. Then nausea gripped him; it was real. Ruth was on the outside looking in once more, alone and abandoned by those he loved most. The room began to spin; the fear of loneliness, deeply unsettling, struck him once more.

Chapter 42

On October 4, 1932, thirty-eight thousand disappointed fans rushed home from the intimate setting of Wrigley Field. The Cubs had offered very little resistance to the Yankees.

Champagne corks popped within the Yankee clubhouse. The Yankee juggernaut dismantled the Cubs pitching staff. In what proved an anti-climactic four-game sweep, the Yankees performed up to their nickname, scoring an average of nine runs a game. The 13-6 win in game four added an exclamation point to the season. The Yankees ran away from their competitors in the American League and did not slow down in trouncing the best the National League had to offer.

Ruth was barely able to keep rookie Johnny Allen out of the starting rotation, thanks to Ruppert interceding with McCarthy yet again.

As the season in which the Yankees won 107 games drew to close, reporters naturally asked McCarthy who he thought was the best player on his team. "Why, Ruth, of course, he's the best in the game," the manager responded without hesitation. "Ruth, unquestionably, Ruth."

Ruth rubbed his chin quizzically as he read McCarthy's comments. He did not expect this sort of accolade from a man he despised, whom he felt had stolen his future. Sticking to his personal vow, Ruth had not spoken to McCarthy in nearly two years. He doubted the sincerity of the statement.

Ruth did not disappoint Ruppert's expectations. Once again, he finished among the top five in pitchers with twenty-five victories. He was losing ground as the best left-hander in baseball, with Lefty Grove posting a second-straight stellar season. Ruth was now an afterthought when it came to hitting, but it didn't matter. Fans still packed the stadium and the other major league parks when he came a-calling.

The Yankees continued their domination into the series. The Cubs, after losing two straight in the Bronx, were frustrated in their play and glad to be heading home. Player- manager Charlie Grimm was confident that once back in their own turf they could win game three.

The series rivalry had been intense, with vulgarities being flung between the clubs with much the same frequency as the pitches thrown to batters. The primary targets of the Cubs' barbs were their ex-manager McCarthy and Ruth, who was now just a ghost of himself as a hitter. Profanity and tempers rose to the threats of physical challenges.

Veeck and Wrigley fueled the intensity, hoping to knock the Yankees off their game. They were helped by the power of the written word, courtesy of the hometown press. The Chicago newspapers served as Wrigley's personal bully pulpit. The Yankees were depicted as cold villains, cutthroat dirty, and chumps and washed up players. The team was empty, nothing more than a shell of its once-powerful self, the beneficiary of Mack's dismantling of the Athletics.

Ruth and McCarthy, oddly, were now thrust together as evil twins.

The Yankees led by one single run in the pivotal game three. Ruth stepped to the plate in the top of the fifth with one out and the bases empty. He had struggled in the game, both hitting and pitching, so far.

The Cubs had hit an ineffective Ruth hard through the first four innings. Outstanding defensive plays kept the Cubs from scoring more runs. McCarthy went to the mound in the bottom of the fourth with runners in scoring position. The ensuing discussion between Ruth and McCarthy was barely civil and very animated.

"I may as well take you out now. You're hitting in the next inning, so it'll be like replacing an out."

Ruth "I said you ain't replacing me! The ball will start moving when the wind dies down some." He held the ball tightly and folded his arm behind his back, preventing McCarthy from reaching for it.

Dickey stuck out his mitt giving himself just enough room so he could step between Ruth and McCarthy, if needed, before the situation escalated.

"Skip, just go back to the dugout, Ruth can get them out." Dickey said, while deep inside he wondered *what the hell am I doing? Ruth ain't got nothing!*

Ruth had tempered his reaction to the situation temporarily; he knew that one more visit from McCarthy would require Ruth's removal from the game by rule.

The next pitch Ruth delivered was driven hard to Lazzeri's right, toward second base, sure to go through to centerfield. A certain base hit from the sound. Lazzeri had the surest set of hands of any infielder in the game. During his teen years, he served as an apprentice boilermaker in an iron foundry. For hours on end, he'd catch an endless flow of glowing rivets, red hot from the furnace, and flip them on to an awaiting steamfitter. Desperately Lazzeri lunged, flying his left arm over to his right with a unexpected quickness, snaring the ball on its first bounce. Scrambling to his knees he fired it sidearm to first. The throw, a little off-line, was scooped up deftly by Gehrig, dashing any Cubs' hopes. Dickey rushed out to Babe and patted him on the back. Ruth, regardless of Dickey's jubilance, knew he had been saved by Lazzeri and Gehrig.

Nothing comes more naturally to hometown fans and players then taunting competitors whose skills no longer matched their reputation or when there is discord within the ranks of the opponent. It was no different on the north side of Chicago. In the top of the fifth, Cub fans had a chance at both.

A rhythmic chorus of boos was delivered as Ruth strolled to the plate. He rarely drove the ball hard. The blue-collar fans who made less than six thousand dollars a year started to resent the highest-paid professional baseball player. The man, who had once attracted thousands to come see him drive the ball out of sight, now attracted those same crowds hoping to see him fail at the plate.

Charlie Root looked in at Ruth. Ready, he delivered the first pitch to Ruth, high and away. Everyone watching the game expected ball one as the call. The umpire, thrusting his right arm, proclaimed, strike one. Immediately, Ruth starting jawing with the umpire, as a storm of trash and rolled-up cups descended on him from the upper level stands. The Cubs players, now on the top step of the dugout, really started giving the verbal jousts to Ruth. He dished it right back with more venom.

"Ruth, what gives, you can't see any more, either? "A voice shot from the Cub dugout.

"Sure enough can see your ugly face; you look just as ugly as your sis."

"Are you ready, Ruth?" Root inquired, "I'll be quick in sending you back to your rocking chair, old man."

"Just throw the damn ball over."

Ruth readied for the next pitch, rubbing dirt on this hands and bat. Root's second pitch swooped an inch above Ruth shoe tops. Ruth stepped from the batter's box, a flash of the right arm followed: strike two! The exhilarated patrons erupted. Cubs' fans were showering the infield with even more litter. Fans who were not throwing things were slamming their wooden seats up and down. The Cubs players began tossing the errant trash that found its way close to the dugout in the direction of home plate. Ruth became incensed, and threw down his bat,

"You useless SOB's, come on over here," he said, and he marched toward the home team's dugout.

"Settle down, big fella," they're not aiming at you, the Cubs catcher said, trying to defuse the tinderbox. Gabby Hartnett jumped into Ruth's path.

The next comment infuriated Ruth further, "Yeah, you fat slob, go back up and try to hit. You're just a no-skill nigger."

Harnett immediately threw his arms around Ruth's barrel chest and held tight. "He didn't mean nothing."

"Hell he didn't! I'll pop his head like a zit!"

McCarthy had charged from the dugout, running over to confront Charlie Grimm, who was playing first base.

"Get your bunch of hoodlums under control or we'll walk and file a protest with the league."

"Go away, McCarthy. I'll manage my team the way I like. You go tend to your own onions."

McCarthy inched closer to Grimm when the bigger Grimm without further provocation shoved him down. McCarthy quickly scrambled to regain his feet and readying for a confrontation with the larger man. McCarthy realized a much larger figure stood blocking the path to Grimm.

"Now try that on someone your own size." McCarthy heard a serious but familiar voice say.

"Ruth?" McCarthy, with his fall, hadn't noticed as Ruth had hustled up the first base line to the side of his manager.

"Stay right there, skipper. Come on, Grimm, try me. You and the rest of the toads in your dugout, let's see what kind of men you really are."

"Go bat, Ruth."

"Didn't think so, you chicken spit. You lay a hand on my manager again or any of my boys, they'll need to put you on a soup diet. And Root, if you're thinking of throwing the next pitch into my ribs, you'll be remembering my fist in your mouth until next Tuesday."

The umpires restored order several minutes later. Ruth looked out toward Root, who was wind milling both arms in an effort to stay loose. Thirty-eight thousand fans roared a chorus of boos directed at Ruth and his Yankees. The jeers and insults were growing louder with each passing minute before the action continued.

Taunts about Ruth's age, physical appearance and heritage emanated from the stands.

Ruth stepped into the batter's box, intensely watching Root, who began to get ready.

Harnett spoke, "You ready, ol' man?"

Just as Root began his windup, "Time," yelled the Babe. The umpire thrust his hands into the air, signaling a stop in play. Babe stepped from the batter's box, looking around the stadium at the fans now rabid with anger. Suddenly two dozen lemons were rolling and bouncing across the grass in the direction of Ruth.

"Grimm, get your team in order or I'll toss you," the home umpire, now frustrated, yelled from behind his mask.

Hartnett chirped, "Now that was an ice-breaker."

Ruth picked up a lemon and fired it just above the head of two standing Cub players.

"We'll see how funny it is after I hit one out."

The Cubs players, once again all standing outside the dugout, continued the verbal assault on Ruth, trying to keep him distracted.

"Are you ready, Ruth?" the home plate umpire asked.

Ruth looked out again. First glancing at Root, and then glancing to the deepest part of the outfield. With the index finger of his right hand, he pointed toward centerfield. "Charlie, the next pitch you'll be watching sail past the flag pole. The next pitch, so put it over."

It had been a long time since Ruth had had this much adrenaline running through him. His right forearm, for the moment, was free from pain. He saw the ball cleanly leave Root's hand. From the spin, a straight ball was on the way and coming in belt-high. With an easy but mighty swing, reminiscent of his youthful days, the ball exploded out toward centerfield, carrying above the stands, floating to the right of the giant scoreboard, past the flag pole and finally landing on the corner of Waveland and Sheffield Avenues. Seventy-six thousand eyes were glued, in awe, following the flight of the ball. Ruth strode quickly around the bases, not taunting or showboating in any way.

A controlled professional crossed the plate, where he met Gehrig with an easy handshake.

McCarthy, also at the plate, was jumping as if crazed; he started hugging the big guy.

"McCarthy," said a startled Ruth, stunned since managers never left the dugout to greet a player after a home run.

"Thank you, Babe, thank you."

Through a simple exchange, unexpectedly, he and McCarthy had had each other's back. Yankee players clapped and congratulated Ruth.

Wounds were stitched over, stemming the emotional bleeding for now.

The Yankees completed the destruction of the Cubs the very next day, putting an exclamation point on the comeback season. It had been four years since they had tasted a victory this sweet.

During the regular season, Babe enjoyed eating out in the South side of Chicago. The cacophony of aromas wafted through the maze of food stands featuring hot dogs, stuffed chili peppers, spiced Italian beef and Cuban-spiced rubbed pork chop sandwiches. But with the series played on the more elegant North side, Ruth decided on a quiet dinner at Via Lago Café, about a half-mile northeast of Cubs Field. From there, it would only be a short cab ride to the Edgewater Hotel.

The weather in Chicago cooperated; there was a hint of warmth still resident in the breeze coming off Lake Michigan. Claire and Ruth covered the distance to Wilson Avenue in less than fifteen minutes.

Ruth grabbed the chrome-handled front door, allowing Claire to enter first. She convinced Babe to have a quiet dinner, promising to join the celebration at the hotel later.

"Why, Babe, how did you ever find this place?" Claire was surprised; this was not the typical smoke-filled, noisy speakeasy Babe was drawn to. Upon walking through the doors, her eyes were immediately drawn to the long mahogany bar, with mirrors behind glass shelving. A row of chrome four-legged barstools covered in tan vinyl stretched neatly from one end to the other. Two idle bartenders stood wiping glasses in an effort to keep their boredom in check.

The tuxedoed maitre'd accompanied them to their table in the far corner as Claire admired the mosaic of red, yellow and green tiles.

"Marse suggested it. Told me they have a good steak. Plus, it's on the way to the hotel."

"This is wonderful; it's been a long couple of years. We sure need a break."

"I am Roberto, your server. What I can get you?" a middle-aged olive-skinned man asked.

"A couple of cold ones for me, and a glass of your best white wine for the lady," Babe said.

"Thanks, Babe, but I'd prefer a dry martini," added Claire. "Babe, you had a great season, and what a World Series! The Yankees could not have won without you. What more do you think you need to accomplish in baseball?"

"Hon, I want to manage, preferably the Yankees. I know I can be a real good manager."

"You realize, Babe, in winning this series you may have sealed your own fate. McCarthy could be in place for a while.

"Claire, if we lose it's my fault for not delivering enough on the field. If we win, McCarthy stays. I'm between the devil and the deep blue sea. I don't have many years left, so I have to put my trust in Ruppert that he'll live up to his promise and give me a shot."

"Do you trust the Colonel?'

Ruth burst out laughing, Clair followed along. "I don't know, but I'm coaching some at third base, so that's an indication that he's at least thinking about it. Well, at least I'm making a hell of a lot of money. So long as people want to come see me play, it'll stay that way."

Ruth was making short order of his porterhouse steak when Roberto spoke, "There is a gentleman here that wants to speak to you. Normally, well, we have a policy not to interrupt those dining with us, but he says it is important."

"Sorry to interrupt your dinner, Ruth, but we have a problem."

"Sit down, Judge, please. Now what is so important as to intrude on my dinner?"

Chapter 43
Ohio 1960

"Kid, you want a few more dogs?" the old man asked Pepe. "I can't believe they're charging thirty-five cents for a hot dog."

"I can get a package of ten down in the neighborhood for $1.10. Players are just making too much money. Some players are asking for as much as one hundred thousand dollars to play. It's a child's game, and that will be the end of the sport. A man will not be able to take his children to a see a game. I make six thousand in a good year. Sir, you've already spent too much on him."

"Where is it you live?"

"North Hill, Akron, Italian section."

"Italians — some great players, those Italians."

"I played a touch of ball when I was younger. Pepe here plays in the little league."

"Good, kid, what position you play"

"Second, second base," said the youngster.

"Stick with it, kid. Let's get some pop and a few more dogs each. Don't worry, my treat. Baseball's not going away, no matter what they pay players; Americans just love to watch a baseball game."

Chapter 44

The depression deepened across the United States in 1932, with no signs of abating. Banks defaulted, closing their doors at the rate of nearly four a day. For unemployed Americans, there was little prospect of work on the horizon. Politicians were predicting more jobs by late summer 1933 while in the meantime preaching austerity efforts to American families.

Baseball finally realized it was not immune to the effects of the economic free fall. It may have been true that Americans did seek solace at ballparks, but the depression was sustained and money had run out for too many families.

The New York Evening Post ran the following headline in late September 1932, intentionally ahead of the opening of the World Series.

"1933 Baseball Season Doomed"

"The 1933 season is in serious jeopardy. Teams not located on the Atlantic coastline are in dire financial straits due to the greed of players, owners and the commissioner himself.

Mountain Landis draws a salary more than the best players in the game. Players' salaries continue to rise with no regard for the out-of-work Americans who scrape pennies together to watch them play. Baseball is on the precipice of a financial collapse as fans will continue to stay away."

Attendance in every city had declined; especially hard hit were Cleveland, Pittsburg and St. Louis. The harsh reality of the depression had finally touched home plate for owners. Fans kept coming, but they migrated from the dollar grandstands to the two-bit bleachers.

An emergency meeting of the owners was held in Chicago after the Evening Post article. All owners attended except Ruppert and Huston, they remained in New York and sent Ed Barrow instead.

Unanimous agreement was reached that the salary of every player and employee would be decreased by at least twenty percent. All agreed that this action would return most clubs to black ink, but it had not accomplished anything for the fans. One day a week, the price for bleacher seats was cut in half. There was a return of the five-cent hot dog and ham sandwich at the parks.

Some owners were worried about players' reactions to the salary cuts, but without any competing league, there was plenty of spare talent to go around if they elected not to accept the new financial terms. What the owners were more concerned with was star players' ability to make money in other ways outside of the game, such as barnstorming, which had remained popular.

The final item on the agenda was to deal with was the commissioner's salary and the cost of baseball's governing office. This was delicate because of the power Landis had secured in his agreement. Under the terms of his contract, he could not be fired. Further, he and he alone determined his compensation.

Comiskey spoke first, "Judge, the owners have seen profits reduced, players will take a cut. We believe that for the good of the game, you need to accept a smaller paycheck and elimination of the clause that allows you to determine your compensation and evaluation of performance."

"Stop right there, Charlie, you came crawling to me when your league was infested with vermin which nearly ruined baseball. I gave you the terms that I would accept to fix baseball. You accepted it and no one put a gun to your head."

Comiskey elected not to debate the issue, "The owners have decided to go back to the Lasker Plan." That plan called for a three-man commission of neutral but influential men. Albert Lasker, a part-owner of the Cubs, had authored the plan.

"A decade ago, you did not muster enough support for that plan."

"Well, times have changed, Judge. To be frank, several of the owners do not agree with all of your highhandedness. Plus, some of your decisions appear biased. We know you have a history of bias in major court decisions." Several of Landis' landmark judicial rulings had been overturned due to a lack of any legal basis for them. Landis clenched his jaw, accentuating his sharp features more than normal. With his wavy hair more wild than usual, to many owners, he appeared a menacing and demonic figure.

"Well, the contract is ironclad. There is nothing you can do. I guess you can take it to court, let some of my friends make the ruling. We're done here. Goodnight, gents."

"Stay seated," the normally-reserved Connie Mack spoke up. "I have dismantled my team so I could make money. I do not take a salary. The press is raising a ruckus about salaries and the cost of baseball's administration. You're shoveling against the tide. Judge, we've hired the best East Coast lawyers for advice. You know there's more than one way to skin a cat. If you don't go along, well, we'll simply disband both leagues due to economic reasons. Then a new league will be formed. The new league will have no need of your services. Judge, don't let your pride stand in the way of what makes sense, *for all of us.*"

Owners stood united against Landis and voted a salary reduction of sixty percent. Otherwise, they would vote to end the Landis reign as sole head of baseball and return to a triumvirate comprised of unpaid owners in a new league, even if it resulted in a long, contentious law suit with Landis.

Landis thought himself above the premise that 'Power tends to corrupt and absolute power corrupts absolutely.' He was put into this position by a corrupt sport, to fix a corrupt sport. He needed ultimate authority to do so. If he were held accountable to owners, how could he possibly rule without bias? A long and arduous argument ensued. Legal threats were tossed back and forth until Landis finally conceded to a forty-percent reduction. He believed the owners had run a bluff, but if they carried through he could lose the argument. The judge was resentful of the actions of the owners; he would extract his revenge, especially from those he disliked. When the agreements were drawn up, he reaffirmed the inability of the owners to fire him and introduced a condition that he would never be paid less than any player and that any vote to disband the league would require his approval and the approval of the United States congress. He not only controlled how the game was played but who played baseball at any professional level.

Landis wasn't simply the commissioner; he was baseball's supreme ruler, the emperor of the game.

Chapter 45

"Good evening, Mrs. Ruth, sorry to interrupt your dinner, but Mr. Ruth and I have some urgent baseball business."

"Mr. Landis, I mean…," Claire began.

An edgy Landis contemptuously cut Claire off before she could correct what she'd said, "*Judge, or Your Honor*, if you will kindly address me accordingly," Landis said, cutting Claire off mid-word standing on his own pomp.

"Well, you are just so formal. All right then, *Judge* it is. What can be so urgent with baseball matters that it requires interrupting a romantic dinner between a husband and wife? The series just finished. Can't this wait for the dust to settle and for us to conclude our evening at the end of a long, hard season?"

Landis curled the edge of his mouth and tightened his jaw, causing his features to become more chiseled than normal.

"If it could, I would not be here, and I wish to talk to Mr. Ruth alone. Women have little understanding of business matters," Landis said, speaking in the tone generally saved for the admonishment of a child.

"Now hold on, *your honor*. That's no way to speak to a lady, especially when that lady is my wife."

"Well, I guess, then, she can hear this, so long as she does not speak up."

"Why, you small-minded little man!" Claire stood and excused herself. "I am going to powder my nose. Perhaps in the ladies' room I can breathe a bit of fresher air." She arose from the table, "Babe, you deal with this wretched ogre of a man. Hopefully, you can conclude with this beast before I have returned."

"Now see what you've gone and done, Judge. You do not want her mad at you," Ruth continued, "Now what is it you want with me so we can continue our dinner without your intrusion?"

"Take a look at this," Landis dropping the newspaper he had carried for two weeks onto the table.

Ruth snatched it up, and stared at the headline. "I tell you, Judge, I simply pay this kind of stuff no mind."

"Well, I see he is still here, so we break bread with the devil." Claire reseated herself, quietly shifting into her chair.

"Hon, what do you make of this?"

"This is business. I doubt your lovely bride will make any contributions to this discussion."

"Well, Judge, you'd be surprised. She does pretty good managing my affairs."

"This is much bigger than just you, Babe. This is about sustaining baseball's popularity in American culture."

"Hold on, Judge, I want to hear what she's thinking."

"Thank you, dear."

"Before you waste too much of your time reading this article, let me tell you what you're going to read in next week's Sporting News if Ruth does not agree with what I suggest. It seems as though thousands and thousands of fans across the country are angry at how much money Ruth, here, makes. Yes, the Yankees had offered Mr. Ruth a contract for $50,000, more than ten times more than the average working man gets. You're going to read how a selfish Babe Ruth summarily refused to sign for anything less. The publicity of you snubbing what is a veritable fortune to many will cascade even more fans against you. Ruth, you will become public enemy number one for the many poor-off Americans. With your skills fading, the hatred toward you will grow more intense."

"Judge, the series just ended. I ain't been offered no such contract. I ain't turned down no such offer."

"That may be the case, but certainly the fans don't know that. They only know what they read, and what they read is what I want the newspapers to tell them. So if you are thinking of barnstorming, well, after reading this, I do not think there'll be many takers. Plus, I will suspend you and America will be on my side."

"I should rip your head off."

"Relax, dear; let me talk to the judge. I know I am just a simple-minded woman, but what is it you want? Let's see if we can find some common ground."

"Claire, there is no common ground! I know a lot more about the judge than he knows. I've never told anyone this. I've held certain things inside me for a long, long time. He protects certain players who gamble on the game, those he likes, but throws others out. I saw you at the series back in '21, all cozied up with Rothstein. Now, I asked myself, what is the commissioner of baseball doing with a man like Rothstein? Then, out of nowhere, my thrower suddenly goes soft. How about the other time when my outfielders who ain't made but a handful of errors all year between them suddenly can't catch a fly or throw? Don't look so surprised, there, Judge. Claire, you ever ask why, after there's a brawl, the judge is harsher punishing the Jewish players than the others? If you don't believe me, go ask Buddy Meyer." (Buddy Meyer was a Jewish ballplayer repeatedly suspended for his participation in fights with other players. Most of them occurred after repeated anti-Semitic comments directed at him. The non-Jewish provocateurs received no league discipline.) "And he wants no part of Negroes in the major leagues. Ain't that so, Judge? He doesn't want professional baseball tarnished with Negroes or Mexicans. No, this is how it will be, *Your Honor*. Ruth will take a small cut, just enough to make more than you. I am going to take my barnstorming outside of the country, to Japan. You will endorse this as an act of diplomacy and the spreading of American baseball beyond our borders. Since we are going out of the country, we'll be taking the best of the Negro players with us. I plan on being in this game for a very long time. I hear the owners are growing tired of your dictatorship. This is your call, Judge. Do you want to gamble or can we work together to each get what we want? "

"Ruth, I see you've grown up a bit. You're finally wearing the pants."

"Judge, I think I got two seasons before I'm forty. You're going to tell Ruppert that after the '34 season. I will be named as the player manager."

"Ruth, I'll tell you what I want from you. I want baseball to expand across the country. I am not going to fight your barnstorming. Take baseball across the country; let the fans come out to see the great Ruth and New York's Murderer's Row. Explore the western frontier. I want stops in two Nevada towns. There's interest in that area and money is flowing into their economy. Plus there are New York connections. Folks will be plenty excited."

Ruth, puzzled by the Landis request, nodded in a simple but dismissive manner toward the judge. Landis brushed back his bushy hair and got up from the table, exiting as smoothly as he had arrived.

Chapter 46

On January 15th, 1934, Ruth emerged from his room and descended as far as possible down the fairy tale-like staircase with its curved white granite railings. A twenty-piece brass band, originally positioned in the vestibule to flank the stairs, now blocked Ruth's descent as the crowd of nearly six thousand crowded the portico. A hero's welcome was being given Ruth on his return home after spending six weeks in Japan. The barnstorming was a success. Americans who were unfamiliar with Asian cultures were anxious to hear from Ruth about his trip. Ruppert and Landis had arranged for the homecoming celebration.

The low ceilings and heavily marbled lobby concentrated the sound; there was nothing to absorb any of it. The noise level from the band and the constant refrains of 'Roll Out the Barrel,' the adopted Yankees theme song, not to mention the cheering throng, were deafening.

Ruppert extended a hand to his star, the most famous face in baseball, at the sixth step from the bottom. Standing about four feet above the crowd, Ruth and Ruppert savored the adulation. The Yankees had financed the trip to the Far East, after getting a surprising approval from Landis.

Several uniformed police officers parted the crowd as the newly-installed Mayor of New York City, Fiorello La Guardia, made his way to the staircase. He was accompanied by Landis.

At Ruth's side was a slightly-built 17-year-old pitcher playing for the Yomiuri Giants. The four Americans shook hands while the youngster bowed slightly to each out of respect.

LaGuardia raised his hand, signaling everyone to settle down. It took a few minutes until the Mayor finally could be heard over the noise.

"Thanks you all for your support," he began. "Since the Yankee franchise was established more than two decades ago, they have steadily gained notoriety for their businesslike approach to the game. Yes, they have, but this organization also has a heart, and that heart is the greatest city in the world, New York." LaGuardia paused and the crowded erupted, throwing rice and confetti at the quintet. As the noise abated, LaGuardia continued, "And the heartbeat of the Yankees is the one and only greatest baseball player ever to put on a uniform, George Herman Ruth."

The band struck up 'For He's a Jolly Good Fellow' and Ruth stepped forward, waving at everyone there to show their appreciation for the big fellow. His fabulous ear-to-ear grin was never more prominent. He reached into his pocket grabbing his handkerchief and quickly dabbed the corners of his eyes. Ruth had never felt more alive or wanted. Claire loved him as a wife should, but this outpouring was more than he had ever expected. Nearing his 39th birthday, he was not nearly the player he once was. He could no longer fight off the thickening of his frame. The extra weight on his spindly legs caused aches and discomfort in his knees from the time he woke each day. The bumps and bruises and the abuse on his insides from excessive eating and drinking were extracting their vengeance.

"Hello to all my friends," Ruth bellowed. "It's great to be back home in America. I thank baseball for giving me the opportunity to serve as its goodwill ambassador for the game we all love so much. I also want to announce that I have signed my contract for 1934, which includes a voluntary reduction of $17,000. With so many of you still suffering, it's the least I can do to ease the financial burden of this terrible depression. Colonel Ruppert and the Yankees will also keep seats in the stadium bleachers at fifty cents and have seven-cent hot dogs until every American is back to work." Ruppert had not made such a promise; Ruth had backed him into a corner. *Let's see the Colonel retreat from this stance.* "Many of you are probably wondering who this little guy next to me is. Well, his name is Eiji Sawamura. He is one hell of a pitcher and a good kid to boot. Landis has promised me he was going to open the doors of professional baseball to men of all races, including my good friends from the Negro leagues; they got some ungodly great ball players there, too." Ruth had to contain himself from laughing, as he now painted the judge into an equally awkward position. "Heck, maybe he'll finally allow some women to play ball. Finally, this will be my final year as a regular player. Next year I have been promised a managerial position, so expect to see me plenty at the third base coaching box, telling those Yanks what to do when they're comin' round second base.

I am readying for the next part of my baseball life, winning games as a manager with my mind instead of my body."

Claire, watching from the mezzanine landing, stood with her mouth wide open. She could not believe what she was hearing. During all their remaining years together, Claire never shared a prouder moment with her husband than when he gave what become known as the Terminal City speech. He fought not only for himself, but for the rights of others to share in the game he loved so passionately. She clapped loudly. *Brilliant, just brilliant, Babe*, she thought. *Who could ever doubt your street sense?* In one well-orchestrated speech, he delivered a knockout blow to those whom he came to see were just using him.

The Yankees had slipped backwards in 1933, finishing the season seven games off the pace of the Senators, with whom they'd developed a fierce rivalry. Midway through the season, Ruth's starts were spotty. McCarthy found a better suited role for him, eighth and ninth inning finisher. With the two teams playing each other twenty-two times, McCarthy studied Washington's manager Joe Cronin's use of Jack Russell early in the season. Serving as the late-inning pitcher, Ruth managed twelve wins from July to season's end, getting sixteen wins on the year.

On January 20th, McCarthy knocked on Ruppert's midtown office door, fully prepared for an expected critique of the season. No one was seated at the secretarial station. Once again, he had fallen short of the ownership's expectations for the team, and with Ruth's Commodore manifesto, he expected the worst.

"Come on in, McCarthy," a voice from beyond the door could be heard.

McCarthy saw Barrow standing by the window, looking out on the busy streets and sidewalks of New York.

Barrow spoke first, "Quite the city, New York. How many people do you think live here now?"

McCarthy, pausing to think, had not answered quickly enough for Barrow, who went on.

"Seven million! Seven million people live in this city. Nearly four million within a fifteen minutes ride on the subway. Joe, you have the most talented team in the league in the biggest city. Our team has not won. When our team doesn't win, we lose fans. The Giants had nearly as many fans in attendance at their home games and they have to battle the Dodgers on every home date. Not you, Joe. When the Yankees play, there is no other New York team at home.

Baseball attendance across the nation had no bounce-back in 1933, continuing to drop throughout the season. Although the fans held a deep anger towards baseball owners and players, wherever Ruth went, one would never see it.

Upon the Yankee arrival in Sarasota for an exhibition series with the Red Sox, three thousand fans stormed Payne Park's newly-constructed chain-link fence in right field to greet Ruth. Even struggling with his swing, Ruth could poke the ball beyond the three hundred thirty foot fence's original barrier. Sarasota's chamber of commerce had planned a huge welcoming event for Boston, and the Red Sox, wishing to divert attention from the beloved star they had traded over a decade ago, moved the field fence back over one hundred feet, just for the Yankees visit.

Ruth, part of three World Series champion teams with Boston, was graciously invited to a ceremonial black tie dinner by new Red Sox owner Thomas Yawkey, who purchased the team in 1933, and previous owner Bob Quinn. Decked out in a white tuxedo, Ruth sat at a table with other past Boston players.

"Well, Babe Ruth, it is so good to see you," Cy Young greeted him.

"Hey, kid, it's good to see you," a surprised Ruth responded.

"How's the wife, children?"

"Claire is back in New York, the girls are growing too fast."

"Well, I expect it isn't easy with three women bossing you around."

Both men chuckled wholeheartedly.

"You know, kid, I like Florida, but there are a lot of old people here."

"Ruth, I appreciate you calling me kid, but I'm considerably older than you. I've got to ask the question. Do you think you have enough left to do it?"

"I don't understand what you mean. Five hundred homeruns, now my wrist is shot it hurts every time I swing. My legs are not as strong and I cannot drive the ball the way I once could."

Young pushed him further, "Ruth, you know very well what I mean. Do you have enough left in you to beat my win total?"

"Well, kid, one thing I know for sure is that I won't pass your number for losses. That one is all yours to keep. Other records are made to be broken, and that's what'll keep the fans coming out."

Yawkey pulled a chair between Ruth and Cy Young and spoke, bringing an end to the conversation between the two. He put his arm around Ruth. "Look at this table of talent we had in Boston. I am committed to getting the Boston Red Sox back to championship caliber. I have enough money to challenge the Yankee war chest. The Red Sox will be back on top within three years."

"Pretty bold statement, kid."

Yawkey continued, "Ruth, you ever think about returning to Boston?"

"Not a chance. Next year I've been promised a chance to manage. I am staying put with the Yankees."

Ruth's tongue-in-cheek admission to Young about his health was prophetic. His arm problems returned. Hitters started offsetting the movement on his pitches by moving up in the batter's box. Whenever Ruth got a chance to hit, his swing was painful to watch. He managed four wins for the entire year.

Ruth spent more time in the third base coaching box than playing. Ruth was a gambler, believing that you force the action, risking the out to take the extra base. McCarthy was more conservative, believing in station-to-station baseball. At times, he accused the batter with more pop in the bat of over-swinging. This clash of styles served to set up the ultimate showdown at season's end.

When McCarthy failed once again to deliver a pennant, Ruth was confident he could deliver a knockout blow to McCarthy. In five years of leading McCarthy's way, the Yankees were bridesmaids four times. For a team loaded with talent, Marse Joe just seemed to find a way to push the wrong buttons, over and over again.

Chapter 47

On February 24, 1935, Ruppert hastily summoned Ruth, his financial manager and Claire to his office. This was it. Ruppert was finally going to fulfill his promise and promote Ruth to skipper; his dream was playing out just as he imagined. Ruth was excited, but thoroughly exhausted from his trip to the Far East.

The crowds in Japan were overwhelming. On January 2, 1935, as a contingent of Americans representing baseball disembarked from the Empress of Japan ocean liner they were greeted by over half a million Japanese who had jammed the streets surrounding Yokahama Harbor. Rickshaws and bicycles were abandoned as fans tried to push as close as possible to the pier. In a few short years, baseball emerged as the Empire's number one sport, thanks to Ruth.

Gehrig and Gomez were the first to head down the gangway, and halfway down they stopped to wave. "Rusu, Rusu, Rusu," the chants rhythmically began as those on hand clearly wanted to see the world's most recognized sports idol.

"Where's the Babe?" Gomez asked Gehrig.

"Brushing up on his Japanese, I guess."

Then screams of "Beibu Rusu," were heard as the Babe emerged with Claire close by his side. Police escorted the first group, which now included Jimmy Foxx and Bill Dickey, to an open-air limousine. It took nearly two hours for the car to drive the three miles to the hotel. Nearly one thousand Japanese fans were hospitalized with serious injuries, but that did not serve to deter fans. Every game played drew a crowd in excess of 60,000. The emotional outpouring was intense, and each standing ovation lasted for several minutes. The Japanese thirsted to see 'the God of Baseball.' The Americans kept their training locations secret, but thousands of fans managed to find the location every time. At one practice near Osaka, a sudden rainstorm swooped in, but rather than cancel and send the fans packing, the team continued with some of the fielders holding umbrellas between pitches.

Ruth had been out of the country for six weeks. He had been informed of the meeting before the train left from Los Angeles, and Ruth was restless the entire way. After the situation with the Yanks was settled and he was home in his Manhattan apartment, then he could rest before heading for spring training.

"This is it, Claire. Ruppert will make me a manager. As manager, I'll get more wins than anyone else, ever. Hurry up. I don't want to be late."

"Settle down, Babe, we have plenty of time."

"He probably heard how good we did in Japan with me at the helm, twenty-three to zero. We packed them in every night."

"Okay, Babe, I'm ready."

"Let's go."

Arriving twenty minutes early for the 11:00AM meeting, the trio was surprised to see Ruppert's office packed. Present in addition to

Ruppert were Barrow, now the Yankees general manager, Ford Frick, the National League president, Will Harridge, the American League president, and Judge Emil Fuchs, president of the Boston Braves.

"Sit down, Ruth; we'll make this as easy as possible. This is an uncomfortable situation."

"Colonel, it is awful nice of you to invite all these fine folks here to help celebrate my promotion."

"Ruth, it's nothing as simple as that. We have concerns to discuss."

The last unseen guest made his presence known as he stepped from the far corner.

"Landis!"

"Yes, it is me, Ruth, although it's Judge or Your Honor, as I've told you and your wife once before. It's a term of respect, which for some reason you two seem to ignore. We have a serious matter that's been brought to our attention."

"What could possibly be a problem, *your honor*?" Claire asked.

"The associations your husband keeps."

"Well, I was with him in Japan for three weeks. I have no id..."

Landis cut off Claire rudely. "Not in Japan, in Nevada. Were you with him there?"

"Of course, Judge, and I still have no idea what the problem is. I was with him all of the time."

"Well, Mrs. Ruth, we know you were there as well. There are some photos I'd like you to look at. "

Landis handed her a set of three pictures. Claire looked at them quizzically without any reaction.

"Okay, *your honor*, let me in on the secret," Claire said, heavily emphasizing the title.

"Well, do you recognize the people in the photo?"

"Local business people we met in Las Vegas. They were very nice and treated us warmly, which is more than I can say for you."

"Perhaps too much so," Landis responded, ignoring Claire's dig. "Have you any idea what business they're in?"

"Judge, we met them briefly. I do not remember all of their names. They ran a small restaurant."

"Let me help you then, Mrs. Ruth. This person here the one you are arm-in-arm with, that is Mayme Stocker."

"That's right; she owns the coffee shop we're standing in front of."

"Coffee shop, Mrs. Ruth, you do forever play naïve so well. That little diner has been the center for west coast gambling and bootlegging operations since the 1920's, well before such activities were legal in Nevada. Stocker is the proprietor. How about the group of gentleman in this photo, you recognize any of them?"

"I remember meeting them but I don't recall their names. The exceptionally good-looking man had a funny name, but I cannot remember it now. Babe, do you recall their names?"

Ruth was never one to remember anyone's name. "Kid something, I don't know."

"The good-looking well-dressed man is Benjamin Siegel. The other two are Del Webb and Gus Greenbaum."

"Even so, Judge, I still do not see the problem. All I remember is that Greenbaum is a bookkeeper."

"Mrs. Ruth, let me lay it out clearly for you. Siegel has strong, documented ties to New York and California gambling syndicates. Greenbaum is a bookkeeper, all right. He keeps the records for the Chicago outfit. Del Webb is not only tied to Siegel, he also has racing interests across the country. The problem here is simple. It is the implication of your husband's association and carrying on business with them."

"Judge, I ain't done no business with them, they're just acquaintances."

"No? Let's look at the second photo. Stocker is handing you an envelope. What were the contents of that envelope?"

Ruth responded, "Fees for the barnstorming."

"Really, Ruth? Perhaps those were payoffs for recklessness in your third base coaching. Maybe you helped the Yankees lose so the gamblers could profit."

"Why you SOB, I ain't ever bet on the game, not once."

"No, it has not been once. We believe you've bet on games for a long time. Maybe you did not bet, you simply allowed others who bet against the Yanks to win. Look at this photo. What is in the envelope Siegel is handing you?"

"This is a setup, Colonel. This dishonest creep came to see me in Chicago to ask that I stop in Nevada."

"Okay, I have one last picture. This one was taken here in New York City, not in Las Vegas." Landis reached into his pocket and unfolded the final photo he wanted to share with Babe and his wife.

"Take a long look."

"Judge, that's my good friend Al Jolson with a friend he introduced me to, a local New York guy."

"Show the photo to your bride. She will know who it is."

Claire stared at the image of Babe and Al Jolson standing on Broadway with a third man. Her jaw dropped. She never for one moment imagined that Babe would ever do anything to hurt the game. He played each inning as it was his last. But the visual evidence was convincing, and she realized how quickly Babe's reputation could be tarnished.

"Yes, I know who that is."

"I do have another picture with you and that third gentleman which was taken a few years earlier in case your memory needs a little help. Claire, I understand he was an extraordinarily close friend of yours. Would you please let everyone here know who he is?"

Claire fearing the next photo may put an uncomfortable spin on an innocent situation responded without any haste.

"Babe, I am so sorry you have to go through this nonsense. That is Charles Luciano. He came to several of my shows. That's all, Babe."

"Thank you, Mrs. Ruth. So, Babe, you see that you and your lovely bridge each have a long-standing association with known members of the underworld and gambling syndicates."

Landis continued with the point he wanted to make, "The Colonel and everyone else here today knows the rules about gambling. Ruth, there is a significant amount of suspicion regarding the possible impact of your associations and who may have benefitted from them. Accordingly, we have made some decisions. You will never be allowed to act in the capacity as manager, owner or have a significant decision-making position in baseball. You are a great ambassador to the game, and the fans do not know of your associations to gamblers. If they did, they would be merciless towards you, since you have been the highest-paid player in the game while they struggle to make ends meet. On top of that, you look like you're throwing games for the financial benefit of you and known gamblers."

Ruth turned to Ruppert. "Colonel, you know I play every game to win. This is complete bull."

"Ruth, I just don't know. Those pictures trouble me. The truth is that I really don't know what to think. All those years, all that talent, the lack of championships; Ruth, this is not easily explainable. Perhaps I was blind to what was really going on."

Barrow finally lashed out, "Ruth, you're finished as a Yankee. You'll never play another game in pinstripes. If I were the commissioner, I'd throw you out entirely."

Landis played the mediator now, settling Barrow a bit. "Ruth, we're going to give you a chance to go home and finish your career where you started, in Boston. You need to be gone from New York and the closeness to temptation. The Yankees are going to release you and then you'll announce that you have signed a personal services contract with another team. It will be announced that you'll have an executive capacity but you'll serve in no such function. You are immensely popular and we will not risk losing fans due to your indiscretions."

"What if we don't agree to this and fight you, *your honor?*" Claire demanded angrily.

Landis regarded her calmly. "Then Ruth's legacy will be torn apart. Everything he has accomplished will be expunged from the records."

Ruth silently sat in place for nearly twenty minutes, not moving, not talking. Landis had beaten him. He could hear everyone in the room speaking, but all of the voices were muffled. His thoughts were cluttered.

Landis walked over to Ruth, leaned in close to him and whispered, "You're finally out of my hair."

Chapter 48

Ruth's release from the New York Yankees shocked the city's fan base to their core. There was no mention of Ruth continuing as a coach or being assigned to lead the minor league team in Newark, NJ. Loyal fans viewed this as simply a callous move by an organization that was all business, with no sense of loyalty or family. Ruppert now became the target of fans' abuse and cruel letters. He was seen as just another cold-hearted Kraut.

For 15 years, he had toiled for the Yankees, bringing the Yanks their first of several championships. Now, clearly, he was unappreciated. Ruppert and Barrow, in the end, had no problem cutting off their ties with him. His purpose for the Yankees was done. Ruth was discarded as easily as dirty bath water.

Seeing the news headlines on February 24, 1935, fans gathered at Ruth's Riverside Drive apartment building entrance. Finally at noon, the Ruth family emerged through the glass doors. Claire, Julia and Dorothy all were at his side for the impromptu press conference.

"Thank you all for coming out. We are on our way to a long-needed vacation. I would stay and talk to everyone here, but our ship leaves in two hours and we'll be on that big boat, heading to Europe. But I will answer a few questions. Just don't ask about my weight."

The crowd roared and a voice shot out. "Hey, Babe, can you ski?"

"Ski? Yeah, kid, I'm the king of the slopes. Heck, I'm the champion of flops!"

Another voice adds, "What are your plans? Can you still play?"

"Well, the first plan is to spend some vacation time with my wife and the girls. Yes I can still play. But I want to manage. I will be going up to see Mr. Yawkey in Boston about managing the Red Sox when I return."

Ruth's family plan for a cross-Atlantic cruise on the Manhattan was abruptly ended. Before the Ruth's could board the ocean liner, a message from Barrow caught up with Babe. The Yankees had assigned Babe's rights to Boston. Upon reading the news, Babe was thrilled.

"Claire, change of plans. We need to head to Boston. You guys go on without me; I have to see Mr. Yawkey."

By noon the next day, Ruth was walking into Yawkey's Fenway Park office.

"Do you have an appointment, Mr. Ruth?" Anne Ruotigliano asked.

"No, but I came here as quickly as I could upon hearing that Mr. Yawkey acquired the rights for my services."

"Oh dear, let me tell me Yawkey you are here."

"Babe, how are you?" Yawkey as he quickly emerged from his office. "Please, let's go into my office. Anne, hold any visitors."

"Sorry I didn't let you know I was coming, but hearing the news, I was anxious to get started with the boys and getting ready for spring training."

"Babe, what in God's name are you talking about?"

"You got my rights from Ruppert. I expect I'm here to manage the team."

"Babe, this is a terrible mistake. We signed Joe Cronin to manage the Red Sox. Worse, we did not acquire you, the Braves did. That team belongs to Judge Emil Fuchs, a very dear friend of Commissioner Landis. You know him, I trust."

"What!"

"Let me call over to him and let him know you're here. Babe, I wish things were different. This is the second time the Red Sox are losing your services. Maybe we're jinxed. We wish all the best to you and Mrs. Ruth. "

Ruth's spirits plummeted as he sat in the anteroom. A friend of Landis was now his boss. The next day at the Copley Plaza Hotel, Judge Emil Fuchs announced the Braves' newest player. Fans flocked to the hotel to see the return of the prodigal son.

April 16, 1935, was opening day for the Braves. Forty thousand patrons, over fifteen percent of the entire attendance for the season, took every seat at the 'Wigwam.' They weren't there to see the futile team that would only win just 38 games that year. No, they had come out to see Babe Ruth. The Fuchs gamble was going to pay off. Ruth's popularity would re-invigorate the struggling Braves and the rest of the National League.

Ruth entered the game in the top of the fifth inning. He retired the Giants one–two-three. Batting in the bottom of the inning, he promptly deposited the ball deep into the right field seats. Gingerly he circled the bases, tipping his cap to the adoring fans. The Braves now held a 4-0 lead as Ruth prepared to pitch the sixth. Two doubles and a single before the first out and the Giants had cut the margin in half. A sharply-hit grounder to shortstop Billy Urbanski resulted in a double play. Ruth was within one out of getting through the inning without further damage. Marty Koenig, his former Yankee mate, strolled up, taking his position to hit. A switch hitter not known for power, Koenig had regained some of his early career consistency after his initial struggles following leaving the Yankees.

The banter commenced. "Hey, ol'man, you got anything left?"

"Plenty to set you down, kid."

Koenig drilled the first pitch to deep center field, the ball carrying nearly four hundred feet, but Wally Berger ran the ball down just before smashing into the wall. He jumped up, holding the ball high overhead, marking the final out of the inning and the final pitch for Ruth.

"You got a horseshoe up that butt of yours, Babe."

"Nope, that was my best pitch, letting the outfielder go get it."

That would be Ruth's last appearance until May 25th. The Braves held on for the 4-2 win, Ruth without fanfare equaling Cy Young's achievement with his 511th victory. The accomplishment went unreported by the newspapers.

For over a month, Ruth sat on the bench. Initially he sat quietly, but as the Braves' losses mounted, Ruth again itched to have a chance at calling the shots. Bill McKechnie, who would manage Boston to a sub-500 record over eight seasons, resisted all of Ruth's suggestions and kept him from coaching the bases. Finally Ruth told McKechnie he was going to talk to Fuchs, to which McKechnie answered, "Who the hell do you think told us to sit tight on you and not let you do any coaching? So sit down and be quiet."

On May 25th, due to the regular players' injuries, Ruth had a chance to play right field. Pittsburg fans applauded for him as he came to bat in the first inning. Urbanski was on first for the Braves. Red Lucas delivered a fast ball which Ruth turned on. Unleashing power he had not shown in years, he lined a drive deep into the grandstands. In the third, with teammate Les Mallon on second, Ruth lifted the ball deep into right field, soaring high then coming down to a gentle landing spot on the roof. A single into right brought in another Braves run. In the seventh, many fans sensed this would be Ruth's final at bat of the day and they cheered and stamped their feet as the grandstand began to sway. Forbes Field had been designed not to allow any cheap home runs. Generous dimensions and high screens kept many a baseball in play.

Guy Bush delivered a pitch low and inside. Ruth completed his swing, his face grimacing in pain as his body contorted, twisting around his slender legs. His hands completed the swing high above his right shoulder, and he held the bat there for several seconds. The clout carried high and far, soaring above and beyond the eighty six foot high upper deck with plenty of room to spare. The ball bounded into the street, rolling into the adjacent Schenley Park. Forbes Field had opened twenty-six years earlier, and that was the first ball ever hit over the right field stands.

"Skipper, I need to come out." Ruth told McKechnie.

Ruth's final game came on June 2, 1935. The team was back in Boston to face the New York Giants. The Braves had lost four straight again and asked Ruth to stop the losing streak.

Facing Koenig, Ott and the rest of the Giants once again, Ruth warmed up prior to the start. Shanty Hogan was the Braves' catcher.

Hogan rubbed a ball while standing at the mound with Ruth, 'This is a good day. "

"What do you mean, kid?"

"It's a good day for history. Today you break Cy Young's record for wins. He's here, you know. He's been following the team around since opening day. "

"What? Why would he want to do that?"

"I think he's cheering for you, Babe. It's a burden, owning a record. People are always asking about the record. The want to know if it could be broken, or not, are you worried?"

"Nah, kid, records are meant to be broken. I hope all of my records get broken."

Ruth's eyes moved to the grandstand, looking at the spot where the Royal Rooters once led the cheers for the hometown boys. He spotted Young halfway up, behind third base.

"You know, Babe, since his wife died, he looks at his record differently."

"What do you mean?"

"Was a time he wanted nobody to break the record, but now he's hoping you will. The bigger the deal it is for someone to break it, the more valuable it was. Something like that. He's been cheering you on for some time. You never noticed?"

"Nope, can't say I did."

"Today is your day, Babe. Let's end the chase today."

"Okay."

"How many people you think are watching today, five thousand, maybe? You know if you win today a hundred times that amount will someday claim they were here."

Through eight innings, Ruth was throwing as if it were 1927. His accuracy was sharp as an aerial bomber, nailing corners of the strike zone. Movement on his balls was exceptional and late, giving hitters no chance to adjust. He looked towards the sky, and thanked Jackie Mitchell after each inning.

The Braves had scratched out a run in the sixth and one more in the eighth for a narrow lead.

"Babe," McKechnie called out, "you want I should bring someone in to finish this?"

"You come out to the mound and I'll choke you. You're a puppet for the judges. I'll finish what I started, so leave me be."

The final inning did not start well for Ruth. Mancuso lashed a double to the left field corner.

Giant pinch-hitter Harry Danning popped to short, reaching for the first sinker Ruth offered. Jo-Jo Moore, the Giants leadoff batter, smashed the ball to third. Pinky Whitney misplayed the ball as it caromed off his foot. Mancuso slid into third safely. With one out and two on, Koenig came to bat. Behind him was deep trouble, the heart of the Giants batting order, Bill Terry and Mel Ott.

"Babe, well, here we are again. I think you're looking tired. I am surprised you've lasted this far."

"Shut up, kid. Just hit."

The first pitch was right down the middle of the plate and Koenig ripped it to the right of shortstop Billy Urbanski. He dove, managing to knock the ball down. The Braves might get one out, but a run would certainly score. The ball was quickly flipped to Rabbit Maranville, who caught it in his right hand and fired it to first. The ball was low and skipped into Buck Jordan, not a slick fielder. He bobbled the ball on the scoop, and then secured it.

"You're out!" pronounced the umpire

Ruth looked toward first. Koenig was only halfway up the line; he had stumbled getting out of the box, in the clubhouse he would later claim he had caught his spike on the edge of the grass. Koenig looked at Ruth and winked. Ruth thought he detected a tiny smirk.

Teammates greeted Ruth as he left the field. Young ran to him and the two men hugged for a few minutes. "You did it, Babe! 512! I'm proud of you. I know you've been railroaded by Landis, but hang in there. You now own a record no one will ever break."

Ruth left the field, dressed without showering, walking away from the game without any hullaballoo or emotional demonstration from the spectators. The unsuspecting onlookers believed it was nothing more than the end of a regular season game, just one of one hundred fifty-four. He never played another inning.

Young met Ruth as he exited the ball park. "Thank you, Babe. I cherished the memory of that record more than life. Now I can cherish the memory of my times with Robba more."

Ruth was never given an opportunity to manage. He never spoke to Landis again

Chapter 49

"Pepe, wake up, Williams is coming up to bat again."

"I must have fallen asleep."

"Yes, you did. Do you think Williams will knock another one out of the park?"

"Where's the old man?"

"He left and told me to tell you so long."

"Is that all he said?"

"Actually, he said to tell you 'So long, kid.'"